The Betrothed Sister

The Betrothed Sister

Carol McGrath

Published by Accent Press Ltd – 2015

ISBN 9781783752935

Printed and bound in the UK

If the bones remain the flesh will come again

A Russian proverb and a meditation on historical fiction

This book is dedicated to my son, Tyrone, and Veronica, his partner.

Acknowledgements

The first of these goes to my fabulous editor Jay Dixon, and, Jay, I appreciate how hard you have worked on editing all three manuscripts with me. Thank you to Rod Fine for suggesting the title *The Betrothed Sister*. A very special thank you to the Neohori Writing Group in Greece where I wrote much of the actual manuscript, having researched the background in primary and secondary sources in England, often in The Bodleian Library, Oxford. Brenda, Mel and Theresa – your input in the manuscript's early stages was invaluable. Thank you, Tim Matthews, for the map and family tree you have designed to illustrate Thea's journeys. Thank you, Rebecca Hazell, for your notes and advice on Medieval Russia. Thank you to the RNA for their support of my writing throughout the years. Thank you, Patrick, my darling husband, for your trusty and steadfast support and for believing in me. Thank you, Accent Press, especially to Hazel, Stephanie, Beth and Greg for all your hard work to bring my novels to readers. Finally, thank you, dear readers, for reviews and for reading these novels, sometimes more than once. They could not happen without you.

The Offices of the Russian Church

Matins	Dawn
Prime	The First Hour
Terce	The Third Hour
Sext	Noon and the Sixth Hour
Nones	Between 2.00 and 3.00, the Ninth Hour
Vespers	Late afternoon
Compline	Before 7.00, early night.

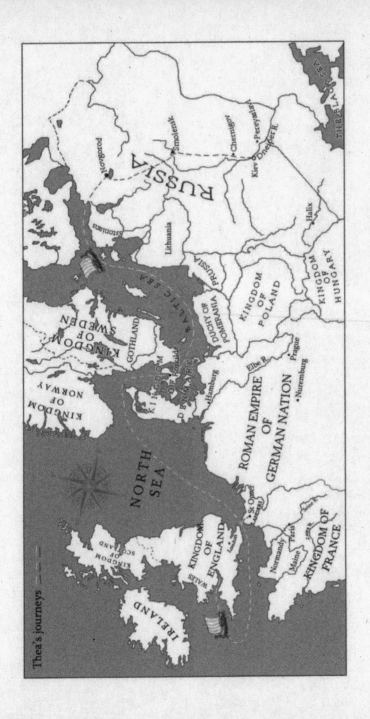

The Kievan Rus Royal Family Tree (The Riurikid Dynasty)

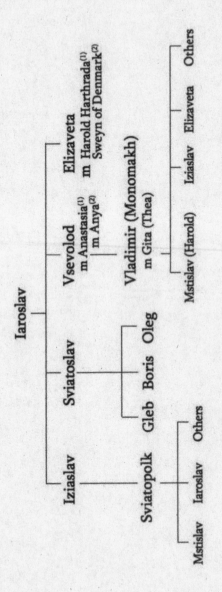

The Godwine Family Tree

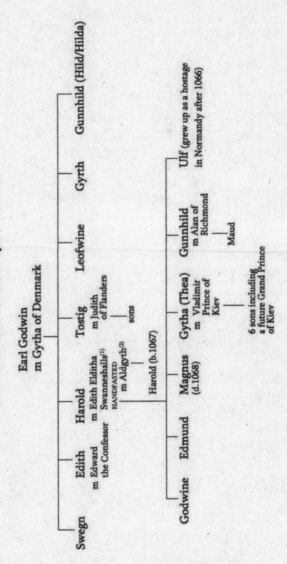

Earl Godwin
m Gytha of Denmark

Swegn | Edith
m Edward
the Confessor | Harold
m Edith Elditha⁽¹⁾ Swanneshals
HANDFASTED
m Aldgyth⁽²⁾ | Tostig
m Judith
of Flanders | Leofwine | Gyrth | Gunnhild (Hild/Hilda)

sons (from Tostig)

Harold (b.1067) (from Aldgyth)

Godwine | Edmund | Magnus
(d.1068) | Gytha (Thea)
m Vladimir
Prince of Kiev | Gunnhild
m Alan of
Richmond | Ulf (grew up as a hostage
in Normandy after 1066)

Maud (from Gunnhild)

6 sons including
a future Grand Prince
of Kiev (from Gytha)

Prologue

My needle slides through the convent's silence as I draw it in and out of my tapestry for the last times. When I stitch the edges with this golden thread it will be finished.

I have sought a life of contemplation in my final years but as happens with the old, my memory flits beyond this cloth where my story is laid out in embroidery silks. I remember the past, but these days I lose sight of the present. A Danish cunning woman once predicted that the land of the Rus would bring me a noble husband and beautiful children. And so it has come to pass because you, my children, have been my joy and Vladimir a truly beloved husband.

Study my embroidery after I am returned to the earth, children mine. My betrothal, my wedding and in those tiny blue and red crosses you can see your name days. Come closer and examine the margins; for if you do, you will discover the story of your mother's adventurous life. Here you can discern fleeing ships, snow-topped trees, pine forests inhabited by bears and wolves, fortress towers and the great cities where we have dwelled. And you will find me, too, amongst the orchards and meadows – my soul a thing of air, a bird, a bee or a moth that draws towards a bright candle. And there are rose gardens, which enclose secrets that only you, my children, who know my heart so well, can interpret.

Yet, this is not only my story. It possesses the voices of others. Look, there is Padar, the Godwin poet, holding Gabriel, his magical Frankish sword. He will speak to you of his part in my tale. See Gytha, your great-grandmother, whom I loved with

1

all my heart, hidden amongst the dragon ships that carried us from England to the land of the Danes. Gudrun, too, my dearest friend, will speak of her love for the poet. See her seated by her loom.

Let me explain. I must point you to the beginning of that journey that brought me as a betrothed exile into the land of the Rus and to your father's bed.

Part One
Exile

And here Gytha, mother of Harold, travelled away to the island of Flatholm, and the wives of many good people with her, and lived there for a certain time, and so went from there across the sea to St Omer.

The Anglo-Saxon Chronicles, The Worcester Manuscript, 1067, translated and edited by Michael Swanton, 1996.

And in the middle of this year [1068] Harold's sons came by surprise from Ireland into the mouth of the Avon with a raiding ship-army, and straightway raided across all that region; then went to Bristol and wanted to break down the town but the townsfolk fought hard against them; and when they could not gain anything from the town, they went to the ships with what they had plundered, and thus they went to Somerset.

The Anglo-Saxon Chronicles, The Worcester Manuscript, 1068, translated and edited by Michael Swanton, 1996.

Flatholm, September 1068

A pale moon was reflected in the still water that lay along the island's shoreline.

Thea took a step closer to the water's edge and for a moment glanced up at the night sky. She stared down at the reflection of the moon that lay on the surface of the sea. For a moment all was silent. It was as if the world had paused to take a breath.

Edmund touched her hand. 'Hurry,' he said. 'Grandmother is waiting in the boat for us.'

Accepting her brother's help, his hand guiding her elbow, Thea ventured into the shallows. She lifted her skirts high in the hope that the water would not drench her gown and allowed Edmund to lift her into the skiff. Taking a place in the stern beside her grandmother, Countess Gytha, she leaned back against the last chest of Godwin treasure. A sense of relief swept through her. They were finally setting out.

Thea's grandmother sat stiff-backed and silent waiting for the boat to cast off, her stony gaze reaching forwards towards the two dragon-shaped vessels that had remained out in the bay as the women made ready to leave their island sanctuary. All that day Countess Gytha had not spoken, not since her grandsons had sailed to them in the shadowy morning light, and had told her about their defeat in Somerset and of her youngest grandson Magnus's death in his first battle.

Godwin and Edmund told her they must leave immediately. Thea had watched the broken-hearted but stoical Gytha staring out to sea from the monastery cliff-side, leaning on her eagle-headed stick as the boys and their Danish oarsmen had worked hard all day long, sweat running in ribbons down their bared backs, shifting chest after chest out to the anchored ships. They must catch the evening tide and sail away into exile in Flanders before the Normans changed their minds about allowing them safe passage out and, instead, attacked their ships and seized their treasure. Now, as well as one sturdy oak chest on their skiff, other coffers containing valuable items were already stowed on board the *Wave-Prancer*, the second of the two great ships that would carry the band of noblewomen and their children and maids to Flanders. Later, Gytha turned around and left the cliff path. She entered the monastery and took up a position by the north window, looking out to sea.

To Thea's relief, Countess Gytha, once the task had been completed, left off her watching from the monastery's north window, attempted to eat a good dinner and at last she, too, made ready for her departure. Embracing the abbot who had cared for them since winter, the countess had smiled sadly as she presented him with a valuable relic, a fragile snip of the Virgin's veil. This holy object was contained inside a small crystal-and-gold reliquary box which she had smuggled from Exeter after the siege, when she and her daughter Hilda, Thea and their women and children had been banished to Flatholm to await exile.

Thea knew that leaving England would bring Grandmother Gytha immense pain. Losing Magnus left a hollow in her own heart which was already brimming with sadness for the death of her father at Senlac, the viciously thorough conquest of their land by the Normans, and her mother Elditha's decision to enter a monastery. Her thoughts moved like quicksilver through the night sky above. My sister Gunnhild is trapped with Aunt Edith at Wilton Abbey. My little brother is a Norman hostage hidden away in one of their dark castles, and now that the Normans have killed Magnus, Godwin and Edmund are all the brothers I have left. So, with those thoughts, Thea looked away from the island of Flatholm, glad to leave days there that had been endlessly marked by prayer and the work of a small monastery.

Though Flatholm had been their home for only six months, since Exeter had fallen to the enemy, she had tried hard to make the best of it. She had gardened, applied herself to her embroidery and told stories to a small group of children belonging to the noblewomen accompanying them into exile. She had even discovered other tales, stories older than those she already knew, from a strange bearded monk who came to visit them from Denmark carrying word to the women of her brothers' summer campaign. He had brought them hope, if only for a short time.

Thea glanced up at the thin, fragile moon. Despite all that had happened since the Normans stole England, anticipation gripped her. By the time that moon grew fat again they would be settled in their new home. She moved her lips in prayer to her name-day saint, St Theodosia. 'Gracious lady, grant us a warm hall, fine furniture and new clothing, and take a care for my brother Magnus.' Surely her saint would answer her prayer.

Yet, Thea did not confess to her saint her deepest and most secret wish. She wanted revenge on William the Bastard. She wanted revenge not only on him but on his whole House for his destruction of her father, the kidnap of her brother Ulf by William, her mother's seclusion and the murder of her brother, Magnus. If St Theodosia knew what lay in her heart, she knew it already. Thea wanted vengeance and until she had it, her life would never be complete again. One day, the Bastard, William of Normandy, false king of England, would die an ignoble death, unloved by his children and preferably in great pain because she, Thea, daughter of the great King Harold, wanted him to suffer for what he had done to her family. And, she added this to her thought – one day she would marry a warrior prince who hated the Normans as much as she did and who would help her brothers recover their kingdom.

She started. Voices were falling towards them, dropping from the direction of the cliff below the monastery, coming closer. She twisted round to see the rest of their women following a monk who was swinging a lantern. Their ladies, who were wrapped in their warmest woollen mantles, came in a snaking line down the cliff path to the beach. All of them, even the five children, were carrying small bundles. When the group reached the shingle the women gathered up cloaks and skirts and, bunching the escaping thick material into their hands, they began wading out to climb into the fleet of skiffs. Edmund and Padar, their warrior poet, took an arm here and a hand there. They lifted the older women, swinging in turn each of a tiny band of confused children from one to the other over the lapping water. Finally they deposited the women and their offspring into the assorted fishing craft that would ferry them to the big-sailed ships which were to carry them over the Narrow Sea.

The women's exile had been arranged months before by Aunt Edith, England's dowager queen, wife to King Edward, whom some called Confessor because he spent so much of his life in prayer. Because of her influence, King William had promised then this safe passage. Of course, Thea mused, he would promise anything that would rid himself of the Godwin threat and hold onto Aunt Edith's goodwill. If he retained Edith's goodwill he might get England's sheriffs and officials on his side, those who had the running of shires in the days of King Edward. Thea could not understand why her aunt was so devoted to Uncle Edward. She shuddered. Never would she wed with such a frost-bitten one, never, not even to please the family.

A final splash threw salty spray into her eyes. She blinked it away, looked around and saw that the skiffs were full. Padar climbed over two rowing benches and sat opposite them, squeezed in on the end of the third bench, wrapped in his old sealskin cloak. He grunted a greeting, and received a glimmer of a smile from Gytha. Edmund came down the rowing boat. He placed an arm about Padar's shoulders. 'Look after them as we cast off, my friend.' Once, it seemed long ago but it was only a year since, Padar had protected her mother and now he promised that he would protect them.

Grandmother Gytha seized Thea's hand and spoke for the first time since Prime. 'Soon we shall be in Baldwin's court.

Just think how he will welcome us with honour. His family was always friendly to us Godwins.'

'Will he be friendly, Countess?' Padar asked, taking his watchful eyes from the shoreline. Raising a bushy eyebrow and leaning forward, lowering his voice, he said, 'Will he really be a friend to you? I'd leave your coffers under guard when we reach St Omer. You'll not breathe a word about it, my lady Countess, either, if you are wise. Given half a chance, Baldwin will be like a crow ready to scourge the wheat field. He seeks the best opportunity. He straddles loyalties.'

Gytha narrowed her eyes, nodded and glanced at Edmund who had taken up oars. 'The boys will need it if they are to get back our kingdom.' She turned to Thea and patted her knee. 'You will need help, too, if you are to marry well. Fifteen, my girl, and high time we found you a match.'

Thea thought to herself that her brothers would use most of the coin and treasures they possessed to buy ships and weapons. But she would need a dowry if one day she were to marry well. She thought for a moment of the day Grandmother had lifted the lids of her treasure coffers and revealed the great family treasure she was hiding in the cellars under the palace in Exeter – the jewels, the gold and silver, Thea's father's valuable books, priceless tapestries, reliquaries of precious crystal – there was more than enough for her brothers' war on the Normans. There had best be some left for her too.

She watched the waves roll about their craft as the oars beat on water and the dragon ships drew closer. How would Godwin get them off the rowing boats and up into those enormous ships? The ships' walls were as high as a giant's reach.

A loud greeting echoed over the sea. Glancing high above her perch Thea saw Godwin waiting at the nearer ship's side. He shouted down to them, 'Grandmother first. Edmund, keep the boat still as you can. I am coming down. I shall carry her up the ladder myself.' Before Gytha could protest, Godwin was on the rope ladder and climbing down to them. He jumped into the skiff, and lifted Gytha as if she were a bundle of fine light wool.

'Hold tight, Grandmother. That's it, arms around my neck,' he urged.

Gytha laughed as Godwin reached out and grasped the hanging thick knotted rope with one hand, his other arm hugging the countess, and began shimmying up it. Gytha clung to him, holding on as if her life depended on it, her skinny legs wrapped around his middle as he climbed the knotted rope one hand reaching above the other. At the top two of his warriors reached out to lift her into the safety of the dragon ship. She was fearless.

Thea glanced at the dark waters below.

'You next, sister,' Edmund said. 'Can you climb unaided?'

She nodded. As she made ready to grasp the rope ladder, Gytha, apparently unaffected by her journey upwards into the dragon ship, stood safely with Godwin supporting her on a rowing bench inside.

Countess Gytha called down, 'Girl, bring my stick with you. I'll need it to steady myself and smash a few sea serpents.'

Padar reached up and handed Thea the eagle-headed stick. Her ascent would be even more dangerous now there was this in one of her hands. Thea climbed, holding on precariously with her left hand, her arm aching. She held the stick up to Godwin who was leaning over the side waiting to help her over the top. He took it and turned to his grandmother with a 'Here it is, Grandmother. Let Gunulf help you down onto the bench before you fall and break something.'

Gytha grasped her stick and accepted the oarsman's help. Once down she waved her stick about her head so all Thea could see of Grandmother Gytha was a carved eagle head poking above the side of the ship, and her grandmother's voice yelling, 'I hope the Bastard King sleeps uneasy in his bed tonight. I curse him, by the Norns' spells; I curse him by Christ's holy blood, by Thor's hammer and by Freya's bones I curse him. I pray that he suffers Hell's fires for his theft of our kingdom.' The eagle-headed stick rose above the ship's walls and was shaken up at the stars as if to emphasise her words.

Godwin's answering call echoed around the waters, 'He will pay for Magnus's death, for my uncles' deaths, for my father's death. We will harry England's shores until he wishes he had never heard of our kingdom.' He lowered his voice and called down to Thea, whose stiff fingers could hardly grasp the rope as she listened patiently to her grandmother's diatribe, wanting it over so that Godwin would get her over the side. At last he called down, 'Now, Thea, come further, hand over hand.'

Thea climbed steadily, crushing her terror of dropping back down, until, to her relief, Godwin grasped her and swung her over so that she fell past the rowing benches and onto the deck. One by one, the other boats drew up to the big ship. Led by Hilda, Thea's other aunt, the ladies courageously climbed into the ships. Finally, the children shimmied up and they were all on board. The *Sea-Dragon's* sails were unfurled and the seamen seated in the ship's body began to row. The *Wave-Prancer* followed. This ship, Edmund explained, carried the rest of their surviving Danish warriors and house coerls, all well-armed and alert. Thea glanced with admiration at their coned helmets and at their great jewelled arm bracelets that glinted through the starlight.

She watched, thrilled, as Godwin raced across the great rowing benches that ran along the ship's length and shouted to the men in the *Wave-Prancer*. There was an answering call as the warriors began to manoeuvre their ship into position beside the *Sea-Dragon*. When they drew closer, Godwin climbed up onto the wall of the *Sea-Dragon*. With a yell he leapt over the narrow channel of sea onto the supply ship and was gone. He would command their protection from the second ship which carried the greater number of his men-at-arms and sailors who were also warriors.

The *Wave-Prancer* moved away again, oars moving in rhythm. It took up the lead position now. The *Sea-Dragon* followed and soon they were out from the headland and the island was left far behind.

Padar joined the women where they made themselves more

comfortable by leaning against Gytha's coffer. Squatting down, he opened his satchel, drew out a large flask and pulled a wax stopper from the skin. He produced a silver cup, and with his eyes twinkling he offered the first draught to Gytha. After the countess drank, Thea and the other women raised the flask to their mouths. It held a concoction of something that tasted of honey and bitter herbs – clashing flavours. Thea did not mind. The liquid coursed through her, for a heartbeat, allowing her thoughts to drift away to far distant lands, to kingdoms that marked the edge of the world.

'A distillation of barley and spices,' Padar remarked as he took the flask back and knocked off the dregs, stoppered it and returned it to his satchel.

'Just what we need,' Gytha said as the ship ploughed its way out of the channel, southwards. 'Now, little man, lull us into sleep with the melodies of my homeland.' It was as if Gytha was remembering places far to the north that had long been hidden in her soul, the land of the Danes and the country of her youth.

As Padar pulled his harp from his big leather scrip, the children squeezed up against their mothers. They were all packed as closely as a line of drying cod, twenty of them in all, women and children, jammed into the stern of the *Sea-Dragon*. Thea looked past them and behind for the necessary. She took note that it must be that covered pail that leaned against the ship's wall just at the furthest end of the ship where the stern curved upwards into a dragon's tail. They would need to be careful if they had to crawl around the chests and over to it. Aunt Hilda was famous for her weak stomach.

The countess huddled down amongst the fur covers. As Padar played his harp her eyelids closed. In sleep Gytha's aged face relaxed and the lines of long years of care settled. For a moment, Thea glimpsed the fine-bred northern beauty her grandmother had once possessed. The water's lapping; the oars' plash; the murmuring of the night breeze and the strains of Padar's music contrived to shift Thea's thoughts to dwarf kingdoms under the mountains. She imagined caves along which rivers twisted through pillars of ice. Gradually, her own eyelids closed as she, too, was lulled into sleep by the skald's melodies and the gentle rhythm of the dragon ship as it ploughed through the sea. She pulled her sheepskin closer and drifted into the territory of uneasy dreams.

2

The Prince's band can pull
Their oars straight out of the sea.

Viking Poetry of Love and War, collected by Judith Jesch, 2013

Thea's eyes shot open. A grey dawn light was seeping into the sky. She sensed a shifting of bodies. Her bladder ached. There was nothing for it. She would have to use the makeshift privy and, no doubt, she must soon help Grandmother Gytha to it as well. Aunt Hilda was fast asleep on the other side of her grandmother. She leaned forward and peered at her gently snoring aunt. Thankfully, her colour still retained a soft bloom.

Thea stood unsteadily and lowered herself to crawl over the other women and around their children who were curled up in sleep. The boat was moving so fast it felt as if they were racing away from somewhere or something, rather than keeping the steady pace it had held during the night. Thea crawled past the sleepers and tried to grab the wooden rail running around the dragon ship's sides. She stumbled as the ship seemed to jolt. Righting herself and looking up, she saw Padar above in the mast calling out to Godwin on the other ship. Godwin called something incomprehensible back.

She steadied herself and leaned against the ship wall. Edging along it slowly, she managed to reach the bucket. With great difficulty, she squatted down behind a curtain that had been hung like a tent from a hook projecting from the stern. The bucket stank of foul odours, of vomit and excrement both.

Moments later she rose and allowed her gown to fall around her ankles again. Despite the ship's roll she managed to extract a ball of lavender that hung from her belt along with her needle-purse and scissors. Trying hard to get the lid back on the bucket with one hand, the lavender ball in the other clutched to her nose, she managed to elbow away the coarse curtain. A moment later she had tripped over, falling into the arms of one of Edmund's helmeted house coerls. His sword scabbard dug into her thighs.

'Sweet Mary, let me free,' she cried out.

'What, my lady, taking the Virgin's name ...'

'Move your great leather-clad hulk now.'

'Steady, my lady, steady now. Get back with the other women.'

An arrow hissed past her to bury itself in the ship's wall.

'That is a warning,' he added. 'It was meant to miss its mark. You women are more valuable as slaves than dead. Next time we might not be so lucky. Keep down and take a look.'

She twisted her head around to see a ship with two black sails gliding out of an inlet, fast catching them up. A crescent moon was painted on one of them.

'Normans?' she said.

'No, Moorish pirates come into our waters from the south.' He tightened his grip on her arm. 'Go back. None of us are safe. They'll be looking for captives and ransoms.'

Edmund had come up behind the Dane. 'That's right, Gunor.' He reached out and helped Thea to step around him. 'Get back to Grandmother and do not move.' He glanced over at the privy with its flapping leather curtain. 'Not even for that.'

A slew of arrows arched from the pirate ship and hissed their way, but went amiss, hitting the ship's sides. For a moment the onslaught stopped. Edmund gave her a gentle push. Bent over almost double she retreated. When she paused, she straightened up again, unable to resist looking out to sea, where she discovered the reason for the brief reprieve. Godwin had set up a response from the *Wave-Prancer* which he had deftly manoeuvred between the *Sea-Dragon* and the enemy. The pirate ship was only yards behind them, gaining on both of their vessels. She bent down again and scuttled back to her place amongst the frightened women, their shivering children and her grandmother. The women clutched each other, then pulled the children under their mantles and ducked low as the pirates returned fire.

'I need the bucket,' Gytha said imperiously, rising from her furs.

'You can't, Grandmother,' she heard herself shrieking. 'We are being attacked! Edmund says ...'

'Never mind what Edmund says, what is necessary is unavoidable. Help me to it. Take my arm, girl.'

Despite protests from Aunt Hilda, who was greening at the gills, Gytha dragged her frightened granddaughter back into the danger zone.

'Grandmother,' yelled Edmund, 'you can't.'

'I can and I must.' Gytha clutched at the wooden rail, pulled herself behind the makeshift curtain and ordered Thea to hold it closed for her.

Thea's legs felt weak. She was shaking. She could hardly hold on. 'Hurry, Grandmother, hurry,' she hissed through her teeth.

It seemed to take Grandmother an age. Curses crossed the water followed by the swish of returned arrow fire from the *Wave-Prancer*. Thea heard screams as men were hit. The battle was beginning in earnest; arrows were fired to kill. Gunor and Edmund shouted orders past the women crouched down behind the coffers, holding their children close, petrified.

The oarsmen momentarily stopped rowing. Gunor came weaving his way past them followed by Padar who had climbed down from the mast. He spoke to Edmund who nodded. Gunor handed him his arrow quill. Agile as a squirrel Padar scurried up the pole again towards the opened sail and nimbly worked his way above it. He lashed himself to the top of the mast, withdrew his bow, plucked an arrow from the quill, set it, pulled back the bowstring and let it fly.

The arrow sped like summer lightning over the *Wave-Prancer* and straight into the enemy's mast. Thea could not see how it landed but she heard Padar's yell of success and their crew's applauding cheer. Gunor stood below Padar and struck a flint into a spark. Once he had set fire to another arrow he thrust it up towards the skald. He followed Padar up the mast. Padar leaned down and grabbed it. Within another intake of breath, he had set the burning arrow into his bowstring.

'Aim for their sail this time,' Gunor yelled up.

Padar was light and fast. A moment later, he had let the flaming arrow fly towards the mast of the Moorish vessel so that it caught the very top of the sail. The wind would do the rest.

Thea was as mesmerised as if she had been watching an archery contest at old King Edward's court. She moved from her post in front of the privy and scrambled up onto a chest. She leaned over and clung to the ship's wall. A second arrow arched. Within a heartbeat it was gone. The *Wave-Prancer* was just to the left of the flaming arrow's trajectory. She prayed that none of the burning arrows would catch Godwin's sail. With amazing accuracy three flaming arrows hit their mark and she let go a breath of relief. As the enemy's sail billowed out it seemed as if it had scooped up a fat fireball.

The pirates tried desperately to throw buckets of seawater up at the gathering flames. A continuous stream of what now looked like wide, burning, linen ribbons floated briefly in the air, turned into skinny black rags and descended to be tossed about and swallowed by the foaming waves.

The *Sea-Dragon* lurched, as with dangerous speed the oarsmen began to row forwards.

There was a roar of complaint from the privy. The wind-filled curtain flapped open allowing a full view of Grandmother Gytha's red woven leggings, tied at her knees, and her bunched-up brown undergown. Gytha pulled herself from the bucket and banged its lid back down with a crash. Straightening her clothing, Countess Gytha emerged grumbling, 'How dare they attack us? Mark this, Edmund, after this wave-dancing and enemy-dodging is over, a seaman must be dispatched up here to empty that bucket. It reeks of pig's innards.'

18

Edmund yelled back, 'Grandmother, get back, we are not safe yet.'

Thea clambered down from her perch by the privy and handed Gytha the lavender ball to hold to her nose. She dragged her grandmother back from danger to shelter again behind the chests where the terrified children were shrieking. Their mothers sobbed as they clung to their children and to each other.

If St Theodosia abandoned them, if the pirates were able to put out the flames and retaliate and their ships were captured, Thea swore an oath. She would kill herself rather than become a hostage or a slave.

Drawing her seax from its sheath, she grasped it tightly under her mantle. Her grandmother pulled her into her bony arms and whispered, 'Thea, there will be no need. We shall outrun them. Those bastards are fighting a fire. Anyway, they will not dare attack further into Normandy's waters, not if a Norman fleet is out.'

'But will the Normans attack us too?'

'They dare not. They promised us safe passage. The Norman bastards will protect their shores, believe me. Besides, Godwin and the *Wave-Prancer* will be more than the enemy's match. He will divert the pirate scum from our ship to give us a chance to get up into the Narrow Sea between Normandy and England. Once we are past Brittany's coast, the devils will retreat.'

'That puts Godwin in danger.'

'He is used to it. Godwin has better marksmen and faster oarsmen than they have on that ship with its ruined sail. By tomorrow morning we shall be breaking our fast by the hearth in a Flanders inn.'

The countess's words proved true. The pirate ship *was* retreating. The *Wave-Prancer* would hold the mid-channel until the threat vanished into the southern horizon.

Edmund ordered bread and buttermilk for the women. He followed the servant back to the stern and crouched beside Aunt Hilda. Pale with shock, their aunt was gabbling prayers as fast as a feast-day goose running around a yard. 'It is over,' he said to her quietly. 'You can put your cross away, Aunt Hilda. God has listened to your prayers. Please eat and drink. We have another day's sea journey ahead.'

Aunt Hilda shook her head but her mouth shaped a wisp of a smile. 'No food, just water.' She studied Edmund for a moment. 'I have come to a decision. Once we are safe in Flanders I shall seek a life of contemplation.'

Countess Gytha reached her jewelled hand out of the covers and accepted the bread the servant offered. She turned to Hilda and remarked with an edge to her tone. 'So God steals another of our Godwin women to be his handmaiden. Well, so be it, if that is your choice, Hilda, my daughter.'

3

St Omer, 1068

The September sun was beginning to streak the sky with gold and pink as late in the afternoon the two ships slid into the shelter of a Flanders bay.

The ships sailed around a shallow grey headland where tufts of sea grass waved in the breeze. Beyond the headland a shore of lichen-encrusted stones served as a beach. A large jetty pushed out into deep water where they could anchor and tie up the ships. Sails were quickly lowered and safely secured on the decks. Their oarsmen rowed the dragon vessels close to the pier so that one man from each ship was able to climb over and moor them.

A large crowd soon gathered to gape at the newcomers and an arrangement was brokered with fishermen who were watching their arrival from the quayside. Ladders were raised against the *Sea-Dragon*'s walls and the women safely disembarked. Once on firm ground, Thea peered past the onlookers and over the low harbour walls beyond the jetty. There, a decrepit town of assorted thatched wooden and stone buildings stretched around the harbour in a semi-circular shape. The town's church spire poked up towards pale yellow puffs of clouds that hung in the sky like unwashed sheep's wool.

A florid-faced man with a head shaped like a turnip pushed forward through the quayside gathering to greet them. His leather apron suggested him to be an artisan. He stared at Thea, Countess Gytha and Aunt Hilda. 'By St Christopher, your women seem weary. I hazard a guess that you are all travellers, pilgrims?' He raised his dark eyebrows. 'Or could you be exiles in search of a place to rest your heads? You would not be the first. You will not be the last now William of Normandy is king in England.'

Their languages were similar enough for them to understand each other's tongues. Thea waited patiently with Gytha and the other women. It was true. They all needed to rest. They could not spend another night on the ship, nor were they fit to travel on to Bruges.

For the time it takes a hunting dog to draw in a breath, let it out and bark, Godwin had taken a step forward, his hand on his sword hilt. 'You are correct. We are from England. Our women are destined for King Baldwin's court.' He surveyed the red-faced artisan. 'So, my good man, who are you?'

The man bowed. 'My lords, I am a humble man, Luc, master shipwright.

Despite his acclaimed humility, master shipwright Luc wasted no time opening up negotiations with Godwin and Edmund concerning lodgings for the night. He pointed to one of the larger stone buildings in front of the church, a hall house with an upstairs chamber reached by an outer staircase. 'My own dwelling is a spacious hall.' Bowing low to them, Master Luc declared his intention. 'I would be pleased to offer my hospitality in exchange for coin.'

'State your price,' Godwin said. 'The ladies can rest here or on board our vessels depending on the cost.'

Gytha leaned on her eagle-headed stick and grunted impatiently through the negotiations until Godwin and the shipwright slapped hands and a deal was concluded. 'The cargo,' the countess said, pointing her stick at Godwin. 'What shall we do? It must be kept safe.'

My grandmother looks like a cunning woman, the way she wields that stick. She will have us all accused of sorcery. I wish it did not possess the eagle's head. I wish she would just rest her hands on it.

Godwin broke into Thea's thoughts. 'I shall stay with our cargo, I and the house coerls; no need to worry. Any threats and they will have my swordsmen to reckon with.' Shaking his long, yellow hair he gave Master Luc an icy stare. The message

22

he intended reached its mark because Master Luc looked anxious and retreated, allowing them to conduct their discussion in private.

Godwin turned to the countess. 'Tomorrow we shall purchase horses. Padar will accompany you, Grandmother, to the convent of St Omer. It is only an hour's ride. If Padar rides on to Bruges, in no time at all Baldwin will send an escort to the abbey to fetch you.'

He asked Gytha, Thea and Hilda to walk with him along the quay, away from Flemish wagging ears. For a moment, Thea felt a sense of foreboding. What if Count Baldwin did not expect them after all? What would they do? They left Edmund and Padar waiting with the other women and children as Godwin guided the royal women further back down the jetty.

He glanced over at the *Sea-Dragon* and nodded at the *Wave-Prancer*. 'We shall watch over your chests, Grandmother, yours and those of the other women, until we know what Baldwin intends. Tell Padar to return to us here the moment an escort reaches you. Only then shall we leave the ships with Gunor and travel on with you to Bruges. Only when we know you will be received by Baldwin shall we bring you the ladies' valuables and the treasure chests.'

Gytha nodded. 'Godwin, keep half of our treasure for your use in Denmark. I shall need a quarter for my own use. Another quarter must be set aside for Thea's dowry.'

'I shall do right by my sister. She will have her portion in silver, gold and jewels, tapestries and our father's precious library. I swear it.' He took Thea's hand, lifted it to his lips and kissed his sister's fingers. Thea felt his strength. She would trust her brothers with her life. If they made her a promise they would abide by it. He smiled, squeezed her hand, dropped it and turned back to the countess. 'Now, Grandmother, this is my plan. Tonight, after the midnight bells ring, we shall take the ships around the headland. We can set up camp up on the cliffs we saw as we entered the bay.' He pointed up towards the grey headland. 'That is where Padar will find us.'

Gytha caught her breath and said, 'God bless you, Godwin, you and Edmund both.' She took Hilda's arm and turning around paused. Thea felt her grandmother's gaze on her from her head to her booted toe. 'Adjust your head covering, girl. We can see those flame-coloured curls and we should not.'

Thea could not resist a smile as she set her fillet to right and drew the hood of her mantle over her veil. When her grandmother said such things to her she knew that the countess was still every bit as indomitable as she had been during the siege at Exeter eight months earlier. Grandmother Gytha was determined to battle on through life undefeated by difficulties and she would never reveal her true age, just that she was of the royal house of Denmark and had come to England to unite with Earl Godwin during the reign of the great Canute. *But she must be at least in her mid-sixty years*. As Thea followed her grandmother back along the jetty, she could not help wondering what trials still lay ahead of them all.

4

Mizzle that had begun to slide from the overcast sky became a cold drenching rain as the women and children reached the monastery at St Omer, most of them travelling in an ancient, rattling long wagon pulled by two nags. They had only been able to purchase three decent horses in addition to the wagon and its ambling beasts. Thea and Gytha rode on two of these. Padar took the third. Thea felt chilled to the bone after they had dismounted. They waited for what felt like an age in drenching rain for grooms to appear at the abbey entrance.

Padar pulled on a bell rope three times before a monk came to manoeuvre the massive outer doors open with much creaking, allowing them to lead the horses and cart into a bleak and very muddy yard. A silent band of servants appeared through the streaming rain. Without a word, they helped the women and children from the wagon and led the horses away to a barn.

'Bah, the Benedictines,' Gytha complained. 'They don't waste their words.'

The equally silent monk pushed another groaning door open into the monastery. Once inside he spoke at last, telling them to wait in the hall. A meagre fire flickered in a raised central hearth, but despite it the room was dim and damply cold. Thea's first impression was that this place felt as austere as Niflheim, a kingdom that skalds sang of, one that was bitterly cold and harsh. Surely they would not have to wait long before they continued to more comfortable shelter in the grand palace of Bruges?

Soon, she heard an army of footsteps advancing steadily towards them from beyond the hall. A severe-faced sister appeared through an inner doorway, followed by another and then another. After a moment during which the lead nun surveyed the bedraggled party, she said. 'I am Abbess Constance, my lady Countess. We have been expecting news of your arrival all summer. You sent us no forward warning. Now that you are here we are unprepared since you take us by surprise.' A pause followed. Gytha frowned and waited. The abbess continued, 'But, none the less, we have certain arrangements in place to welcome you here.' There was no expected deference to Countess Gytha, and, though clearly, she knew who the countess was, there were no warm welcoming words.

Thea and Hilda hovered behind Padar and her grandmother with the others and their band of clinging children, all shivering uncontrollably in the chill air, wet through and frozen to the bone. Thea wondered what was to come next. She had not long to wait.

Gytha drew herself up straight and held the abbess's eye with a direct look. 'We do not intend to inconvenience you for long, Abbess Constance. Count Baldwin will be sending an escort for us to travel forward to his court in Bruges.' She nodded towards Padar. 'Our messenger will be on his way to him in the morning at first light, rain, wind or hail.'

Padar bowed. 'Lady Abbess, if we can avail ourselves of one of your monks to guide me there…'

'No need. Count Baldwin has sent me instructions.' She seemed to soften a little as she said in a kinder tone. 'Well, you are here at last, so come this way, Countess, and I shall explain his plans for you in the privacy of my chambers. My nuns will show the women and children the hall where they shall sleep tonight.'

Gytha gave her a formidable look. 'What needs to be said can be spoken in front of my ladies, and now.'

'Well then, if you insist.' Abbess Constance's voice softened further as she surveyed the drenched party of women and children. 'Your exile will be here, where you will all become lay sisters. The children can be educated by our monks until they are of an age to either take orders or go out into the world to households chosen by Count Baldwin in his boundless generosity to your family and your noblewomen.'

Gytha opened her mouth to protest and Thea felt as if a stone had settled in her breast when the abbess raised a hand to silence her grandmother.

'No, it is the count's wish that as part of his protection you rest here indefinitely and that whatever goods you bring with you are to revert to the abbey as payment for your keep. My lady Countess, at your great age you may wish to take the veil.' She smiled thinly. She reached out and touched Gytha's arm. 'It is none of my doing, Countess. We hope you will join our order.' Her voice contained a sense of pity for the women as if she felt their disappointment. 'We shall welcome you.'

'That is *not* our plan. If this is all the count can offer us then I refuse. We shall continue to Denmark and my nephew's court.' The countess turned briskly and looked searchingly about her shocked ladies and children. Her eyes lit on Thea. 'Those who wish to remain in this abbey may do so, of course, but, you see, Abbess Constance, I have my granddaughter's future to consider. We ask for just a few nights' shelter so that the children can rest and my ladies can see for themselves exactly what Count Baldwin is offering them.'

I certainly have no desire to stay here. Thea glanced from the cold-faced nuns to her grandmother.

'As you wish, my lady Countess; but consider this carefully, we have much to offer you at St Omer – a library, a herb garden, great kitchens, weaving rooms, embroidery, contemplation and peace. Naturally, our lay nuns may have their own private chambers which they make most comfortable.'

But it is cold. Thea glanced down. She was standing in a puddle of water. She looked at the children who were clinging to their mothers' mantles. They were dripping water too. *Would this discussion ever end? Would they ever be warm again?*

'More comfortable than this hall, I dare hope,' Gytha retorted.

The abbess inclined her head, giving a shadowy hint of a smile as she said, 'Indeed, the evening is chill. Follow me. You can dry out in the guest dormitory. The servant man can rest here in the hall. I shall arrange bedding and food for him tonight. Tomorrow he must go back to wherever it is he has hailed from.' With those harsh words, Padar was dismissed and the disconsolate group of women had no choice but to trail after the abbess and her nuns out of the hall.

They processed through a lime-washed covered corridor to a guest dormitory where cots were ranged in formation along a wall with very small, high-set windows and little light. A weak flickering fire burned in a corner, this time set into the wall at the end of the room.

The abbess opened her hands and lifted her palms in a sweeping gesture. 'Until you decide your future, this great room is yours. Sister Ann will come for you so you may sup with us in the refectory. Our day here ends with Compline, which every visitor attends but we shall not disturb your rest for early morning Matins.' With those words she inclined her head again and moved away. Momentarily turning back, she added, 'Tomorrow, I shall take you on a tour of our nunnery. It might help you decide.' She smiled. 'It is not such a bitter existence as life can be in the world. The worldly life is harsh.' With those words she swept away, escorted by her band of nuns.

The countess sank down onto the nearest bench, groaned and leaned against the wall. 'Apparently, Abbess Constance has given you all a choice. Choose well, my ladies.'

'Let us see tomorrow, Mother. It will be better by daylight,' Hilda said, taking charge. 'Come to the fire such as it is. That this is certainly no welcoming house is surely so. Tomorrow we can return to the shipwright's hall.' With that, she gently took Gytha's arm and pointed to the cot beside the hearth. 'Rest there, Mother, and get warm. I shall see to the children and their mothers and decide who sleeps where tonight before Sister Ann returns for us. Supper may be better than we think.'

Thea thought how kind her aunt was. She settled her

grandmother on the bed, helped her remove her drenched overgown, found a dry shift in her satchel pulled it over Grandmother's head and covered her with blankets from the other cots. She glanced around the chamber as Grandmother fell into an exhausted doze. Despite the impoverished fire it was clean, airy and contained a peaceful atmosphere. With sudden realisation, she thought again. This may be where Hilda will want to end her journey. *Not me though and not my grandmother.*

Padar waited patiently in the hall, seated on the bench as close to the fire as he could get. After some time, an elderly servant hobbled through another door with a basket of logs and threw a couple on the fire.

'Chill night,' Padar said as he opened his hands to the meagre blaze. The servant nodded and began to retreat with her basket. 'No, don't take them away.' He drew out a purse from his belt and offered her a few coins. She grabbed the coins, clutched them tightly and set the log basket to rest on the floor with a thump. 'My family will be grateful,' she mumbled in the Flemish tongue. 'The sisters must not know. They'll have the coins off me.'

'What kind of sisters are they?' he enquired, also speaking in Flemish.

'They are kind enough and too often on their knees, but there are others such as your ladies who will be made comfortable as long as they have silver in their purses and devotion in their hearts. The nuns are friendly enough when you get to know them.'

'That is a comfort.'

The servant shuffled off before he could ask when he could expect his supper. As if reading his mind, she turned around to face him. 'I'll bring you a bowl of broth in the Compline hour.' With that she disappeared through the doorway. Padar waited a while, threw another log on the fire and, wondering what lay beyond the hall, he crossed to the door the servant had exited and pushed it open.

He was in a courtyard where various tile-roofed buildings stood in a rough square. At various stages, steps ascended to second floors belonging to the various buildings. Smoke hung about the first of these and rain splashed onto the tiles above it. He could smell fish cooking. Carp. Perhaps it was fresh carp from their fishpond. His stomach complained. He would like carp, or was it pike? Whichever, no matter, and if the servant could be bribed to give him logs for the fire, perhaps she could bring him a plate of fried fish with his soup.

As he stood within the shadow of the doorway, a hot tasty dish on his mind, he saw the Godwin ladies walk along the cloistered walkway towards an arched door at the end of the yard. He longed to call out but instead drew back into the shelter of his doorway. The children were bunched together. All five of them looked miserable with their heads hung low and their small hands grasping their cloaks tightly around them. Lady Hilda led the band toward what he assumed was the refectory. The countess and Lady Thea were not amongst them.

He waited as they vanished through the doorway. Thea may have stayed back with Countess Gytha. The countess had looked care-worn. Perhaps she would rest tonight and tomorrow return to the port. They could be away from Flanders and sailing to the royal court of Denmark by evening. After all, King Sweyn Estrithson was Countess Gytha's own blood, her nephew. If she had any sense, that was where she would go, and Thea too.

The next morning, accompanied by Lady Margaret and Lady Hilda, Countess Gytha made her way into the hall. She had taken her supper in the dormitory and after it she had slept long, thankful not to attend Matins in a freezing church. Apparently the skald had slept in comfort, judging by the lingering warmth in the receiving hall. Her sharp eyes noticed the large basket of logs sitting by the hearth.

She leaned over her stick, studied Padar for a moment and

said, 'We've seen the abbey and the library here. It is not as bad as we thought it would be. The nuns are not unkind. Abbess Constance assures me they will provide well for my ladies, though I am not persuaded to remain here. Those ladies who have relatives in Flanders will rest at the abbey with the smaller of our children until they are fetched away to better halls. Abbess Constance is in agreement.' She sighed before adding, 'My daughter, Hilda, and her maid wish to take orders. What a decision, Padar, but so be it.' She glanced over at her daughter. 'She says that St Omer is as good as any other abbey, better than some, and close to the coast should I ever need to return to them. Bah! Their goods will be received into the abbey's care in return for the abbess's goodwill.' She contemplated the crackling fire. 'And plenty of wood in their chambers for the fire.' She nodded. 'Indeed, that is one of my conditions. My ladies must not want for good food, their own chambers and warmth. Lady Megan wishes to stay too. Her sister, Gudrun, who is younger, fourteen summers old, only a year younger than my granddaughter, will accompany us to Denmark as Lady Thea's handmaiden. The boys will remain in the abbey until they can join their mothers' new households. Lady Margaret will accompany us to Denmark.'

Lady Margaret smiled and nodded. Countess Gytha drew breath and folded her hands over the eagle head of her stick. 'So as you see, we are four, Padar, and we shall depart this place tomorrow.' She smiled. 'You, Padar, may have another night here by the hearth.'

A bell rang with a low clanging from the tall abbey tower. Padar waited until it ceased ringing, before replying, 'Countess, permit me to return to the port today and make my lords aware of your decision. With a guard and the cart I can bring the Lady Hilda's goods to her, and the chests belonging to the other women. After that we can leave.' He flexed his fingers and closed his hand. 'It will be the day after tomorrow.'

So the little man was anxious to be off, thought Thea. He had a warm fire and so should they. Gytha remarked as if reading her mind. 'My dear, I shall ask for more firewood for our use today.' The countess glanced from Thea to Hilda to the basket by the hearth. Thea smiled. *Padar was no fool. Neither was Grandmother.*

The arrangement was not a bad one after all. Perhaps it was as well to be out of the new young Count Baldwin's clutches. The Abbey of St Omer was austere but, by day, it had a strange beauty. They had looked around. Hilda had said to Gytha, 'Perhaps it *would* make a final resting place for you one day, Mother. I shall stay here and so ought you. My nephews can take Thea with them to Denmark, and anyone else who wishes to continue the journey.'

'Not yet,' Grandmother had replied saying that she was not of a mind to close the doors on the world this year. The Norse Norns, the three sisters of fortune, continued to weave her fate in the world beyond the cloister. 'After all, I have a marriage to broker.' She had grasped Thea's hand and squeezed it and Thea felt glad that she was to have her grandmother with her a little longer.

'Yes, Padar,' Grandmother now said aloud. 'I agree your plan. Make what arrangements you must and bring Edmund back with you so he can see where his aunt chooses to dwell. My grandsons may well return here with me after we settle Thea's future.'

Padar bowed his head. 'I shall be back in a few days, Countess.'

Countess Gytha said brightly with obvious effort, 'Come, Margaret, Hilda, we shall use this delay to our advantage. We can take the children to see the abbey school. And, Hilda, the abbess promises you and your maid a chamber together. I am afraid the others will remain in that bleak dormitory for now.' She sighed. Thea knew it would be hard for her to say goodbye to the ladies who had been with her in Exeter and on Flatholm but the time for partings was drawing close. She continued, 'We can demand our firewood. Your possessions and silver will be on their way. The sisters here are assured of a great deal of wealth.' With that final word Gytha swept away with her ladies, leaving Padar to gather his pack. She set her wrinkled mouth into a determined line that even the formidable abbess would not dare to challenge.

In the end Countess Gytha had arranged all. Two days later, Thea stood in the yard waiting for Padar and Edmund to unload the noblewomen's possessions. The women of Exeter who chose the life of the cloister were promised great comforts in return for a portion of their goods: a tapestry, books for the library, a golden plate or two and a bag of silver. With this bargain, Christ was promised three new brides.

Though they clung to her, Thea hoped that the children would settle and find hope in their new lives. *Perhaps I can marry well. One day, I shall have my own children,* she thought with longing, when sad-hearted she pulled away from the last little boy and finally departed from her small surrogate family.

Grandmother simply did not feel strong enough to ride again. She climbed into the cart with Lady Margaret, and fourteen-year-old Gudrun. Padar shook the carthorse's reins. Thea touched her mare's flanks with her heels. Edmund clicked his tongue and moved his gelding into place by his sister's side. Today she was protected by her brother, but was her future safe? *She was to become a dispossessed princess sent to Denmark begging for a husband. They had best find her a youthful, handsome prince for nothing less would do. Her prince must win her heart if he was to win her. She was already fifteen years old, and grandmother was right – it was time she had a home of her own and a husband who adored her as her father had her mother. Yes there had been that other wife the earls had made her father take to his bed, but it was her mother whom he had loved. She, too, would have a prince who loved her and one who would love none other, ever. She would be his only wife and his only love.*

She gave her mare a determined flick of her switch and trotted through the abbey gates thinking these thoughts as she glanced back over her shoulder and waved until her aunt was just a grey speck standing by the abbey wall.

5

Schleswig, Denmark, October 1068

Denmark's low shores slid into visibility. They had passed four queasy days and nights on the dark rolling waves and she had felt sick for most of the journey. Even Gytha had been so ill she could only lie under her furs and moan and complain that this was not how she remembered the seas from her youth. As they sailed into the port, Thea suddenly felt the journey's agonies vanish. She clasped her hands together so tightly she felt her knuckles click. Beyond the grey lapping sea, she could make out the town's harbour wall, church spires, and gradually houses with brightly painted door posts came into her view. This sea town was called Schleswig. 'Look, Gudrun,' she said to the girl who quietly stood by her side. 'Our new home. We are away from those who killed our fathers at last.'

Gudrun said solemnly, 'But I shall never forgive them. They stole our lands and they murdered our fathers and brothers.'

'Yes, but now we must find a new home, Gudrun. It doesn't mean that we forgive or forget what happened to our families. Look at the life out there waiting for us.'

The port's curved harbour was packed full of colourful ships with strange beasts surmounting their prows. As their oarsmen rowed through the collection of handsome vessels, guiding the *Wave-Prancer* and the *Sea-Dragon* into their designated mooring places by one of the many quays, Thea's attention shifted from the port buildings to bands of labourers who were loading and unloading cargos.

Danish words ricocheted back and forwards between great-prowed ships and the merchants on the quays. Gytha whose hearing was acute said, 'I feel at home here.'

At last the *Wave-Prancer* had docked. Bursting with

excitement, Thea waited patiently for a ladder to be laid against the ship's hull so they could reach the wharf. To amuse herself as she waited, she studied the prows on the nearest vessels. These bore the carved heads of various-sized dragons painted with green and gold and blue and silver. She had never seen so many griffins, mermaids, sinister orcs, grinning ogres and yellow bears' heads jostling about in one place before.

The men secured ropes, lowered sails and dragged coverings over their weapons and cargo. Edmund and Godwin set a guard of their trusted house coerls on the treasure coffers. Then, and only then, were Countess Gytha, Lady Margaret, Thea and Gudrun allowed to climb down the ladder that Edmund and Gunor dropped into place against the *Wave-Prancer*'s hull.

Once she stepped down onto the quay, Thea noticed the white ermine fur that trimmed rich merchants' mantles. Their brightly dyed knee-length gowns were edged with miniver. Many wore cone-shaped, felt, beaver-trimmed hats, and boots that were decorated with intricate patterning.

These wealthily clothed men moved around the harbour with confidence and purpose, pointing here and there at barrels and sacks with their silver-topped riding whips, selecting this and that to be transported away on various large wagons. Horses with extravagant flashing silver decorations on their bridles restlessly pawed at the earth and shook their manes. Carts with brightly coloured swirling patterns painted on their sides rattled through the hubbub.

No, the people of Denmark did not appear poor. Surely they would find a welcome at her uncle's house? Thea's cousin, King Sweyn, had no love for the Norman king of England. Nonetheless, they all were wary ever since Gunor had said to Padar it was likely that King Sweyn of Denmark had an eye on a slice of England's wealth for himself and Padar had agreed. The king was not to be trusted. Grandmother warned, 'Godwin, trust him not. He is one of the locust princes.'

Padar remarked, with a smile twitching his mouth, 'Remember this, when passing a door-post, watch as you walk

36

on, inspect as you enter. It is uncertain where enemies lurk or crouch in a dark corner. It is just the same with kings as with the common man, my ladies.'

'Indeed,' remarked Countess Gytha. 'Think ahead.'

'Look ahead, the palace lies over there.' Edmund pointed towards a shallow hill to where large gabled building dominated the town. He shook out his hair, ran his fingers through it, tied it neatly back again with a leather thong and turned to Gytha. 'A royal palace indeed, though the king, of course, might be at Roskilde. If so we can send messengers ahead to announce our return.'

Despite her mistrust of the 'locusts', as she called princes who had an eye on England's wealth, Grandmother Gytha's eyes filled with tears. This was her first home, the place of her birth. She was prepared to be sentimental today, an emotion which was rare. 'Sweyn was a child in shifts, last time I saw him. Now he has fifty or maybe more years.'

Feeling great affection for her grandmother, Thea took her arm and whispered, 'Tonight we shall sleep under goose-feathered quilts.' It would be welcome after long days sailing over the rolling seas into the northern lands.

Gytha replied, 'By the looks of it everyone is well off enough to have a dozen goose quilts.' Then she grunted, 'Well, they were ever pirates!'

Thea started at the clatter of horses' hoofs and the sound of their jingling bells. Sensing a growing excitement, she looked beyond the wharf to where a band of riders was trotting along a dirt road that swept towards them carving its way through raised walkways fronting the harbour buildings. Merchants, sailors, and slaves with collars about their necks scattered as the newcomers came trotting along the quayside. The riders rode swiftly onto the stone quay, calling to Godwin and Edmund. Godwin raised his hand in greeting.

The horses swaggered towards them, followed by a long wagon drawn by two magnificent high-prancing white ponies. It was painted white and decorated with a row of tall golden crowns. Gorgeously patterned pennants fluttered from each side as it rolled down along the quay on smooth, well-oiled wheels. A dwarf held the horses' reins and despite his low stature appeared completely in control of its movement.

Godwin and Edmund stepped protectively in front of the women as a stout, thickly bearded man, garbed in a richly fur-trimmed cloak, swung down from his mount. His grey-and-white-streaked hair fell thickly to his shoulders under his tall jewel-studded crimson velvet crowned hat. His companion, tall, fully armed, wearing a leather tunic under his short mantle, leapt off his mount to stand behind the older man, his hand hovering menacingly over the pommel of his sword.

Edmund and Godwin fell to their knees. 'My lord king,' Godwin said, looking up at Sweyn Estrithson. Merchants stopped their business. They turned and bowed low in obeisance to their king. Thea and Gytha inclined their heads followed by their two ladies, Margaret and Gudrun. Godwin lifted his eyes and announced, 'We have arrived from Flanders, my liege. I have brought my sister and grandmother with me. They seek your protection.'

So this was Sweyn Estrithson, King of Denmark. He scanned their small company with sharp, piercing, blue eyes before speaking. 'You have returned, Godwin Haroldson, and safely, I see. Well, back in Denmark safely. May God be praised! Informants gave me a sad report about the loss of your brother, Magnus. What was King Dairmaid of Dublin thinking of when he allowed that fledgling to fight before he had first broken in his sword?' He waved a huge gloved hand at Thea's two kneeling brothers. 'Get up off your knees, cousins, obeisance in the offal and dirt does not become us. And you too,' he called over to the kneeling merchants. 'Get onto your feet and be about your own business.'

As Godwin and Edmund scrambled up Sweyn Estrithson studied Countess Gytha, smiling from his aunt to Thea his cousin. 'Now, who do we have here? By Christos, tis indeed Aunt Gytha, who looks as if she could do with a long rest in a soft bed.'

Gytha inclined her head. 'That can wait.' With a jerk of her granddaughter's mantle, she pulled Thea forward. 'Nephew, I bring with me my granddaughter Thea and our two attendants. Our request is a simple one. We ask that we may join your court, for a time.'

'For a time?' the Dane said stroking his beard and looking thoughtful. 'What other plans do you have?'

Gytha impatiently tapped her stick. Her voice was strong as ever as she said, 'England will shake off the Norman pestilence and when that day comes we go back to whence we came, to our own lands.'

Sweyn narrowed his eyes. 'Let us pray then that it will be soon.' He smiled, showing a set of strong though yellowed teeth. 'Meantime, welcome, Aunt Gytha.' He turned away from his aunt, reached out, lifted Thea's tiny hand in his great bear-like paw and said, 'Welcome, my lovely cousin.' Thea felt his eyes slide up and down her person, as if he was already appraising her for a marriage market. Well, did she not want a husband? Yes, indeed she did, as long as he was a prince and handsome and kind and not one of Sweyn's burly warriors who stood about watching, their eyes following their king's as he greeted her.

Humbly bowing her head, she wished that there had been time to change their travel-stained clothing. Perhaps then she would not feel so exposed. A gift too, perhaps, would make her feel as if they were not so dependent on this king's goodwill.

King Sweyn smiled broadly. 'Well, now. There are many who have come from other places dwelling at my court, merchants and slaves from the Slav lands and we have your father's disgruntled thanes ...' he looked hard at Thea, '... from England, too, all looking to make their fortunes in my country, but none as comely as my little cousin, Thea. We shall have to find you a husband.' He *was* speculating. And, in that moment, she determined that she would have her say in what happened to her.

39

He turned from Thea and gathered Grandmother Gytha into an embrace. Releasing her, he remarked that she was as delicate as a bird, adding, 'So now we shall make room in our humble house for the courageous Godwin women.' At this, Gytha's tears flowed, a sight that Thea had not seen since her father and uncles were slaughtered at the Battle on Senlac Hill, not even in the worst days of the siege at Exeter. Gytha dabbed delicately at her eyes with her veil. For a moment, Thea thought her grandmother had lost her wits and her sense. Surely Grandmother did not trust him after all.

Sweyn said, 'No need for sorrow today. You are safe here, Aunt Gytha, and look, I have a wagon for your comfort.' He swirled around, fleet of foot for such a large man and pointed to the elaborate cart where the dwarf sat on its driving platform watching their exchange, his small eyes blinking at them. Sweyn's hands flew opened in an elaborate gesture, 'Come, ladies.'

After he had ushered them towards the cart and helped them and their two women climb on board, he turned to Godwin and Edmund. 'We spotted the *Wave-Prancer* and the *Sea-Dragon* from the high rooms of my palace. Soon enough messengers rode up from the port to confirm that you were back.' He clapped his great hands together and looked over at some merchants who were clearly half-listening as they finished checking the unloading of barrels. 'Now let us be gone where we can talk without being overheard by flapping great ears.' He glared at the merchants. How quickly his facial expressions change, thought Thea uneasily.

Godwin hesitated. 'I need to finish securing the ships first. Padar will escort my mother and sister.' Padar bowed to the king, who slapped him heartily on the back. 'Good to see you back safely, Padar; you little cat with many lives.'

Padar said, 'A cat that moves silently if he scents danger.'

Sweyn frowned and muttered, 'No fool there.' Turning to Godwin, he nodded. 'As you wish and I shall send carts down from the palace for the weapons and your luggage. I expect the ladies travelled light. We can feed and clothe you all here. My new queen, Elizaveta, will see to that.' With those words, he swung back up onto his stallion.

Padar grabbed his pack from the ground where he had dropped it and climbed up onto the richly decorated royal wagon beside the dwarf. With a crack of a silver-headed whip the little man with the reins manoeuvred the wagon around with ease and they were off.

The air in the women's room was thick with chatter. This room took up the upper floor of the sea-side palace and pleasantly looked out to sea. For two long days Thea had sat quietly close to a window with a table napkin poised on her lap. She was bored with stitching it. Tired of the sewing and the sound of women's constant voices ringing in her ears, she watched out of the window, looking for ships sailing into port, rarely speaking unless spoken to.

Occasionally Gudrun, who had become her obedient shadow, helped her select threads for the napkin that she was embroidering with wool in garish bright colours that the Danes seemed to favour. She longed for the delicacy of silk and the precious silver and gold embroidery threads she had used in England.

In the centre of the group of women sat Ingegerd, a sharp-faced young woman who was Harald Harthrada's daughter and recently both Sweyn's stepdaughter and his daughter-in-law. In the year following her father's death at Stamford Bridge, Ingegerd had married Olaf, one of Sweyn's many sons. Shortly after, her mother, Elizaveta, who was also Harthrada's widow, had married King Sweyn. Elizaveta and Ingegerd had travelled to Denmark from Norway after the defeat at Stamford Bridge. It had long been rumoured that Elizaveta had disliked her Norwegian marriage and was not sorry to be rid of her berzerker husband, King Harald. That bit of tittle-tattle had even reached Exeter. Thea believed it. Elizaveta had been particularly kind and welcoming to the Godwin exiles. Not so her daughter. Thea felt that Ingegerd, who always looked so haughtily at her, would never warm to them. Nor could Thea warm to Ingegerd, but she determined to rise above the slights, and slights there were, but then Thea thought maybe Ingegerd had her reasons.

Ingegerd's father, King Harald of Norway, had given battle to Thea's father at Stamford Bridge while the Normans had landed in the south, in that fateful late summer of 1066. Thea considered it only just that King Harald and her treacherous Uncle Tostig, who had allied with the Norwegian king, had both died in the battle at Stamford Bridge. Between them, they had deliberately weakened the English army by their attempted invasion. Was it because Harald of Norway was planning to carve England up with Duke William of Normandy; for him the Danish north and for Duke William the south? Nobody knew the truth of it, but whatever Harald of Norway was planning when he sailed down the Northern sea road with his war fleet, he was, at least in part, responsible for her father, Harold of England's defeat, his death at Senlac and that of her two noble uncles, Uncle Gyrth and Uncle Leofwine.

Somehow she must dwell in peace with this difficult woman. She must try to put her own ill will behind her. If only Ingegerd would show her a little warmth, perhaps the chilly Danish princesses might also welcome her into their circle. But this cold-hearted daughter of Norway, black-eyed, dark-haired Ingegerd, threw confiding smiles at her sisters-in-law when Thea entered the stuffy, carpeted sewing chamber. As they stitched, she cast polite looks cold as winter frost in Thea's direction, and Thea despaired because she could not penetrate those unsmiling obsidian eyes; eyes that held not a scrap of emotion and clearly wished her ill.

Thea had to sleep in the women's chamber in a curtained-off boxed bed that she shared with Gudrun. The Danish princesses had a whole room to themselves, one that was set apart from the women's work chamber, whereas in the women's room there was little privacy. Thea felt the princesses' maids watching her at night until she pinched out her candle and pulled the coarse linen curtain against their sidelong glances. She suspected that they sniggered behind her back when they lay down on pallets close by.

Although the princesses had maids to wait on them, Thea had to fetch her own washing water and empty her own chamber pot before the Danish princesses arrived each day to sew. Grandmother Gytha, on the other hand, had been allotted her own chamber. She passed her days with Queen Elizaveta in a private antechamber behind the king's hall, comfortably ensconced far away from the tensions of the sewing room.

When she complained to Countess Gytha, Gytha drew her close, stroked her hair with her skeletal fingers and said, 'Thea, raise your head and ignore them. Wait your time for action with patience. When it arrives you will outshine them all. If you do you must have a degree of humility and elegance. There must be no childish tit for tat. Now smile.'

'Yes, Grandmother. I promise to behave with decorum. I shall try.' She smiled, though tears filled her eyes as she did.

Thea had never felt so alone. She prayed to St Theodosia daily that her situation might change; even hoping that Sweyn might find her an acceptable husband very soon so she could escape.

After a week of prayer her saint answered her plea. No husband in the offing, but the talk was of their removal to a royal palace at Roskilde. It was apparent that this was where the princesses spent their winters and, since Roskilde was an island, soon they would be making another sea journey. Then, thrilling news reached the sewing chamber. As they prepared to leave, the princesses announced that a visit from the court of Kiev was imminent.

Thea stopped sewing. She looked towards the closed circle as the girls' chatter became even more interesting. Prince Vsevolod, brother to the Grand Prince of Kiev and brother to Queen Elizaveta, sought a wife for his son, fifteen-year-old Prince Vladimir.

'He is exactly my age, well, probably a few months older,' Thea ventured, attempting to join in the conversation.

The princesses haughtily looked her way. The eldest of them said, 'She speaks. Well, Thea, he will seek a rich dowry.'

'I doubt you have a dowry,' Ingegerd said, throwing a supercilious glance in her direction. 'Any silver your grandmother possesses will go to my father as payment for your brothers' ships. Much good has that done them.'

'My brothers will reclaim our kingdom,' Thea said, trying hard to swallow her fury. She decided impulsively that she wanted this prince. He was young and he would without doubt be handsome. Elizaveta, who was his aunt, was a very handsome woman. So it went without saying the family were too. Aloud she remarked quietly, 'It is just a matter of time. My brothers intend to capture the north.'

'So I hear,' said the Danish princess. 'But if my father helps them he will expect the crown of England for one of my brothers or maybe for the English Aetheling, Prince Edgar, as my father's under-king. So you see, we have great wealth and shall marry well.'

'Of course, maybe Prince Edgar would have you to wife, Thea,' the second eldest princess added. 'He is as penniless as you are. You could live on gruel in the Scottish hills.'

'Is that so?' Thea said, remembering the gangly prince from Uncle Edward's days, a pasty looking boy with little to say. 'I have no doubt that the English will not accept a young man with no fighting skills, one with no experience of government and who hardly speaks English, a prince who has lived most of his life in exile.' She made one more careful stitch, looked up and added, 'My brother would be a competent king, like my father was.'

The princess shrugged. 'Godwin has experience, does he? I doubt that. Besides, I don't think the Prince Vsevolod of Kiev will want an impoverished exiled princess for his son. He will choose one of *us*.'

Thea bit back her retort. She had been ordered by her

44

grandmother not to speak of their treasure coffers. She had overheard Godwin whisper to Countess Gytha, 'Our goods, including my sister's third portion, are stored away in a safe building with strong doors, a guard and secure locks.' Padar and Gytha were not alone in their mistrust of King Sweyn.

'Good,' Gytha had whispered back. 'I do not know my nephew's mind yet. It is for the best he does not know our wealth. Godwin, bring me a golden cup as a gift for him. There is a ruby-studded chalice in my chest, find it, and a psalter too, the one with St Luke's gospel. Its cover is emerald-studded. You will discover that amongst your father's collection of books on hawking. I shall present it to Bishop Vilhelm when we remove to Roskilde for the winter. Oh, and, Godwin, bring me a jewelled arm bracelet for Queen Elizaveta. Choose that gift well. It is a peace offering. Harold was responsible for the death of her first husband.'

'She deserves nothing. Her first husband attacked my father's kingdom,' Godwin had retorted, then reconsidered, adding, 'Grandmother, consider it done.'

Ingegerd was saying, 'My uncle, Vsevolod of Pereiaslavl, and his two brothers, my other uncles, are the richest princes in Christendom. They will choose appropriately for their sons.' Taking Thea by surprise, she rose from her sewing chair, glided like a swan to the widow seat, lifted Thea's embroidery, and cast a sharp eye over a line of uneven red stitches. Holding it up, she spun around with it for the others to see. They raised four pairs of eyebrows. 'I think you must unpick that, Thea, my dear,' Ingegerd said, turning back. 'Your cross-hatching work is wanting.' Thea felt her face colour when Ingegerd dropped the sewing back into her lap and handed her a small pair of silver scissors. 'Keep them. I have others. You will have need of them here.'

At those words the four Danish princesses smirked. Thea felt her face redden with anger. She bent her head over her needlework but could not resist commenting as she undid her row of embroidery, easing out the stitches carefully with the

45

point of the silver scissors. 'The prince will never choose shrews for his son's wife. He will consider a woman who is refined and gentle.'

Thea's sarcasm had not missed its mark. The four princesses looked haughtily away as if she was not worth the effort of a comment. They began to discuss the gowns they intended to wear when they were presented to the ambassadors from Kiev.

Thea held her work up and examined her re-worked, now perfect, stitching, turning it over as obviously as she dared, allowing the others to see her neat work. She handed the scissors back to Ingegerd. 'Thank you, Ingegerd. I have no further need of these today. My grandmother has many that are sharper than yours.' Ingegerd snapped them up and returned them to her belt purse without a word.

Placing her embroidery carefully into the work basket by her chair, Thea raised her head proudly and said to Gudrun, 'Come, Gudrun, let us seek pleasanter company. We shall go and see if Padar is in the hall. I want him to teach me a new tune for my flute. His music will be sweeter than the air in this chamber.' With those words she had drawn her sword.

Thea swept from the sewing room, adjusting her veil to hide her escaping tresses. She knew that the moment she departed, the princesses would discuss her. She smiled to herself. Her dowry would surprise them but, more importantly, it should please Elizaveta's brother and his son. She longed for a prince such as this one. He was young and surely he would be kind. 'Vladimir.' She whispered his name to herself as she left the chamber. 'Prince Vladimir and Princess Gytha.' She used her formal name. It sounded right. As she tripped down the staircase into the hall with Gudrun, she thought of the beautiful Godwin christening gown which Elditha, her mother, had given her when they were departing from Exeter and which she kept wrapped in soft linen in the bone-plated silver box set amongst her own treasures safely at the bottom of her travelling bag. One day it would be used for a prince. 'Wait and see, my lady Ingegerd. I shall wed my prince.'

6

Roskilde, October 1068

Church bells began to ring, obliterating the sounds of the street, the hawkers selling trinkets and merchants selling spices, eels and bread. The countess rose from her chair and gently closed over the shutters. 'I have something to say to you, Thea, so listen carefully.' She returned to her chair.

Thea glanced up from her embroidery. She was glad to spend a morning with Grandmother at last rather than in the sewing room. 'Oh?'

'Our visitors from Kiev seek a bride. Queen Elizaveta thinks they will select one of her stepdaughters.' Thea took in a deep breath. If only he was to be her prince. The countess lowered her voice. 'But this marriage is dynastic!' And I am highly connected myself and wealthy.'

Grandmother was plotting, but what and how? Thea wondered at her old grandmother whom she so loved for a moment. 'And?'

Gytha's thin lips relaxed into a smile. 'King Sweyn is organising a grand reception. You will, of course, be presented with the other princesses. You must behave perfectly.' Thea's embroidery slid from her knee onto the floor planks. This was her chance. She must seize it. She would hold onto this opportunity as she now held onto her stool, grasping it with both hands. Her heart battered hard against her rib cage.

Gytha raised a thin eyebrow. 'Sweyn's daughters are well connected to royal houses throughout Europe,' she remarked. 'But none can hold a candle to you, Thea.' She gripped the head of her stick and seemed to concentrate hard. 'And our visitors from Kiev shall see you at your best.' She clicked her tongue against the few yellow front teeth she had left to her. Thea gasped at Gytha's forthrightness. And why should she not consider a brilliant marriage? She had put up with much unpleasantness here from those princesses with great patience. Not only was this her big opportunity to win a prince, it was also her chance to escape them, all of those smug, rude and spoiled girls.

As if reading Thea's mind Grandmother Gytha said, 'You have put up with slights from those princesses. I have intended speaking with Elizaveta since it became obvious that they have been cruel in their behaviour towards you but she only sees goodness in Sweyn's daughters.'

Thea nodded, there was never proof. The girls were subtle.

'So we shall work together on this. It is time we removed you elsewhere.'

'I have no gown in which I can be presented, Grandmother. There is not enough time to have a seamstress make me one.'

'We *can* make you look elegant and beautiful. In my travelling chest there is a valuable silk gown, tunic, and an equally fine matching ermine-trimmed mantle. Perhaps the gown and its tunic can be adjusted to fit you.' Gytha creased her brow into thin pleats. 'Though I may have shrunk with the passing years, like you I was tall in my youthful days.' Gytha rapped her knuckles decisively on the arm of her chair. 'The tunic may not need adjusting, just the gown's bodice and side seams. You are very slim, my child, too slim. You eat like a bird.'

The more Gytha described the gown, the more Thea longed to wear it. It had been so long since she had worn beautiful clothes. The blue gown had a tunic of damask silk, its borders encrusted with pearls and decorated with silver embroidery.

'Now let me see. What else will you need, shoes? No you must have slippers, slippers with embroidery to match the gown. And there is a long veil stitched with silver threads hidden in my travelling chest that surely can be cut into a more fashionable shorter veil. I believe there may be a jewelled fillet as well, to hold it in place. Once we find them, hang them, stitch them, brush them, you will look like the princess you truly are, my little bird.'

Gytha rattled on. There was the question of Thea's dowry. She was sure that Sweyn suspected her wealth after she had given him and Elizaveta expensive gifts. But her nephew was much too preoccupied with the delegation from the lands of the Rus to ask her about a dowry for Thea. He wanted the prince for one of his daughters. Again Gytha's voice fell into a whisper. 'It is well our treasure chests are placed in a warehouse under constant guard because we shall have your dowry to hand.'

Gytha lifted up Thea's chin so that Thea found herself looking with wonderment into Gytha's smiling eyes. 'Did you know, Thea, that noblewomen in Russia are expected to glide like swans? So Elizaveta says. Ingegerd may have a cunning look about her, but her elegant manner of walking, head held high, moving forward as if she barely touches earth is to be commended. You, my granddaughter, will walk in an equally stately manner tomorrow.' The countess lifted her little tinkling bell and rang it. When Lady Margaret bustled into the chamber from the next room, a tiny antechamber where she slept, Gytha told her to seek out the garments for Thea from amongst the clothing she kept in her travelling chest.

Lady Margaret nodded and without hesitation, hurried to the clothing coffer and did as the countess commanded.

Bending over the opened chest, she began to search for the silk gown her mistress had described, scattering long-unused, fennel-scented mantles and robes all over Gytha's bed. Thea jumped off her stool and ran over to help Lady Margaret.

'My lady, I should shake these out, brush them all and hang them on the pole behind that curtain,' she offered.

Lady Margaret stretched up again, this time holding a woollen mantle lined with squirrel fur. 'Here, Thea, take this and shake it over there.' Thea diligently took the mantle and hung it over the clothing pool and began to beat at it with a rod, creating clouds of fine dust. Lady Margaret lifted up a pair of felt mittens from the chest. 'Winter is coming, Countess. You will soon need these again.'

'Leave them out.' Gytha rose stiffly from her chair and tapped her way over to the chest. She pointed with her stick and poked at a roomy grey gown that Lady Margaret was now holding up. 'Grey, dull. Drab, but then drab I am, too old for the bright silks the young can wear.' She bent over the chest. 'Keep looking, Margaret. I know it is in there.'

'This may be it,' Lady Margaret exclaimed as she lifted out a linen bundle.

'Ah, good,' Gytha said. 'So it is.' She withdrew the dress and tunic from the linen clothing bag and held both up to the light. 'They will suffice,' she remarked, letting her aged arms fall again. She allowed the silk and damask garments to drop onto the clothing lying on her bed. She examined the silk gown again. 'Nothing your needle cannot do.' Thea was striking the dusty cloak with a stick and at the same time watching the contents of the coffer as they appeared. As the overgown slid onto the bed she had felt a surge of anticipation. Grandmother leaned heavily on her stick and smiled. Then she rapped the top of her clothing coffer in a decisive manner. 'Close the lid, Margaret. Thea, leave off thumping at that mantle. You will have us choking with dust soon. Come over here, girl. We have your gown.'

Thea, to her relief and pleasure, possessed her own chamber at Roskilde. She rose when she wanted and avoided the princesses as much as was acceptable and now felt increasingly thrilled about the arrival of the ambassadors who hailed from a snowy, forested land. Russia seemed as distant as Jerusalem and as unfamiliar as the far away countries to the east where spices were purchased.

It was like something out of the stories she had told the children during the siege of Exeter. She would be that magical princess. What was her prince like? How could she find out? Perhaps Gudrun could find out about him from a servant attached to the ambassadors. There were English servants amongst them, she had heard, girls whose fathers had taken them into exile after the Great Battle. She must enquire.

Gudrun at first resisted. But a few days later she came rushing into their chamber carrying a basket overflowing with their freshly laundered undergarments. She dropped the basket onto the floor. She was out of breath. Her words came rushing forth. 'My lady, I've done as you asked. A girl called Greta who washes the ambassadors' personal linens approached me in the laundry …'

Thea jumped up. 'What, you know his appearance, Gudrun. Is he dark? Is he handsome? Is he tall, as tall as me? What does he do all day? Is he generous? Is he kind? Does he have a hunting dog and a hawk? Has he taken a mistress …?'

'Too many questions, my lady. I cannot find out all those things. It would be too bold.'

Thea folded her arms and tried to look nonchalant. 'Well, I don't really care. But what did you discover that made you race back here and tumble the laundry onto the rushes?'

'Well, my lady, he is tall and he is courageous, so says Greta, who has only seen him once. He is proud of bearing and he speaks many languages. He is dark and his eyes are velvety brown. His skin is clear and he is neither fat nor thin and his hair is black and glossy.' Gudrun looked down at her toes and up with a mischievous smile. 'She says that everyone admires him and that the young Rus noblewomen all want him to husband.'

'Oh,' frowned Thea.

Gudrun said quickly, 'He has fought in battles since he was fourteen summers.'

'Gudrun, you have done well. If you find out anything else …'

'My lady, I shall tell you the moment I discover it.'

On the morning of the ambassadors' reception, Thea hummed an old English song about love and blackbirds to herself as she bathed in a tub of tepid water carried by servants up two narrow staircases in heavy wooden pails. As she dried her hair with a linen towel by the opened shutters she could glimpse the church steeple and the thatched lower roof of Bishop Vilhelm's two-storeyed palace building. If she leaned out and peered around the sides of the window opening she could see an image of a cow's head carved on one gable, a dragon's head on another, a bird, a stork on another and a golden swan rising up in the distance. Elizaveta said that Russian noblewomen glided like swans. Well if they could, she could also and, after all, her mother had often been compared to a swan. She would be as a golden swan with her gold-red hair, long neck like her mother's and her mother's fashionably pale skin. Thea touched her throat. I am like a swan. I am gold, I am rich and I am told that I am handsome. Pray God, I shall win my prince today and he will love me and in return I shall have his children and help him rule his lands as a princess must.

The pearl-encrusted silk gown and tunic lay across her bedcover. Lady Margaret had neatly and expertly adjusted the gown. Brushed and scented, the old fabric was as well preserved and as bright as it must have been twenty years ago when Grandmother Gytha wore it at King Edward's court in Westminster. She cherished the hope that the sapphire-coloured material would reveal its subtle sheen in the hall's candlelight. She touched the silver circlet studded with sapphires and the delicate, transparent veil that lay beside it. Queen Elizaveta had insisted that at this private reception she should not wear a veil. Her hair would be her only adornment.

In that moment Thea decided that she did not like the idea of being surveyed by strangers alongside the Danish princesses, her tresses loose as if they were in a slave market. Gytha's shortened veil was delicate and it would frame her hair to advantage. She would wear it.

Gudrun broke into her thoughts exclaiming, 'The princesses will never compete with you no matter how they dress this afternoon.'

Thea dropped the veil on top of the gown. 'I hope it does not give them any more cause to dislike me than they have already.'

When King Sweyn had confirmed yesterday that the Russian ambassadors expected to see the recently arrived Saxon princess whom they called Gita, the Danish sisters had been openly rude, repeating that Russian princes liked Danish princesses. Danish princesses knew every household task so that they could oversee their household servants. What did Thea know of bee keeping and cheese-making, brewing and baking cakes?

Thea had coolly replied, 'Nothing that cannot yet be learned.' At this retort the princesses had looked away with scowls on their faces, and she was sure she had heard one of them mutter 'Shrew,' beneath her breath.

When Elizaveta had entered the sewing chamber she admired the embroidery on Thea's napkin. The four princesses had smiled sweetly at their stepmother and nodded. Ingegerd remarked that, thanks to their help, Thea was improving her embroidery skills. Thea had bit back her angry retort. Elizaveta was blind. How could she not see through her stepdaughters' behaviour? How could she not see that her own daughter was lying? Thea was teaching *herself* the colourful Danish embroidery, though any possible enthusiasm for Danish embroidery had been quelled by the Danish princesses' cruel behaviour.

'My lady, I am always delighted to learn new skills,' she said to Queen Elizaveta with a smile playing about her mouth. The princesses had the grace to look away. Ingegerd raised a haughty eyebrow and said, 'She learns our ways very well, Mother.'

'And Thea is a lovely young lady, always gracious.' Elizaveta frowned at her stepdaughters. 'I am sure you can learn much from Thea too.' Dutifully the girls nodded. 'Yes, my lady,' the eldest of them said, speaking for them all. Thea managed her most gracious smile at them, though she did not feel in the least courteous.

The princesses were to demonstrate a dance for the

ambassadors and they would present gifts to them. Thea knew that in this she could excel. She could outdance them all and if they were asked to play music, Padar had taught her an intricate and haunting tune on the flute. She asked her grandmother if she would present a gift too. 'No, Thea, but I shall on your behalf and it will be a great gift. I shall present them with a relic for the Patriarch of Novgorod.'

Thea wondered if the countess had stripped the Exeter minster of all its precious relics. When she asked, Gytha replied, 'Only the three that I had given to the Exeter minster. I had no intention of them ending up in a Norman cathedral.'

'May I comb out your hair, Lady Thea? I think it is almost dry,' Gudrun was saying, lifting a comb from Thea's little table.

'I think you may, Gudrun. I shall sit on your stool so that you can reach.' Thea replaced the silver and sapphire fillet and gossamer-thin silk veil carefully on her bed as Gudrun scrambled from her seat.

The royal family attended midday prayers. When afternoon arrived, Thea felt her heart hammering against her ribs. She took a deep breath to steady her nerves. The royal princesses swept from the chapel and entered the porch that opened into the great hall, led by their governess, Lady Eleanor, a strict woman just returned from France, where she had remained all summer with her own noble family, attending her mother's funeral, helping her younger sisters by settling two of them in a nunnery and the third into a marriage with an aging widower who kept the neighbouring lands. Her only brother was young and her father was surely dying, she told them with sadness in her eyes.

On her timely return, order filled the sewing room. Under her strict rule the princesses behaved with decorum. The preparations for the girls' appearance in front of the ambassadors had proceeded pleasantly. Lady Eleanor had warmed towards Thea and during the few days preceding the presentation, Thea had relaxed. 'It's actually enjoyable now we have Lady Eleanor with us,' she had confided to Gudrun.

Gudrun laughed and said to her, 'Well, is it because the princesses have been so unkind to us or is it because you want love that you wish to win this prince, my lady?'

She had replied solemnly, 'I want to be loved, Gudrun, and I think I shall love *him* with all my heart.' She had bitten her lip and tasted the salty flavour of blood. I can't be sure of that though, she thought to herself. Nothing in my life has ever been sure. Those who once loved me are gone from me. I only have grandmother, maybe Gudrun and possibly Padar. How long will they remain in my life? My brothers will leave me too, but one day, I will have my own beloved companion to share my life and he will love me back.

Lady Eleanor was flat-chested and dressed simply as became her station. She was swathed from head to foot in pale linen which did not become her pasty complexion, or what could be seen of it, because her wimple tightly framed her face, making it look grotesquely shrunken. Her gown was girdled by a silver belt from which dangled a small bunch of keys, a pair of golden scissors and a purse. Thea supposed Lady Eleanor's presence would give the impression that her charges were serious young women, well-educated and carefully schooled in household duties, thus the purse, keys and the scissors.

The king's eldest daughters, Helene and Ragnhild, directly following Lady Eleanor, glided through the outer door wearing scarlet gowns that were much too elaborate and did not suit them. They wore bright emeralds, sapphires and garnets set into rings and bracelets and sewn onto the sleeve borders of their gowns. Gunnhild and Guttorm, the younger sisters, tripped in behind their sisters, their overgowns blue as was her own, but as Thea noted, they were overly decorated with garish embroidery.

Thea walked slowly to her assigned place at the rear of the group. The princesses knew, and she knew, too, that she outshone them all in her rich blue gown with its simple pearls and her circlet of silver and sapphires. They looked her up and down; they looked away and at each other. The eldest girl remarked, 'Pity she is so tall.' It was as if she was not there, a ghost girl, an intruder.

Before they passed through the tall doors into the great feasting hall, Thea removed her circlet. She set it down on a side table in the entrance porch, unpinned the gossamer-fine veil from inside one of her sleeves and carefully placed it on her head. Replacing the silver circlet, she felt her hair fall in coils below it. The effect would be remarkable. Her delicate veil would frame her perfectly symmetrical oval face and yet it would allow her russet hair to show to advantage. As she walked forward, she glanced into the surface of a silver urn and nodded.

Guttorm turned to her and gasped rudely, 'What *are* you doing?'

Thea smiled, knowing with not a little satisfaction that she was disobeying their father. I mark myself out, she thought. I am not prepared to be herded in front of them as if I am a slave at one of the auctions these foreigners hold in their Russian ports, though she conceded to herself that at least her Uncle Sweyn never kept slaves, since the Church disapproved vigorously of the practice. Yet this was, in effect, how they were being presented to the wealthy Russian diplomats.

Once inside the great oak doors, her eyes were drawn to her uncle, who was seated on his great carved throne, presiding over the sumptuous hall. Today he wore a tunic of purple edged with gold embroidery, as if he was an emperor from olden years. Her eyes glided to the three Russian ambassadors seated to King Sweyn's right beside Elizaveta. Grandmother Gytha was honoured today since she had been placed at her nephew's left hand between him and old Bishop Vilhelm. The Bishop smiled benevolently when the five girls progressed forward. He was as fat with goodwill as he was thin and small in stature. What a bizarre way Sweyn had of marketing his daughters, parading them as if they were about to enter Noah's ark.

With another sweeping glance Thea noted that Ingegerd and

Olaf and her brothers Edmund and Godwin and those sons of Sweyn, so many of them, too many names to remember, were seated together down the side.

All eyes followed King Sweyn's daughters as they glided through the centre passage between two wide-set rows of leaf-painted pillars. Thea observed that while the Danes were watching their princesses, all three pairs of diplomatic eyes were looking beyond the Danish princesses at her. She took a quick breath. Sweyn was whispering into the nearest ambassador's ear. The ambassador nodded and looked away from her.

Lady Eleanor led them to their places below the king's table. Behind them hung a rich tapestry with a series of graceful ships that were embroidered with stitches of gold and silver thread, stitching that was different from the gaudy embroidery she had recently worked. These stitches glinted in the candlelight like a myriad of stars. It occurred to her that the crimson, blue and greens of this hanging were intended to become a gorgeous background for the princesses' flowing fair hair. The daughters of Denmark held their heads high. There was no giggling or smirking here as there was in the upper chamber. This was serious.

Though it was afternoon the hall was dim and candles had been lit. That morning, the princesses had discussed this feast. They had boasted of pears from the king's orchard, dates from southern Europe and sweetmeats, such as would usually only be served in distant realms where there was always sunshine, but which often mysteriously appeared in Sweyn's kitchens. Glass tumblers glinted on the linen clothed table and jewelled eating knives sparkled in the soft candlelight. The princesses had napkins of linen to dab their mouths daintily after every bite and silver finger bowls set by their places so their hands remained spotless. They must appear as pristine by the end of the meal as they had at the beginning.

The first dishes were carried to the table by servers. As the feast proceeded, Thea glanced down at her silver plate and slid her fish about it with her knife. She had no appetite. Fowl breasts and tiny pastries stuffed with soft cheese arrived on the table. These were accompanied by various dishes of beets, radishes, and beans that had been cooked soft in oil and served with herbs.

The napkins the visitors lifted to their mouths were those that they had embroidered in the women's chamber in the king's house at Schleswig. She wondered if what Elizaveta was whispering into the ear of the ambassador seated by her would be, 'My stepdaughters' work, so fine.'

Thea shrugged, lifted a date from a golden dish and popped it into her mouth. Ouch, it had a stone. She tried to spit it out onto her plate but failed and it landed instead on the table linen. Princess Gunnhild wrinkled up her nose. She grinned smugly. Her rude smirk quickly vanished the very moment the important, tall-hatted ambassador stared down at Thea and seemed to smile. Thea reached over the cloth and carefully lifted the errant stone between her finger and thumb and daintily placed it on her plate. When he looked away again she watched him. She thought that the diplomat looked pale and unwell. He was not eating anything. Occasionally he removed his furred hat and wiped his brow with one of the embroidered napkins.

A small band of musicians began tuning their instruments. Soon the music struck up. The princesses were called upon to perform an elaborate slow circle dance with four of their brothers, one that Lady Eleanor and the minstrels had adapted from dances they had observed at the French court in Paris. The governess nodded at them and they rose. 'Remove your veil,' Ragnhild hissed at Thea through her teeth. 'You will spoil our effect.'

'I intend to remove it,' Thea said. 'I shall not spoil anything.' She lifted the circlet and veil from her head, folded the veil neatly, laying it on their bench, replaced her silver circlet and glided, her head held high, from the bench to take her place before the king's table where Edmund awaited to partner her. Grandmother's lessons had paid off. She felt that she walked as if floating on a cloud.

Edmund smiled, leaned over and lifted her hand. He was an accomplished dancer and she knew they stood out from the others. He was fair, very handsome and she noticed that often women looked longingly at him. 'Ready,' he whispered.

'Yes,' she whispered back.

They turned to face the high table. But as they spun around again he said so low into her ear that his utterance was like the faint rustle of a soft silken mantle, 'You are doing well, my sister. Now that we are dancing, their curiosity will be wetted, as if you are a fine wine. Was this Grandmother's idea?'

'No, and wetting appetites is not my intention. Winning a prince is,' she whispered back, glancing sideways at the tall, elaborately hatted Russians. Did they ever wear other hats? Their robes were furred. Under them they wore embroidered baggy shirts; they probably hid sharp daggers beneath those broad belts that gathered the material into folds, even though her uncle never allowed weapons into his hall. She slipped around Edmund and around again, and as they stepped lightly she smiled at them all – her grandmother, the king, the queen, the ambassadors and old Bishop Vilhelm, whose face was as red as the embroidery on the napkin with which he persistently mopped his brow and who appeared uncomfortably smothered by his stiff decorated gown. In contrast, the Russian ambassador seated by her uncle looked ghostly pale, as if he were ailing.

Afterwards, one by one the princesses presented their gifts to the ambassadors. These were four caskets each containing a different jewel. Thea stood back with her handsome brother watching this performance. Helene, the last princess to step forward, presented her golden casket. The tall, pallid ambassador stood to receive it, looking tired and pale as bleached linen. Suddenly he sneezed loudly. He instantly fell back onto his chair again, apparently choking. Elizaveta's face creased with concern. She spoke to the Russian diplomat seated by her side who immediately lifted a goblet to his companion's lips. The ambassador seemed recovered but he was gripping the arms of his chair as if he was about to collapse.

Consternation and frowns of concern gathered on the other diplomats' faces. The one with the tallest furred hat, seated nearest the king, leaned across Queen Elizaveta and said something to King Sweyn that she could not hear.

Lady Eleanor nodded at Thea. She stepped forward and began to play her flute accompanied by Padar on his harp. Thea paused. Padar plucked his harp's strings and sang a verse about love. She lifted her flute again and played the final notes of their song. From the corner of her eye she saw two pages help the ailing ambassador from his place and out through a side door. She bowed to Padar and returned to her seat.

The evening continued as Padar recounted an old story of how long ago the Norse hero, Sigurth of Sweden, killed a dragon called Fáfnir and how Sigurth's horse Grani cooked the dragon's heart for him to devour. When Sigurth tasted the dragon's blood he was miraculously able to understand the song of the birds in the trees above him. The sparrows warned him of a treacherous smith in their community. Forthwith the hero killed this smith too and by doing both these deeds he saved his people.

Shortly after this, Lady Eleanor led the girls from the gathering. None of the princesses spoke to Thea as they hurried towards the outside staircase leading up to the women's hall. Instead of joining them, Thea climbed a second narrow staircase up into the gabled end of the great building, far, far away from their glares and unkind remarks. She would stay away from the sewing room that evening. She would not attend Compline, the last evening service of the day to be observed in the chapel, and where, no doubt, the king and his guests would gather before retiring. Instead, she sent Gudrun down to the courtyard kitchen for a jug of watered wine and some leftovers. When the girl returned with a laden tray, Thea spoke of the afternoon's events – the dishes she had hardly touched, the dancing and her concern for the ambassador who had collapsed during the presentation of gifts.

Gudrun said quietly, 'You will have impressed them all and I am sure the Russian ambassador will recover soon.'

Feeling her appetite returned at last, Thea shared the small feast with her handmaiden.

Until it was time to sleep Thea sat, dressed in her finery, by her window dreamily watching the moon rise, wondering if in one of his palaces, Prince Vladimir of Kiev, her raven-headed prince with his liquid brown eyes, was watching the moon rise too. For a while she practised her flute as Gudrun nibbled on a last chicken wing and listened.

As the moon rode high in the sky, Gudrun helped her remove her gown and slip on her linen night shift. She allowed the girl to soothe her into drowsiness by combing out her hair. When they had both climbed into the big comfortable bed, Thea blew out their candle.

'Will they choose you for the prince, my lady?'

'I wish it with all my heart,' she said thinking of the ambassador who had smiled at her. 'Go to sleep, Gudrun.'

She sighed as she looked at her beautiful gown now hanging from her clothing pole, its pearls gleaming in the moonlight. What if she was never able to wear it again? She longed, how she longed, for a prince's love.

It was two days before Thea discovered what was ailing the ambassador from Kiev. He had fallen grievously ill with a contagious disease they called the little pox, which was as deadly as it was terrible, since it spread quickly wherever it appeared. It had been fortunate that she had stayed away from the women's room after the reception and that she had avoided prayer in the chapel that same night, otherwise she might have taken a more serious dose of the pox than she was to suffer.

7

At first, the pox threatened those who had been sneezed over by the ill-fated ambassador. Princess Helene sickened. The ambassador had sneezed on her as she had presented her gift. A few days later her sister Ragnhild became ill. They shared a chamber. Poor Lady Eleanor, so recently returned from France and troubles that had beset her own family, took to her bed sneezing and within days, like the unfortunate ambassador, she was covered from head to toe with white pustules.

Doctors flocked to the palace with cups, poultices and herbs. The ambassador recovered within a few weeks but he would carry terrible scars on his face and body. The two elder princesses slowly recovered but it looked as if they, too, might wear disfiguring scars for the rest of their lives.

A month passed and, before winter set in, trapping them in Denmark, the Kiev delegation made ready to depart, with their gifts, but with no promises of a betrothal for any of the princesses. Unable to let them away without a word on the subject, King Sweyn, who remained healthy since he had once had the pox many years before and wore the scars to prove it, held counsels with the two remaining Rus ambassadors and Countess Gytha. Countess Gytha wanted decisions and she wanted them before those who could make them died. The small delegation announced that they would return from Russia with a decision when the spring sailing season opened up the Baltic Sea.

Shortly after a final meeting, they packed up bag, baggage, and servants and sailed away. The ill Rus ambassador and his five servants who had also taken the pox sailed from Roskilde in a separate ship along with their own doctor, herbal remedies that included comfrey and coriander to keep the fever under control, and an old crone who was rumoured to cure the disease with spells and witchcraft.

Thea sickened on the day they departed. She felt hot and cold all at once. She ached. Her back was exceptionally painful and she vomited up her dinner. When the tell-tale small reddish spots appeared on her mouth and her tongue she knew she was ill with the disease. Gytha put her to bed and prayed. She summoned doctors to Thea's chamber daily and tended her herself. She wrapped her granddaughter in coloured cloths and draped them about her bed to keep the light from her skin. Gudrun, who fortunately did not sicken, placed aromatic bouquets about Thea's chamber and bathed her mistress's skin with infusions of comfrey and liquorice.

'I am dying, Grandmother,' Thea said. 'I am dying and all has gone bad.' She said nothing more for days. She dreamed though. She dreamed of a wedding to a dark-headed prince who turned into a glossy jackdaw and looked down on her with pity. She looked down at her wedding gown and it was soaked with blood. When her fever lessened she felt as weak as a baby chick and as helpless as a newly birthed kitten.

Countess Gytha came to Thea's chamber to find Thea improving. She recounted what had taken place while Thea had been ill. '"Thea is not so ill,"' I said to my nephew. She will have no scars. Her face is clear of spots.'

Thea heard her grandmother recount how she had told King Sweyn that she wished to return to St Omer. Gytha patted Thea's arm. 'I said to him, that assuming they are spared the devil's pox, my grandsons intend sailing back to King Dairmaid's court in Dublinia.' She took a deep breath. 'I told him all this.'

Thea's heard her voice crack. She did not want everyone to leave her again. 'What did he say? I wish you would stay with me here, Grandmother.'

The countess said, 'Listen, Thea. That was not the sum of it all.'

'Oh,' Thea managed.

Gytha told her quietly how Sweyn had grunted at her, '"What are you suggesting, Aunt?"

'"Either my grandsons can take Thea with them to Dublinia or you must send her to a place of safety until she is wed with the Russian prince.'"

Thea raised herself up. 'Is it decided? Am I to marry the prince? What if I am scarred from the pox? I want a looking plate now. Am I scarred?'

Gytha carried the silvered glass over to Thea. 'See, no, you are not scarred, my child. Listen to the rest of it, Thea.'

'The rest?'

Gytha laughed as she took the polished surface away from Thea. 'Sweyn's nose reddened, his face grew more ruddy than usual. If his eyes had been eating knives they would have pierced me through, my granddaughter. "What have you told the ambassadors, Countess?" he asked me. "I know you had meetings with them behind my back. You gave them gifts, I hear.'" I told him that I had informed the ambassadors of your dowry but only because they enquired.'

'What did he say to that?' Thea croaked, now feeling utterly exhausted by her grandmother's visit.

'He said, "What dowry?'" and stroked his white-streaked beard. He asked, "Why have you not told me of this dowry? You mean that I am not expected to provide for my niece?" I told him that I had never concealed my wealth, only its value. King Sweyn then frowned, "Which consists of?" I said, "Gold, silver, jewels and tapestries, all of greater value than the Russian Prince Vladimir could ever expect to see in a lifetime."

'"That I doubt," Elizaveta then said. "Let me remind you that my family are extremely wealthy.'"

'"So am I," I said.

'"So, then, with such wealth, more than I am prepared to provide, perhaps the Rus prince will ask for Thea after all?" Sweyn steepled his hands. "Well, well. Who would have thought that it was Thea's dowry that you stored in that warehouse. My son, Eric, does not have a wife. He is comely

65

enough … Would he not be a better prospect for your granddaughter?"'

Thea started. 'No, Grandmother. Perish the thought.'

Gytha snorted before she replied, 'I told him that the boy is only nine years old and not likely to inherit a throne. I told him that you have the possibility of the Kiev prince when you recover. And recover you have. I said to them, "In return for your support I shall give you my support. If you wish to be united with us, you might ask for my grandson Godwin for your youngest daughter, Guttorm. He likes her."

'"So Godwin for Guttorm," he said. "What exactly do you propose?"'

'"A wedding in summer next," I said.

'"If you have enough silver to set him up with his own hall and if he swears loyalty to the royal house of Denmark, then it is an acceptable proposal."

'"This I can do. Moreover, when my grandsons recover their lands in England they will repay you generously for your kindness to us."

'Queen Elizaveta spoke up. "I think, Countess, when she can travel we can send Thea to my husband's farm at Søderup. She will learn to play more songs, become accomplished on the harp and there she will become expert in embroidery and household skills. If the ambassadors from Prince Vsevolod return for Thea, I shall give her betrothal my blessing. When my stepdaughters recover there will be other husbands for them. The Grand Prince of Kiev, my eldest brother, Prince Iziaslav, may soon seek a wife for one of *his* sons. There are two brothers nearer the throne of Kiev than Vsevolod and his son."

'King Sweyn said in response, 'Yes, my dear, you are right. There are the German princes. There are many, many other princes and princesses besides the only son of your youngest brother, Elizaveta."

'"It is decided then." Elizaveta folded her hands in her lap. "When she has recovered Gunnhild can accompany Thea to Søderup. Gunnhild is only twelve years old and has much to learn. There are women on the farm who will care for our princesses and teach them much. As for Kiev, we shall leave the choice to Vsevolod for now."'

'Grandmother, you are leaving me and it is not quite decided.'

'I think it is very much decided. You will marry the Prince of Kiev. I am sure of it. I shall return to St Omer. And you shall go to Søderup and completely recover your health, my granddaughter.'

Thea sank back into her pillows. Gytha was resolute and when she was so firm, no one quarrelled with her decisions.

After Grandmother tucked her back in bed and she found herself drifting uneasily towards a weary doze, Thea's last thoughts were, *Poor Godwin. He was to be granted a hard bargain in return.*

Gradually, slowly, Thea recovered her strength, and both Gytha and Thea felt saddened that the two older princesses of Denmark had not been so fortunate. They remained in darkened chambers, still very unwell. Elizaveta said it could be worse, much, much worse, since there were not so many marks on their faces as to suggest their removal to a nunnery. They would still make great marriages.

Edmund climbed the staircase thinking. 'What now?' He wanted to be away from this court. It was a miracle that Godwin and he, himself, had not caught the pox. They needed to sail south and soon. Gytha and Queen Elizaveta sat in the countess's receiving chamber with Godwin, and King Sweyn. 'Ah, here you are, Edmund. Have a cup of French wine.'

Edmund declined. Sweyn waited until a servant had filled his own cup with honeyed wine and had discreetly slipped from the chamber before opening a discussion.

The king popped a sugary sweetmeat in his mouth, chewed, swallowed and turned from Edmund to Godwin. 'Your sister has been very fortunate to have recovered her beauty, more fortunate than Helene and Ragnhild.' He leaned forward, setting his cup on a dragon-footed side-table. 'Until the ambassadors from Kiev return to us Lady Thea can rest on my farm. It is a place with women who are skilled in everything she must learn if she is to marry well.'

Godwin said, 'So, Uncle, you agree that she will become wife to Vladimir of Kiev?' Supporting his brother, Edmund nodded.

Sweyn shrugged and rolled his eyes towards the ceiling beams. 'We can all hope for the match. I shall do my best,' he said. He smiled at Godwin and Edmund and looked jovial, as if this had been his intention all along. Gytha pursed her mouth. Edmund was sure it was not. However, apparently Sweyn would support her now if he might bring Godwin further into his sphere of influence. Poor Godwin, thought Edmund. *Thankfully not me.'*

Godwin looked at the cross hanging on his cousin's tunic. 'You swear on the cross that you wear about your neck, lord King, that you will protect her and help her to this marriage with the Rus prince.'

For a moment Sweyn's smile vanished. Edmund thought he would not swear to it. The king was a religious man despite all his cunning. If he swore on the cross it would be binding.

At last King Sweyn spoke, 'I do.' He lifted the jewelled cross that hung from his neck. 'This was given to me by Pope Gregory when I was in Rome many years ago.' He bowed his head, kissed it and swore to protect Thea. Godwin nodded. Edmund smiled as Gytha let out a sigh of relief. 'We can hope for the Prince of Kiev,' he said.

Sweyn lifted the cup of wine, sipped a little and said with a bit of a gleam in his eye, 'Godwin, you do not possess a wife. I hear that you are fond of my daughter Guttorm. Her mother was my concubine and I promise you a dowry for her if you will take her to wife. She is fourteen, old enough to wed. What say you?'

68

Gytha bit her lip and turned away.

Edmund wondered what Godwin would say now that Sweyn asked him directly. It was good for him to be connected to the Danish royal family and the marriage link would strengthen their position. Sweyn would continue his support for their cause. Surely Godwin must see it.

'I have lands to recover before I think of a wife. Yet, I like her well enough. Maybe I could come to love her,' Godwin replied.

'Then it is settled. Elizaveta will speak to her.' He reached over and patted his wife's knee. 'If you are to wed her when you return in the spring from King Dairmaid's court at Dublinia then you must first make *me* a promise.'

'Which is?' Godwin said cautiously.

'Loyalty, just that.'

Godwin knelt and said, 'King Sweyn, your grace, uncle, cousin, you have that already.'

'I must be sure of it whether you win back your English lands or no. Your Godwin treasure can buy you a farm in Gotland, an estate as well as men and ships. Here, swear on the cross, as have I.' Sweyn pulled his gold chain over his head and pushed the jewelled cross into Godwin's hands. Godwin swore loyalty to Sweyn. Edmund noted that his brother did not actually swear to marry the Danish princess.

'And now you, Edmund.' Edmund hesitated, but he, too, followed his older brother's lead. He swore to be loyal to the King of Denmark, his uncle and cousin.

He had best keep his promise.

Before the supper hour, Edmund watched as Gytha wrote a message to be sent to the Patriarch of St Sophia in Kiev. She used the dragon seal that had belonged to the royal house of Wessex to secure her letter. Giving it to Godwin, Gytha said, 'This must go to Kiev with a gift, a great gift. Have you someone with whom we can entrust with this task?'

He leaned forward from his stool. 'I do, Grandmother Gytha, I have a ship travelling to the Vistula. It will be the last chance this season before the ice comes. From there my merchant travels south by Kiev to Constantinople. It is a long journey but if all goes well he will be there by Christmastide. What is the gift?'

'It is a finger bone of St Nicholas encased in gold and crystal. Christmas will be timely. Are you trading, Godwin? You have never talked about it.'

'Edmund and I have bought a ship with a merchant of Norwich who had the good sense to move his valuables to Denmark before he fought at Hastings. He survived the battle and escaped to his Dane relatives as soon as he was able to take ship from England. The merchant is a landless exile, much like us.' Godwin sighed after he spoke of exile.

'And you purchased this with ...'

'Ah, I was going to tell you, Grandmother. I used silver coin, a little of our treasure. There is still much, much, much more, safe in my friend's warehouse, well-guarded by my own people. Thea's dowry is intact.'

'Well then, a sound position.' Grandmother put her seal away in its velvet purse. 'Two good ships and a share in another. What will your merchant bring back for trade?'

'Spices, olive oil and silks.'

'Do you trust this merchant?'

'My father trusted him. He nearly gave his life at Senlac for our family. He forfeited his lands in Norfolk when he fought that day. If he fails me my house coerls will kill him. He will protect your letter and the reliquary. Warriors travel with him.' Godwin tucked Gytha's letter deep into his satchel. He glanced up. 'Come, Edmund. We have a task to do for our grandmother.'

'Grandmother, the reliquary will reach its destination,' Edmund said in a gentle tone. He stood, kissed her rough cheek and took his leave.

Thea complained ceaselessly. Although she was recovering, she felt despair not joy. 'This red robe, I have no need of it now,

Grandmother. It caused me to have terrible dreams.' She had not forgotten her dream of a blood-infused wedding gown and the prince who looked like a jackdaw and who smiled down on her with pity in his brown eyes.

Countess Gytha leaned over and propped her up with pillows. She gave her beer to drink. 'Drink this. It will speed your recovery, Thea.'

Thea grimaced. The beer was laced with bitter herbs. She swallowed and spluttered, 'It is foul.' Gytha handed her a napkin to wipe her mouth.

Her grandmother had told her that Godwin had agreed to marry Guttorm, one of the detested princesses. How could he? And she was to travel with the fourth princess, Gunnhild, to Søderup, wherever that was. At least Gunnhild was the youngest of them and, away from Ingegerd's influence, she might be almost tolerable. Padar and Gudrun were to travel with her too.

As she had lain ill, others had planned her life.

'And when do you depart for St Omer, Grandmother? Will I ever see you again? Will you ever return to us?' She began to weep. Everyone she trusted except for Padar and Gudrun intended leaving her here with the Danes.

Gytha said gently, 'You and I, my precious, have been together since the great battle. Now I must think of my future as well as yours. You will marry soon, if not the Prince of Kiev then another great prince. Your uncle promises to protect your future. He swore on his cross. When you marry, you will travel far into a distant land. I am too old for such travel. If Sweyn fails us, I shall return for you. I promise.'

Thea had to accept that. It was her wyrd, her fate, that she must make a great marriage. Since the ominous dream she was not so sure that she wanted Prince Vladimir after all. She wiped her tears away with her napkin. 'When will you set out?'

Gytha took her in her arms and embraced her. 'Soon, my sweet girl; not before you depart for Søderup.' She drew back and Thea saw concern in her grandmother's pale eyes and on her brow. *I must be brave for her sake.* 'I think you may be able to travel within two weeks,' Gytha said quietly. 'Lady Margaret and I must sail for Flanders before December grips us with cold and storms. You will not be without your brothers for long. Godwin and Edmund will return in the spring.'

'It will be a sorrowful winter-tide without you, Grandmother.'

'You will be in my prayers and thoughts every day, little pearl.'

'And you in mine, Grandmother, for ever.' Tears threatened again. She swallowed them back, and for the remainder of the afternoon they talked about how Padar would teach her more stories and songs, and of how he would watch over her as once he had watched over her mother, Elditha. The mother I lost, Thea thought, raising the linen cloth to dab at her eyes again, and now I am to lose my grandmother too.

8

Søderup, December 1068

At the beginning of December, on a frosty morning with spider webs clinging to hedgerows, Thea sailed from Roskilde. It took a whole two days to travel back in the direction she had come from a month earlier.

King Sweyn's manor was situated on an inlet north of Schleswig where there nestled a special harbour for the king's ships. After they disembarked they travelled through the bitterly cold countryside in a covered cart. Thea was swaddled in a fur cloak. Princess Gunnhild complained constantly that her father should have given her a fur mantle as well.

'You don't even look ill,' she said nastily to Thea.

'I wish I did not feel so tired all the time. You were fortunate to escape this pox.' Thea turned to Gudrun, 'And you too, Gudrun.'

She archly turned away when Gunnhild, still muttering complaint, burrowed deeper into her cloak, a rich mantle which Thea noted was, in fact, warmly lined with sheep's wool.

The clip-clop of a horse drew up beside them. Padar peered in through the wagon's curtain. 'Is all well here?' He glanced at the Danish princess, who scowled back at him.

'Oh, has the milk curdled, Princess Gunnhild?'

'No, it has frozen.'

'We shall be there soon.'

'Thank you,' Thea said. 'I shall be glad to lie down.'

'You will not have long to wait now, Lady Thea.'

A wide gate drew open. Through the parting in the curtain Thea saw a sprawling farmhouse with two storeys. A collection of snow-sprinkled wooden buildings was set in an orderly semi-circle about it. Trees stood around the farm yard, their branches shivering in the wind. Then she made out figures wrapped in heavy cloaks chopping wood, carrying pails and lifting straw with pitchforks from an open cart. Their wagon drew to a halt in the yard. Grooms ran forward to hold the horses steady as the girls dismounted. Two smiling figures appeared in the yard and a moment later, a broad-shouldered, heavily cloaked man stepped forward.

'Good to see you, Princess Gunnhild.' He bowed graciously. 'And you too, Theodora Gytha, welcome to Søderup. I am Jarl Niels. My wife, Lady Ingar, will make you comfortable while I see that these dolts of grooms do the same for the horses.' He waved for his wife to come forward and meet King Sweyn's cousin. Moments later, after friendly greetings were given and received, Lady Ingar ordered servants to carry the girls' belongings to their chambers. She ushered the three girls into the hall where flames danced brightly in a central hearth. Servants took their mantles, hung these on pegs close to the entrance, and Lady Ingar settled them by the fire and sent for possets and cakes.

'When the king comes here he throws himself into the life of his farm,' Jarl Niels said and looked over at Princess Gunnhild who sat closest to the hall fire, clutching a cup of hot milk laced with honey. 'Is this not so, Gunnhild?'

'I suppose so.'

Lady Ingar, her warm brown eyes glowing below her wimpled brow said, 'Now, Gunnhild, no sulking. Here we all work for our bread. Last time you were here you enjoyed learning to make cheese.'

Jarl Niels nodded at Thea. 'The king wants life to be ordinary here. His message insists that I am to address you as Thea. You will observe that Princess Gunnhild is referred to here as Gunnhild.' The steward of Søderup continued, 'I am Jarl Niels. You will use my name in full when you address me, Theodora Godwinsdatter. My wife is Lady Ingar. Remember that. My daughters,' he broke off to wave a hand at two neat, plain-faced women in their twenties who were dropping

74

spindles across the hearth. 'Now, Thea, look at how modest my daughters are and how busy their hands remain. They are Elizabeth and Mary – called so for the holy family. Their husbands – well, you will learn their names in time.'

'Yes, Jarl Niels,' Thea said, too tired to think. 'If I may, I must lie down.'

'Nonsense, no one lies down before supper is served.'

'Jarl Niels,' Lady Ingar began, 'I think tonight is an exception. Thea's maid can bring her soup up to her. She has been ill. I do not wish to be responsible if she relapses.'

Jarl Niels softened. 'Well, well, if you insist, dear wife. You know best. Take her to her chamber.'

'Thank you, Jarl Niels,' Thea said as she set her milky drink aside and thankfully rose to her feet. 'Come with me, Gudrun.' She was thankful when she found out that she was to have her own bedchamber that was reached by an outside staircase.

Thea stood in the middle of her new chamber. The rafters reached down towards the floor from a high point in the roof and the floorboards were scrubbed. The room was plain but it would do, and she did not have to share it with Gunnhild. Its walls were lime-washed but undecorated except for a carved Christ with enormous eyes hanging from a wooden cross. At the bottom of this cross, instead of a weeping Madonna, a snake-like creature was carved into the wood. It had one foreleg. She recoiled from it. It was hideous. If she could, she would ask for a replacement. Surely that cross was not Christian? She told Gudrun to take it down and hide it under the bed. She could not bear to look at that every day. Instead she hung a little ivory cross that had belonged to her mother in its place.

For a week Thea kept to her room, sending excuses down the stairway daily, until Lady Ingar came to her one morning, whipped the padded cover from her bed and tossed her a work gown of rough wool. 'Today, you must join the other women who are spinning in the hall. In the afternoon you will work in the dairy making cheese. Everyone here is expected to work. If

75

you do not work you will not eat.' Lady Ingar seized Gudrun's arm. 'You too, my girl, enough tripping up and down the stairway with bread and honey and titbits from the kitchen. You will assist Lady Thea in every one of the tasks we give her.' She turned back to Thea. 'You will eat with the rest of us today in the hall below.' She looked at the tiny ivory cross on the wall and arched one of her eyebrows. 'Where is it?'

'Under the bed, Lady Ingar. The snake is a frightening, pagan image,' Thea said, shuddering. 'I could not sleep with that snake at the cross's foot ready to reach out and snap at me.'

'Nonsense, it is the way our craftsmen work and it is a warning to sinners. Nonetheless, if it disturbs you I shall have it removed from under your bed.'

'If you would, my lady, I thank you,' Thea said, reaching for the work gown.

Gudrun was visibly shaking with fear as Lady Ingar stomped down the stairway in her great boots. These, Thea remarked, looked more suitable for a man than a woman. Climbing down from the high bed, she said, 'We have no choice. We have to join the other women. I hope they are kinder than the princesses were.' She sniffed the gown. 'At least it is clean. Come on, Gudrun, help me,' she said and they pulled the itchy gown over her shift.

Thea decided not to hurry. She drained her cup of buttermilk and ate her bread roll. Concealing her hair under a linen coif she was dressed as simply as a peasant who had always worked on a farm. Over the past few days she had been thinking about Prince Vladimir again, as the terrible memory of her fever-inspired blood-red wedding had faded. Instead, when she dreamed of her wedding, she wore a pale blue overgown of samite silk and blue slippers of the softest leather. She was as pure as the Virgin, a perfect beauty with her pale skin and golden-red hair, her veil as delicate and transparent as a skeleton leaf. What would her prince think of her today? She shook her head. Ready to face whatever Lady Ingar demanded of her with stoicism, she descended the staircase into the icy cold of the yard.

She had had no idea of the bitter December cold that had gripped the outside world in the week she had lain in her warm bed, missing her grandmother or thinking about the Prince of Kiev. 'This cold is biting,' she complained, hugging her arms about her body.

'It is no worse than during the siege we suffered in Exeter, my lady. That was a hard winter too,' Gudrun said as she trailed after Thea into the hall.

'It was, I shall never forget it, nor do I want to suffer it again, ever.'

Thea wrinkled her nose on entering the hall. The smell of damp wool mingled with the unwashed smell of many busy bodies. The women stopped working and looked up at her.

'Sit here,' Lady Ingar said, moving over on a bench close to the hearth. 'Here, take this and this.' She handed Thea a spindle whorl and a handful of soft, oily wool from a basket. 'Gudrun, you will help your mistress.' Lady Ingar glared around at the others, who included Princess Gunnhild, and signalled to them to continue working.

Thea lifted the spindle and wool and began the work of teasing wool into thread. As she finished one lot Gudrun handed her more wool to spin. She was glad that she had done this task before in Grandmother Gytha's hall. Soon the knack of dropping her spindle returned to her and she noted the admiration and surprise in the eyes of Princess Gunnhild as she swiftly produced woollen threads that Gudrun nimbly wound into skeins.

There were no unkind comments or snide looks on the women's faces. They concentrated on their task and as they worked they conversed. Soon a sense of togetherness developed between them as they asked Thea about England and said how they were all welcome here at Søderup. Princess Gunnhild, away from her sisters' influence, smiled at the conversation as she worked, although she was not as nimble-fingered as they were and often broke threads.

As the dinner hour approached and candles were lit the morning's work was cleared away into huge baskets. Servants pulled out trestles and laid them with food. The men came into the hall and soon the hall was full of people. Servants bustled around setting out bowls of the steaming meat stew that had bubbled all morning in a cauldron over the central raised hearth. They brought in freshly baked bread from the outside kitchen and cheese from the Søderup dairy. Thea discovered that she was very, very hungry.

It was at that dinner time that Thea noticed how Padar smiled across from the men's trestle at Gudrun. She observed too how Gudrun's eyes seemed to light up like glowing stars when he looked her way. Gudrun had turned fifteen on the day they had arrived in Søderup but she had been too tired and miserable to mark her name day. She must make her handmaiden a belated gift, perhaps a belt purse, if there was felt to be had at Søderup. And, she mused as Padar's twinkling eyes looked across the hall towards them, Gudrun was old enough to admire and be admired. She must speak to the girl, find out what had been going on while she had lain in bed thinking of her grandmother and her brothers; worrying about her brothers' long sea journey back to Dublinia so late in the year; missing Grandmother Gytha whom she loved with all her heart, dreaming her own dreams of longing and love. She bit her tongue to stop the tears welling up as she thought of her grandmother now. This was life and she must just get on with it. Swallowing back her longing, she bent her head over her bowl and scooped up another spoonful of stew.

Thea had no time to think again about Padar and Gudrun. That afternoon they worked in the dairy, hanging sharp-smelling cheeses to drip over vats. When their day ended and darkness brought an end to their work they processed into the tall wooden chapel where she shivered through a candlelit Vespers. Supper followed. She glanced about the candlelit hall, remembering Padar's smiles for Gudrun, searching deep into the shadows, seeking him. He was not present this time so she said to Lady Ingar, 'Where is Padar tonight, my lady?'

'Oh, Padar, well, my dear, the skald has been called back to Roskilde. He took an early supper and galloped away from us for the coast.'

'He is *my* skald. He has gone without a word to me.'

'He will return soon,' was all that Lady Ingar said. 'There was no time to explain anything to you and besides, I gather that his mission is secret. Your three house coerls remain. You are well protected here.'

Thea glanced over at her protectors, all three men deep in conversation with Jarl Niels. She wondered if they too had to earn their supper. There was a frown on Jarl Niels' face. She caught him looking over at Lady Ingar and signalling for her to join him in the private chamber behind the hall. A little later, as plums were served, both master and mistress took their leave of the company and disappeared through the leather curtain that divided the back chambers from the manor hall. As Thea supped on her plums and thick cream, she wondered if the secret conversation between Jarl Niels and his wife had anything to do with Padar's departure.

'Come with us, Thea,' Mary said to Thea after the empty dish of stewed plums had been removed from the table. 'We shall embroider for an hour before we go to our rest.'

Thea followed Mary and the other women into an alcove, far from the central hearth but warmed by its own brazier. Mary pulled forward an embroidery frame that Thea had only given a cursory glance at before. The frame before her was such a feast for the eyes, she forgot all about Jarl Niels' abrupt departure at supper.

She peered closely at it, bending her head, gently touching the threads. Shapes were marked out in charcoal for them to work on. A part of the work was completed already. She made out the central picture first, a tree that sprouted many branches and oak leaves and to either side two ships in full sail, both with miniature warriors aboard them. The ships faced each other across the tree. There were crosses on the ship masks and one of the vessels seemed to possess a dragon figurehead at both its prow and stern. The other was simpler with an anchor balanced at the stern. At the prow stood a strange creature that she thought must be a griffin. Her eyes followed the embroidery to its borders where she now saw a patterned band and below that a series of interlocking oak leaves.

'It is the story of Olaf Haraldson and his brother Harald of Norway, Queen Elizaveta's first husband. We are embroidering it for the queen's chapel at Schleswig – a gift.'

'Harald of Norway was another thief after my father's kingdom,' Thea said crossly.

'He did not win this time either.' Mary laughed and pointed to the ships. 'This is the story of Olaf's sailing race. You see they raced their ships to Trondheim to win the crown of Norway. They were half-brothers. Olaf,' she indicated a figure with a bow, 'won the race and so swiftly that he was able to take part in the church service, reaching the church before the arrow that he shot from that bow during the voyage had arrived.'

'Impossible,' Thea said.

'We think God smiled on Olaf who was a well-respected king and a good Christian. Look, Thea, at the way we show the waves. The ships look as if they really move. Many now say Olaf should be a saint.'

'And the tree?'

'The tree of life. We do not displease the fates.'

'Which bit do you wish to work on Thea?' Elizabeth said brightly.

'Not the dragon prow. I am working on that,' Princess Gunnhild squawked up.

'I am happy to work on the waves,' Thea said dreamily. 'I like the sense of moving forward with the tide.'

'Good, let us sort out needles and wool for you. And, you, Gudrun, run into the main hall and fetch us a sconce to see by. These tallow candles won't provide enough light.'

Once Gudrun returned and the sconce was secured in a wall

bracket, they settled on sewing stools to stitch. Waves, oak leaves and dragons, the anchor and a great billowing sail all took on life from the women's nimble fingers. Thea forgot Padar. She forgot everyone as she drew her needle with its woollen thread in and out through ink-coloured waves, until she remembered other warships that had crossed the narrow seas carrying the duke who was intent on stealing her father's kingdom. She glanced up at the tiny arrow set in Olaf's bowstring and cursed the thief King of England and all his kin.

It was not until she was contentedly tucked up beneath her fur covers that night that she wondered again where Padar had gone and how Ingar and Niels had glanced over at her as they retired from the hall after supper.

What did it all mean? She turned onto her side and curled up as if she were a small creature like a kitten and fell asleep pondering the mystery. Her last thought was that maybe Padar's disappearance was connected to her future, though she could not fathom how or why it was a secret. If it was not a secret there would be more explanation and fewer furtive glances between Niels and Ingar when she had asked for him.

9

Novgorod, Russia, Winter 1068-1069

There was snow in the heavens. Breathing in the crisp air after a week at sea, Padar huddled into his sealskin cloak and followed the king's messenger from the ship and along the wharf. He had no idea what King Sweyn wanted with him, though he suspected that this summons concerned Lady Thea.

His thoughts, as he walked, turned to the girl for whom he was beginning to have feelings, and whom he had left behind in Søderup. 'Pray God I can return soon,' he muttered as he trailed through cold streets behind the king's man.

He had never felt such interest in a girl before. When he had first spoken with Gudrun a year ago in Exeter she had seemed wise beyond her years, one who thought before she spoke and who weighed her words carefully. In another world she would be betrothed or married already, but her future had disappeared with her father's death at Hastings and her mother's demise from a broken heart soon afterwards. Now that Gudrun was growing into a woman he found that he had an affection for her and he did not know what to do about it.

As he walked through fluttering flakes of virgin snow, a wisp of hope began to surface. There had been women before. They had passed into his life and out again as fast as a candle burned down, a short time snatched and easily forgotten. There had never been time in his life before for love. His had been a life of service to the Godwin family, but now that his life was changing, he was changing too. If Lady Thea travelled to Russian lands to marry one of their princes, since he had promised Countess Gytha that he would look after her granddaughter's interests, it made sense that he planted roots in that distant land too and, of course, if Lady Thea travelled to

Russia her handmaiden would accompany her.

Almost thirty years old and he was in love, and he wondered at it. *Gudrun with her little swelling breasts, her golden hair and eyes that were such a deep blue that they looked like the sea on a summer's day. St Olav's whiskers, I could be her father. She is only fifteen to my twenty-nine summers.* He drew the hood of his cloak over his head and hurried after the messenger. *Her father was a thane and she has nothing now. If times were settled, if I had a trade, I would ask for her. I have nothing. I am just a poet, a warrior and a spy, unless of a sudden, riches fall from the sky and that is unlikely.* He sighed as he walked on the wooden walkways through the merchant quarter and past the silent cathedral to the king's house.

The king's man left him at the palace entrance. Just inside the hall, Padar shook snow from his mantle and stamped slush from his boots. He glanced around the king's receiving hall to where groups of Sweyn's house coerls stood in knots, talking quietly. Since the little pox had stolen lives, a worried hush had descended on the palace. They seemed subdued rather than boisterous as they often were. Pungent smoke, herb-infused wafts of it that was intended to stave off the pox, floated towards the rafters.

As his eyes became accustomed to the hall's dim rush light his attention was drawn to a pair of bearded men seated over a game of strategy in an alcove close to the raised dais. He peered through smoke that was curling from braziers towards holes in the rafters. Both men seemed familiar. His eyes searched through the spirals of smoke into the alcove again and this time recognised the two men hunched over a Hnefatafl board. One was Merleswein, once the most important Dane in York; he could not forget the man's disdainful laugh, and heard it now. Sitting on a stool opposite the arrogant thane was Bjorn, a burly bodyguard. What were they doing here?

Padar had held his suspicions about what was happening in England's north close to his heart for weeks. Tales had filtered through to Denmark all through that autumn that William was targeting the northern shires, determined to build more castles and stop rebellions. If York had fallen foul of King William, as was rumoured, then these men were exiles. If so, then he wanted to know the how, when and why of it.

He strolled over to the pair. For a heartbeat he paused before speaking. They were the sort of men that even Padar did not want to encounter unannounced in one of York's narrow lanes. You did not want to be at the other end of one of their double-edged seaxes. However another glance, to his relief, assured him that today the pair did not carry swords. He coughed to attract their attention without risking physical contact. Who knows how they would react to a hand on the shoulder?

Merleswein looked up, his eyes boring into him. Recognition crossed his dark countenance. He leapt up and clapped Padar's back. 'Infernal smoke,' he grunted gruffly. Padar coughed again, this time because he could not help it. The Dane laughed. 'So, Padar, what brings you here? Not in Ireland with the Godwin boys?'

Padar cleared his throat. 'I was about to ask the same of you, Merleswein. Not in York?'

'York is angry, my friend. King William's men have levied a new geld on the city and that bastard, Robert of Commines, his governor, has permitted their mercenaries' pillage on those who refuse the tax.' He spat onto the floor tiles. 'York wants another king, not the Norman bastard. They are talking about young Edgar.'

'Edgar?' Padar repeated. It took only a moment for him to grasp the state of play here, what these men were really up to. Sweyn had always had half an eye on England. He had always considered himself part of the English royal family. King Sweyn was not only a nephew of Countess Gytha but he was also a relative of the fearsome Danish king, Canute, who had conquered England more than half a century before. He would look for the best chance and seize it.

'That fine young Aetheling is in Scotland and been there since last summer. He has had enough of William the Bastard's charity. He has run away from the Norman court, got his mother and sisters out too. He wants his crown. The people of York want a leader.'

'And you choose that youth rather than a son of Harold Godwin? The people of York want peace. They need to trade. That boy won't bring them peace.'

'That *boy* as you call him is a young man of seventeen summers near enough and, moreover, he is a descendant of Alfred. We need such a one at the head of our army.'

'Your army,' Padar was now perplexed. Where was this army coming from, Scotland or Denmark; perhaps from both? Clear as torchlight, Padar saw the depth of Sweyn's cunning. Edgar's mother, Agatha, was, in fact, Queen Elizaveta's sister. He frowned at this significance. Edgar, the prince returned from Hungary, related to the Russian princes, had accepted William of Normandy as his king and had sworn allegiance after that October battle in 1066. Last Padar had heard of the young prince was that Edgar had been in Normandy with King William. Now he was planning to lead an army and take the throne from William.

'Does King Sweyn intend to help him?' He broached this crucial question carefully. His voice was calmer than he felt. He had a suspicion that Sweyn was about to embark on an act of betrayal.

Merleswein nodded. 'The lords of the North, Gospatrick, Waltheof, Edwin and Earl Morcar have all pledged their allegiance to the boy. They want their lands back.'

'What about Godwin?'

'What about Godwin Haroldson? If he joins us he will get his Wessex lands back. Without us he is useless. England's woods are crawling with the dispossessed, thanes without land, the hungry and the poor. There are those who call themselves the silvatii, men of the forest, and they *will* fight back. My friend, think on this, if we can get help from the sea there is more chance of destroying our enemies.' Merleswein grinned, showing teeth set like stout white rocks into his gums. He caught Padar's arm. 'You should join us, Padar. You may be small in stature but you are sharp and quick. I remember your ability with the sword, with the arrow, never mind your agile mind. And you were always a trustworthy scout.'

'Once upon a life,' Padar said. He shook off Merleswein's grip. 'Now my life is pledged to watch over Princess Thea. What does Sweyn get out of this pact?'

'Interests in the Danelaw, the Eastern part of England once ruled over by the Danish Viking earls. Though they became English they followed their own customs and laws and for the sake of peace the kings left them to it. They feel a Danish king like Sweyn might help them out. The Normans are moving north and we don't like it.'

'I understand Danelaw,' Padar said. 'I own Danish blood and I have been on King Harold's business often enough up in the north when he was our beloved earl and then our noble king. So what is Sweyn after?'

'Simple, skald. That young Prince Edgar will recognise him as Danelaw's rightful overlord; well, only if he provides us with a fleet.'

The northerners were fickle, or maybe just desperate, thought Padar to himself. Aloud he said, 'Beware. Another Northland king tried that at Stamford Bridge just over two years since. He had no proper horsemen, used ships, and *he* was ill equipped to win a land battle. Remember his sorry ending.'

'We shall see, Padar. We shall see. Now you did not answer my question. I have told you our business. What is your business here today?'

To his relief, he did not need to answer. The hall hushed except for the noise of shuffling feet and the swish of a curtain. Sweyn himself entered the dais from behind a tapestry hanging. On seeing the king, the thanes pushed forward, turned towards the dais and bowed to Sweyn. Even Merleswein sprang to his feet, knocking the gaming pieces over with a clatter. He shoved his way through the gathering and knelt before Sweyn. 'My lord king …' he began to say looking up at the dais. There was no opportunity to finish his speech because at that moment the king's searching eyes picked out Padar where he stood by the Hnefatafl table.

Waving the burly Dane back, the king called out, 'Later … Padar, my messenger told me you are here so I come to find you.' Merleswein frowned darkly. 'Merleswein, we shall talk later.' The king waved in the direction of the Hnefatafl board. 'Go back to that game. The winner plays me after supper.' He made a guffaw as Merleswein bowed and retreated. 'Padar step up here.' King Sweyn called for a servant and demanded apple mead to be carried through to the antechamber.

Once Padar was seated in the chamber behind the hall, on a stool beside the king, who reclined comfortably in his throne-like chair amongst a pile of furs, feet on the hearth rail, he was asked about Gunnhild and Thea. Padar reported that both were well and then inquired politely, 'Noble king, how are your other daughters?'

'Recovering; Christ's mercy, thank heavens, the bastard pox is departing my court with this cold weather.' Sweyn tugged at his beard. 'The reason you are here, Padar, is that I have a mission for you. I wish the mission you are to undertake to remain secret.'

The servant edged his way through the tapestry with a jug. Sweyn told him to leave the jug on a table by the hearth, dismissed him and offered Padar a cup of apple mead. After he poured himself a cup as well, the king leaned forward and threw a log on the fire. It hissed and spat. For a moment there was smoke. The wood settled and the fire crackled.

'It concerns Lady Thea,' Sweyn began. 'I made a promise to Aunt Gytha that I would do all I could to help her marriage to the Russian prince. As a Christian king I intend not to break my word and if you sail now you will beat the ice.'

This at least was good news. Padar recognised quickly that he must not, nor could not, broach Sweyn's possible change of alliance, since he did not wish to jeopardise Thea's chances with the Russian prince. He leaned forward and listened to the king's proposal intently.

King Sweyn had gained intelligence that Prince Vsevolod had sent diplomats to Hungary and to Poland seeking a bride for his only son. The Rus prince was worthy of the best match in Europe. Through his mother, Princess Anastasia, Prince Vsevolod's first wife, the boy was the grandson of Constantine Monomakh. As such he bore the name of this great Byzantine emperor, one of the noblest names in Christendom. Padar must persuade the Russians that a match with Thea would please the Danish king and bring the Rus princes new lucrative trade agreements with Danish merchants. It would be a suitable reciprocal arrangement.

As the king talked and the fire blazed, Padar became excited at the thought of a new adventure, at the trust placed in him, and he even felt relieved to be away from Denmark for a season once he discovered that he would not return before Eastertide. For Thea and Gytha he would move rocks. He would put his own life at risk for them. He would place their needs before a little girl's affection even if she looked like sunshine and was as sweet as mead. Padar bowed to the king and decided to do all that was asked of him.

He determined to avoid Merleswein as he waited to sail to Staria Lagoda and then by river to Novgorod. He would not tell that thug his business nor that of those whose interests he protected. He hung around the quayside, made friends with merchants and gave the impression that he intended to take up a merchant's life himself. One day Merleswein found him saying goodbye to a Rus merchant and remarked, 'So you are off to trade for furs, Padar?'

'It will be a good living,' Padar replied. 'You should consider it yourself instead of kicking up trouble between cousins.'

'Those Godwin boys can join us any time they wish. But their cousin Sweyn will make a better king. The father lost a kingdom. Who is to say the cubs will do any better?'

'I doubt Edgar Aetheling will bring anything of value to the

89

table.' Padar shrugged and strolled off along the quay to find more convivial company. Godwin, he suspected, would never marry a Danish princess now, not if Sweyn supported Aetheling Edgar.

A few weeks later Padar found himself, guarded by one of the king's trusted bodyguards, a man called Odin, and a small band of King Sweyn's warriors, whisked by sleigh pulled by fast-running woolly dogs along the frozen river they named Volchov, towards the northern Rus city of Novgorod.

As he peered out from his furs over the frozen woods and fields, he was reminded that deep midwinter had gripped the world. He glanced uneasily through the dark spindle-like trees that lined the river banks. God only knew what nature of malignant spirits and flesh-eating creatures lived within the forest's secret heart? Padar turned away from the frightening landscape that edged the river and tried to think forward to his arrival instead.

He travelled with gifts in his pack. These included one of King Harold's priceless rings set with a large opal, and a great number of silver arm rings. After he showed these to the Danish King and Queen, Elizaveta had suggested a gift for Prince Vsevolod's new wife, a Kypchak princess from the Northern Steppes. Her name was Anya. Padar stole back secretly at night to the guarded warehouse and carefully selected a lovely gold brooch set with garnets. Elizaveta looked on it with approval when she examined it next day. 'You chose as well as I myself would,' she said.

As the pack of dogs pulling his sleigh barked, and raced on like possessed demons over the ice road, Padar pondered his mission to the Rus princes. It was too cold for conversation. Odin silently sat beside Padar. Determining that he would return in spring with a positive response, Padar crept down lower under furs. Sweet Christ, it was cold in Russia. If only he could drift off into sleep, time would not hang so slowly about his frozen journey.

Church bells were ringing when, some bitterly cold days later, they arrived outside the great river gate that led into Novgorod. There they were surrounded by a waiting group of curious, helmeted, sword-carrying warriors, the younger members of Prince Vsevolod's personal guard. 'We have come to guide you to the fortress,' their leader announced and Odin translated.

The buildings they passed seemed recently built. Their roofs were high with many overhanging gables. Many houses opened onto streets made of logs split in half lengthways, built up higher above the central roadways than similar walkways in Denmark. They had been constructed on stout pillars and were swept clean of snow. Peering from the sleigh, Padar saw that some buildings belonged to craftsmen and glass-makers. He caught flashes of glass being blown just inside their doorways; others were smithies. Some obviously belonged to bakers because he could smell the loaves baking and began to salivate.

Set back inside gates and courtyards, there were grander two-storied hall houses, much taller than the rest. Odin told Padar that these belonged to noblemen and merchants. 'Novgorod is a wonderful city and Kiev even nicer. You could make a good living in these Rus cities, my friend. Well, if they were at peace.'

'You mean there is fighting here?'

Odin glanced in a guarded manner about him, clearly checking that the guards who ran alongside the sleigh were not listening, though noticing this hesitance, Padar remarked, 'If they do not speak Norse they will not understand us.'

'Well, hear this then,' Odin began. Padar leaned in to listen above the swish of the sleigh runners. 'A few years ago there was an attempted invasion of the city by Vsevolod's cousin, a prince called Vsevslav. His warriors burned down Novgorod and stole the bells of St Sophia. Mstislav, the governor here, fled, just ran away. He was only a youth then, not fit to rule this city. Now, they have rebuilt Novgorod.'

'How was the city recaptured?'

'Vsevslav and his sons were arrested after they lost a battle south of the city. But, there is an even stranger story. They were to be forgiven. You know, like us, the Russians lay great store by cross-kissing oaths, but, and this is the terrible thing,' Olaf lowered his voice. 'It seems that Prince Iziaslav of Kiev broke trust. Prince Vsevslav and his sons are now imprisoned in Kiev where they can do no mischief. But a broken cross-kissing oath …' He crossed himself. 'No good comes from breaking oaths, Padar.'

Padar shook his head. 'No.'

By the time Odin had finished, his breath rising into the icy city air in white puffs, they had entered through the fortress's formidable gates. 'What happened to the bells?' Padar asked.

'Returned after the Battle of Wemiga River where Vsevslav was defeated by the three princes of Kiev and where that cross kissing occurred.'

'So who is in charge here now?'

'Prince Vsevolod is in charge.'

'And, Mstislav, no return for him?'

'Not a good move. The merchants don't want him. Their veche, the town assembly, that is, have denied him Novgorod.' Odin shrugged. 'The youth is in Kiev with his father, the Grand Prince. The youth will get control of another city, a lesser one.'

'So are you here, Odin, to be my ears and eyes?' Padar said.

Odin laughed heartily. 'To keep you right, little man…and safe. We will be in Novgorod for the winter.'

'It looks as if I am going to need your help. I cannot understand a word of their Rus tongue. You had better teach me some useful words.'

'Here's one.' He mumbled an incomprehensible word. Padar gave him a quizzical look. 'It means, "clear off, you cunt".' Odin laughed again. 'You will find English fur-trade merchants here, Padar. Their knowledge of the city and the Rus is limitless. And many of them winter here.' He slapped Padar's back. 'Not so bad to be a guest here. Tomorrow their midwinter feasting begins. It is a good time to be in Novgorod. You will see. They treat us Danes well.'

The guards were waving them forward. Padar swung his travelling pack from under the fur coverings and sat it on his knees. He intended to keep it with him since it not only held his harp but also a casket with the gifts.

They entered through a second set of wooden gates and proceeded into an inner courtyard, Padar clutching his bag, Odin rattling on beside him about the feasting he could expect in this very impressive city over the winter.

The sleigh dramatically drew to a halt with a spray of snow jerking them forward. When Padar raised his head, he saw that an enormous turreted building loomed up in front of them. He drew an impressed breath. Their escort barked something at the gatekeepers. The gate opened and the sleighs passed into a courtyard. They crossed this yard and the procedure started over again, another gate and another courtyard. At last Padar and Odin were able to climb from the sleighs. They waited with their Dane escort before the fortress's entrance door as one of their helmeted guards banged on the heavy door. When it opened, two servants, who were clad in beautifully decorated, though somewhat inadequate, woollen garments for winter, appeared from the doorway. A slave who followed offered to carry Padar's large pack but Padar shook his head. 'What was that word, Odin,' he muttered.

'I would not use it to the prince's servants. This palace hums with intrigue. You want the servants and slaves on side. Only use it with proven enemies.'

'I think you are telling me a load of crap,' Padar whispered back.

'I am not,' Odin protested.

'Well, I'm keeping the bag with me.' He shook his head at the servant and clutched the heavy pack even more tightly.

The Rus guards led their Dane attendants away to their living quarters in the courtyard and the servant escorted Odin and Padar into the hall of what was apparently a highly guarded kremlin or keep. The great three-aisled and pillared hall was filled to bursting with merchants, noblemen and their servants.

Members of the prince's guard, his druzhina, loitered about the tiled floor. They craned their necks curiously to view the newcomers.

'Come on, Padar, we must ensure an audience with Prince Vsevolod before the Nativity services and feasts commence. And we want somewhere to rest our bones by nightfall, believe me.' He threw a glance at the heavy pack which Padar was clutching. 'And you want rid of that.'

'Too right,' Padar said with a weary grunt. 'Yours is light as a sack of goose feathers in comparison, I'll warrant.'

A long, thin man with a high forehead and greying long hair, dressed in bright wool and fur, appeared out of a knot of fur-hatted men and greeted Odin like an old friend. Odin turned to Padar. 'He is a steward. They call him Michael. He is Prince Vsevolod's man. We are to have a place in the West Tower to sleep and we are promised an audience with the prince after evening mass.' He groaned and raised his eyes heavenward. 'I think we must attend that.'

Steward Michael nodded. Odin turned back to him and spoke in the incomprehensible language that was buzzing all around the hall. Padar glanced behind him to ensure that the servant was still there. The man was waiting for them. Moments later they politely bowed to the steward and were following the slave to a side door and along a walkway to a wooden staircase that zig-zagged up through a tower. 'It is one of many belonging to the fortress,' Odin informed Padar as they climbed higher.

Padar grunted and wished he had allowed the servant to carry his pack.

'We will winter well here,' Padar said, setting his pack on one of two comfortable feather beds.

He looked around their chamber, examining every corner as if danger lurked in them ready to pounce. A wood-burning stove stood in one corner and in another Padar discovered a carved cupboard. He tested out the low stools and remarked on

94

a strange wooden carving set upon a table. It depicted St George.

'An icon,' remarked Odin. 'They pray to those pictures as we do to our saints.'

Padar had no intention of praying before this image. In fact, he rarely had time for prayers. The old gods were as good as the new God to him. Whichever suited his mood at a particular time was where he placed his belief. He shrugged and dug his hands deep into his pack, under his spare tunics and leggings, and drew out first his harp, then the casket. 'I hope they appreciate the gifts.'

'We shall take them down to the chapel with us. The sooner we are rid of them the lighter our load here will be,' Odin said, scratching his head thoughtfully. 'And less chance of theft.'

Padar nodded his approval of this plan. He opened the door a slit. The slave was standing outside their chamber as if on guard. 'He looks as if he is to be attached to us with fish glue.' He shut the door. 'I'm going to purchase a padlock for our door.'

Odin laughed. 'Not a bad idea, but he won't steal. Even the suspicion of theft will get him gutted.'

The kremlin's small church was a gloomy space that smelled of expensive frankincense. Padar was fascinated by its strange pungent atmosphere, the gilded pictures of saints and a procession of heavily cloaked women who were moving in a ritual way around the church's perimeter kissing icon after icon. 'Women of the court,' Odin said. 'Pity we can't see their faces. Many of them are beautiful.'

'More beautiful than our own women?'

'Different beautiful.'

The priest in charge wore a stiff, dark red robe covered with gleaming silver and gold embroidery. His white beard flowed and his great cross looked as if it would topple over and crush him.

'There's Prince Vsevolod with our bridegroom,' Odin

whispered into Padar's ear.

Padar turned away from the important priest and peered through the candlelit gloom at the group of nobles. Steward Michael hovered in a distinctly obsequious manner behind Prince Vsevolod. Priests stepped gracefully forward and bowed to them. Other nobles flanked the princes, their eyes lowered.

The older prince must be Vsevolod, Padar thought, peering through the gloom from one to the other. Both were lavishly dressed in loose, long, straight coats, opened at the front to reveal undergowns of stamped velvet. Their robes were stiff and fell from their sides in a triangular manner. Both held large amber prayer-counting beads in their hands. Padar noted that Vsevolod, though tall, was not as tall as the youth who stood with him. The dark-haired youth with the haughty countenance rattling his amber counting beads was surely Prince Vladimir. Poor Lady Thea, he thought momentarily. She could be out of the Danish frying pan into the Russian fire with that one.

Evening prayers seemed even more drawn out than Compline was in the Latin world. There were long readings from scripture read in the language of Rus, not in Greek or Latin. Padar had no understanding of what was said, nor did he understand the further icon-kissing that followed, but he approved that what he assumed were Pater Nosters and Hail Marys which were sang in the Rus tongue to the rattle of beads marking out the prayers. Ordinary people could follow if they knew Russian. Fascinating as it was, when the time came to leave, he was glad to escape the smell of incense, wet leather, fur and sweat.

A guard ushered them from the chapel, through the courtyard to the hall they were in earlier and into a spacious room beyond where Prince Vsevolod was waiting for them, standing by a long window that was covered with isinglass. Olaf tugged Padar's sleeve. 'Down,' he whispered. They prostrated themselves and when they rose they saw that the long-legged youth was warming his toes by an opened stove set into the wall.

A shape emerged from the shadows by a wall. As the figure came further into the pooling sconce light, Padar felt his eyes widen. He had not seen the Irish Earl Connor, who ran merchant ships throughout the northlands, since they had separated after the siege of Exeter.

Prince Vsevolod opened his arms. 'Welcome to Novgorod,' he said in Norse. 'I believe we have much to discuss. Earl Connor has already given me a fair account of your lady. I hear that the Princess of the English is fair of face, her eyes grey and that her hair is red gold, that she is intelligent and courageous.' The prince paused. 'What can she otherwise bring to our family? I hope we can do business.'

The youth seemed to watch Padar closely through his sharp brown eyes, which, Padar noted, were at that moment hard like bronze. When Padar opened the casket's lid to reveal its treasures, Prince Vladimir pushed back his stool and ambled over to his father's side. Prince Vsevolod bent down and peered into the opened casket. He lifted out the jewels one by one and turned them over in his long, delicate hands. He held the brooch up to the bright torch light glowing from a wall sconce. 'My wife will be delighted with this. The craftsmanship is delightful. Saxon silver. German garnets. Beautiful.' As he examined the other items in the flame's glow his face beamed his approval.'

Laying the casket on a table, Padar took a deep breath. 'The princess possesses a valuable dowry and she is well-connected to both the Danish royal family and to England's ancient aristocracy.'

He was not quite sure how far back Thea's noble roots went, so he took another breath wondering how he should give credence to his boast. 'She is the granddaughter of the great Godwin, King Edward's advisor and once the wealthiest man in England.'

The Prince turned to Earl Connor. 'Can you give an account of this lady's character, Earl Connor?'

Earl Connor did not hesitate. 'She is a devout Christian and though she has suffered much she bears her troubles with great

97

nobility. The Lady Gita speaks well of all. She glides through the world like a swan, but if she must, she can hiss like one too.'

The princes both laughed. 'She has spirit,' Vsevolod said. 'She will need it in the terem.'

'The terem?' Padar said. 'What is it, my lord?'

'The ladies' chambers,' Prince Vsevolod said.

He picked up an extravagantly engraved arm bracelet rich with decoration and considered it. He said absently, glancing up at Padar, 'Christ's Nativity falls the day following tomorrow. Rest and enjoy our festivities. Earl Connor will guide you in our ways. I promise you my answer by the Feast Day of St Basil. After it, I must depart for Kiev.' He slipped the bracelet onto his forearm and removed it to this time let it hang from his wrist. 'I hear the Godwin countess sent our patriarch in Kiev a very precious reliquary on her granddaughter's behalf. He is well pleased with the sliver of the true cross and St Nicholias's finger bone, and he is delighted by the reliquary crystal which protects it.'

Padar bowed. The youth spoke in English, his voice clear and firm, his bronze eyes softening, his English careful. 'I wish to know this Saxon princess. My nurse always told me that red hair is fortunate.' He glanced at the silver band that his father was admiring and when his father handed it to him, the young prince slipped it over his own tunic sleeve and up his arm. He turned to his father and said quietly, 'We should consider their offer, Father.'

'And so we shall, my son,' Vsevolod said. He addressed the earl. 'Take these men away now. It is past suppertime. My wife is in the women's tower and I promised I would sup with her tonight.' He addressed Padar. 'I shall bring her Princess Gita's gift. She will be delighted.'

Odin excused himself as they entered the hall where trestles were set out for supper. He had friends to see.

'Do you think the women's quarters, that terem place, is like a Moorish prince's harem or is it more like the sewing room in

Roskilde?' Padar said to Earl Connor.

'A bit of both,' the earl replied. 'The Russian princes do not take more than one wife at a time. Their women do not mix freely in public places except in church or at very special feasts. They have private meals with the family. Family is important.'

'Isn't it always,' Padar said as they found places on a bench squeezed in between two fat boyars, noblemen. 'I expect the Nativity feast will be held publicly. I mean, are we all invited?'

'You guess correctly.' Connor lifted a jug. 'Here try this kvass. It's a fermented rye-bread drink. You will like it.'

Padar made a face, but nonetheless accepted a bowl of the strange drink. He was thirsty.

'I think you will succeed in marrying off Lady Thea to the young prince. The wedding will be very grand. Now, Padar, tell me about everything.'

'A drink and food first. I am starved.' Padar lifted the bowl to his lips, drank deeply, smiled and nodded. 'The kvass is good, tastes of bread, honey and mint,' he said, setting his bowl on the table and pulling his eating knife from his belt. He speared a hunk of reindeer meat from a platter on the table and began to chew. That was not bad either.

Connor helped himself to some roasted eggs. 'How are the boys?'

Tears welled up in Padar's eyes as he told Earl Connor of young Magnus's death. He felt choked as he spoke of it. The earl's eyes, too, swam with tears as Padar talked. He remarked that he had known Magnus well in Ireland when the boy had been fostered by King Dairmaid. 'I have been trading. I had no knowledge of the boy's death. He was too young for that fight,' Connor said sadly.

'It was a time we thought fearful, but in comparison to what came later Dublinia was a safe haven.'

Connor shook his head and wiped his eyes with his sleeve. 'How could they have sent that youth into battle? His mother will be saddened by his loss.'

'They all are,' Padar confided. 'Lady Thea swears revenge.

Godwin and Edmund are more determined than ever to recover their lands.' Padar looked around for Odin. It would not do to confide his suspicions of King Sweyn anywhere near him. Fortunately, Odin and his friend had finished their supper and were retreating into a candlelit alcove with a bag of dice.

'It is good to see you again, Connor,' Padar said.

'And you, Padar. Here's to Lady Thea.' He lifted his bowl.

It occurred to him that Connor and he would have weeks, months perhaps, to remember the past. Padar confided in Earl Connor, 'I think King Sweyn intends to help Aetheling Edgar. The northern earls have given the boy their support. I am not sure how Godwin will fare, though there are plans being mooted that he marries one of Sweyn's daughters.'

Earl Connor munched at a hunk of dark bread and said thoughtfully, 'I think we should concentrate on Lady Thea's betrothal. That alliance with Aetheling Edgar may all come to nothing. Unless an attack on England is co-ordinated the English will not dislodge the Normans. I sail to Ireland in the spring. Godwin and Edmund should be encouraged to deal with both Malcom of Scotland and the Aetheling. If Sweyn's interest is plunder, the Aetheling will have made a poor alliance. If he and Godwin unite it could be to both their advantage.'

'Possibly,' Padar replied and yawned. 'Sweyn has more ships to give than Godwin can get from Ireland. Both need King Sweyn.' He wiped his eating knife on his tunic and tucked it into his belt. Odin was drinking with his friends but he longed for his rest. It had been a long and eventful day. 'Connor, I must find my way to my tower room and sleep.' He looked up. The tall slave hovered close by. As if he read Padar's mind, the servant reached for a torch. 'Ah, Connor, look, and take note, I apparently have a shadow and would rather I didn't, but tonight I am glad of him. Without him, I am lost in this labyrinth of a fortress. The West Tower ... I have no idea where it lies from here.'

Connor laughed. 'You will soon find your way around. I shall introduce you to the English exiles tomorrow. You could settle in this land. Trade is good.'

'I shall consider it, but now my soft feather pillow calls my weary head.' Padar scrambled to his feet, bowed and with a nod to the slave, set off after his guide through the dark rambling fortress towards the right tower.

10

It seemed as if Christmas had only been a moment ago. It felt as if February passed by within a turn of the hour glass, then March. Easter came and went with services and feasting. Thea's birthday passed quietly after Easter during the season of the ram. She was sixteen that year. Her gifts were simple but beautiful – Lady Ingar presented her with a silver brooch engraved with flowers, Gudrun a new felt purse, and a fillet from the sisters that like the brooch pin was embroidered with green tendrils and minute blue flowers. She wept with delight. Her pleasure was complete as summer edged into their lives. At last, the beech trees were bursting into leaf and the days were lengthening again.

As the winter had flown by, Thea had learned to cook, to spin, weave, make cheese and brew beer. She did not mind her days on Sweyn's farm and although she applied herself diligently to every task Lady Ingar set her, wanting to please the strict but kindly mistress of Sweyn's estate, her true delight was music. She practised her flute every day. To her great joy at Christmas the instrument makers who had a workshop attached to the manor had presented her with a harp. After that the best part of her day came to be late in the afternoon, just before Vespers, when Jarl Niel's skald drove a brightly painted cart to the manor's hall from his cottage by the river, to give her lessons. With his help, she began to set some of her stories to music, plucking out suitable notes to accompany her clear, high-noted voice.

Grandmother Gytha had sent her a letter during Lent. It was short. Thea's eyes dripped tears onto the parchment as she read her grandmother's words and in them heard her grandmother's

103

voice speak.

To my granddaughter Thea also named Gytha for myself,
Greetings, I am safely residing at the monastery of St Omer and
find it is a pleasant place – peaceful after the tumultuous events
that have tracked my life. Now it is time to rest. The young boys
thrive here, learning more every day. The young girls are with
their families in Flanders. We are thus a small company of lay
nuns. Your Aunt Hilda sends you Easter greetings. I have every
faith that you will soon be betrothed and that your new life in
the lands of the Rus will bring you every happiness. Prepare
well for it. Learn every skill you can master. Always remember
you are a Godwin and a king's daughter. The years remaining
to me may pass all too quickly. We may not meet again this side
of heaven. Promise me that after my fates have spun out my life,
you will remember my advice.

Your brothers intend passing the summer in Ireland. They
hope King Dairmaid will help them again. They fear that Sweyn
may have other interests.

May God and His angels protect you.
Gytha, Countess of Wessex

What other interests possessed Sweyn? Her grandmother did
not say. Thea wept, folded her letter and drew together its
familiar Godwin dragon seal. She carefully placed it in the
small casket that contained the precious Godwin christening
gown. As she lifted the gown out of its soft cloth wrapping and
looked once again upon its pale fabric she made a wish that she
would soon marry Prince Vladimir and if Prince Vladimir was
to be her betrothed, they could learn to love each other and have
many children together. She imagined him to be Odin, brave
and wise, god of wisdom, battle and poetry but also like Balder,
Odin's gentle handsome son. Sometimes he became Tyr, the
god of war, justice and order. She touched the tiny linen gown
with the tip of her right ring finger. For a heartbeat she thought
of her father and mother. Then she made a third wish. This was

that her mother, Elditha, would write to her. William feared that the Godwin women might ferment rebellions in England, and so kept them apart. Maybe, just hopefully, Elditha would find a secret way to speak to her eldest daughter. Instead of writing to Elditha, she swallowed her tears and wrote a reply to her grandmother.

Dearest Grandmother Gytha,

I hope this finds you and the ladies of St Omer in good health. It is my greatest wish that you are happy and that sometimes the stern-faced nuns who dwell there smile, that you have plenty of firewood and good food. You say you have found peace in the lay community there. I pray to St Theodosia you speak the truth.

Words cannot describe how much I miss you. I am, none the less, content to be here. The farm is a pleasant place and everyone who dwells here is kind. Princess Gunnhild returned to Roskilde. She missed her sisters. Padar vanished on a secret mission soon after we arrived here. I heard that he was sent to the Rus to visit the court and my future husband, if indeed my husband is to be the Rus prince, Vladimir of Kiev. Indeed, if it is to be he whom the ambassadors spoke of then I am very happy. Thus, I prepare with great diligence here learning how a household is well ordered that I may organise my own with great care ...

She was careful not to criticise Sweyn because she suspected that her letter might be read before it was sent and after all it would be sealed by Jarl Niels and sent with merchants visiting Flanders. If their journey was a guide it would take several weeks, perhaps longer, to reach its destination. She took care to press some blue flowers and include them as a keepsake for Gytha. She wrapped a cheese she had made and prayed that it would not spoil on the long sea journey. Finally she included a needle-holder that she had embroidered with a dragon ship sailing over waves, just like the *Wave-Prancer*, so that Gytha would not forget the journey they had made in it to Denmark.

'Gudrun,' she said a morning later as they walked to the weaving sheds with baskets heaped up with newly spun wool. 'I think Padar will be back soon. I feel it.' She glanced up at a flight of sparrows crossing the sky. 'Look, they are returning. If Padar has been to the lands of the Rus, surely he will bring back news of my betrothal. Grandmother was sure that I would be betrothed to Prince Vladimir. She arranged it.'

'Really, truly. Then, Lady Thea, will I travel with you to Russia?'

She smiled. They had become close companions, genuine friends rather than simply mistress and maid. 'Yes, my dear girl. If I am betrothed; Prince Vsevolod might choose another princess for his son, one better connected and wealthier than I.' She sighed and feigned sorrow. 'I could lose my handsome, devoted prince yet and grow into an unwed crone here in Søderop making cheeses and butter, embroidering altar cloths and pillows for Jarl Niels grandchildren.'

'Nonsense, Lady Thea, that will never be so. You are much too beautiful. If Padar describes you well ...' Gudrun looked sheepish as she spoke Padar's name. She blinked and said softly. 'I hope that one day I can find a husband too. I, too, wish for love, my lady.'

Thea felt a sense of reality enter her dreams. 'But in truth, my friend, we never actually marry for love. It grows. It did between my mother and father. Theirs was a handfasted wedding in the old way. She was the daughter of a wealthy nobleman and he died leaving her a great heiress. I never knew my mother's family. My father's family became her family and just look what happened to his brothers. Uncle Tostig died a traitor, Uncle Gyrth died at Senlac and my favourite uncle of all, Uncle Leofwine, also fell in the great battle.'

'And my father too.'

They continued in companionable silence across the courtyard. Thea pointed to the bench outside the shed where men inside were busy working the table looms. They sat down.

106

The rhythmic noise of shuttles clacking and the oily smell of new wool escaped from the shed. 'There is something I cannot say in the house.'

'My lady? I am listening,' Gudrun said quietly.

'Before she left for Easter at Roskilde, Princess Gunnhild told me that there was a cunning woman here who was clever with ancient spells. Gunnhild said that the woman might help me make an invocation to disturb William's enjoyment of our stolen English lands.' Thea glanced down at her tightly clenched hands. 'If I cannot marry well then he is to blame.' Thea's eyes stung as if pins were pricking them. 'Do you think God will punish me if I ill-wish that Bastard?'

'That is twisted thought; it is as twisted as an old snake, my lady. It will curl about your heart like a serpent and choke you. My lady, be careful what you wish for. It is more honourable for us to hope that King William just keels over and dies or that he is defeated in a battle. Sorcery and witchcraft are dangerous.' Gudrun shuddered. 'I am not sure that Princess Gunnhild has your interests at heart. If you were discovered dealing in spells, you could jeopardise every chance of a good marriage.'

'But, Gudrun, if it was only a small spell, if we can find the woman, will you help me?'

'Yes, I suppose, but only if we pray devoutly that none of her evil can taint *us*, only those who have committed evil.' She sat still thinking until she added, 'King William killed my father too.'

'Then we shall go into the shed and deposit these baskets. After that we must walk down to the river and follow the sycamore pathway into the woods.'

'But we shall be outside the palisade.'

'Yes, and we can say we are visiting the dyers. They have been dying fleeces.'

'Do you know how to find the cunning woman, my lady?'

'She has a hut by the great rune stone marker where there was once a chieftain buried in his ship.' Thea frowned. 'She delivers herbs and charms for the sick but she has stronger magic too; so Gunnhild said.'

'We must take Ghost,' Gudrun said firmly. Ghost was the fiercest hall hound. He was completely white and wore a studded collar.

'We can take Ghost. Let us ask for salt for the dyers, a good excuse to get outside the palisade. I heard Lady Ingar say they need salt and that no one would be available to go to the river today. *We* can offer. That way no alarm will be raised and I do not have a music lesson today until after Vespers.'

'They'll look for us during the dinner hour.'

'We'll say that we plan to eat down by the river.' Thea stared up at the cloudless sky. 'Lady Ingar will be so pleased about the salt that she will allow us to take meat and cheese with us. Everyone is busy today. She will let us go if we take Ghost. That hound can be really fierce. I've watched him catch rats in the hall straw.'

Just after noon, with Ghost trotting along by their sides, occasionally snuffling in hedgerows, Thea and Gudrun hurried towards the mill. Gudrun pushed the sack of salt, a sack of corn for the miller and their dinner in a wheelbarrow along the palisade pathway. Thea swung Ghost's leather leash from her hand.

Organised shelves with large sacks of milled flour lined the walls inside the mill. In the centre of the room ladders ascended up the mill's interior to the floors above. Gudrun shouted up the ladder to the miller who came lumbering down the ladders to greet them.

The burly miller seemed surprised to see Thea standing in her mantle in the middle of the space below amongst sacks of un-milled grain. Bowing, he said, 'My lady, what brings you to the mill?'

'Lady Ingar sends her greetings and a sack of last September's corn to be ground into flour. She will require it by tomorrow.'

'Will she now?'

'She expects company. There is not enough flour left for the bread. She asks that you send it over to the hall kitchens when it is milled.'

'It will be done.' The miller followed them outside, lifted the corn sack, opened it and thrust his hand inside. 'I suppose it is cleaned. The last sack took an age as it was full of grit.'

Thea shrugged. 'I do not know that, Jacob. I am just delivering it. We must be on our way now.'

'God speed, my lady,' Jacob shouted above the roaring of the millstream and the clunking of the mill wheel. 'Tell Lady Ingar I shall have her flour up to the hall by noon on the morrow.'

Thea and Gudrun waved their good byes and skirted the mill pond. They passed by a dam that Jacob was always strengthening. The river lay beyond the cut leading to the mill stream's dam. They trundled the wheel barrow along the river trackway. Ghost raced after them, then before them frantically wagging his long tail.

Thea wrinkled her nose as the pungent stink from the dyers' longhouse reached her. But she did like seeing the coloured fleeces stretched over the hedgerows where they were thrown to dry. Today, dyers were using woad which was particular smelly although the result was pleasing, a deep blue like the sky.

After handing over the precious bag of salt, one of the dyers thrust a bone for the hound at her. Thea shoved it into the wheelbarrow and hurried them along the river away from the stench. 'Come on, Gudrun. Let us find a secret place amongst the bluebells to eat our picnic. Ghost can chew at his sheep's bone. And, you know what? We can leave the wheelbarrow here and fetch it on our way back to the hall.'

'You are still determined to find her, my lady?' Gudrun looked thoughtfully at her mistress.

'Yes. We shall find her, so let us look for a log to sit on and eat that cheese.'

She chose a spot amongst the bright blue flowers that was shaded by elders and pushed the barrow out of sight into the trees. She pointed to a log, flat on the top, conveniently close to the river bank where they could sit, drink their ale, eat and rest for a short time. After they had eaten their share and given Ghost the rest, they were able to tug off their boots, slide down onto the riverbank and cool their feet in the fast-flowing stream. Moments later, Thea pulled her feet out, dried them on her mantle and said, 'Now, Gudrun, we must hurry.' She pointed into the wood behind. 'Let's try that way, in through those beech trees. They should open out onto a pathway. Dry your feet and come on.'

Thea glanced up at the trees by the stream. They were bursting into leaf. Verges were filled with lacy cow parsley. Hawthorn clung in snowy clumps to the hedgerows. Spring was already turning towards the summer season.

Thea discovered a rough trackway that led into the woods not far from where they had been resting. It was as if it had intentionally opened for them, as if something was drawing them forward onto it, an invisible force that she did not wish to resist. In the distance she could hear the peal of bells. 'The monastery of St Olave,' she said, delighted that the track wound through the trees close to the comfort of resounding monastery bells. She turned to Gudrun. 'As long as we stay on the track within reach of the bells' ringing we cannot get lost.' Logic told her that since woods around the king's estate were not very dense the path would take them towards the ship burial.

She called Ghost to her and walked forward into the beech trees. Keeping a few steps behind, Gudrun followed her. 'Are you sure this is the way, my lady?'

Thea turned. 'No, I'm not sure, but I shall soon find out, and besides, is it not a wondrous thing to have the afternoon to ourselves; not to be surrounded by people and their work, endless work. Listen to the birds, Gudrun. You can really notice them here.' She stopped and raised her hand to her ears. 'I hear woodpeckers knocking on tree barks and, listen, there is the finch. I think I can imitate that call.' For a moment they both paused and listened. Thea pursed her lips and made a perfect imitation of a finch calling to its mate. Stopping, she breathed deeply. 'It is *so* good to feel part of the woods, as if we were Ghost or even the animals he chases along the verges. Just look at Ghost now. He's enjoying his freedom too.' Nonetheless, she held onto Ghost's leash ready to slip it through the hound's collar in case he deserted them and bolted into the thickets. She only promised Ghost conditional freedom.

Ghost clearly knew his freedom's limitations for he stayed within them, faithfully shadowing Thea, only darting into the undergrowth sporadically, returning to rub against her legs.

The woods opened into a wide clearing and the stones that marked an old ship burial stood just as Princess Gunnhild had said. 'See, I am right. It's somewhere here. The cunning woman's house is close. I feel it.' Thea stopped and gazed around her. 'I think the path stops here.' She pointed into a stand of trees. 'Look, a track continues over there.' She pointed into an avenue of beech trees, convinced that she discerned smoke floating up into the branches.

The cunning woman's low, lime-washed hall lay behind an ancient oak tree with spreading branches. 'There it is,' she whispered to Gudrun. They stopped by the tree. Thea took a deep breath, wondering should she call out a warning of her presence? There was no need. A heartbeat later, the lady herself came out to greet them. She waited for them by the cottage entrance. Immediately Gudrun made a sign with three fingers behind her back. When Gudrun muttered, 'Hail Mary, Lady of Grace, protect us,' Thea ignored her maid's fear and marched forward.

Ghost bounded up to the lady, raised his head, sniffed and retreated, barking and leaping around Thea as if a bee had stung him. He crouched low, making a strange gurgling sound in his throat that was not exactly a growl. 'Stay, Ghost,' Thea urged, fearful now that the cunning woman had disturbed the hound. Gudrun drew closer and instinctively reached out for Thea's mantle.

The lady did not appear how Thea imagined a witch would

111

look. She was not old, nor was she poor. Her linen dress was blue, a deep blue, and was attractively embroidered about the hem and neck with red threads set down in intricate patterns of interlaced swirls. A gold necklace hung about her neck, made up of gold discs or perhaps coins. Her hair hung in two thin braids below a plain, neat, white linen cap. She leaned on a stick that was carved with tree leaves but, although the cunning woman's braids were silvered, she did not look old. Her face was unlined and her eyes were hazel and kindly.

So this was Ragnar, Gunnhild's witch.

For a moment the lady said nothing. She gestured with her stick for them to come forward. They tentatively took a few steps closer. Ghost pulled back momentarily and bared his teeth.

'So what is it you need, my lady? A love potion or a candle to make your lovers more loving?' The gentle laugh that followed possessed a light clinking cadence. It made Thea think of all those elf stories she had told the children on Flatholm. And for a moment she was sure she saw Prince Vladimir himself materialise before her, clad in a brown mantle with his glossy black hair spread about its hood and she was sure he held aloft a gleaming silver sword. He was smiling. His mouth opened to show gleaming white teeth. What was he trying to say? Was he warning her? As quickly as the vision formed it disintegrated. She was standing on the track with a witch staring at her.

Ragnar studied Thea's startled face and for a moment Thea felt uncomfortable. She slipped the leash about Ghost's collar. The act of bending concealed her nervousness.

The witch spoke again. Her voice sounded young. Perhaps witches never aged. 'Come, my ladies, I know you require something. I see it in your countenance.' Thea stared at her, holding the leash so tightly that she was sure her fear must show. 'Something is bothering the Lady Thea, I believe.'

'You know who I am, witch?'

'Yes, my lady, I know much that happens here. And I know

your names, Lady Thea and her maid, Gudrun.' She smiled. 'I live in the king's woods with his permission. I am the guardian of that ship burial over there.' Ragnar pointed into the trees. They both instinctively turned to follow her gesture. When they turned back she said, 'Many come to me for cures and for advice. Some seek spells, others incantations. Some want a lucky token.' She looked into Thea's eyes. Thea drew back from her penetrating stare. 'I think you want the future. I am right, am I not, my lady?' Thea nodded. She wanted more than the future. She wanted to make the future.

'Well then, come inside. Bring the hound. Or, no, best leave him. He may not like the parts of the dog, the heart, the liver, and paws that I use in my cures.'

'Ghost, stay by the entrance.'

Thea shuddered. There was no turning back. She slipped the leash over a post and Ghost growled again and sat still, marking a mother duck and her ducklings waddling towards the pond by the side of the witch's dwelling.

Once inside Thea and Gudrun sat together on a bench, their knees touching. Glancing nervously about the room Thea noticed a row of jars on a shelf opposite and shuddered at the thought of what else they might contain besides parts of pickled dog.

The woman's hearth was neat, she observed with a sharp glance. A rack of drying herbs released a pleasant scent of rosemary, thyme, fennel and hennebelle. She could not recognise the other aromatic smells discharged from a second drying line above the hearth. Her eyes slid along the fireside to a pot cast from iron, suspended from a bracket hanging to the right of the smouldering fire. Beside the pot she saw a great bronze basin. The witch must use this one for her conjuring. It was huge and decorated with a circle of naked dancing figures. Other forms engraved on its surface held drinking horns. Some dangled bunches of grapes. As Thea studied it, the bronze seemed to glow right at her. At length, she tore her gaze away and across the small room. Sunbeams from the window fell on

113

an elegantly carved chest opposite. An opened silver-plated box sat on the chest, pouring out a heap of gold and silver jewellery.

'I was polishing those when I heard you come. They are talismans. Step closer, my lady.'

Thinking of the vision she had earlier, Thea stood on shaky feet and crossed the hall room. She lifted a silver swan's foot hanging on a fine chain from the casket.

Lady Ragnar smiled. 'It has chosen you. You will wear it in the lands of snow and summer meadow. Take it with you when you leave today. It will bring you good fortune, a fine marriage and many children.' She looked at Gudrun. 'Now, girl, you may choose something.'

Feeling less jumpy, Thea found herself saying, 'Gudrun, you must. You are here now and cannot deny Lady Ragnar's kindness to us.'

Gudrun rolled her eyes, but left the bench to stand by her mistress. Diffidently she reached into the casket and drew out a long cloak pin. She touched its apex and immediately drew her finger back. A spot of blood was blossoming on the tip of her pointing finger. Instinctively she sucked the crimson bead away. Thea lifted the pin, which was decorated with swirls that seemed to have no beginning and no ending. She gave it back to Gudrun. ''Tis beautiful.'

'It is for your cloak, Gudrun. Be careful with it,' Lady Ragnar said with a smile hovering about her mouth. 'The pin has its own life. Its name is Needle. You will journey far, child, and I think you will discover the love of a man who will bring you great joy and I suspect a terrible danger. Yours may not always be an easy pathway but do not worry because in the end you are promised great happiness.' She drew a breath after she spoke those words. The room grew silent. Motes of golden dust floated above Thea. She clasped the silver swan tightly in her hand and felt Lady Ragnar's gaze penetrating her heart.

At length Lady Ragnar said, 'So, Lady Thea, why *do* you come here? I feel it concerns more than your own future. I sense your sorrow and loss. Perhaps in the telling of it you will find comfort. Sorrow can become happiness. Loss can turn into gain. Tell me your sadness; nay, it is anger, Lady Thea. Sit again and speak with honesty. Only then can I help you.' Tears were clouding Lady Ragnar's green-rimmed hazel eyes as if when speaking she had felt Thea's own anguish.

Thea and Gudrun returned to the seat below the window. Thea made a play of hanging her swan's foot about her neck and tucking it below her gown. What should she say? Where could she begin?

She began slowly. 'I pray that I do not have unwarranted darkness in my heart, Lady Ragnar. I truly believe in justice.' Then she could not hold back. Her words tumbled out in a passion. 'My father lost his kingdom. My brother Magnus died fighting to recover our lands. My brother Ulf is locked away in a castle in Normandy, a prisoner and he is only nine years old now. That is, if he still lives. My mother is as good as a captive. She is hidden from the world in a nunnery in England and she may not ever write to me. My grandmother is an exile. She has known suffering, too much of it. So, you see, I want help, Lady Ragnar. I want a spell, an incantation perhaps, conjuring words on a scroll, something that will make the king many call The Bastard, who is responsible for my family's sorrow, recognise his wickedness, the cruel hand he has dealt us, without thought for all those people of England who fought for my father and whose families now suffer exile and loss. I want a conjuring that will protect the weak, the poor, the landless and the needy from that Norman's evil doing.'

Ragnar sank down onto a stool beside her beautiful bronze basin. For a moment she looked at the small glow in the raised hearth. She leaned towards Thea and Gudrun, who grasped Thea's hand. *Stay strong, Gudrun,* Thea willed. *Do not falter now.*

Ragnar spoke again. 'A noble speech, my lady. I believe you mean every word of it. But, you see, change is the only sure thing in life. We are as pebbles on the earth's great beaches. We cannot turn tides. But, Lady Thea, wait for a moment. There may be something in the future that I can sense. I can show it, but I do not change the future.'

Ragnar took an urn from a shelf and dipped it into her water bucket. She poured the water into the bronze bowl and waited for it to settle. Sitting on a stool, she allowed her head to lower as she looked over it. Thea leaned in closer. The water was clear as a crystal casket, as pure as a flame glowing by a church altar, as calm as an angel's smile.

Yet, Lady Ragnar saw something in its surface. She studied it, her face serene. After a little time she looked up. 'As he has destroyed one family, then his own will never live in peace. Sadly, sons can turn against fathers. His eldest son will become a warring prince. He will wield swords and shields. He will create blood and darkness against his father, the king. King William of England, Duke of the Normans, will not die a peaceful death.' She set the basin aside and held Thea's eyes with a stern look. She shook her head. 'I do not need to curse that king. Listen to me, my lady. You must not attempt to tamper with fate. Let fate be and she shall find her way. We cannot save those who are already dead; may your father and your brother rest in peace. As for your little brother, he lives. Of this I am sure. And I promise you this. I shall pray to God and his angels for Ulf's safe keeping.'

Ragnar rose from her stool and said, 'Now you must both return to the hall. Jarl Niels is my cousin but he will not like you visiting my home. May God and His holy angels care for you too, my dears; may the Sisters spin you a kind fate.'

Thea fussed with awkward fingers about her mantle. She pulled a silver coin from the sewing purse that hung from her belt. It was a special coin, one of several that the coiner Alfred had given to her once. She had concealed them in her travelling chest because her father's image was stamped on them. They were a legacy from the year he had been king. 'Keep this, Lady Ragnar, and think about my father's journey to whatever heaven he travels towards; remember my brother Magnus too. I loved him dearly.'

Ragnar inclined her head and when she looked up Thea saw that her eyes were once again moist. The sorceress did not grant another word of comfort but Thea knew in her heart that her brother Ulf would one day return to his own family. Her hand flew to the swan's foot pendant. Everything that had fallen into chaos would fall once again into some new place and settle.

As they walked home a burden seemed to leave her heart and she felt lighter. Gudrun's colour had returned and she was smiling to herself, as if her heart held a secret. The bells from St Olave's monastery rang out. If they hurried they could slip into the chapel in time for Vespers. She would pray to St Theodosia that one day Ulf would return to their mother, who must miss her youngest son every day of her life.

'Gudrun, we cannot leave the wheelbarrow behind. We'll push it back to the hall. Everyone will think we have stayed by the river all afternoon.'

'She was not like a witch, my lady, not frightening at all.'

'No, but put that cloak pin away. And do not wear it here. Remember never to speak to anyone of what you heard this afternoon, not even Padar if he returns to us. You don't want him to think you a superstitious ninny.'

'No, never, my lady.'

After they had passed through the wicket gate set into the palisade, Thea glanced quickly along the pathway past the stables towards the kitchen building. She was surprised to see horsemen dismounting and grooms running forward to seize their reins.

'Gudrun, look, leave the barrow there by the kitchen building. If Lady Ingar looks for us, the church is where she must discover us. It seems her visitors have arrived a day early and they do not look like her cousins.'

'Oh, my lady, are we in trouble?'

'None we cannot deal with. Go, Ghost, go and find your friends.'

She wiped the dust and grass stains as best she could from her gown and strode forward.

11

The estate church steeple rose up through the trees. Thea and Gudrun hurriedly made their way along a narrow pathway that servants usually took to the church. Thea breathed easily when they encountered no one. The bells stopped ringing. As they reached the porch they could hear the priest intoning. Apparently, Vespers had begun.

'Let us slip into the back of the nave.'

'Will they see us?'

'Not if we are careful to keep out of Jarl Niels' sight, Gudrun.'

They never reached the nave. Lady Mary waylaid them by the porch. 'There you are. We have searched everywhere for you. Important men have come seeking you.'

'Come for me?' It was not the greeting she had expected. She had not considered for a moment that the horsemen she had seen were anything to do with her.

'Mother is with them.' Mary nodded in the direction of the altar. Following Mary's nod, Thea's eyes glanced along the nave. As her eyes adjusted to the church's dim interior she saw four strangers who wore embroidered tunics with wide sleeves and broad belts. 'The Rus ambassadors?' she said, turning back to Mary.

'Correct, Thea. You are not totally addled by your day in the sun. Their guards are in the yard. You may have noticed horsemen. Queen Elizaveta has come to speak with you. You will find her with Father in the hall. Everyone has been waiting for you to return. Mother brought the foreigners into our church, just to keep them busy until you were found.'

Thea felt an anchor was weighing her heart down, dragging her deep into the depths of a great unknown sea. What would Jarl Niels say to her? Her mind worked quickly, composing a lie. Where *had* she been?

'To the hall now. You look a mess. Is that a bramble tear in your gown?'

Thea glanced down. Her saffron gown did have a rip near the hem. 'Oh, it must have got caught when we paddled in the stream.'

Mary's answer was to prod Thea in the back and send her hurrying out through the church door. Gudrun followed, trying to keep up. Thea could hear the girl's stout boots clatter on the tiled floor of the porch. The priest intoned on, singing a long prayer. Thea turned her head and looked back through the opened door at those gathered in the nave. No one had shifted their attention from the priest.

'Hurry; the skald has returned,' Lady Mary said as they crossed the yard. A group of armoured men were sitting with their backs against the stable block wall, their weapons by their sides. These must be the guards they saw a while ago before Gudrun pushed the barrow to the kitchen lean-to.

Lady Mary paused by a crab apple tree close to the hall entrance. She lifted up Thea's chin, forcing her to look into her darkening eyes. 'You had better have a good excuse ready for Queen Elizaveta. Where have you been, child? You were not at the mill. Nor were you at the dyers.'

Thea fumbled about for words of explanation. 'We had a picnic and then fell asleep under bushes close to the river bank. It was hot and we were tired. The bells for Vespers awakened us.' The lie had easily tripped off her tongue.

'Just look at the state of you …' Lady Mary began.

'There they are …' A familiar voice reached out from the shadows beyond the open, great, studded hall door. Thea peered through it, trying hard to see him. She stepped closer and there he was. Padar, wearing his familiar red mantle, was sitting on a stool inside the hall doorway; his harp lay across his knees. He was twiddling the strings. Standing up, he carefully placed the harp on the stool.

'What does the queen want with me?' Without even greeting

Padar, the question tumbled out of her mouth.

His eyes slid past Lady Mary to Gudrun then back to her. 'Queen Elizaveta and Jarl Niels are waiting to speak to you.'

'About what?' She stood on the hall threshold momentarily frozen, cold despite the warmth of the afternoon.

'Your betrothal, of course.'

'They can wait a quarter of that candle notch longer,' Lady Mary said, glancing at the fat candle standing in the hall porch gloom marking time. 'Look at her, skald. She is not fit to be seen in those garments.' She turned to Thea again. 'Go and change your gown, Thea. We shall tell Jarl Niels you are on your way. There is to be a feast in your honour. Wear your best gown.'

Thea peered past the hour candle into the hall. Figures were rushing about. She now heard the bumping of benches, the clanging platters and the noise of servants' chatter. She peered past Lady Mary. She stepped past Padar and looked about. Two of their servants were hanging fresh tapestries showing sailing ships and river scenes from beams by the walls. The king's pennant hung behind the top table on the raised dais. Servants and slaves were bustling about carrying loaves of hastily baked bread and barrels of ale. There was the smell of fowl roasting.

Lady Mary, who had followed her inside, said in a cross voice, 'Yes, you are to be betrothed to Prince Vladimir. You can see the hurried preparations we have been making for the queen's visit, while you fall asleep by the river.' She lifted Thea's hands. 'Wash those. You are not a slave.' She seized Thea's arm and propelled her out of the entrance and along the outer wall to the staircase. Trembling with excitement, Thea began to mount the stairway. Padar, who had followed them, momentarily smiled up at Gudrun as she placed her boot on the first step. 'Come on, Gudrun,' Thea said irritated at them both. 'We have only a quarter of the candle notch.'

That afternoon, Thea, who had hastily washed and changed her overgown, stood before the queen, feeling a sense of fear as the queen told her that she was to return to Roskilde and warned her how she was to behave that evening.

'You must look your best tonight. We have a few weeks and a little more to prepare, my dear. One of the ambassadors will stand as proxy for Prince Vladimir. This evening you will be veiled and you will say nothing. It is discreet. Nothing, my dear. You do understand. They will be watching you. You will behave like a princess. You eat daintily if at all and you must lower your eyes. You will walk gracefully, not like a country woman but like a noblewoman.'

'My child,' Jarl Niels broke in and spoke gently to Thea, 'important matters of trade with the Rus are at stake. There is a little disappointment that they have chosen an English princess rather than a Danish princess. However, for you it is a grand marriage. Queen Elizaveta has your interests at heart and she intends that you will understand the way a Rus princess must behave. We want no misunderstandings.'

Elizaveta nodded and Thea wondered if she resented the fact that she was to marry Prince Vladimir rather than one of her stepdaughters. 'Are the princesses recovered?' she politely ventured. 'Are they well, my lady?'

'They are recovered and as well as can be expected but all our hopes, my child, are with you. Do not disappoint us. Now go and prepare yourself. Lady Ingar will fetch you when we are ready to introduce you to these new ambassadors.' She sighed. 'They are a serious group of men, more serious than those who carried the pox to our palace.'

Gudrun's hands were shaking as she pulled the sapphire blue gown from the coffer. Moments later, she lifted out the silver, sapphire-studded circlet and its luminous veil. Both had been folded into a rose-coloured gown that Thea rarely wore.

Thea seized the circlet from Gudrun, allowing the rose gown to fall onto the floor. She would soon be betrothed to Prince Vladimir and travel to Novgorod where she would marry the prince in a great, no doubt exceptionally magnificent, Russian wedding. He would appear as he had this afternoon in a fine mantle. Soon she would meet him. The vision in the wood was an omen, a good omen. Her prince was not warning her, he was greeting her. Tonight was one of the most important of her life. She must impress them all.

She stood still in the middle of the floor, her hands flying to her face. 'By the Norns, how could the witch's magic work so quickly? Do you think she had intelligence of their coming here before we went to her cottage? Or is it coincidence?'

Gudrun bent down to rescue the gown that lay in a heap on the floor rug. Clutching the garment, she said, 'Coincidence maybe, though she clearly can see things we cannot. But, my lady, Padar is back, however it has come about.'

Thea raised an eyebrow. Her maid's eyes were shining and her face was glowing with pleasure.

'You may keep that rose overgown. It becomes you. When I am Princess of the Rus, I shall have all the dresses I could ever desire. You must have that one. The undergown is still in the chest. Wear both this evening. My handmaiden should complement her mistress.' She instinctively touched the swan talisman that lay cool and comforting between her breasts. Should she wear it or keep it hidden? Better it remained hidden.

She lifted her polished mirror from the coffer, peered at her face, pinched her cheeks and laid the mirror down again.

Gudrun blushed, her creamy skin taking on a lovely glow. 'I am pale beside your beauty, my lady.'

'We must both look radiant tonight. Once my betrothal is settled, you will travel with me into the country of the Rus.'

Gudrun's eyes looked anxious and her skin paled to the colour of church candle wax. 'But Padar?'

'I shall request Padar's protection. We shall see if he is the one Lady Ragnar thinks will bring you joy.'

Gudrun removed the brooch from her belt purse and peered at it. 'Needle will remain in my belt purse as my talisman.'

'See it does. We are in enough trouble.'

Gudrun lifted Thea's comb from the chest. 'Shall I braid your hair into two plaits or fold it into a neck twist?'

'Two braids will suffice. There is no time. They are waiting for me. And I think use the sapphire clasps. They will show beneath my head covering.' She smiled happily. 'I feel, Gudrun, that our visit to the witch was a good omen. Our lives are changing.'

'And about time too, my lady.'

Ingar was mounting the staircase. Thea recognised her tread so she placed a finger on her lips, composed herself, raised her head and arranged her veil.

Part Two
Betrothal

The son of Prince Vsevolod and of a Byzantine princess of the house of Monomakh, Vladimir married Gita, the daughter of the last Anglo-Saxon king, Harold, who was defeated at the Battle of Hastings in 1066.

Medieval Russia's Epics, Chronicles, and Tales, edited by Serge A. Zenkovsky, 1974.

12

Roskilde, Calends of August 1069

The day of Thea's betrothal feast arrived within a month of her return to Roskilde. Since Prince Vladimir was helping his father to keep order in Kiev, the Rus diplomat, Lord Igor from Novgorod, stood proxy for him. If Thea had hoped that the prince, himself, would come for her, he did not and she was disappointed when she discovered that she would not travel to the Rus lands before the spring sailing season.

She asked Padar to describe Prince Vladimir. Padar confirmed that he was tall and dark with brown eyes that sometimes looked hard but quickly added that they were more often softly hued. He told her that the prince could be distant but that was his sense of how a prince should behave. Her face fell. She had hoped he would be lively and fun to be with. Padar raced on, 'Oh yes, my lady, he is very devout. He attends all the services.' So he was serious. 'Yes, a learned prince,' Padar said. 'He is much loved by them all. I think him fair and kindly. My lady, you must not be disappointed that after your betrothal you cannot travel over the seas at once. There will be time for you to make ready for your journey to the lands of the Rus.' She wondered for a heart-beat if Padar was being diplomatic and if there were other reasons that she must wait.

This is usual with betrothals, she told herself, chasing off her disappointment as if it was a bothersome fly to be flicked away. She spun around. She was ready. Followed by a group of fussing maids, she swept from the chamber where she had dressed and down the stairway. *Great princes are busy, fighting battles or caring for their peoples, and I am sure my Vladimir is already a great prince.*

As Thea stood at the bottom of the stairway she found that she had difficulty breathing. Her new overgown of gold damask, embroidered with silver crosses, was stiff, tight and uncomfortable. She disliked the hardened damask, its tight sleeves scratching her skin. She resented the fact that it hung badly on her because it had not been made for her but, long ago, for Queen Elizaveta.

'It is suitable and becoming,' the queen had said firmly.

Thea thought otherwise. It itched as if it contained a host of crawling creatures, though she knew it had been kept carefully in lavender and its seams were ruthlessly checked for lice by maids before she had her fitting for it.

As she had prepared for the ceremony, Elizaveta had explained that a Russian husband did not look upon his bride's face until the third night of their wedding.

'Even though Ambassador Igor is only standing in as the prince's proxy?'

'Thea, you must observe the Rus custom.'

Elizaveta held up a fine silk veil, so fine that, in fact, Thea was relieved when she realised that she could see through it. She smiled to herself thinking, surely if I can see through it, *others* might see *my* face.

Her maids discreetly withdrew into the shadows. Thea paused momentarily. Through her cobweb-fine veil, she observed the gathering of Danish noblemen and women waiting by the whetstone close to the hall entrance. Sweltering in the wretched gown, Thea stepped forward from the stairway. Flanked by Elizaveta and the king's older daughters, Helene and Ragnhild, she walked sedately up the length of the hall, past the central hearth and took her place close to the nobility and the Danish princesses.

She felt the princesses glowering at her from behind closely drawn silk wimples. Only their cheeks, noses, chins and eyes showed. Thea knew well how Lady Fortune had smiled on her. She had escaped unmarked from the previous year's attack of the little pox, except for a few tiny scars on her body.

Guttorm, the third princess, had remained sulky ever since Thea had returned from Søderup. Her petulance, on this betrothal day, Thea knew did not stem from the illness suffered by her sisters during the previous autumn. Godwin had not returned to Denmark from Ireland with Edmund during the spring sailing season.

Guttorm had said bitterly, 'Lucky for you that *your* betrothal goes ahead. Your brother has not fulfilled his promise for *our* betrothal. It was part of my father's agreement with our great-aunt.'

Thea had replied diplomatically, 'Princess, I am sorry, too, that he has not returned with Edmund. Perhaps the Pope considered you too closely related.'

'Pah! Others marry cousins twice removed.'

In contrast, Princess Gunnhild, who had passed some months at Søderup with Thea and Gudrun leaned forward and squeezed Thea's hand.

'Thank you,' Thea whispered just in time.

King Sweyn snapped his fingers and the ceremony began. She took her place facing the Rus diplomat. A cleric unfolded a scroll tied with scarlet ribbons that hung damply in the heat, falling from the parchment's seal like tired streamers. He pinned it to the small table with four glossy black stones.

Old Bishop Vilhelm, ready to witness the signing, leaned over the scroll and began to read in a low, mumbling voice. Thea strained to hear him, her curiosity aroused as to what treasures she was to bring with her to Russia.

She possessed a wealth of jewels, tapestries and a small collection of exquisitely decorated books from her father Harold's collection about hawking. She would bring to Russia several bibles scribed in English and a jewel-covered gospel of St Mark that had once belonged to Grandmother Gytha. There was a hoard of silver and gold coin, valuable double-edged swords that long ago had been forged by the Franks and a collection of seaxes with handles carved from tusk, decorated with intricate patterns.

She would bring linen and woollen cloth and a collection of beautiful household items to her marriage. All were valued in

Russia. Thea wondered who gave her these. She suspected it was Edmund who was now trading between Denmark, Flanders and Ireland in wool, linen and highly decorated metal utensils, walrus tusk combs, silver boxes engraved with intricate designs and beech wood coffers.

Thea rustled her stiff gown impatiently. There were no lands attached to her dowry settlement. She was a stateless and landless Saxon princess but now, like a phoenix greeting the sun, she must be raised out of exile to be reborn a new princess in the land of the Rus. In Russia she would find her new home. I want a home of my own, she thought as she waited for the bishop to give her the pen.

She leaned over the table and signed the betrothal document, writing her official name, Gita Godwinsdatter, Princess of the English, with a flourish. She stretched up and drew a relieved breath. The Rus called her Gita, not Gytha. She smiled to herself at this formality. She was neither Gita nor Gytha. To her family and friends, she would always be Thea.

After the exchange of rings was over, Thea sat on a padded winged chair close to the whetstone as the Danish and English nobles who had known and fought for her father presented her with gifts to take to her new land. None of these treasures was as important to her as the silver and sapphire betrothal ring that Prince Vladimir had sent to her. As her hand hovered above a bone-plated casket the swirling patterns on the broad silver band seemed to move of their own accord and its huge pale blue sapphire stone gleamed in the candlelight that flickered by her shoulder. She could not stop her mind wandering to the prince who had sent the ring. Was he really as handsome as Elizaveta said when she had helped her dress for the ceremony? Was he as Padar had described, kind and fair in his dealings with others? Would her prince find her to his taste, as beautiful as this precious ring which he had sent to her for their betrothal?

She concentrated on thanking the gift-givers who had presented her with such beautiful objects: an ivory-covered prayer book, a purse of uncut garnets, a crucifix with amber insets, bolts of cloth, wolf furs, sheepskins, a collection of carved spoons, skins, tapestries, and cushions for her comfort on the long journey deep into the Rus lands.

An unexpected gift arrived at her feet. She looked long at it, studied it, puzzled at it. This was a birthing chair with an embroidered foot rest. Since it came from the sulky Danish princesses who would never forgive this marriage, she felt a frown crease her forehead. She stood and walked slowly around it, admiring its craftsmanship, praising it but pondering it.

'I think it a thoughtful gift,' Thea said carefully to Ingegerd as Queen Elizaveta began ordering servants and guards to take the presents to a storeroom.

'Wait!' Edmund shouted. 'There is another from my thanes.'

Everybody looked towards the entrance. A breeze blew into the hall as the heavy doors were pulled wide open by Edmund's retainers and two English noblemen carried a litter through. They carefully lowered the litter onto the floor tiles.

'My lady, we want to ensure your safe carriage when the dragon boats travel the great Rus rivers and must be carried overland between them. Look beyond the curtains,' one of Edmund's thanes said, clearly thrilled to do such a service to King Harold's elder daughter.

She parted the heavy woollen curtains and peered inside. There on the great padded seat on which she would recline lay a silver fox bedspread. 'Thank you, it is exquisite.' The birthing chair forgotten, Thea embraced the two survivors of the Great Battle who presented it to her. 'Come and visit me in the palace if you should find yourselves trading in Kiev. This silver fox will grace my bedchamber. It is far too beautiful to remain in a palanquin.'

Queen Elizaveta whispered in her ear, 'You must now take your place at the top table.'

With the ambassador following just a step behind, Thea glided forward to sit in a place of honour at the table on the raised dais. The trestle table had been set as if by an enchantment, with silver platters and intricately carved spoons.

Helped by a steward bearing a long staff, the court found their places. Edmund and his men were placed on the lower trestles with the princesses, Danish nobles, their wives, daughters and many of the priests of Roskilde, a handful of Rus diplomats and their retainers.

After King Sweyn and his queen joined Thea and the ambassador, course after course was served, placed before them by a dozen servers. There were pigeons in cream, chickens stuffed with eggs and nuts called walnuts from the south, hunks of boar, beef, various roasted birds and a salmon dressed in a sauce made with a fruit which Ambassador Igor said were called lemons. She tasted everything, discreetly lifting her veil aside so she could eat.

Musicians strummed harps. Long, lean dogs wearing glittering studded collars circled the trestles looking for scraps. Thea noticed that two of the king's hawks sat placidly on perches by an un-shuttered window, jesses jingling, as their guardians fed them titbits. Every time the falconers paused feeding them, they looked as if they would take off from their perches and circle the hall or fly out of the window. She knew they would not since they were hooded and chained to their roosts.

King Sweyn leaned across her towards the Rus ambassador, 'Ambassador Igor,' he said. 'Today is a great day for Denmark, another Rus alliance for us Danes.' He stroked his white beard thoughtfully. 'My ally, Pope Gregory, is reforming the Roman Church throughout Christendom, tightening our church practices, you know. He is putting a stop to intermarriage amongst great families but he will never object to *this* marriage. Even though my little cousin, Gita, as you Russians name her, is to unite with a prince of the Byzantine persuasion the Pope will be pleased because she is marrying out of her own blood. Her children's blood will be fresh and untainted.' He lifted his cup of Rhenish wine. 'May our allegiance continue to flourish.'

The ambassador lifted his cup and smiled at Thea. 'Krasivee Dama, beautiful lady, our prince is fortunate.'

He is indeed, Thea thought to herself, not just because she was beautiful as people often remarked, but because she was educated and could read and write and she would understand matters of state in her new country once she mastered their language.

Two musicians clashed cymbals together. Thea started. One blew loudly on his bagpipes and another began to play a fast swirling tune on a flute. The noise of music invited shouts for refills of Rhenish wine in cups and drinking horns. Any further conversation was challenged by male bellowing and female laughter. Sound gushed upwards and outwards around the trestles like steam from the earth's depths bursting through the floor rushes from below the hall's foundations. Sweyn raised his drinking vessel to the ambassador again. Likewise, the ambassador raised his cup to acknowledge Sweyn's toast.

Later, as the servants carried out pastries and fruits, the uproar around the trestles subsided as guests seized them. King Sweyn took the opportunity to resume his previous conversation. He leaned across Thea and reminded the Rus diplomat that his cousin, Gita of the English, was of noble blood, a Saxon princess. He reminded the ambassador that it had taken the Bastard King of England years to get permission from Pope Alexander to remain married to Matilda of Flanders whom every king considered to be of high birth, pious and beautiful, tiny, non-threatening and a complacent wife to the undeserving Duke William. 'And they were fifth cousins.' Sweyn stretched his velvet-covered arm along the back of Thea's chair, patted her shoulder and said that Thea was every bit as religious, modest and devout as Matilda of Flanders.

What nonsense, pious and beautiful? How could he praise that dwarf, the bastard king's wife? How dare he compare them? Did he not know that the wife of William of Normandy was a harridan who had had her bared backside paddled by the cruel duke in front of his nobles when she had refused to marry him, that Duke William had dragged Matilda by her plait through the Flanders mud, and that she was a great joke

133

amongst the English ladies? The story had run through Thea's family like a cornfield on fire. Perhaps it was a widespread rumour!

Once tamed by that Bastard, so the entertaining tale went, Matilda would have none other than Duke William to husband. He will never tame any of our women in such a manner, she angrily thought to herself, well if that is the truth.

King Sweyn ran on, 'Ambassador, you will inform the prince that my cousin must remain Catholic, loyal to my friend Pope Gregory in Rome.'

The ambassador sharply replied. 'That is for the lady's conscience, Sire'

And not if my prince's religion is better. Thea glared at King Sweyn.

A troupe of actors bustled about the trestles. Sweyn shoved back his great chair. He stood steadily and waved his arms about, insisting that his court ceased their noise and watch. He gestured to the actors to set up their props in the central open space in the hall. Sinking into his chair, he leaned forward and rested his large face and white beard on his folded great paws.

Thea felt relief when Sweyn's attention shifted away from her to the play. She watched as the play unfolded. The drama was a favourite story of how a magician who, for a handsome fee, charms the moon from the sky and brings a clay image of cupid to life to win a rich woman's favours for his client. He succeeded, but the prince concerned might have accomplished his love quest by simply giving a pure white gelding to the lady as a gift. The actors spoke in rhyme and elaborated on the theme of wooing and betrothal. They ended the piece by leading a pretty white foal wearing a decorated bridle, its mane plaited with ribbons, around the hall.

As the colourful cavalcade paraded past the dais, Thea found herself smiling at the characters, a shifty-looking play magician, the lack-lustre prince, fat cupid, a golden-clad dwarf, equipped with a tiny bow and arrow, and finally the lady riding the foal, who was a boy disguised as a rich lady with false red-gold hair and who wore a disdainful countenance.

'One should not mock magicians,' remarked the ambassador quietly. Thea wondered at his words, but moments later, she noticed Sweyn's eye roving from one court lady to another to rest on a rosy-cheeked young lady. She felt uncomfortable for the queen who was intently watching Sweyn from her place further along the trestle.

Elizaveta had not loved her first husband Harald of Norway. The Norwegian king had been greedy and cruel, but her real complaint was he had elevated his concubine, a woman of noble lineage, above her as if she, Elizaveta, the Queen of Norway, was already a dead wife. Thea reflected, *I hope my prince does not treat me this way.* Her own mother had been set aside by her father for a new political marriage after he was chosen by the nobles to be King of England after King Edward died.

'If Harald could have set me aside for his mistress he would have. Can you imagine how I felt, Thea?' Elizaveta had confided as they prepared for Thea's betrothal, touching Thea's lips with cochineal, even though no one would see her mouth today under her veil. 'Harald of Norway was a brute, and his manners at table, by the Holy Mother, are not worth remembering. He was uncouth.'

Thea watched Elizaveta watching Sweyn. Elizaveta did not deserve a repetition of such treatment from her new husband, a man who was known to have fathered daughters and sons by his many concubines.

Thea's attention eventually returned to the Rus ambassador seated by her side. Ambassador Igor was an old, stooped man who wore the customary Rus embroidered felt hat trimmed with fur.

'I hear the winters in Novgorod are bitter,' she said, not able to think of anything else to say, wishing that Gudrun and Padar were seated with her at the dais table tonight. She peered along the tables. She could not see them. They were lost amongst the servants who thronged the lowest uncovered trestles. 'I shall be glad to travel north in the spring, ' she said, though she wished she could travel before winter set in. After all, Padar had travelled late in autumn.

'Princess, you will find our homes comfortable, your chambers warm and snow in winter a beautiful sight to behold as if God, Himself, had taken up a painter's brush to cleanse the land and paint it anew.' He waved his arms emphatically as if he, too, was painting the land with God's paint brush. He had spoken to her in English, and she felt touched. She hoped he would live long and remain close to her household, though that was unlikely, given his advanced years.

She smiled. Clearly encouraged, he ran on, 'I wish you much happiness. Prince Vladimir is admired amongst the Rus people. He is courageous and honourable.'

'So everyone tells me,' she said quietly.

From the corner of her eye, she noticed the Danish king lean forward, ale cup in hand, slowly raising it to his lips as he studied yet another lady who sat near his older daughters. In the time it took for a dancer to twirl, his eyes roved back to the dark-haired, rosy-cheeked girl. To her surprise, she saw that Edmund was studying the pretty girl too. He was asking her to dance with him and the king was glaring at Edmund!

'Princess Gita, our country is unsettled.'

'What? How?'

'Our grand prince, Iziaslav of Kiev, Prince Vladimir's uncle, is exiled in Poland. Kiev is unsafe. Even Novgorod, with its impenetrable kremlin fortress, is not safe these days. His cousin, a sorcerer they say, was prisoner in Kiev. With the help of merchants who felt threatened by Steppe tribes the sorcerer prince usurped Prince Iziaslav in the spring. This evil magician threatens the peace of our lands from Pereiaslavl in the south to Polotsk, which is a fortress north of Novgorod. Our three princes, Iziaslav, Sviatoslav and Prince Vsevolod, are determined to protect Novgorod and Kiev.' The ambassador speared a tiny sweetmeat with his knife and daintily nibbled it.

'What is the cousin called?' Thea asked, now curious and determined to commit to memory all these complicated names.

'He is named Prince Vsevslav. Just call him the magician. Everyone else does.' The ambassador laid down his eating knife, dabbed his mouth with his napkin and began to tell Thea the history.

Servants passed by their table with pastry coffins filled with cream. Thea nodded her head and accepted one. Musicians struck up with flutes and small drums.

The ambassador continued his story. 'Ask your harp-player, Padar, about him. He heard all about it in Novgorod last winter. He was there when tribes from the south attacked Kiev. Our enemies, certain untrustworthy nobles, whom we call boyars in our land, released the sorcerer and set him up as their prince instead.'

'The nobles had such power?'

'Yes, they do have powers on our councils. And remember this prince was of royal blood and many thought he should have been elected as Grand Prince of Kiev, not Iziaslav. His father had been the eldest of the princely brothers but he died before he could inherit Kiev. Iziaslav was the senior prince.'

Thea frowned. It was confusing. Beyond the table in the centre of the hall, Padar was playing the harp softly. They listened for a moment.

The ambassador remarked, 'The skald plays well.' Then he resumed his tale. 'The rule is that a prince's father must rule in Kiev as grand prince before the son can inherit. Otherwise the throne goes to the uncle whose father had ruled. The boyars of Kiev thought Prince Iziaslav a weak grand prince. However, many think that these boyars were subject to an enchantment.'

'You mean the magician who was his nephew enchanted the nobles of Kiev.'

The ambassador tapped the table with his wooden spoon. 'Indeed it was so but, Princess Gita, all improves we hope. We expect to reclaim Kiev very soon but you see it will be some time before things are settled and I hope you can travel to Russia soon.'

'I hope so too,' Thea said.

The ambassador took a breath and continued, 'The magician is set on dividing the three brothers of Kiev but now they have united to banish him from our territories. You see, Princess, we Russians dwell in troubled times. It is certain that your wedding will be delayed.'

'Does King Sweyn know this?' Thea asked, thinking that Russia was every bit as dangerous as the land she had fled a year before.

'Your uncle needs our trade routes through to Byzantium. King Sweyn knows that marriage into our princely families is of great benefit to him and to us. His warriors will help our warriors. Our families are already united.' The ambassador glanced along the table at Queen Elizaveta. She was sister to the three princely Russian brothers and an aunt to Thea's affianced prince.

Ambassador Igor said in a firm voice, 'King Sweyn will want your marriage to happen soon. However, he must be patient.'

Thea felt disappointed and it showed because Igor said in a kindly manner, 'Princess Gita, I am certain that you will travel to our lands no matter the threat.' He smiled with old wisdom in his eyes and Thea recognised that he had seen much unfold in his long lifetime and suspected that he sensed that she could not wait to escape from the Danish court. 'You, of course, must be used to danger, Princess, since you were in England when the Duke of Normandy swept through your land. Assuming that our great city of Novgorod is safe you will travel there to await your wedding.' He leaned closer to Thea, so close she could smell a whiff of mint waft off his breath. He touched the sapphire ring on her middle finger with his own mottled one. 'The young prince is fighting in Ukrainia but he will come to Novgorod when things are settled. He will take you south for your wedding ceremony in Kiev's magnificent Cathedral of St Sophia.'

'But if there is strife in your lands I could be betrothed for years?' She tried not to let her impatience show.

'You will enjoy your betrothal,' he said, avoiding a direct answer. 'The prince's stepmother will take you into her terem and teach you our ways. You will learn to be a Russian princess.' He smiled in a kindly and very reassuring manner. 'Kiev may be a troubled city, but when it is peaceful it is the most wondrous city of all our Rus cities. It is a Jerusalem, a great city of Christian churches, craftsmen, merchants, people of many nations, including exiles from your esteemed father's court.' The diplomat paused and crossed himself before continuing, 'You, lady Princess, will be safely hidden from any outside turmoil in the Lady Anya's terem in Novgorod until you travel to Kiev for your wedding.'

'Lady Anya's *terem*?' Thea was both curious and anxious. A terem sounded like a cooking pot. She was to be hidden away!

'Our women remain more sheltered from the world than women here in Denmark. But you will find her palace quarters much to your liking and the atmosphere pleasant. Princess Anya is only twenty-two summers old. She will teach you the ways of our land – the rules we expect our wives to understand. '

Thea had wanted her wedding to follow her betrothal. She wanted to be a princess of the Rus and not to be ruled by a stepmother who was only six years her senior. She wanted her prince. She pushed a pastry coffin around her silver plate until a creamy filling oozed out. She lifted her veil aside and spooned a little of the custard neatly into her mouth. *She would learn to be a good wife and mother, yes, but she wanted to help her prince rule his lands. Together they would be strong. No enemy would steal what was theirs and do as the Normans had done when they had crossed the Narrow Sea, entered her homeland, massacred her father's people and razed their homes to the earth.*

She glanced up from her pastry. Padar had finished playing. The musicians with bagpipes, drums and cymbals were back. So were the poor. They had crept into the hall doorway from the courtyard beyond begging food, leftovers, creatures seeking betrothal alms and who were almost as noisy as the guests with their whinges, cries, begging and blessings until they were shooed from the hall by two of Sweyn's servants who carried enormous baskets of leftover loaves and scraps high on their shoulders. She felt sad for those unfortunates who needed alms.

Once the musicians had resumed playing, two men began leaping about the lower tables in a wild dance. She turned her attention from them. To her side, Ambassador Igor was studying the rosy-cheeked woman who was seated again between two of King Sweyn's female cousins. Edmund was conversing with his friends.

What was so special about that woman? She looked at the ambassador with a question she did not form, but it was one he answered anyway.

'The woman sitting amongst the Danish women is from our land. She travelled here with her father, a well-respected merchant of Kiev. I have asked for her to serve you and teach you our language.'

'She is beautiful. But I think it best we keep her very busy and away from the king.'

'I fear it is so,' the ambassador whispered conspiratorially. 'Her father would kill the king should he lay a finger on her.'

'That would signal her father's death for sure.'

Ambassador Igor leaned close to Thea. She strained to hear him above the dancing warriors, the women on the lower benches, who were now clapping and banging drinking cups in encouragement, and the loud conversations that competed with the racket below.

Igor whispered close to her ear, 'Not if her father snatches her from under the king's nose and sails away, He knows all sorts of tricks to elude King Sweyn's greatest fleet. Dimitri is one of our most valuable spies as well as a wealthy trader. He works for Prince Vsevolod himself.'

'What is her name?'

'They call her Katya.'

'Katya,' Thea murmured to herself. 'I hope you will become my friend.'

13

Autumn 1069

Thea liked her new position at the Danish court as the official betrothed of Prince Vladimir of the Rus. Katya was soon established in Thea's new household as her personal teacher.

Thea enjoyed studying the strange symbols that made up the Russian alphabet and she strove to read simple words as she spoke them. Katya was a good teacher and Thea was quick to learn. By November Thea had begun to knit together simple sentences in Russian.

One afternoon Thea said, 'Enough for today, tell us of your life in Kiev, Katya. I am curious.'

Katya sighed. She glanced at the seamstresses who were sewing new garments for Thea. Her sorrowful dark eyes darkened into two pools the colour of bog-land peat. 'Sometimes I long for Russia. Others, I want to be as far away from that terrible country as I possibly can be. I like sewing. Perhaps I should not return to Russia when you travel, my lady, but instead stay here in Denmark and earn my living as a seamstress.'

'Oh, Katya, was it so terrible? Why does thinking about Russia bring tears to your eyes?'

'It was.' Katya brushed her tears away with her fingers and told Thea how in the springtime a fierce Steppe tribe called the Cumans attacked Kiev from the Steppes. 'It was a terrible time. It is why my betrothed lost his life.'

Thea's eyes widened as Katya told her story.

'There was an uprising in Kiev because the Grand Prince did not allow his noblemen to have an army to protect their trading vessels from the Cuman tribesmen's attacks. The boyars banished Prince Iziaslav and chose his nephew to rule the kingdom.'

'Ambassador Igor told me about it. What happened to your betrothed?' Thea urged Katya.

'The sorcerer prince, you know about him, enticed many of Kiev's nobles to follow him. He cast spells and magicked the Cuman invaders away from the walls of the city. In truth, he is no sorcerer, just a thug who used bribes to win his way out of prison and into the boyars' hearts. The nobles armed themselves and even Iziaslav's own army turned against him. The magician prince negotiated with the tribesmen and gave them promises of trade.'

'Which, perhaps, Iziaslav should have done.' That seemed one solution to Thea.

'He would not spend the money.'

'Your betrothed, Katya, how was he involved?'

'My lady, my betrothed was a young nobleman in Prince Iziaslav's employ. When Prince Vsevslav, the wicked sorcerer, was released from prison and his followers attacked Prince Iziaslav,' Katya paused and swallowed, 'a swordsman struck my love down in the street as he helped Prince Iziaslav flee the city. I miss him every day.'

'Oh, Katya, it is so sad. If I meet that prince I shall thrust my eating knife into his evil heart.' Her hand involuntarily strayed to the silver eating knife that hung with her scissors and purse from her belt. 'I hope my Vladimir is safe from his cunning.'

'Did your betrothed die in the street?'

'They carried him to my father's house. As is our tradition, when the match-makers led us together for our betrothal, I was veiled so my fiancé never saw my face. He *did* see my face on the day he died, my lady. He looked upon me as he breathed his last breath. He was alive when they brought him into our house, but his life was draining from him, so when he asked for me I was brought to him. He said, "I want to see your face before I die and I shall keep it with me when I travel into God's Kingdom". My lady, I lifted aside the head covering that cloaked my face, my head and my neck. I let him look upon my

142

face. I did not weep. Instead I smiled and so my beloved died with my smile in his heart. I can never forgive those who murdered him.'

Thea thought of the vengeance that lay in her own heart. She thought of Lady Ragnar's calming words to her as she had looked into the still water in her beautiful bowl. She said to Katya, 'Perhaps God will extract his own revenge on this man. I hope it is so. Such wickedness will not go unpunished.'

The circle of life did not pause for a wicked sorcerer but somehow God's mysterious justice might have a way of evening things up.

Katya looked at her fiercely. 'If I can, I shall kill him.'

'No, Katya, set aside revenge and allow fate and God to find a way. One day another man will want to marry you and perhaps then you will let sorrowful memories of your first betrothed rest.' Thea held Katya's hand. 'I, too, have lost many whom I have loved.'

Gudrun shook her head. 'If the one I love was murdered in the street I would have revenge in my heart.'

'And who is your love, Gudrun? ' Katya asked, a small smile beginning to brighten her sad face.

'I cannot say because he has not spoken yet. Perhaps he never will.'

Thea felt her mouth open and then closed it firmly. If she could speak to Padar for Gudrun she would. First, she must be sure that it was what Padar really wanted. And she must think of a way to provide them with a home. The life of an exile was precarious. The life of two exiles with no home and land of their own might be impossible.

'Have you ever seen Prince Vladimir, Katya?' she asked.

'Only once. My father works for his father. He carries messages. He watches for him.'

'And …?'

'Are you asking me about my father or Prince Vladimir?'

'Well, the prince. Is he heroic? Is he kind? Is he as handsome as they say?'

143

'I really cannot tell, my lady. He is a warrior and his father worships him though his father is recently married again. The prince's mother died. His father may have other sons.'

'He has never written me a letter.'

'It is not our way. He cannot even see your face before you are married.'

Thea could not believe that Vladimir's uncle, the ruler of Kiev, had had to flee his kingdom, but worse, she was saddened that Katya's betrothed had been murdered during the rebellion.

Hearing footsteps, all three looked towards the doorway as Padar entered the room, pushing awkwardly though a blue-and-crimson door tapestry. He carried a new harp with him.

It was time for Thea's music lesson.

'An ancient lyre, very like the harp you have been practising. Your first lesson will be today, Lady Thea. Besides I have news for you.'

'Go and fetch my seamstresses some refreshment,' she said to Gudrun who had flushed crimson. Katya, too, was staring at Padar with interest in her eyes. 'You too, Katya, my dear.' Thea gestured towards the end of the long chamber. 'Just look how my sewing women are busy around the hearth working on my wedding garments. They are hungry.'

After the girls had slipped through the same curtain that Padar had entered by, Thea said, 'What news, Padar?'

'In a moment.' Padar pushed the codex that Thea had been using for her lesson aside. He placed a kinnor, a wonderful lyre from the East, on the table. 'I brought it back from Novgorod in the spring. It is just like the harp of King David.'

Thea reached out and plucked the strings. The instrument was in tune. She longed to play it. 'Padar, what is your news?'

He lowered his voice. 'It is both good and bad but more bad than good. The English North rose up. King Sweyn's warriors burned down the castle at York. They took York, my lady. That was good.'

'The Aetheling will be king, not my brother, and that is not good.'

'The bad news is that King Sweyn made a truce with King William. The Bastard paid him to leave York. The Aetheling fled back to the Scots.' He paused as the wall candle above him spluttered. 'The other bad news is that Godwin attacked Exeter and failed. He has returned to Ireland, tail fallen.'

Two days after her betrothal feast, Edmund had sailed back to Ireland. 'And Edmund? What news of him?'

'Edmund will join Godwin.'

'And you, Padar? Will you go to Godwin?'

'No, my lady, I shall sail with you to Novgorod next summer. I wish to settle down. I may trade in the Russian lands.'

'Tell me more.' She was thinking of Gudrun.

'The earl, that is Earl Connor, and I intend to join in an enterprise. I shall become his agent in the Rus lands. I learned their language last winter; not a great deal of it, but enough to stop translators cheating me.'

'Perhaps you should take lessons from Katya.'

'I think not, my lady. It might encourage her.'

'Encourage her?'

'Those dark eyes follow me. She smiles at me at supper and she steps into my path around the courtyards. She becomes bold.'

'Nonsense, she is, in truth grieving for a lost love. You would choose another, Padar?'

'If she would have me. I have nothing to offer a wife.'

'Padar, if it is Gudrun you speak of, she will take you and with my blessing.'

Padar appeared startled. 'She likes me?'

'I believe if you asked for her she would be very happy.'

'Thank you, my lady.' Padar bowed from the waist.

The curtain moved. Her maids had returned. She glanced over at the door. Gudrun held the tapestry curtain aside for Katya, who carried a laden wooden tray. Observing how Gudrun turned at the first wooden pillar to peer back at Padar, she said quietly into his ear, 'You do have my blessing. Soon we shall travel to Novgorod and both you and Gudrun will be part of my household.'

Padar's countenance was so joyful, looking at his happiness took away the melancholy she felt for her brothers' failed attempts to recover a kingdom.

'When the time is right, I shall marry her, my lady.'

'Do not leave it too long, Padar. Now, show me this instrument. I wonder if I can make David's harp sing songs of joy.'

That evening, Thea fell on her knees on the chapel's stone flagged floor. She prayed to St Theodosia for Godwin, then Edmund. She prayed for the Atheling who had fled through woods and mountains back to Scotland, bitterly disappointed at Sweyn's double dealing. Her prayers turned towards little Ulf and to her mother and to Grandmother Gytha.

The cunning woman's words floated in and out of her mind as she whispered her prayers and counted them off, clacking a simple ring of stones that hung from her belt. The past was past and though it still caused a deep ache in her breast, she felt at peace because it would be God's will that William of Normandy would reap punishment for the evil he had sown. And Lady Ragnar, who saw far into the future on water as still as a clear night sky, had said, 'In time, King William will suffer for his crimes.'

14

Russia, April 1070

On a late spring day, filled with the scent of lilac, Thea's retinue – her guards, their horses, and wagons – clip-clopped and rumbled their way through the streets of Novgorod. Her white mount, an Arab horse with a plaited mane and a proud stance, was a gift from the ambassadors who had met her party at Lagoda. His name was Starlight. She loved him from the first moment she met him and he had nuzzled her hand. Padar and Earl Connor trotted to either side of her on their sturdy destriers. Rus guards rode behind with two Russian ambassadors.

Thea occasionally glanced back to reassure herself that the wagons with her maids and wedding goods, including her beautiful palanquin, followed close behind. She could see the wagons' curved covers rise above a host of armed men in conical hats. The Godwin dragon pennant, her father's fighting man and her mother's swan banner, fluttered from the palanquin where Gudrun and Katya sat behind a servant who occasionally flicked a light whip at the horses pulling their carriage. Her family's silk banner depicting the dragon of Wessex was carried by a page that walked before her horse and led her cavalcade into the city. She felt today that she really was a princess.

Katya had instructed Thea that she should be veiled as she entered Novgorod. If her husband could not see his bride's face before their wedding, then his people should not see her face either. Thea could feel the spring breeze lift the delicate silk to fan her face. Her loose linen gown fell to either side of Starlight's flanks and her matching blue woollen mantel lay elegantly over his rump. She knew she looked well and she did

147

not care if the Rus ambassadors gave her disapproving glances when they caught glimpses of her hair. She asked Earl Connor if Vladimir would be waiting for her at the fortress.

'My lady, unless a magician can whisk him to you with a twitch of his wand he will not be here. His stepmother and her court will greet you and make you welcome until the prince and his father can leave Kiev and fetch you south. Sadly, Kiev remains a dangerous city. Since the prince's uncle has returned from exile and reclaimed his kingdom, his two brothers have come from their cities to support him, but the tribes are still a danger to the city's security. It will not be safe for you to travel south. Nor will your prince come north for some time.'

Thea felt disappointment. 'So I am to be like a prisoner here.'

'There will be much to occupy you, Thea, and you will soon get to know the royal ladies in Princess Anya's retinue.'

'I see.' Thea turned away. She did not want the royal ladies, she wanted her betrothed. She wanted him to greet her wearing a mantle trimmed with ermine, with his glossy black hair falling onto his shoulders and his soft brown eyes only for her.

Earl Connor led the procession into Novgorod's main square where merchants and peasants alike stopped to stare at the English princess as she passed through the lower city. A peasant woman threw flowers at Thea, crying out, 'Welcome, Princess of the English.' Padar caught the straw-wrapped posy and handed it to Thea. She dipped her nose into the pleasantly scented little red roses, lifted her face and smiled back at the woman who had tossed it to her. 'Speciba,' she called back in the Russian language. 'Thank you.' She held onto the posy with one hand as she rode on, its pleasant scent lessening the fishy odours of the street that mingled with the stink of cattle dung, horse and human sweat. When a second posy was thrown Padar picked it up and offered it to Thea. She took it and then found holding her reins and the posies awkward. Starlight side-stepped and she almost dropped her flowers as she tugged the reins to control him. Padar leaned towards her and said, 'May I, my lady, give this to …'

'Gudrun. Of course, take it to her.'

Without hesitation he trotted back to the palanquin where Gudrun sat with Katya. Thea smiled to herself.

Once they had passed through the large town square Connor resumed his conversation. 'The people seem to welcome you, Lady Thea. And you will have time to adjust, become familiar with the ways of the Rus and, my lady, Novgorod in summer is a pleasant city. It has become my home of late.' He turned his laughing blue eyes towards her. 'As I am a merchant trader, I am often here.'

'And no wife, Earl Connor, not yet?'

'No wife, Lady Thea. That hope died two years ago, as you must know.' She felt him searching her face. She did know.

'Yes. I would have welcomed you as a stepfather.'

'Thank you, my lady.'

Thea had been delighted when she discovered that Earl Connor was to be part of her escort to Novgorod, just as she had felt sad when her mother, Elditha, declined his suit two years before and had instead retreated into a nunnery in Canterbury. If she could not have her father, Earl Connor would have become a very acceptable substitute. 'My lord, will you reside here again this summer?' she asked, departing from a difficult subject. All she had left of her mother's life was secured in her travelling bag – the Godwin christening gown and a little book of riddles, her swan necklace, and a portion of the precious healing mugwort root. She wondered if she wrote a letter would her mother ever receive it? Perhaps a Rus messenger would be permitted to deliver a letter to Elditha.

Did her mother know about her betrothal yet? Would anyone tell her?

Their horses turned onto an incline. Earl Connor was saying, 'I shall not remain here long. It is the sailing season. Look.' He pointed up to a tall keep surrounded by whitewashed walls and turreted towers. It dominated the strange tall-roofed wooden city below.

She gasped at its splendour.

'You may well be impressed. For all its beauty it is a fortress. You are safe behind its walls. It is impregnable.'

'So everyone tells me.' Thea could not resist a shudder as she looked at the kremlin, as this keep was called. As their cavalcade approached the gate, she fancied for a moment that once she was shut inside it she might never ride out again. She patted Starlight's mane. 'You, too, Starlight. You feel it also.' Her horse snorted. She leaned down and whispered, 'I shall never be shut away!'

Padar, who had caught them up again, glanced at her with concern in his eyes. 'It looks more austere than it actually is, Lady Thea. The chambers within are comfortable and the terem ladies do have their own garden, I hear.'

As if a garden was any consolation for incarceration. This splendid castle did not resemble King Sweyn's manor or his large sprawling house in Roskilde, nor did it resemble the palaces she had known in England with their open gates and the beautiful wooden halls of her childhood. She determined not to allow memories to possess her spirit. Soon she would marry her prince, and it was for him that she had crossed the wild Northern sea road and had ridden through mysterious and haunting, dark forests to Novgorod.

The temporary governor and a noblewoman called Lady Olga had welcomed Thea in fluent English. Lady Olga explained that Thea's mother-in-law to be, Princess Anya, was about to give birth to her first child. 'The princess is in Novgorod for her safety. Prince Vsevolod's home on the Steppes south of Kiev, holds many dangers these days,' she said as servants presented Thea with a sweet cherry drink, savoury pastries and delicate little honey cakes.

'I hope I meet her soon,' Thea said in halting Russian.

'Indeed, when the princess is purified and everything in her chamber has gone through the ritual, you may meet her.'

Thea was confused and determined to ask Katya later why

150

the princess had to be purified. She did not like to show her ignorance to the tall, thin, severe-looking Lady Olga.

Soon after her welcome, Lady Olga led Thea away to her new chamber in the terem tower where a bath was prepared and a long rest was promised. After her three-week long journey by sea and forest roads, Thea felt grateful.

Olga escorted Thea through long, sconce-lit corridors to the guarded Terem Tower.

Thea tried to make conversation, to find out why she could not meet the princess now. 'It is customary in Denmark and in England for the ladies to assist at a birth. Is it so in Russia?'

'Midwives will look after the princess.'

'I see. When is the birth expected?'

'Within the month. She is very large. The summer heat is exhausting for her now.'

'My mother had six children who survived. One of us is a prisoner in Normandy and he is only nine years old. My brother Magnus was killed in a battle nearly two years ago.'

'I am sorry,' Lady Olga said. Thea noticed that by her casual tone Lady Olga did not really mean it. Lady Olga did not know her brothers, so how could she understand Thea's loss?

When they reached the tower, and a guard opened the terem door, Thea felt uneasy. It was as if she were to be locked away like a princess in a fairy tale and Lady Olga the wicked witch.

Lady Olga lifted her skirts to mount the wide, curving staircase. The servant that followed with Thea's clothing coffer waited as she explained to Thea, 'The kitchens and a refectory are both here on the ground floor. Steps lead down to the store rooms. Except for special occasions and some of our feast days you will not leave the terem.' She turned around and placed a finger on her thin lips. 'Princess Anya resides on the first floor so your servants must climb up and down the staircase quietly as mice in the granary.' She turned back and quietly cautioned the servant bearing Thea's clothing coffer on his shoulders to travel upwards slowly. She frowned at Katya and Gudrun when their boots banged against a step.

When they entered Thea's chamber after several turns of the staircase, Lady Olga drew Thea over to her chamber's window. 'I shall care for you, Princess, until your wedding. My husband is an important courtier here. He is Princess Anya's steward.'

Thea nodded, hoping she would remember who everyone was.

The sun shone through the window glass with a soft glow and a distortion of what lay outside. Lady Olga remarked, 'I make it my business to know everything that happens in this castle and further beyond its walls. If you need anything send for me.' She smiled in a kindly manner. 'Call me Olga,' she added before Thea had time to thank her. 'That is when we are alone, my dear.'

'Olga, when we are in private as we are now you must call me Thea. The governor called me Princess Gita. That is not the name my friends use. You see it is my grandmother's name also.'

Olga placed a hand over her hand which rested lightly on the deep window ledge. 'You will eat with us in the terem. I shall send you my own maids in the morning to escort you up to our large chamber.' She swept her hand around the vast room that Thea was to share with Gudrun and Katya. 'This is the best room in the tower. It will be cool in summer and warm in winter.'

Thea glanced around the spacious room. One wall was decorated with a fresco painting of the Madonna and her ladies seated amongst painted meadow flowers. A high bed with steps covered with thick counterpanes took up much of the space. Two pallets had been left for her maids.

Olga walked over to a wall opposite and flung open a low door. 'The pallets must be hidden from sight by day. Come.' Thea crossed the room, followed by Gudrun and Katya.

They peered into a shadowy alcove set into the thick walls. Olga picked up a lamp from a chest and held it up so that it illuminated the wooden clothing rails. 'Your maids may start unpacking your coffer. This must be kept as you now see it.

Their own travelling bags must be kept here too, out of sight.'

Olga lifted lamp higher. The room reached deep into the wall where shelves held linens and useful items such as needles and embroidery silks. There was a chest for the sleeping pallets and covers, and further along behind a screen stood a covered glazed pot for the necessary.

Olga turned to Gudrun. 'Empty the chest of clothing. Shake the garments out and hang them. I shall inspect this chamber for perfection after morning prayers tomorrow.' She returned to Thea. 'After your bath, which my maids will now prepare for you, I shall send food for you. Tonight, you may eat in your chamber. After tonight you will join us in the terem refectory for all meals unless you are indisposed.' She sniffed delicately. 'We do not eat with men. It is not our way in Russia.'

'Thank you, Lady Olga,' Thea said.

Lady Olga bowed her head, 'Goodnight, Princess.'

Thea could hear her padding down the stairway and telling the terem maids to be quiet as they carried something heavy towards her chamber. She supposed it was the bath tub and welcomed it.

As days and nights passed, Thea began to understand the rhythm of the terem. She came to like the women who dwelled there. She grew used to the spiced meals that the terem cooks prepared for them. She spent secluded days in the work room above her chamber. She studied the different traditions of the Rus Church. However, no matter how hard she tried to conform to the rhythms of the terem, she became restless. When would *her* prince come to free her? The more she thought about Prince Vladimir the more magical he grew, so magical that he was increasingly like a prince from a story than a man made of flesh and blood that she would one day reach out to touch. She confided in Gudrun and Katya and they exchanged looks. Finally Katya said, 'My lady, try not to dream too much lest your dreams cause disappointment.'

'I shall never be disappointed by Prince Vladimir, Katya.'

Every day during prayers in the chapel Lady Olga sent two slave girls to inspect Thea's chamber. Thea thought sadly, I have no secrets but if I had any Lady Olga would tear my secrets from the very walls. It is just as well that my life here is so predictable that I have nothing to conceal. What if I did have secrets? she thought to herself.

Life was too predictable. There was a garden and she walked in it. There was the work room. There was a beautiful church which she came to love. But there was no freedom. Perhaps I can ride out on Starlight, she thought, but when she asked, she was told she was not to ride out of the fortress. There was no one to escort her.

'Padar could,' she said. Lady Olga shook her head. Anyway, Padar was setting up his trading business with Earl Connor. Padar rarely visited the fortress. She felt so alone.

If she felt alone, she noticed how Gudrun pined. Gudrun's appetite was like that of a sparrow. She was turning into a little bird before their very eyes. 'I do eat,' Gudrun protested when Thea tried to tempt her with delicious honey sweetmeats.

'Padar will return soon,' Thea said as she tried to forget her own longings.

We are both pining, Thea thought to herself, and we feel our confinement but what can we do about it? The other women are kind but they are so content to pass their days in a beautiful gilded cage, or they will sew, help with making kvass or supervise the endless work of the ovens. They play with their children. Their men come and go but they go more often than they come. I wish I could feel content as they do.

'This is the way of it,' Katya said when she complained.

'I hope I get used to this life,' Thea sighed, and tried to study her new prayer book.

15

June 1070

The possession of a secret crept up on Thea.

Lady Olga had introduced her to the ladies who lived in the terem and had then set her to work on a linen embroidery that was to record the most significant events of her life.

Lady Olga presented Thea with a length of linen as long as the stretch of her arms and as wide as the window opening above them. 'A rushnyk is very individual. You will use stem stitches and cross stitches. It is important that you stitch carefully.' Thea opened her mouth to speak, to ask more about it.

Lady Olga stopped her question. 'Before you ask any questions, it is a sacred towel, sacred to God and sacred to you. You will keep it with you all your life. It will follow you into St Sophia on your wedding day. One day it will be used to lower your coffin down into the grave.'

'Just that, just a linen towel?' Thea said in her halting Rus as she stared at Olga, and at the length of linen lying across her knees, shocked at this new information, puzzled by the skeins of red, blue, yellow and white embroidery threads neatly set out on the low table by her designated sewing chair. 'Wh-what must I embroider on it?' She was bewildered.

'You embroider your path of life from your coming to your new land until your wedding and, in time, significant events after it. It tells your life, your life in perfect –' she touched Thea's hand and repeated, '– mind, in perfect cross-stitch work, just as the Norns spin out the lives of the Norse people under their tree of life. We also have a tree of life in our tradition. You can embroider the tree into your rushnyk.'

Thea nodded. Lady Olga knew so many things for a lady

whose own life was apparently spun out in a closeted terem.

'What else do I embroider?' It would not do to make mistakes here and embroider the wrong thing.

'For your wedding, you should work a duck and a drake to symbolise Prince Vladimir and yourself. Ducks represent water which gives us life and I hope your marriage begets plenty of new life.' She lowered her voice. 'Many children, of course. Your husband expects it of you.' Olga swept her hand over the table with the needles and skeins of thread. 'These needles are special.' She lifted a bone needle with a blue silk thread dangling from it and passed it to Thea. 'Take it. It is particular because it is your needle and it is yours alone. They are all new. If the needle breaks, you must have a new one for the blue thread to replace this one.'

She lifted the piece of fabric from Thea's lap. 'Now you are ready to begin. If you work on your arrival here in Novgorod at the top, then I think you could stitch a ship and a horse, a girl with a crown of course as you will marry our prince, and a castle and church.' She looked thoughtful and her mouth pursed. 'Just your life here; nothing else is of any consequence. Yellow is the colour of the sun, black is the earth and for your wedding you will use red and blue.'

Olga wrinkled her brow in thought for a moment. 'You could stitch a sun at the bottom corner as you have come to us in the summer.' She paused and turned to the two watching girls, Gudrun and Katya. They were seated on stools beside their mistress. She said sharply, 'You two are responsible for the care of your mistress's sewing threads. None must go missing. They are silk. They will be delivered carefully to her chamber every day and never left here by night.'

Now Thea understood why a whole shelf in the wall alcove of her chamber was set aside for embroidery threads and needles.

The girls nodded. 'Yes, my lady,' Katya ventured.

'Good.' Olga glanced down at the silks again and stretched out two long, slim fingers towards the threads that lay on a low table. She touched the red. 'For the large wedding section you embroider the duck on the left and the drake to the right. Your drake, Thea, will be stitched in red. It represents his energy.' Her fingers momentarily hovered over the blue skein. 'The duck is blue, blue representing purity, sky and water.' Olga then lifted the red thread and showed it to Thea who felt defeated before she even began to sew.

'There is also a new needle for the red thread.' Olga set the small skein beside the blue and lifted the white. 'Now, the white.' She held up the white skein. 'White is the scared colour. When you stitch the Cathedral of St Sophia, you use white. Angels, too, are white. This thread also has its special new needle.' She threw Thea a steady gaze and repeated, 'Your needles are never to be loaned or carelessly left here in the sewing room.' Olga gave Katya and Gudrun a stern look. 'Your handmaidens must never use them. The needles possess your energy and none other.' The two girls lowered their eyes demurely to their hands folded neatly in their laps.

Olga went on, 'Thea, we purchased all these needles for you Monday past. It is the day of the moon and the moon's energy will transfer into whatever your needles touch, into your bride and groom, into the fortress and into your new life here in our lands.'

She indicated the yellow threads. 'Yellow is never used alone. Yellow represents wisdom. Little yellow stitches do make a beautiful border.' She stroked the silks in a covetous manner and finally said in a gentler tone, 'All your threads are of silk. They travelled here from Byzantium. Make sure your handmaidens guard them carefully for you.' Olga looked again severely at Gudrun whom she clearly considered careless, though the truth was Gudrun was thinking of Padar, Thea mused. Lady Olga glared at Katya who perhaps was not quite good enough to be so close to the betrothed of Prince Vladimir, not from the elite of Russian maidens. She does not like me either, Thea thought with realisation. She does not make this task pleasant. She speaks of my wedding as if she resents it.

'Thea, I shall leave you to make a small cross-stitched border in blue, a ship and a procession towards a kremlin. You will be seated on a white mare at its head. Let us see how you begin. I shall check it later. Tiny stitches because with many tiny stitches you can create the rushnyk's powerful energy…'

Olga never finished her sentence because an agonised shriek blew up the stairs as if a flying witch was chasing the cry with a besom. Thea looked startled. Gudrun clutched Katya. The women of the terem lifted their heads and gasped. Olga calmly inclined her head and listened. The cry continued, stretched out like a spider's long, sticky thread.

'Princess Anya,' Olga then said. 'Her birthing has begun.' She waved a hand towards the ladies who obediently picked up their embroidery again. 'Carry on with your tasks.'

Thea lifted her needle secured the thread neatly on the back of the linen. She began to sew several rows of little blue crosses to represent the summer sea she had crossed from Denmark to Russia.

Stitching was a distraction from the cries in the chamber beneath them. Thea tried to concentrate on her embroidery. Katya and Gudrun advised and helped. The cries paused. The other women crossed the room one by one to admire her first stitches. Just as Thea had relaxed again, further agonised wails funnelled up the stairway. She murmured a prayer to St Theodosia for Princess Anya.

Lady Olga announced the obvious, 'That will be the princess again.'

The ladies dropped their sewing into their laps. Their maids ran to the opened doorway and stuck their heads out. Lady Olga sent them scurrying back to their stools.

Olga smiled around the chamber before saying, 'By evening we may have a new prince or princess. Put away your sewing. You, Lady Sabrina,' she looked over at a plump blonde woman of at least thirty years of age. 'Lead the others to the church. Pray for the safe delivery of a prince. I shall visit the midwives.'

Without a further word she hurried from the chamber, wooden-soled slippered feet clattering down the stone stairway. Once her footsteps had receded, the women began to pack away their sewing. Thea instructed Gudrun and Katya to place her threads and her rushnyk in a bag set aside for this purpose, to take it to her chamber and store it away safely. 'Then you may join us in the church.'

With childbirth anything could happen and Thea had an ominous sense that this birth might be difficult. She could not help feeling scared. As the women descended the stairs moving down slowly, gracefully as swans, Thea began whispering her own prayers and fingering the counting beads that hung from her belt; she recited Roman paternosters, because they were the prayers she knew best.

They glided past the refectory where daily they ate together like nuns, the hall where nursemaids supervised children and where the children ate, the curved archway that led to kitchens, and past closed chambers, dormitories and a spacious antechamber. All of these rooms belonged to the terem household. Lady Sabrina opened a small doorway that led outside into the garden. One by one the women lowered their heads, adjusted veils and drew mantles close about them as they filed onto a pathway leading to the back of the fortress's lime-washed church.

They sped through poplar trees that shed pollen pale as snow, scattering it over the women's veils and mantles. They entered the church through a side door set into its long wall. Inside, a priestly guard nodded the veiled women into the church's nave. It was cool and it was empty. Led by Lady Sabrina, the women moved slowly about the church kissing icon after icon, praying for Princess Anya and the safe delivery of her child, their soothing murmurs echoing around the nave.

Thea clutched her veil to her nose.

Every day, the kremlin's inhabitants said their prayers here, both men and women. It was impossible to miss the reek of human habitation, sweat and stale clothing, despite the pungent

159

smoke wafting through the church from its many incense burners. Instructed by Katya, Thea was quickly learning the ways of the Rus Church. However, as she kissed the icons of saints whose names she had not yet assimilated, she prayed instead to her own saint, her lips moving with no sound escaping from them for others to overhear. 'Please protect this princess whom I do not yet know.' Then, she whispered other prayers. 'Protect my grandmother in St Omer and all her ladies. Care for the children I have left behind. Guard my brothers Godwin and Edmund and watch over Ulf, who remains a captive in the land of the Normans and is now lost to us. Keep my little brother safe.'

16

July 1070

The day felt so long and tense. Thea prayed until she could pray no more. It was late in the afternoon, the hour of lengthened shadows. Exhausted, she slipped out of the church followed by her two maids. They were standing by a poplar tree inhaling fresh air when a priest wearing a dark brown khiton rushed past followed by Lady Olga. She paused and said sharply, 'Clearly, you have abandoned your prayer. It is of no consequence. Princess Anya has given birth to a daughter.'

Before Thea had a chance to show her relief, Olga turned away and following the priest's rushing feet, disappeared after the cleric into the church. Bells were ringing, high noted, as bird song on a summer's dawn. Thea stood listening until Katya touched her arm. 'We should return to the others, my lady.'

Other bells joined in, deeper and louder. Thea said with excitement, 'They must be ringing bells all over Novgorod.' Their resonance reflected power and musicality both. 'Oh, Katya, I have never heard so many ring like this in unison. I love your churches. Their bells entrance me.' She turned and walked back into the church, thinking how Padar had said that Prince Vladimir was religious. She could understand why now. The church was both mysterious and comforting. It drew her in.

The new princess was called Eupraxia. The princess's seclusion had passed. A priest purified her chamber with prayer and incense. Finally, one summer's morning, Lady Olga introduced Thea to Princess Anya.

She led Thea into the princess's beautiful apartment on the bottom floor of the terem, introduced her and, rushing off to visit the cooks, left her with the princess. Thea and the princess sipped a glass of cherry cordial together. They made halting conversation in Russian and managed to communicate with many smiles and much goodwill.

After a little while had passed, Thea lifted baby Eupraxia from her cradle and held her carefully in the crook of her arm. She was glad that the baby was not bound to a board to straighten her limbs as many English babies were but instead simply wrapped loosely in a soft embroidered shawl. 'She is beautiful,' Thea sighed.

'I think so too,' Anya replied with a doting smile on her lips.

Thea thought to herself, soon this will be me. I cannot wait to hold my own first baby.

Thea peered at the little bundle in her arms. Little Eupraxia had dark eyes, so soft a brown they looked like rich velvet fabric. 'How can a baby have such eyes within a month of her birth? I thought new babies had blue eyes.' She spoke in Norse.

Princess Anya, whose own eyes were dark and whose hair was loosely braided and black as polished ebony, called Katya from her footstool to translate for them. The princess laughed and said, 'It is not always so. My child's eyes changed colour quickly, darkened so soon.' She leaned over Thea and touched Eupraxia's cheek. 'She will be as bright as her eyes.' Anya paused and looking lovingly at her daughter said quietly, 'And I think my little Eupraxia will grow into a spirited young woman.' As if in agreement, a whimpering issued from Eupraxia's rosebud mouth and quickly grew into a loud protest.

The princess called for a nursemaid to take the tiny bundle from Thea's arms.

'She has my Kypchak blood.'

'Kypchak?' Thea asked, after the nurse had lifted the crying baby and sat in a quiet corner to give her suck.

'I am a princess of the Turkish tribes,' Anya explained and Katya translated. 'But since my own mother was Russian I speak Russian too. I understand this people.' She glanced over at the nurse. 'My daughter has the dark eyes and the rebellious blood of her grandfather, who is a great prince of the Eastern steppe-lands.'

'I understand. My grandmother is from Denmark and my mother was once a wealthy lady of Wessex in England. Both are of a rebellious nature. I think I am as well.' Katya frowned, translated and Thea quickly added, 'My mother was fair and green-eyed but my eyes are the shade of stones. My colouring came from my grandmother's family.'

The nurse placed a sated Eupraxia in a fabulous gilded wooden crib large as a winter sleigh. Another nursemaid clad in a neat vinegar-coloured gown began moving her boot up and down on one curved foot of the cradle setting it into a gentle rhythm. Eupraxia appeared to drift into sleep.

Anya lifted her eyes away from the cradle. 'I have good news for you, Princess Gita.'

'Oh, what news, my lady?' This, Thea understood, and responded in Russian.

Princess Anya nodded. 'You see, my husband will come to visit his new daughter and Prince Vladimir will accompany him. So, for this very special occasion, as is our custom, you will wear the dress we usually wear for important celebrations. It will be heavily embroidered with gold and silver thread. We usually wear five underdresses but we are in summer so I think we can let you off with four.'

'Four,' Thea said, dismayed. She remembered how uncomfortable she had been during her betrothal ceremony of the previous September.

'Yes, a chemise, a short garment, a long narrow-sleeved garment which will have much embroidery and finally the dress. Your hair will be bound in two braids under a high hat and a veil will fall over your face.' She studied Thea. She reached over and touched Thea's hair. 'Red hair is very fortunate. I think if we can find brocade that is green and covered with gold embroidery you will look very beautiful.' She looked at Katya. Katya translated.

'But if no one can see my face or my hair …' Thea said in clear Russian.

Anya lowered her voice and said mischievously, 'I think your plait might just peep below the veil. The tall hat will be becoming.'

Katya's hand flew to her mouth as she stifled a giggle. Thea understood and touched her head laughing along with Katya.

Then just as she felt they were having fun, Thea felt another presence and glanced over her shoulder. Lady Olga had returned silent as a creeping cat and was standing behind her. She has been listening, thought Thea to herself.

'Lady Anya must rest now. We shall send the tailor to you this evening and two seamstresses. All will be done according to our customs. I think yellow will suit her better than green.'

'I prefer green.'

'We have discussed this already. She will wear green brocade,' said Princess Anya.

Olga smiled. It was not a sincere smile. She looked from Thea to Katya. 'Thank you, Katya, you have done well. You may go down to the kitchens and join Gudrun who is learning to pot plums in honey syrup.'

It was the first time Lady Olga had actually praised Katya, though Katya's translations had not entirely been needed on this occasion.

Thea rose to follow Katya from the airy room. She was loath to leave this happy chamber, one that was not perfectly tidy but filled with cushions, shawls, scent from the garden and new life. 'Thank you, Princess Anya. May I return soon to visit baby Eupraxia?'

'Yes, of course, come soon.' She gestured towards the garden door. 'I shall show you the herb gardens, the pear tree garden and the cherry tree garden. And I shall be pleased to talk to you about our ways. You speak good Rus already, Gita.'

'My friends call me Thea,' Thea said in good Rus.

'Thea then,' the princess said.

Olga spoke in a severe tone. 'She must learn to speak perfect Russian. We shall teach her.' She looked at Thea from head to toe, slowly. 'Thea is tall for a woman. She could learn to walk in a stately manner, and not bolt like a deer.'

Princess Anya raised her eyebrows. 'I have no doubt that a princess as intelligent as Thea will learn quickly. Her beauty will enchant my stepson.' Thea knew then that Princess Anya was her ally.

Olga clearly had to have the last word. 'In time, with instruction, we can make Princess Gita into a Russian princess.' She closed the door into the garden. 'The opened door will allow a draught through which is not healthy for a new-born baby. I lost one infant to a chill. Your women should close it.'

'Thank you, Olga. I can close a door if I wish to have stifling air about me. As for Eupraxia, no fear of her taking chill. There is only the lightest of breezes today.'

Olga inclined her head and hurried Thea from the chamber as if she, too, was a danger to the baby, her continued presence a burden on the beautiful olive-skinned princess.

Thea wondered to herself why there was no evidence of Olga's children in the nursery rooms. Perhaps they were already grown up and living in other households.

A week later the two princes galloped into the courtyard and the kremlin was thrown into a great stir of activity.

The terem ladies were as excited as children anticipating New Year's gifts. That afternoon, the ladies arranged Princess Anya in a throne-like chair in a spacious receiving hall attached to the terem tower. They placed the sleigh-like cradle beside her and retired to sit on a padded bench behind the throne. Lady Olga, Thea and their maids were decorously arranged amongst the terem's noblewomen on various cushioned benches about the hall. Most of the ladies looked hopeful. Thea mused, *they cannot wait to see their husbands.*

Into this excited gathering of women swept the two princes, accompanied by a small group of richly clad boyars wearing sweeping mantles, with jewels on their fingers, on their cloaks and decorating their hats, gleaming and sparkling as they stepped into the sunlight that filtered in through the isinglass windows.

There he was, the young prince with his father. He was tall. His hair was black. His jaw and chin looked carved with strength. He was very handsome. The prince was looking about the hall with searching eyes. She longed to speak to him. His eyes were seeking her out, of that she was sure, but she was seated in the shadows behind a noblewoman whose headdress was as tall as a steeple and kept obscuring her view. She twisted her neck to see better and slid along the bench a little away from the colourful steeple. His father only had eyes for the princess seated on the throne and the cradle by her side. Even if Prince Vladimir had seen her in her elaborate dress, he would not see her face and etiquette demanded that he greet his stepmother first. That was it. She must wait her turn. Her heart quivering like a bird waiting to burst from a cage, she watched him leave off his searching and turn towards Princess Anya's chair. Lady Olga stepped forward to welcome the princes. Surely now Lady Olga would fetch her forward, When she did not Thea felt a sinking feeling, as if a stone had lodged in her heart, weighing it down. She was not to speak with her prince today it seemed. Tears pricked at her eyes. She blinked them away and tried to will the prince to see her.

She had time to study them further as the princes bowed to the princess. As both princes bent down and peered into the cradle, she forced herself to concentrate on their garments which were different to those worn by nobles at King Edward's court. The two princes both wore matching greenish-hued, loose, straight coats. Their gowns had swirled out like women's gowns as they walked up through the hall towards the princess and the cradle. Thea touched her own overgown. She had never possessed such expensive clothing before. It was green brocade, rich and loose. Under it she wore a second straight-sleeved matching silk gown. The outer garment surpassed Grandmother Gytha's blue dress that she had worn years before in Roskilde. It was superior to the ugly gown embroidered all over with crosses that she had worn for her betrothal. The Rus must be the wealthiest people in all of Christendom. She forgot to sit up straight and instead strained forward for a better glimpse of her prince. Her position had not improved as the headdress was slightly to her left. For a flicker of a candle flame she was sure Olga was glaring at her from her place by Princess Anya's side. Thea straightened her posture and inwardly cursed the woman.

Prince Vsevolod took his wife's hands, raised her, gave her the kiss of peace on her forehead and folded her into an embrace. He released his young wife, reached into the cradle, and this time he lifted the baby, holding her aloft so his boyars could see their tiny princess. There was a rumble of appraisal followed by applause. Eupraxia gurgled and, as was typical of her character, howled at her father. Vsevolod quickly gave the baby over to her wet nurse. He bent down, took his wife by the hand, helped her to her feet and led her through a doorway, into rooms set aside for their privacy and comfort. Thea observed a haughty look cross Lady Olga's face as the prince and princess departed accompanied by their retainers, leaving Lady Olga in the hall to introduce Prince Vladimir to his future bride, as surely now she must. Thea drew in a deep breath, exhaled and composed herself. It could not be long now.

Vladimir appeared to be looking for her. Women, some younger than she, were exchanging appraising looks as they watched the handsome prince's every movement. Two boyars bowed to Prince Vladimir and excused themselves. Thea watched from behind her filmy veil as they hurried to join their wives. Her back so rigid that it ached, she waited patiently on her bench. Still Olga did not make the introduction.

One of the prince's servants bent down and spoke to Lady Olga, who nodded and came to Thea's side followed by a tall, thin nobleman. Vladimir stood back watching and waiting. Closer up, it appeared that her prince was slim, athletic, serious-faced. His hair was dark and tied back in a clasp. She tried not to stare, though she knew that she need not worry because with her high head-dress and veil he could not see her eyes.

She stood when Lady Olga spoke. 'Princess Gita, this man is

167

the father of my children. He is my husband and he is also Prince Vsevolod's steward. He is Lord Michael and he will introduce you to Prince Vladimir. Then, I am afraid that, Princess, you must retire with the other young ladies, those who are not greeting their husbands today.'

Thea could feel everyone's eyes upon her as the prince, who had in a trice crossed the room, was already by Thea's side. He bowed to her. She sank to her knees before him. He raised her up and turning to the white-haired boyar said in perfect English, 'I expect you must have conversation for your wife, Michael. I wish to speak with Princess Gita privately in the garden.' He addressed Lady Olga. 'One of your ladies may follow at a suitable distance.' Olga looked surprised. The prince smiled. 'Do not fear. I shall not upset the princess, nor shall I ravish her, though she looks delightful. I think the gown might get in the way, never mind the veil.' He bowed again to Thea. 'I will not impose myself on her for longer than it takes for us to feel comfortable in each other's company.'

The silence that followed could be sliced with a sharp knife.

Michael broke the hush by saying, 'It is not seemly.'

Prince Vladimir raised an eyebrow.

'Oh, well … as you wish, my Prince.' The steward glanced desperately about the room at the older women until his eyes lit on Lady Sabrina, a widow whom Thea had come to like more and more as they sewed together in the mornings.

He summoned Lady Sabrina from the flock of women. 'Lady Sabrina will accompany the princess's maids, yourself, and Princess Gita into the garden.' He glared at Vladimir. 'I warn you, Prince, the bells for Nones will chime soon. You have little time.' He lowered his voice. 'Less time than it takes to sup a bowl of kvass.'

Thea, delighted, found herself walking through a scented garden shaded by fig trees, accompanied by her handsome prince. Her dream was coming true at last.

'This way,' Lady Sabrina said, guiding them along. A little further along the garden track she stopped and exclaimed, 'My roses are in bloom today.' She clapped her hands. 'Quick, there is not much time. Go and fetch my cutting shears, run, Gudrun and Katya. They are in the shed in the first terem garden. Go now! These roses must decorate our receiving chambers.' Dismay haunted the girls' faces. Sabrina fixed them both with a firm look. 'Go through the herb garden and no one will see you. It is shorter.' The girls glanced at Thea for assurance. She nodded. They sped off to fetch the cutters.

Lady Sabrina pointed to a stone bench by a shady fall of vines. 'My lord, if you and Princess Gita sit there you will have a moment to yourselves. I shall be just by the fig trees here, just for a moment or two.'

The prince smiled conspiratorially at Lady Sabrina. Thea realised that while she may not be out of sight, she had turned her back on them and was poking around bushes filled with pure white roses. Her prince led Thea to the stone bench. Amused at this break with terem rules and tedious protocol, Thea relaxed and decorously arranged her skirts, determined to show no simpering coyness. She held her head high. After all she was an English princess.

'Lady Sabrina was my mother's friend,' the prince began. 'She came from Constantinople as a girl of fourteen and I have known her all my life. Her husband died in my father's service. She is doing us a kindness today.'

His English was fluent. He appeared composed and Thea decided to match his composure with her own self-possession. She looked directly at him through her veil. 'She is very kind to me.'

He said, 'I am sorry not to have come to Novgorod before. But, we have troubles in our lands.' He lifted her hand. She tingled at his touch. She could not snatch her hand away.

'Are you happy in Princess Anya's terem?' he asked politely.

Thea replied in halting Russian. 'The women are kind. I am busy.'

'And how are you busy?' He gently placed her hand on the

bench.

She glanced about the garden before answering. No one was in sight, not even Lady Sabrina who had disappeared amongst the rose bushes. She said, 'I stitch a rushnyk for my wedding day. I learn Russian. I pass time tending the herbs in the garden and …'

'You like gardens?' He leaned forward to ask the question.

'And music. I play the harp and sing and I tell stories,' she said quietly.

'Your voice is musical. Do you sing like a nightingale also?' He moved closer to her. In that moment she was glad of the veil. It concealed the blush that was fast rising up her neck.

'That is for others to judge.'

'Lady Gita,' he said with urgency in his voice. 'Sabrina will only allow us a moment or two. No one will know.'

'Know what?' He was staring into her face, trying to see through her veil. Suppressing a longing that was creeping up through her body, she moved further along the bench. She realised what he meant. He wanted to see her face.

'May I?' he said. She nodded. Slowly and gently, his long gentle fingers lifted back her veil and he looked at her face. He gasped. 'By the Virgin, you are beautiful.' He touched her cheek, her hair where it was plaited by her left ear. He touched her ear. 'My people think red hair brings great fortune.'

Just a breath later, as if he were a dragonfly flitting around the head of a flower, he dropped her veil again. He folded his hands in his lap. 'Princess Gita,' he said slowly, 'it may be some time before we can marry. I wish to get to know you. What I mean is that I just want to speak with you, to understand you. It must be different for you here, and, you see, I do not wish to find a stranger in my marriage bed.'

She did see. It was odd to share your sleep with someone you had never talked to before. Yet it happened all the time. In noble families it was expected. 'It is the custom. If we break with it I could be in trouble.'

He moved closer to her again. 'But if I can arrange a

meeting, would you meet with me secretly?'

Thea loved his flouting of these stupid rules. 'If the meeting were like today, in a church or a garden, perhaps it can be possible.' She desperately wanted to meet him secretly.

'I shall send you a message. No one must know.' He frowned. 'Importantly Lady Olga must not know anything. Do not speak to my stepmother. I shall leave a message for you concealed by the vine behind this bench.' He reached behind and separated the vine from which hung ripening grapes and showed Thea a little niche set into the wall behind them. 'I used it when I was a child in the terem. I hid things here: little treasures, a shell from the shore – if I listened to it I could hear the sea – a scrap of cloth that I imagined was my own relic as it came from Byzantium – my mother told me it long ago belonged to the gown of a great pope from Rome. I had a little jewelled knife too. Look for a piece of birch wood. Can you read and write?'

She nodded.

'Reply to my note with yes or no. Do not sign your name.'

Lady Sabrina had placed six cut roses in Gudrun's basket. The bells for Nones had begun chiming. Lady Olga was hurrying through the fig trees followed by her skinny husband. 'There you are. Thea, come with me.' Her suspicious eyes surveyed them all. They lit on the basket of roses, the cutters and the three women by the rose bushes. The prince rose. 'Thea? My lady, why does Lady Olga call you Thea?'

'It is the name my friends use for me.'

'Then I shall use it also.'

The prince bowed and moved into the fig trees, Lord Michael in attendance. Thea stood calmly with Katya and Gudrun. Lady Sabrina smiled through eyes as innocent as those of the Virgin Mary. Olga turned on her slippered heel and briskly led the ladies back through the gardens, past the long, low receiving hall and the church by the poplar trees, to the door that led into the terem.

Thea bubbled with excitement. She wondered when he

would leave her a message. And he had called her beautiful. Now she had a secret. She hugged her secret to herself as she followed Lady Olga through the terem doorway.

17

1071

For weeks Thea walked alone in the garden with the sole purpose of discovering a letter, but although she often slipped her hand into the niche in the wall she never discovered one. Had her prince forgotten her? Official reports arrived from the north saying that Prince Vladimir was keeping peace amongst the tribes. She had expected her wedding to take place the following summer but autumn had passed and Christmas had arrived and gone. No messengers came to order her to Kiev. No date was set for her wedding. She felt as if their encounter had been a dream. She recollected how Padar had said the prince was aloof. Yet he had not seemed so when they had met. As for Padar, he was trading in the north and before he had set out with Earl Connor, he had pledged himself to Gudrun. 'I shall marry you, little dove, on my return,' he had promised and Thea hoped that they would set up home together and find happiness in their new Russian world. For now Padar's betrothal was a secret but he had said, 'I declare my troth to you, Gudrun, before our princess. She is my witness.' It was enough. To Thea's relief Gudrun began to eat again.

She forgot her own longings as her thoughts moved to him and hoped that he was not trading too close to the northern battles, because if anything happened to Padar, Gudrun's heart would break into a million pieces. She whispered a prayer to St Theodosia. 'Beloved saint, bring him back to us soon.'

Thea took lessons from the Bishop of Novgorod so she could understand the liturgy of the Rus Church. As church services were sung in Rus, she was quickly improving her language skills. Lady Olga supervised her lessons in deportment, forcing Thea to glide up and down the terem stairs with prayer books balanced on her head so that she learned to walk in a stately manner. 'If you drop these the bishop will send you back to Denmark,' she threatened unreasonably. Although Thea felt tears stinging the backs of her eyes she never betrayed her true emotions to Olga. She proudly glided about the tower pretending not to care.

During the long, snowy winter slaves lit stoves every day. The noble ladies gathered around these to sew, converse and practice their musical instruments. Thea was amused when they teased her about her handsome prince. They would surround her as if she were the bee in the centre of the hive. 'He will come soon, Thea,' one or other would say. 'Your duck and your drake are almost ready. He must come for you this summer.'

'When he returns he will bring his handsome captains with him,' another young girl remarked with hope in her voice.

'You will need attendant maidens for your wedding day, Princess Gita. Choose me,' they all would chorus.

'But how can I choose, you all are so lovely?' Thea would reply pragmatically.

Princess Anya told the girls to leave off teasing Thea. 'Girls, I shall help Princess Gita choose,' she said. 'There are six of you maidens. We shall have a competition.'

Olga frowned, though she never gainsaid Princess Anya.

The girls were beset with enthusiasm. A competition would ease their boredom when days stretched ahead like long winter icicles. 'We shall choose those who can tell us the best story,' Princess Anya announced because so many noble ladies begged to be Thea's maidens on her wedding day.

'Who will judge?' Thea asked.

'Your skald could judge when he returns to Novgorod,' Anya said. She set her sewing aside and folded her hands in her lap. A smile played about her mouth. 'You all speak of desire, though often it is impossible. You must marry where your guardians and families decide. So let us have a little fun with storytelling. Girls, you can write and you can read. You will write down a story of your choice. We shall send your stories to the skald.' Princess Anya picked up the chemise she was stitching for Eupraxia.

Thea said, 'I can help Padar decide.'

The girls agreed and began to secretly compose their tales.

As Katya moved about the fortress, in and out of the terem, she was able to listen at doors. She caught snatches of conversations every time she carried their linen basket to the fortress laundry. Many of the laundrywomen had husbands in the prince's army. Soon she was able to report that Prince Vsevolod and Vladimir were extending their territories north of Novgorod. The tribes dwelling in the woods were more like trolls than Slavs. In return for protection they made peace with the Russian princes and accepted them as overlords. Vladimir would return soon.

In March just as snows melted into slush, on her return from the church by the garden wall, Thea could not resist looking behind the woody empty vine. She felt around, her hand numbed by the cold, her glove in the other. There was something there. It was wrapped in oiled sheepskin. She withdrew the small package. *At last, at long last*. She glanced about the snow-dripping garden and thrust it into the purse that hung from her belt.

On entering the terem workroom she sat amongst the other women for a moment, and then, with pretended urgency, she said, 'I must excuse myself today, Lady Olga. I am unwell.'

'Unwell, Thea? You don't look poorly. What ails you?'

'My menses have come, I think.' She gripped her stomach. 'Early, as it happens.' Lady Olga knew everything and she knew when Thea needed rags.

'Umm, you must rest today. I shall send you my maids and a posset.'

'No need, Lady Olga.' Thea summoned Gudrun and Katya to her side and hurried them down from the sewing room to her chamber. Gudrun made a mistake. In her haste to follow her mistress she forgot to bring the sewing box with its precious needles and threads with her.

175

When Thea confided in her two friends, Katya became anxious, wondering how the prince had managed to get the letter into the garden.

'Never mind how, Katya. He has sent me word. Gudrun, stay by the door and keep watch while I read it. It would not surprise me if Olga sends her maid down to my chamber.' She opened the parcel and withdrew a piece of parchment. 'Look, Katya, it is in Russian.'

Nervously, her hands shaking, Katya took the tiny piece of parchment. 'Princess he has folded it into a bird.'

'I know. I can see that. Just read it to me.'

Katya unfolded the minute parchment bird and read it aloud. *Meet me at noon on Saturday in the Church of St Nicholias. A priest will escort you there from the Church of the Holy Virgin. Wait for him by the icon of Mary Magdalene. Wear simple clothing and a warm mantle. Your maid will accompany you.*

Thea could hardly contain her excitement. 'Katya, just write *yes*. Hurry. Then take it to the niche behind the vine in the garden. Be quick.'

'But, my lady …'

'No buts, just do it.'

Katya just wrote the word *Da,* yes, on the message. She had just folded it back into the bird shape when the door was pushed open, knocking Gudrun off her feet.

'Careless servant,' Olga began to say. Thea saw that Lady Olga was carrying her sewing box.

Gudrun started to apologise. Olga ignored her. She looked critically at Thea and back to Gudrun. 'And why is your mistress still on her feet? If her time is come, girl, fetch linen paddings from the laundry. Find her a belt and ties.'

Olga turned to Katya. 'Unlace your lady's gown and help her into her bed. Draw the curtains.' She glared at Thea, 'You, Princess, are lax with your servants.'

'My servants are mine to command, my lady. Please leave us.'

'This sewing box was left carelessly in the work room.' Olga

176

marched past Gudrun and went into the small side cupboard of a room, intending to set the sewing box packed with precious threads on its shelf, beside Thea's sewing bag.

Katya took the moment to slip Gudrun the note. Gudrun folded her hands around it and bowed her head humbly. She pushed the note into her sleeve and ran off down the stairs. Katya tried to help Thea to the bed.

Thea shook Katya off. She hissed through her teeth, 'I shall deal with that person once and for all.'

She stood tall as a crane, her head high on her long neck, summoned up her courage and said to Lady Olga as she exited the cupboard, 'Leave us, Olga. My maids are concerned for me enough as it is without you entering my chamber because of a sewing basket which I intended to send for as soon I was comfortable. Go away. You add to my discomfort.'

Olga's eyebrows seemed to cross in her narrow forehead. 'I hope you never speak to the prince in this manner. His father will provide him with the birch rod on his wedding day,' she said unpleasantly. 'You are clearly unprepared to marry one of our most important princes.' She looked pointedly at the silvery wolfskin that covered Thea's bed. 'That is a primitive and unsuitable cover,' she added nastily.

Thea gasped at Olga's appalling threat. She glared at the noblewoman. 'I am well prepared to greet my future husband on my wedding day. I am trained in music, dance, language, deportment, religion and in the running of a terem household,' she said archly. 'Know this, Lady Olga, when I am married I shall have my own household. It will have noblewomen of my choosing. And there are many young and pleasant faces to choose from.' She waved her hand towards the door. 'Now, go, my lady. I shall take my meals in my chamber today.' She waited for a moment while Olga stood rooted to the floor. 'I do not want to see your servants in my chamber again, ever.'

'We shall see what Princess Anya has to say about your rudeness.' Lady Olga set her back and marched out of the chamber muttering incoherently.

'Lady Olga will be your enemy now. If you go to the church of St Nicholias you will be discovered,' Katya fretted as she fussed around Thea.

'She never was my friend. She won't find out if I'm very careful. Besides, I am meeting my betrothed, not just any man.' Thea reached out and took Katya's hands. 'We can escape the terem for one afternoon and return by Vespers without Lady Olga discovering us.'

'In that case we must make a careful plan and let us pray that we are not discovered,' Katya said thoughtfully.

'And, I do feel that I must lie down after all.'

Thea lay on top of her wolfskin bedcovering, stroking the silver fur, her thoughts on Saturday.

18

As the day began to lose light, concealed in heavy cloaks, Thea and Katya slipped into the Church of the Virgin, the smaller church that opened into the garden and was often used by ladies of the kremlin. Priests were lighting sconces. Women came and went from the terem. Thea glanced at them as they passed her by. Thankfully, no one took notice of the two heavily veiled women praying before the paintings on the iconostasis screens.

It was not unusual for Thea to spend chill winter afternoons in the church dedicated to the Virgin. To Thea the iconostasis was mysterious. Three doors led into the sanctum: the beautiful gates which were shut when offices were not observed. To either side of the beautiful gates, the north and south doors, the entrance and the exit for the deacons. Her favourite was the door beside which she knelt, the north door where she imagined the Archangel Gabriel might exit while she knelt in prayer. She often studied the depictions of the Archangels Michael and Gabriel as bells rang out time's passage, as Vespers merged into Compline or until Lady Olga sent a servant to disturb her and fetch her back to the terem for supper.

Today it was important that she was not fetched back to the terem. As she waited for Vladimir's priest, it was as if the small dove she saw in the frescoes depicting Noah's flood had entered her heart and fluttered in an attempt to escape. The second bell after midday passed, the third, and finally after this, they were alone with icons and statues. If the messenger did not come soon the office of Vespers would creep up on them. Olga might appear with her watching eyes everywhere and escape through any door other than that into the garden would be impossible. Her head throbbed. She closed her eyes.

'My lady.' Thea started. She glanced up. A priest was standing beside them. For a short moment she thought he was the angel. He was holding a lantern. The smell of fish oil from it assaulted her nostrils as he approached. This priest belonged to the world of men. He was indeed a worldly priest. He had slipped into the Nave through the iconostasis' north door when her eyes had momentarily closed.

He bowed his head. 'I am your guide. Keep close and follow me.' As he smiled into the gloom, the lantern lit up his features. He was young and his face was kindly. 'My name is Sebastian, a martyr's name. *I* am no martyr. Hurry before we are discovered. I would not wish to see the inside of the fortress cells as a punishment for this deceit.'

Thea did not give Katya the opportunity to change her mind but nodded, scrambled to her feet and stepped ahead of her maid. She followed Sebastian out through the front door of the church hoping that Katya was behind her. They walked across the busy, icy courtyard and paused by the postern gate. Father Sebastian asked them to allow the passage into the street beyond. The guards smiled at Father Sebastian. One called jokingly, 'Chaperoning the ladies now, are you?'

'Escorting two maidens who must select a prayer cloth for Lady Sabrina.'

'I hope their boots are strong and their cloaks thick. There is a freeze going on up there.' The guard who spoke glanced up at the heavens. 'It'll be a chilly walk back.'

'I shall have them back before the sun sinks.'

'What sun?' The guard shrugged his shoulders and stamped his feet as they passed through the low postern gateway. They entered a street that led by the river route towards the town square. Father Sebastian remarked they need not walk far.

Katya looked nervous so Thea whispered, 'Never fear.' Clearly, Katya did fear for she looked uneasy as they walked close to the river. Merchants' houses rose up on either side, some with yards that sloped down the hill on their right to the bank. Thea could glimpse the gleaming cupolas of St Sophia visited on important saints' days by everyone from the kremlin and which lay to the other side of the fortress, peeping to her left up beyond the high kremlin walls. She watched the wide, fast-flowing river where melting ice-flows drifted by. Though a thaw was beginning spring had not arrived.

'Watch your steps.' The priest said, glancing up at the sky. 'It's darkening already.' He tapped his lantern. 'This slush may yet freeze over. We have this.'

It was only a short walk to the Church of St Nicholias. Thea had forgotten what it was like in the world beyond the terem. If only she could linger to watch boats unload cargos by the wharfs. If only she had time to explore the streets and the many shops that surrounded the kremlin castle.

Father Sebastian led them down a side street into a tiny square, gliding ahead of them, his robes sweeping over the icy slush. The Church of St Nicholias rose up in front of them and as they caught him up, the priest led them forward, unlocked a low door and ushered them into the nave. Thea's heart leapt as her eyes adjusted to the shadowy interior. He was kneeling by the altar to St Nicholas. A candle flicker later and he turned around and saw her.

'You are here.' He scrambled to his feet and opened his arms wide. 'And you did not forget me all those months. You looked out for my message.'

Thea nodded. 'My lord, I received your message and left your answer.'

The priest set his lantern down on the ground and turned to Thea. 'I have closed the door. You have until Vespers. Your servant and I will wait here in the nave. I can hear her confession too should she so wish to confess.' He glanced at the curtained confessional to the side of the nave.

Thea felt herself smiling. Nothing ever happened in Katya's life. Thea wondered what her maid could possibly confess – her thoughts perhaps. Gudrun, who was staying behind to guard her chamber, well, that would be different, she mused, the smile hovering about her lips. Gudrun longed for Padar's company always. Thea suspected they had seen each other secretly before Padar had gone north that winter to trade for furs. He was

181

expected home any day now.

'We shall pray while you and Prince Vladimir profess to each other.' Father Sebastian laughed mischievously at his own jest.

Vladimir waved him away. He drew Thea out of sight behind a pillar, placed his mantle on the floor against the wall and bade her sit. The cloak was of dark wool and lined with sheepskin. Sinking into its softness, she immediately felt comfortable in his presence. She had chosen not to wear a veil but had carefully concealed her hair under a wimple in case she was recognised as they passed through the kremlin courtyard. Today, her disguise rendered her more like a servant than a noble lady.

Vladimir touched her face gently and said, 'Well concealed, my lady, but at least I can see your green eyes.'

'They are really grey but evidently change depending on the light. No, I'm told grey with flecks of green.'

'Who said?'

'My mother, and she and my sister Gunnhild really do have green eyes, completely so, like cats' eyes and their hair is fair, not at all like mine, though both are tall in stature.' Thea involuntarily raised her hand to where her wimple concealed her hairline.

'We consider red hair fortunate and I am fortunate to know you, my princess.' He leaned back against the wall. 'How has your life been since last summer?'

'My life has been tedious.' She told him how she had passed her Christmastide and how she had many friends amongst the women in the terem. When she told him about the storytelling competition to choose her wedding attendants he said, 'You must think of a story to tell me. You must set a standard. It can be a story you will tell me on our first wedding night.' He shuffled closer to her. 'You do know that you have to wear a veil until our third night?' He put his head in his hands and moaned. 'How shall I wait? I suppose I must.' He lifted his eyes and with mischief playing in them said, '*Silent is my garment*

182

when I touch the ground, when I tread the earth ...'

Thea interrupted, *'or dwell in towns or stir the waters.'*

He added, *'Sometimes my trappings lift me over the habitations of heroes and this high air, and might of the welkin bears me afar above mankind.* You know the riddle?' he exclaimed. 'You *are* as beautiful as that swan.'

She rolled her eyes. 'Well perhaps, we shall see, my lord.' She looked at his dark glossy hair. As quick as a turn of an hour glass she said, 'Since we speak in riddles, I have a riddle for you.'

He nodded and said, 'Try me.'

'I bring joy to the men who dwell in towns. When I sing out with my flexible tones they sit at home silent. Tell me my name who brightly imitates professional singers and loudly foretells many welcome tidings.' Do you know it?'

'If I don't think too hard, I shall know it.' He tapped his fingers in the air as if playing a tune on a pipe. 'No, it does not come to my mind. "Welcome tidings".'

'You must think on it.'

So you like to sing and play music, my lady?'

'Indeed, my lord, and tell stories.' She shifted closer to him, just a tiny bit. 'But which creature is this? Guess now. I think you do not know the answer,' she teased.

He could not tell her. Delighted that she had won the contest she said, 'Then I must tell you some other time.' She looked pointedly at his glossy black hair again and still he did not pick up a clue. 'I shall tell you on our wedding night.'

He lifted her hand and studied her countenance. 'You are a tease. But another time is good. It might give me time to consult the skald Padar when he returns.'

'Tell me this, when are we to be married? My uncle will call me back to Denmark with my dowry if I must wait much longer for our nuptials.'

'Not this summer as I had hoped but my father now says it will be next spring. We have just secured Kiev. There is still much to arrange there. We intend bringing the bones of our founding fathers Dimitri and Gleb to Kiev for the translation of their relics to St Sophia.'

'Translation. What's this? '

'The movement of their bones to a new resting place before they are beatified and are created saints. These saints are Russian, not Armenian, Roman, nor Greek. They are ours so it is to be an important ceremony. Everyone who is anyone will be there. So ...' he paused and lifted her hand and kissed it through her glove.

She shuddered. She did not like this talk of moving bones and sainthood attached to her wedding. She said quietly, 'What "so"?'

'So, because it is such a grand occasion and every important noble in the land will be in Kiev, our wedding will follow within a week. Everyone will be present.'

'When will this be, Vladimir?'

'Next Eastertide.'

'It's a long time away. More than a whole year.'

'It is, but afterwards we shall have a very long time together and many children.'

He lifted her right hand and removed her mitten. 'You are wearing my ring, the one I sent for our betrothal,' he said. He turned her hand over and kissed her palm. 'And the waiting is exciting because you are brave and clever. Longing to know you makes you even more desirable.' He reached over and planted a feather-light kiss on her lips. She felt her lips parting. His tongue explored her mouth and touched her own. The sensation almost made her want to swoon with desire. Just in time he released her. She caught her breath. So this was what it was like. She was confused. Prince Vladimir touched her hand. 'I should not have perhaps, not yet.'

What could she say? What dared she say? 'The priest,' was all she could say. 'I must go.'

The priest was hustling forward to collect her. 'The day will be darkening, Princess. You must not be discovered here. Come.' The prince helped Thea to her feet. She almost fainted as he held onto her hand a moment longer than was necessary. 'I shall see you again soon, little bride.' He whispered into her ear, 'My beautiful swan, keep searching for me in our wall niche.'

The priest rushed Thea and Katya back through the church. Using the key hanging from his belt he slid open the door's barrel lock. No one had yet arrived for Vespers but a group of priests were approaching the church from the opposite side of the tiny square. Father Sebastian passed a bundle to her. It was a prayer rug wrapped in plain linen. 'Take it, my lady. Take turns carrying it. When you get it into the terem you must give it over to Sabrina. She will understand.'

As they set out of the church and stepped into the small square, Thea shivered and stared up at the sky. Clouds hung there like leaden sacks. The temperature had dropped further. It was bitterly cold. Thea hoped that Gudrun who had remained behind to guard her door would keep the wolfish Olga from her chamber.

The hunting season always began in November with the first snow falls. Already Padar and Earl Connor had shipped their early consignments to Denmark. By late December that year the rivers had frozen and ice flows floated down into the Danish seas. Padar's return had been delayed. Earl Connor returned a week before and had moved into the fortress where he would negotiate with the steward over which furs he wanted to purchase. When Padar arrived back in Novgorod on the very same day that Thea met with Prince Vladimir, he took up residence in the warehouse ready to sort through and grade the consignment of furs he had brought by sleigh down from the forest lands west of Lake Onega. Padar's boys excitedly lifted lids off the half-dozen basket coffers to reveal piles of glistening pelts – the skins of martens, beavers, hares, squirrels and foxes. Padar laughed his delight as he looked through them. These would make him a fortune. He scratched his beard as he thought of where he could sell them. The kremlin steward would purchase much of Earl Connor's share but there would still be plenty more to sell. Winter was deep in the Rus lands but now the snow was melting perhaps he should trade south into Germany.

Padar lifted up a stretch of grey skin that had been taken from a reindeer, thinking how it would make Gudrun a fine pair of slippers. All she needed to do was to line them with soft wool. He set the deer pelt aside. How he longed to see Gudrun. Thinking about it, this grey reindeer skin made a perfect excuse to take him right to the doors of the terem.

When it was possible for Gudrun to leave her mistress they would marry and set up their own home. Lady Thea's marriage had been delayed and delayed. He had travelled back to Denmark and returned again and still not a word of it. Earl Connor had said *he* could not understand why the marriage had been delayed. He hoped that Prince Vsevolod was not looking for a reason to send Thea back whence she had come.

'No,' Padar had reasoned back to the earl. 'He needs the Danish king's support. He wants taxes from Danish merchants who pass through his lands. The prince just has to see her to want her.'

'But he cannot see her. She is veiled in his presence.'

'Ummph,' Padar grunted. 'He will not be disappointed when he does see her face.'

Padar glanced about the narrow hall room that smelled of wax-polished birch wood furniture, candles, oil and charcoal. He wondered at what he had accomplished since he had visited Russia to broker Thea's betrothal. At long last he had a place to call his own. He smiled to see six Russian boys working under his carefully chosen English foreman. He clapped his hands with joy to see the braziers that made his trading hall warm and dry, glow, and that on a damp day prevented his furs from decaying. I am settling down for the first time in my life, he told himself. Life is good to me. Yet, and he sighed at the thought, *Yet Lady Thea still remains betrothed and unwed. And this means I shall remain unmarried too.*

He gnawed at the problem. Why had there been such long delay to her wedding? The prince was fighting on the Steppes, in the forests that bordered Bohemia, helping his father and his uncle keep peace in Kiev in case the wandering scoundrel, the so-called sorcerer, Prince Vsevslav of Polotsk, returned to cause trouble. That was surely why, and meantime Thea had to wait, just wait and wait.

Padar plucked a pine marten pelt from his heap of furs. It would be a beautiful addition to a mantle, as a hood lining with enough left over to edge the cloak, a gift to raise Lady Thea's spirits, with Prince Vladimir galloping around the family's many fortresses demanding loyalty to his uncles and father.

There were great cities scattered about the Rus lands, towns with odd names that sounded distant to his ear. Padar knew not where these cities lay, but, as he held the soft pine marten pelt in his hand, he determined to break into their trading communities.

One day, he promised himself, Gudrun would be wife to a great merchant and they would have many children. *How could he advance his plan?* Possibly he could join a caravan travelling south-west towards the German lands. He tugged at his beard, deep in thought. He could take those furs even into Flanders. If he did this he could try to see Countess Gytha again one last time, for she was, without doubt, approaching her end years.

He pushed the thought into the recesses of his mind. Today he would make a visit to the fortress. He would bring Thea the pine marten fur and Gudrun the reindeer skin for new slippers.

He carefully wrapped the furs in oiled linen. He looked, with meaning in his eyes, at the boys he had set to unpack the baskets of furs. 'By the time I return I want all those pelts packed again,' he said to Dirk, his foreman. 'Make sure they are hidden in chests safely underneath the copper pots.' He rubbed his hands together. 'We do not wish to risk thievery. Goodness knows what mischief lurks around the corner. They have to be sold before the competition gets an edge on us.' He scratched his head and added, 'We shall be making a journey soon.'

The boys stopped sorting, their eyes opened wide. 'Are we coming too, Master?' one ventured.

Dirk laughed. 'Those of you fit to use a sword when we are attacked.'

Padar said, 'You will come with me, Dirk, you, you and you.' He pointed to the boys one by one. 'And the best band of English mercenaries we can find to protect us from here to Mechlenberg.' With those words Padar stuffed his package into a leather sack and pulled on his sheepskin-lined leather boots. He tied up the woven laces over his woollen leggings, tugged his long tunic down and lifted his old sealskin cloak from its peg. Grabbing the sack with the pelts, he pushed out of his entrance door into his slippery courtyard.

He hurried past the guards he employed and who were walking about his yard with stamping feet and exhaling white puffs of breath that seemed to hang as if frozen in the air before vanishing. He called to one, 'Bring a torch. Walk with me. We are off to the castle.'

A few moments later accompanied by a burly guard, an exile who limped along behind brandishing a flaming torch, Padar sped forward as if he was a sinner being prodded across the frozen landscape of his courtyard by a devil's spear. He hurried to his gateway, yelled up to an elderly English warrior who now resided in the gatehouse above Padar's gates. The old thane opened his shutters and poked his head through the opening. 'Unlock the gates, lads,' he shouted. 'The master needs to pass through.'

Two gatekeepers appeared from the shelter of the gatehouse and battled for a moment with a bulky barrel lock that secured it.

'Lock it behind me.' Padar swept through followed by his torch-bearing companion.

The sun was setting and patches of frozen slush appeared reddened by its glow. Padar loved this city. On a torch-lit, snow-filled evening it was an ice-trimmed gleaming Valhalla. Carvings on door posts appeared like goblins, trolls and elves guarding the kingdoms that lay behind their entrances.

Many shopkeepers had already pulled down shutters and were padlocking them for the night. He was far too late for dinner but if he hurried he might make supper in the great fortress hall. He passed through the goldsmith's quarter, not far from the kremlin, when he saw a shortcut through the square by the church of St Nicholias.

As he neared the church, a priest and two women were emerging from the church entrance. The church door was set low into the church wall and their hoods brushed against the top of the lintel. He watched them turn towards the door and draw up their hoods again to cover their faces. Why were they familiar? The thought slipped into his mind and out as he hurried on towards the castle path.

A moment after he noticed the women he heard a crowd's shouts. A figure came fleeing along the street, sliding, slipping and righting himself again, his scanty mantle flying behind him. Observant as ever, Padar saw he was a youth. The fleeing boy hurtled by him pursued by a mob. Padar flattened himself against a wall. He saw from the corner of his eye that the cloaked and hooded women across the track were frozen in fear by the church door. Padar peered at them again. Though they had drawn their hoods close over their wimples, Padar was sure that he recognised Katya, and the other was surely Lady Thea. Before he could cross over to them, they hurried away from the mob towards the river path below the kremlin. They were apparently chaperoned by a tall priest who seemed to push them onwards towards a track that paralleled that which the mob had raced along.

Gudrun was not with them. He was puzzled. Perhaps he was wrong. Something was surely amiss. What would Lady Thea be doing at the church of St Nicholias with Katya and a priest? He shouted at his lantern carrier to hurry and chose another short cut amongst the warren of narrow streets, one he knew could bring him to the kremlin gate closest to St Sophia.

Padar and his limping lantern bearer entered the inner

courtyard as the bells rang for Vespers. He heard the stamping of horses. A party of noblemen had gathered in front of the great hall's entrance door. Pennants emblazoned with bears and snow leopards, reindeers and moose, animals that lived in the northern folds of the world, flew on long poles held aloft by pages. The band of richly clad nobles were handing over their horses to stableboys.

Before he could move aside, the patriarch's low wagon pulled by two fine grey horses came rushing into the courtyard, knocking him and his lantern bearer into a wall. The vehicle skidded to a halt. Dogs straining on leashes pinned to stakes began barking fiercely. Servants kicked the dogs and helped the patriarch dismount. The elderly cleric rushed forward towards the nobles carrying his staff high. 'I was only intending to conduct Vespers for Princess Anya and her ladies.' His staff bobbed up and down like a puppet on a stick as he bowed. 'And here you are, my lords, returned to us at last.'

Prince Vsevolod and his party spun around to greet the patriarch. The prince clapped his hands, stamped the slush off his feet and said in a voice clear as a blue sky day, 'I have come to visit my wife. We shall celebrate our Easter feast here in Novgorod.'

'The young prince too?' The patriarch looked about the nobles and Padar also searched the gathering for Prince Vladimir.

'He is in the town. I have sent out to find him. I had sent my son into Novgorod on an errand.'

At that moment the doors leading to the hall were dragged open by servants. The new governor of Novgorod exited, followed by an excited host of retainers and a few of the terem ladies. Shouting greetings to the newly arrived riders, they immediately surrounded the prince and his retinue, the ladies seeking out their husbands.

'I have come to visit my wife and the Lady Thea. Where are they?' the prince said loudly to Lady Olga who had stepped forward from the group of women. 'Are they well?'

'Both ladies thrive, my Lord Prince. I shall send for them.'

'We shall attend Vespers. Hurry, go and find them. The patriarch is waiting.'

Noble Rus ladies were never permitted to go out alone into the city streets. Yet, he had just seen Thea and Katya slip out of St Nicholias. Remembering how wilful Thea could be, he felt a sense of alarm. Whatever they had been doing in the church, it was secret. He must find Gudrun and warn her. He looked down at the parcels he was carrying. Lady Olga was organising a maid to go and find Princess Anya, waving her hands and shooing the maid towards the terem tower. He would take the furs to the terem kitchen entrance and ask for Gudrun.

'Wait here in the courtyard until I return. Just keep to the shadows.' Seizing the lantern from his servant, keeping close to the wall out of sight, Padar sped after the maid.

19

The mob passed through the square, vanished out of sight and their cries faded. Thea's legs trembled. Katya was shaking. Thea huddled deep into her mantle and drew her hood further over her wimple. She grasped Katya's hand tightly.

Father Sebastian said, his voice low, 'We must get away.'

He drew Thea and Katya from the shelter of the church out into the little square. When he held his lantern high, she could discern the anxiety in his eyes by its light.

'What were they shouting?'

The priest adjusted the lantern, holding it higher. 'They want blood for something.' Father Sebastian glanced about the small square with fear in his eyes. 'If they catch the person, I may well get drawn into this. If they find out who you are, we are all undone and there could be dreadful consequences. I need to get you back to the castle before we get caught up in something we cannot control. I shall alert the castle guards once I see you in through the gates.'

'Is he a thief?'

'Maybe, my lady, maybe not.'

The late afternoon chill had begun to set in. Father Sebastian glanced up anxiously at the setting sun. Church bells rang.

'The fifth hour; Vespers will begin very soon. This way.' He led them along a street parallel to the one they had followed into the square.

They made their way out of the square and into a narrow lane, treading carefully over the freezing slush, without talking. Just as they rounded the next corner, Father Sebastian stopped and opened his arms wide as if to shield them. At the bottom of the wide street stretched the river. There, the mob had caught up with their prey. They carried sticks and brooms and those who had nothing in their mittened hands were scrabbling about on the icy pathways for stones, loose planks and anything else that they could turn into a weapon. One young woman stood out a little apart from the others. Her legs were covered with grey woollen stockings and her feet were stuck into leather shoes but she was clutching a blanket closed like a mantle with one hand. With her other hand she was pointing at a cowering youth and screaming an onslaught of crude expletives.

Thea stopped walking. 'What is she shouting? What is going on?'

'He has raped her and she curses him,' Katya said, lowering her voice. 'By the law laid down women's accusations are always believed.'

'That is just.'

'Perhaps, my lady.' They peered through gaps created in the gathering crowd as the mob bent down to seek out more stones from the frozen ground. Katya clutched Thea's mantle. 'But not always. I think I recognise him. The youth worked for a friend of my father. If he is the same he is no rapist.' She looked up at Thea with fear in her eyes. 'We cannot stay here. They will make him take the test. If he fails it they will kill him.'

'What test?'

At that moment, a red-faced, bulbous-nosed man in a fox-fur cap carrying a chisel in his belt came towards them and seized Father Sebastian's arm. 'You will witness this, Priest.' The man, an artisan by the look of him, was furious. His chisel was tucked into his belt. His other hand hovered over it.

'I am escorting these women to the fortress,' Father Sebastian said.

The artisan's eyes lit on the priest, studied him briefly. His glance skimmed past Katya and blazed into Thea. There was to be no argument. 'They can wait.' Two peasant women were dragging a brazier from a courtyard and were jumping up and down blowing at it with bellows.

The man with the fur hat tied under his chin said, 'They can wait. There was a rape and the punishment is fire.' He dragged Father Sebastian away from Thea and Katya and towards the brazier. Thea could not see where the priest was taken. Was Father Sebastian to be a witness to the youth's branding?

A crowd was swelling around the fire basket. A group of yokels pushed past her, separating her from Katya, and as more people joined the spectacle, Thea found herself swept further up the hill and towards the fortress. She could not see Katya anywhere.

She stopped when the mob paused. She stood on the tips of her boots trying to make herself even taller than she already was. Slightly elevated by the slope leading towards the castle, she could see over the heads of others. Though she could not catch sight of Katya she could now glimpse Father Sebastian as he was hauled closer to the fire by two burly artisans. A wave of anticipation swept through the crowd. One of the two artisans who had dragged Father Sebastian forward, raised a vicious looking pair of tongs. She gasped and turning to the woman to her side exclaimed, 'What is it?'

'Iron.' The woman who was toothless had turned and was staring at her. Stubby fingers reached out and touched Thea's mantle. 'Watch, rich girl. Watch and learn. He is a pup of a merchant's son, one of your own, but by our prince's laws he will suffer for his crime.'

'What has he done?'

'Taken that girl –' she pointed 'see her watching; the child wrapped in a blanket; took her away from her home and used her. Says he is innocent but, watch, rich girl, and we shall see the right of it.'

The old woman elbowed herself forward and shoved Thea to one side. Thea swayed, righted herself and, unable to look away, watched, peering through a space that opened between heads.

She saw that Father Sebastian was trying to argue with the artisan. The artisan ignored him and shoved the tongs into the fire. Two men held the merchant's son. A hush followed, except for the terrified cries of the pleading youth. 'What if he is innocent?' Thea cried out, unable to bear the cruelty she was witnessing.

'We shall see,' her neighbour said.

The artisan withdrew the tongs from the coals, raised them momentarily and laid them across the lad's bent and bared back. The boy screamed and tried to free himself from his captors. Even at a little distance up the hill, Thea thought she could smell his burning flesh. She heard the boy scream again.

'Guilty,' cried the two women who had stoked up the brazier.

'Hear his confession, Priest,' another called.

'The iron burns his flesh. It is seared black.' The artisan had laid down the tongs and shouted above the heads of the mob. The boy collapsed. Father Sebastian was kneeling in the slush by his side.

He stood up and raged at the mob. 'No, this is not the right way. It is not God's way. Nor did the princes of the Rus nation ever intend such barbarity without an investigation. I will bring him to his home and their families must decide his fate, not a mob. They may pay reparation if he is guilty; if they can afford it. That is the law … if they wish to save his life. A judge must mediate.'

It was a just plea, and Father Sebastian's words did not fall on deaf ears. The girl who had accused the youth was led away by a group of women into the cheering crowd who parted to allow her passage. The artisans nodded at the priest and Father Sebastian knelt again and took possession of the weeping boy. Apparently he was to be spared for now.

'What will happen to him?'

'Rich girl, that which should happen to all your kind.' The woman looked back at her, drew her hand across her throat and then spat at Thea's mantle. Others jostled forward. Thea desperately tried to push her way back, to escape, but she was trapped on all sides. She pushed and shoved and managed to darn her way through the crowd until thankfully a gap opened. A breath later she felt herself shoved again. This time she fell down onto the slippery slush. Boots were trampling over her.

She would die here.

At last a hand reached out and pulled her up. She could hardly stand. Her legs could not support her. 'We must get away, now,' Katya said in a breathless voice, then, 'Lean on me.'

'I cannot walk.'

Katya hauled Thea away from the furious crowd and into a narrow street that led up to the kremlin. 'Father Sebastian will help the boy. We can manage our return without him.'

A moment later they slipped through the postern gate. Katya called a greeting to the guards. Clouds passed over the thin moon as Katya hurried a hobbling Thea into the church. 'We are fortunate that the hour for Vespers is over. We can say that you slipped in the garden and fell. Do you have the prayer mat, my lady?'

'No, I thought you did, Katya.'

'I must have dropped it, but no matter.'

They were just about to slip past the terem guards, when Gudrun stepped out of the shadows.

'Padar is back. He came to warn me. He saw you. They have been asking for you,' Gudrun said. 'I told Princess Anya's messenger that you could not be disturbed. I drew back the curtain a little from your bed and shoved a pillow below your coverlet. Princess Anya's servant accepted the lie. He thought you were asleep. I have been waiting in the garden for you since.' All this fell from Gudrun's lips in a great rush.

'Why did Princess Anya want me?'

'Prince Vsevolod and his retinue have come to the fortress. What has happened, my lady?'

Thea sank against the wall, exhausted and shocked.

Katya tugged Gudrun's hand. 'Let's just get her into the bedchamber and under the covers. We'll need to check her for bruises. She was trampled on by a mob.'

'Not after Lady Thea surely?' Gudrun said.

'No, by St Stephen's bones, no.'

Thea felt Katya supporting her. 'It is my ankle,' she said.

197

'Hurry. They will think we are just three servants. Let me speak for us all. It is so dark they will not make out who is who,' Katya said.

'The guards have torches,' Thea gasped for breath.

'No matter, since we are only are going where we go every day.'

As they passed the two guards who lounged about the doorway into the terem, Katya called out. 'We are delivering a new prayer rug for the Lady Sabrina.' And in a lower voice she said, 'More's the pity we lost it to the mob back there.'

The guards nodded and continued to pace about the tower walls, taking no further notice of three women who mounted the wooden staircase.

The doorway into Thea's chamber was flung open. Lady Olga emerged, took one look at them and said sharply, 'What, by the saints, *has* been going on? Where *have* you been?' She pointed at Gudrun. 'You will be whipped for your lies. You told our messenger that your mistress was in bed.'

Thea said firmly, 'I was resting and then got up to take air in the garden. It is icy. I slipped.'

'You, Princess, will get into your bed and you will stay there until I return. As for you, Gudrun, clearly you are not telling the truth. A man was seen conversing with you earlier. It is not permitted.' She turned to Katya. 'Go to the kitchens and fetch a bowl of warm water and cloths. Your mistress needs bathing.' She turned to Thea. 'Prince Vsevolod has come. He will want to know what is amiss with you. He will demand an explanation as to why this servant girl lied to his wife's servant when clearly you were wandering unprotected around the fortress.' Olga lifted up a suspicious-looking pillow and showed it to Thea. 'Subterfuge!'

'I was walking in the gardens. If I chose to place a pillow in my bed I shall,' Thea said quickly, her heart hammering on her rib cage. 'Go, Lady Olga, my maids will attend me. I do not wish to take you from your other duties and I *do* wish to lie down.'

Olga looked at her with fury rising in her obsidian eyes. Thea could have cut the chill atmosphere with her seax. 'Make sure you are presentable and rested when Prince Vsevolod summons you tomorrow.' Lady Olga swept from the room.

Thea's foot throbbed, her knees ached and she felt bruised all over. She sank into her armed chair by the small stove. 'Gudrun, she will not dare to have you punished. You must stay in the church all day tomorrow. Keep out of her sight.' She stretched out her hand to Gudrun. 'I am sorry if this means that you may not see Padar for now. When I am married this will change.' She ventured a half-smile at Gudrun, who was white with fear. 'Now what do I see on my side bench? Bring me that parcel.'

Gudrun tried to smile back and gave her mistress the oiled linen package. Thea gasped at the beauty of the gift. 'Pine marten for a mantle trimming!'

When Gudrun showed Thea her own gift, Thea said, 'It is worth every difficulty just to know that you are loved, Gudrun. Put the furs in one of the coffers that locks just in case Olga starts rummaging through my possessions.'

After Gudrun had locked their gifts away she whispered hoarsely, 'My lady, what happened to you?'

'I saw something terrible, a hard kind of justice.'

By the time she had finished telling Gudrun her story, Katya had returned with healing herbs and warm water and was bathing her feet, dabbing her cut knees and massaging her stiff shoulders. Katya whisked the muddied mantle away for brushing.

Thea obediently sipped a soothing draught of poppy. That evening she drifted into a deep sleep, thankful to be safely in her soft bed and covered with the skin of a silver wolf. She was bruised but safe. She was happy because her prince cared for her. Lady Olga was but a wart on their landscape. If she stuck to her story ... anyway Prince Vladimir would not let her down. Gudrun would not be held to account.

Convinced that all would be well in her world, she dreamed

happily of swans and swallows, cuckoos and jays, and it was as well that she did because her days of relative freedom were closing as a net catches a bird on water.

20

Shortly after Noon service, Prince Vsevolod summoned Thea to his receiving chamber. Lady Olga ordered her to wear a full veil and to walk straight, which was very difficult as Thea was still suffering from a sprained ankle. Thea asked Katya for her veil and her fur-lined mantle, and as Lady Olga tapped her foot impatiently, she deliberately spun out the time that she needed to make ready for this audience. Olga began to pace the chamber.

At last they were ready to leave her large, safe room. Led by Lady Olga, followed by Katya and Gudrun, Thea hobbled across the courtyard, through heavy carved oak doors, along a corridor lit with sconces, into the heart of the fortress. She was sure she saw Earl Connor in an alcove speaking to a group of boyars as they crossed the great hall. There was no time to stop. Olga urged them through the hall as if she were driving nanny goats to slaughter. Thea stumbled. Every time her maids tried to help her Lady Olga snapped, 'The princess must walk unaided.'

Her journey to the prince was torturous, notwithstanding that she had an ominous feeling about what was awaiting her once they arrived. What could Prince Vsevolod know about her activities? She went to church diligently. She was preparing for her wedding. She had been befriended by Princess Anya and the other women of the terem. Her only adversary was Lady Olga. But then Lady Olga was sly. She was inclined to snoop and try to discover Thea's shortcomings, though Thea wondered at this. She could not work out Lady Olga's true motivation.

At last, they entered the receiving chamber. Prince Vsevolod, Princess Anya and Lord Michael were all seated behind a heavy table. They did not smile and she felt that she was the object of their displeasure. On the table lay a prayer mat. *By St Theodosia, it was the one they had dropped during the attack on that boy.* For a moment Thea thought about the boy. Surely he would be safe with Father Sebastian? Her glance returned to the table. A crumpled piece of parchment lay beside the prayer mat, one that had once been shaped like a bird. Her hand flew to her mouth and she was glad of her concealing veil. She felt the colour of guilt creeping up her neck into her face. *How had they come by that prayer mat and how could they have they come by the note she had exchanged with her prince?* If they knew that she had secretly met with the prince what would her fate be now? She glanced around. Olga and her husband were the only other occupants of the room apart from two guards hugging the wall by the door. A recess opened behind Prince Vsevolod but she could not see into it. Where *was* Vladimir? He should be here to defend her. The prince's angry-looking father held aloft the crumpled note.

'This was discovered in my son's pouch last night when he came to join us for the Easter Masses. I can only suppose it is addressed to you, Princess Gita.' Thea opened her mouth. He glared at her. 'Do not protest. My son has confessed. He has been sent back to the fortress from whence he came to Novgorod.' The prince turned to Katya. 'Translate, girl. I shall speak Russian,' he ordered. Thea did not dare admit that she understood enough Rus to understand him. She turned her head to Katya. Katya translated. As she did, Thea had cause to be further glad of her veil. Lady Olga was smirking. So it was Lady Olga who had drawn Prince Vsevolod's attention to her.

The prince scooped up the prayer rug. 'This was discovered this morning by a fortress guard who saw you pass through the gate, Princess Gita. The guard was under the impression that you were a servant from the fortress sent by Lady Sabrina to fetch a prayer rug from the Church of St Nicholias. We have discovered that you were caught up in a terrible incident.' He banged his fist on the table. His countenance darkened further. 'You will never, ever leave this fortress accompanied by only a maid and a priest ever again.' He paused while Katya translated. He dropped his voice pitch a tone. 'Your stay here in the terem in Novgorod is over. You are to go into the Convent of the Holy Trinity outside the city and remain there. I fear that it is questionable as to whether I can allow your marriage to take place. That will be dependent on my spiritual advisors. It will also be dependent on my son's contrition. As it is, you cannot remain here in the Novgorod terem. My wife Anya has spoken up for you, but we cannot have a disgraced princess amongst her company of women. We guard our women. We respect them … that is, when they are deserving of respect.' He pointed at Gudrun. 'And *she* is dismissed from your service. Please make alternative arrangements for that one's future.' His long finger moved to Katya. 'And the daughter of my good friend Dimitri, the saffron merchant from Constantinople, will accompany you to the Convent of the Holy Trinity.'

Olga smirked. Anya wiped a tear from her eyes with the corner of her veil. She appeared very saddened by what was happening. Thea lifted her head high after Katya had translated her response. 'Since I wish to study further the Russian faith, a convent will suit me well,' she said with a confidence she did not feel. She thought she noticed a brief smile hover about Princess Anya's mouth despite her tearful eyes. It was the right response.

The prince said without emotion, 'Then go. You depart today with a guard and in your own litter. Pack a small travelling coffer because you will have no need of worldly goods at Holy Trinity. Your other goods will be stored carefully until I decide if you are a proper bride for my son.' He waved his long fingers dismissively at Gunnhild. 'Make arrangements for your girl.' Looking down at his manicured nails and glancing up again, he added, 'Perhaps the kitchen will give her a place.'

She heard Olga cough. She saw Anya shake her head at Olga. Olga leaned down and whispered into the prince's ear. She passed an object to him. She pointed at Gudrun. The prince hesitated for the moment it would take to brush away a bothersome insect before taking a cue from Lady Olga. His face clouded with anger. 'She is a bad influence.' He held Gudrun's brooch pin aloft. 'It has cunning markings engraved on it. Where did she come by this?'

Thea had suspected that Olga had picked her locks and raided her coffers but she had not suspected that Olga would attack Gudrun in this way. She had her response ready, the only response and the true response. 'It was a gift from a healer in Denmark. It is not intended for magic or for the making of spells. It is simply a talisman. Please allow my maid to keep it in her possession.'

'*That* I cannot do. This smacks of spells and witchery. We have had enough of wizards and witchcraft in this land. That girl will spend today within the walls of the church under the guidance of our bishop. We must turn any evil trait in your maid into good through prayer. Plotinus says in his *Enneads* that magic and prayer may work through natural sympathetic bonds within our world. There may yet be hope for her redemption. She has this one chance to banish any evil magic that may have entered her through the talisman. As for the object, we shall destroy it. I like not its markings. '

As Katya translated the prince made an expressive gesture, the furred cuffs of his wide sleeves falling back. 'Every action may have magic at its source. There are those who consider the entire life of man as a bewitchment. Yet, God witnesses all. When a person prays to the saints, their prayers may be answered and that person can become immune to the magical forces directed at him ... or her.' Prince Vsevolod stood and pointed at Gudrun, who now appeared to be shaking in terror. 'If we see further evidence of sorcery she will face an appropriate fate. Make arrangements for her future. Go, Princess Gita, and prepare for your journey. I hope that when we meet again you will have learned humility and sensibility.'

The prince sank down into his great chair. As he did, Thea became aware of another presence beyond the prince. Thea reached out and caught Gudrun's hand as the shadow became a wide silhouette, slowly emerging into the candlelit room from the gloom of the mysterious recess set deep into the wall. The figure grew into a bishop clothed in stiff robes. He was not one she had seen in the court of Novgorod before. Like the others, he was extravagantly gowned in triangular-shaped, highly decorated skirts and each seemed layered over the other. An enormous decorated cross swung on his breast. His white beard reached his chest making him look like the painting of the Prophet Isaiah that was painted on the second layer of icons on the wall of the church dedicated to the Lady Mary. He had, Thea saw too, a great hooked nose which just made him further resemble the ancient prophet. She swallowed. He was a priest who sought out wizards.

'Bishop Xantes has accompanied us to the city. He will look after the maid, hear her confession, help her from darkness into light. He will protect her from evil. Go, Princess Gita. Go, before I change my mind and send you back to Denmark in disgrace.'

Thea touched Gudrun and whispered, 'I shall send for Padar.' There was nothing else she could do. At least Gudrun would be free soon. She nearly collapsed once she began to move her frozen legs and attempted to walk away. Holding herself stiffly, with Katya taking her arm, she managed, with some dignity, to walk towards the chamber entrance. As she reached the great door, she cast a quick look behind her shoulder. Lady Olga was not watching her exit because her eyes had lit on Gudrun. They had narrowed to malevolent slits.

In that moment Thea saw that Gudrun was in great danger. By evening prayers, she must smuggle her out of the fortress. Padar and Gudrun must marry and leave Novgorod until the prince, his steward and his bishop were on their way to whatever campaign was next on their list of campaigns. As Thea returned along the corridors to the terem entrance her heart was sinking into the depths of an aching sorrow that could only be a little alleviated by the thought that Padar would protect Gudrun. She knew Earl Connor was in the fortress. She had seen him. Now she would ask for him to come to her, to come to the terem without delay. Katya would send a message by one of the pages who hung about the terem doors especially for this purpose. As she wrote her note she felt angry with her prince and not a little disillusioned. It was a terrible disappointment that Prince Vladimir had not disobeyed his father and stayed in Novgorod to guard her from his father's wrath.

21

Usually, Padar slept lightly, alert even in slumber, ready to confront trouble. Tonight he had fallen asleep instantly, dreaming of Gudrun, wondering how he could manage another meeting, wondering if Thea had returned safely to the kremlin and without discovery. When the midnight bells rang, Padar was unprepared for the commotion beyond his courtyard. His outside doors were being dragged open; one of his boys was calling out, 'Who goes there?' Throwing his sealskin mantle about his shoulders he wearily climbed down the ladder into his hall.

'Who is that?' came several voices from the bottom of the staircase.

'Me, you fools, be quiet. And unless I return and kick you, stay quiet. If I kick you, get to your swords as sly as the fox stealing a hen from the roost.'

Padar walked calmly to the door, edged it opened and peered into the frozen yard. The elderly English knight who kept watch over the outer gate was up. The light from the lantern which swung beneath his hand cast drifting shadows over the yard. He was talking with a tall, heavily cloaked figure. Behind them, the gate guards waited to allow a band of soldiers inside his courtyard. A smaller person, standing in front of them, was concealed in a hood and cloak.

Padar drew a sword and sheath from a sack of furs by the door, buckled his sword sheath around his cloak and pulled his door wider open. Holding the unsheathed sword in front of him, he stepped out into the courtyard. Gripping it tightly, he momentarily surveyed the group by his gate. To his surprise, two of his gate guards began shoving the heavy door closed, bringing what he had wondered could be an enemy into his courtyard. He lowered his sword, his sharpened Gabriel, purchased on his return to Novgorod, a sword of Frankish origin of which he was very proud. Perhaps he would not need it tonight.

He felt a presence behind him as he crossed his courtyard. Glancing back he saw that his boys stood in a tight knot, almost though not quite a shield wall of dwarf creatures without shields. They were positioned close together, holding small daggers. He snarled at them. 'Wait here.' He raised Gabriel once again into the air.

The tall man shouted at him, 'Padar, sheath your sword: it is only me. I bring you a great treasure.' The visitor was laughing. He spun around to face Gabriel, shook back his hood, revealing more of his face and Padar saw that the stranger was none other than Earl Connor. The Irish earl turned to the little shrouded figure and said in a gentle voice, 'Lady, you are safe now.'

'Gudrun.' Padar, recognising her, hurried forward with haste, sliding on the ice, reaching out for her, the long sword, still unsheathed, threatening to drop further and trip him up. 'Why are you here?'

Connor indicated the heavily armed guards. He spoke for Gudrun. 'These men are here by my request and will protect us. Padar, my friend, we are travelling south to sell our goods and Gudrun is coming with us. So you had better get a wedding over and done with.'

Padar said. 'Why is Gudrun here in the darkness of midnight?' He looked at the frightened girl. 'What happened?'

Connor put his arm around Gudrun. 'No time. And, a priest's blessing later. Lady Thea says you are betrothed to the maid. For now let us witness you pledge your troth. Trust me, it is necessary. Gudrun is in danger.'

'Just like this. Why?' He stared at Gudrun. Her face, what he could see of it, looked yellow in the light of the lantern. Her eyes seemed haunted. 'What has happened to you, Gudrun?'

Something was deeply amiss.

Connor kept his arm protectively about Gudrun's shoulder. 'She has been accused of possession of a magic object. In

Novgorod, they think magicians cast evil spells, so this puts your betrothed in great danger. It is safer if you marry her, safer for her and for you.'

Padar thought quickly. He would do anything to protect Gudrun. 'This is not how I imagined our wedding would occur. But, I marry you willingly, Gudrun. I marry you this night.'

Gudrun nodded. 'And I thee,' she said, her teeth chattering from cold, or was it shock?

'No more time wasted. She needs rest.' Earl Connor pushed his hand into his mantle. 'Have you a ring?'

Sheathing Gabriel, Padar shook his head. 'Inside, lots of them maybe.' He kept silver and jewels locked away in a small coffer in his loft chamber.

'Take this. It was stolen off a maiden seized by an Irish dragon. Fairy silver. Perfect for her. My wedding gift.' He laughed, breaking the tension.

Gudrun smiled at last and Padar reached for her and hugged her to his breast. 'Oh, my love, my sweet, sweet girl.'

Connor handed a velvet pouch to Padar who drew the silver ring from the purse. It had flowers and runes engraved on it, spelling the maker's name, FRE. Runes could contain magic, Padar mused as he held the ring.

Padar lifted Gunnhild's hands into his own and swore to be her husband. They exchanged a brief kiss. It was done, the hastiest wedding in Christendom.

'Thank you,' Gudrun whispered, as he slipped Fre's ring over her third right finger. 'Thank you for saving me from the terem kitchens, or worse.'

'Now,' Connor said, 'my guard will sleep in the barn with the animals.' He turned to the ancient English knight who lowered his lantern and nodded. 'Padar, find me room in the hall for a few hours' rest. I have sledges arriving at dawn. After that we use horses and boats. We have the warehouse to secure while we are away. It may be some time before we return.'

Padar called to the gaping, nudging boys. 'Meet Gudrun, my wife. Obey her as you obey me. Now, get to your beds.' Inside the hall, he pointed to an alcove. 'There is a couch behind the curtain, Connor, as you well know.' He took Gudrun's hand. 'Our chamber is up the ladder. Come.'

He took Gudrun by the hand and helped her to climb up into his loft chamber, his scabbard thumping up behind him. He pulled a wolfskin curtain aside to reveal the upper chamber where he slept amongst packs of cured ox hides, pots of olive oil, and opened coffers filled with elk tusks, reindeer horns and walrus teeth. 'All for trading,' he said, on seeing Gudrun stare wide-eyed around the chamber. He drew her closer and said into her ear. 'We are going to be rich when this lot is sold south, Gudrun. If you do not want to return to Novgorod we shall have enough wealth to set up in Flanders, go into cloth, or return to Denmark. There are many places for a wealthy merchant, song-maker and spy to live these days. '

She said quietly, 'Not a spy, I hope.'

'Those dark days are behind me.'

He sat Gudrun on his low, wide, wooden box of a bed, unstrapped his sword and carefully leaned both sheath and sword against the lime-washed wall within reach of the bed. He removed her cloak and her shoes and her outer dress. He unbraided her hair, laid her on his linen sheets and covered her with a soft bearskin. It was a relief that the night was so cold, the fleas that hide in the sheet seams must have surely died of it. Shedding his mantle, pulling off his boots and removing his outer garments, he climbed in beside her.

As the thin moon's light slid through the shutters' cracks, in the safety of Padar's arms, her body angled into his, Gudrun grew warmer to his touch. Soon she was whispering a brief explanation as to the horror she had endured. She related how Lady Thea was travelling that night to the Convent of the Holy Trinity. For long hours she, herself, was forced to pray on her knees in the Church of the Virgin. 'All because of a brooch with strange markings on it,' she said sadly. 'Bishop Xantes told me I must pray hour by hour, by the bells, to escape its evil possession.'

As she spoke, Padar could feel the wetness of tears seep through his under- tunic. He held her even closer. 'How did you get away?'

'When Earl Connor discovered from Lady Thea what had happened, he came to the Church of the Virgin. He said to Bishop Xantes that he would take me with him back to Denmark.' She sat up, allowing the fur rug to slide from the bed linen. 'Earl Connor promised that I would make a pilgrimage to those places where pilgrims gathered. I had no time to say goodbye to Lady Thea. Nor had I time to send her a message thanking her for my deliverance.' She heaved a sob and, falling into Padar's arms, murmured, 'Without heed for her own safety, Lady Thea had arranged everything. She told Earl Connor that I must marry you and stay with you. But, I did not know if you would want me. After all they have accused me of magic's evil grip. They took Needle, my cloak pin, from me,' she half-whispered, half-sobbed. 'They stole my talisman.'

'How could you doubt me, my love? All will be well. I shall find you another. Your talisman watched over you more than we all can know. What appears good in one place may own a different meaning in another. You have committed no sin.' Padar stroked her loosened hair. It was fair and soft, and its silk sorely tempted him to intimacy, but not tonight. Instead he said, 'We have each other, a great packet of furs to sell in the south and my sword Gabriel to protect us. When we cross other lands to the Flanders coast a priest will bless our marriage. You will be reunited with Countess Gytha and with many of our old friends from Exeter.' He stroked her forehead, kissed her eyes and then her mouth. Responding she moved closer into the circle of his arms. 'Not tonight, my sweet. Believe me, I want to take you, but, for now, you must sleep. Morning will arrive sooner than a bird pecks a worm from the earth. Gudrun, I love you more than my own life. Never again doubt my love.'

Gudrun drifted into sleep, but Padar lay thinking that there was more to this than he knew. How had Gudrun come by her talisman? Why had she been accused? Was Lady Thea safe in this strange country, in a convent that was even more secure than a terem, a convent with its strange icons, silent nuns and bearded priests? He must find Katya's merchant father and see if he could discover the truth of it all.

Thea sat in an upright chair close to Katya, who had fallen into an exhausted deep sleep. She watched the moonlight sweep over the quiet herb gardens that lay below her window, casting shadows on the wall beyond. A night owl hooted. For a moment she fancied she was in Exeter. It was not such a bad fate, she decided. The convent was peaceful. Rather than being greeted by Mother Sophia as if she was an outcast, she had been welcomed into this gentle community of women as if it were an honour for them to receive and instruct her. Prince Vladimir may have had no option but to wait patiently for their wedding too. Maybe he would send her word.

She fell to her knees and prayed to St Theodosia for Gudrun and Padar. 'Dear Saint, protect them. Bring them back safely to me one day soon.'

After that she climbed into the bed beside Katya and drifted into an exhausted sleep, glad that the following day would offer her a day of instruction, prayer and work in the herb garden clearing away the last of the early spring snowfall from the pathways.

Some weeks later, escorted by guards, accompanied by one of her ladies, Princess Anya rode on a gorgeous caparisoned white horse into the convent to see Thea. The day was pleasant. It was one of blue skies and scudding white clouds that flew about the sky like cupids' wings. They met in the refectory. At first a sense of betrayal haunted Thea. Anya had not come to see her before her departure from Novgorod. Now, here she was with only Lady Sabrina and her guards in attendance.

After their greetings had been exchanged and Mother Sophia had left them alone, Thea held her head high. 'I am happy here, though I wish to know my fate. Am I to be sent back to

Denmark in disgrace?'

Princess Anya took her hand. 'No, Thea. Your wedding will take place next spring.'

'Another year? So long a betrothal is unnatural.' Thea tore her hand away.

'Make a positive experience of your time in Holy Trinity. It is a period for preparation, gathering knowledge and reflection. Many of our women love the sanctuary the convent provides for them. In the Rus lands women who enter convents are revered as if they are clergy themselves; surprising, of course, in this dominant world of men.' Anya took Thea's arms and pulled her round to face her. 'Please know that I am your friend. Know that I have no love for Olga, who possesses a mean spirit.' Anya broke off. Before continuing, she glanced along the refectory table at Sabrina who was bent over a piece of embroidery and lowered her voice. 'I do not even want Sabrina to hear me. Olga is bitter because she wanted Prince Vladimir for her own eldest daughter.' She squeezed Thea's arms gently, dropped her hands and allowed them to rest on the table.

'Where is Lady Olga's daughter?' Thea asked quietly.

'She dwells in a wealthy princess's household far away in the city of Chernigov. The princess is with the wife of Prince Vsevolod's elder brother. The girl will marry another wealthy noble. The mother is bitter. She wanted alliance with the prince. Rest assured, Vladimir is still your prince, Thea.'

The air in the refectory stilled as Thea absorbed Anya's words. She had been hurtled from thinking she could be sent back to Denmark to knowing that she was to marry her prince. She heard bird song in the garden beyond and the hum of prayer from the midday service in the Church of Holy Trinity. Somewhere servants were sweeping. All these sounds had become her normal everyday currency. Her heart lifted. She sent a swift prayer to St Theodosia. 'Thank you. So many women desire marriage with him,' Thea said sadly, thinking of the cruel Danish princesses.

'It may be so; many sought him, but Vladimir wants you.

213

The prince has explained his note and his misguided impatience to see you. He wept when his father threatened to return you to Denmark. Vladimir is his father's only son by the greatest princess of us all. His mother was a Monomakh, a princess of Constantinople. God will protect you. He will keep you safe.'

Thea could not resist saying, 'They sent Gudrun away.'

'No, you sent Gudrun away, and you were right to do that. She will return one day, safely, with our friend, Padar. They have, according to Earl Connor, travelled to Flanders. Earl Connor spoke with my husband about her marriage. Appearances must be observed. It would never have been safe for her to remain in my terem. Olga would find a way to destroy you through your maid.' At this Princess Anya leaned over and whispered in Thea's ear. 'We have let it be known that she has been removed from court. Padar has taken her on a journey south. Even Steward Michael does not know their true destination because he thinks they travel north to Denmark. Gudrun will be safe and you will be safe from Olga's scheming.'

'And they will visit my grandmother,' Thea said with hope in her heart. 'They will return one day with news of her.'

'We shall see,' Anya said softly.

Before she left the convent, Anya placed a kiss on Thea's forehead and gave her a tiny cross studded with garnets to protect her. 'Wear it and think of me. Put all your cares behind you and grow even more beautiful.' She took Thea's hands in her own and added, 'Katya will watch over you. Her father will visit her soon and bring you our news.'

Thea had the prince's forgiveness, it seemed, and Vladimir still cared for her and insisted on their wedding. She could not contain her joy. She would endeavour to learn new things but one thing she promised herself. Never would she allow Lady Olga to join her terem when she lived with Prince Vladimir in their palace in Kiev.

What had Prince Vsevolod said? *Evil can be defeated by prayer and observance of the faith.* Perhaps there *was* truth in those words, she thought, and dug out the weeds that jumped all over the herb garden that summer with renewed determination. Still, he had directed his words at the wrong person.

22

Convent of the Holy Trinity, December 1071

Thea had not made progress with her embroidery. She had lost interest since she had been sent to the convent. Instead, she had passed autumnal mornings working in the herb garden and quiet afternoons in her chamber improving her Russian and writing down stories using an old bronze stylus on sheets of birch bark purloined from the convent's workshop.

It took her days to master writing on birch bark with a stylus. She persevered and succeeded. At first she penned little stories in her native English, the first language she had learned to write, glad that she had learned the art of writing. Later, she practised writing in her new tongue. The Russian letters looked as if they were enchanted, as magical as the runes and swirls on Gudrun's forbidden brooch pin. The written word held power, she mused. Long ago people had thought that letters were indeed as powerful as those etched into Gudrun's needle.

Early in December a first fall of snow, between Nones and Vespers, drove Thea and Katya from the herb garden into the communal hall. Snowflakes drifted against the windows and through the door into the long room the moment they opened it. Inside a blast of heat that burst from a large wood-burning stove felt welcoming and the scent of pine resin created a sense that Christmas and St Basil's Feast Day were drawing closer.

The other women glanced up from their sewing and smiled. One nodded. 'Not a day for the soil! Better in than out. Come and sit with us, Princess Gita. We are sewing feast-day gifts for the orphans, belts and purses.' She patted the bench and threw some little sticks into the stove. They burst into flame and crackled.

Katya blew on her fingers and fetched their sewing bags

from a shelf.

'Tis a day for the hearth.' Thea found them a place close to the stove.

She had no sooner threaded her needle than Mother Sophia bustled into the hall. For a moment, Thea watched the Mother flap around the convent's lay guests commenting on a colour, correcting a stitch here and praising a composition there.

When Mother Sophia reached their bench, in what seemed a quick turn of the hour glass, she passed a finger over Thea's embroidery, remarking, 'My child, you have made more progress with your study of religion and writing than you have with this embroidery. Still, there is a long winter of time before us.' She turned to Katya and touched the maid's shoulder.

'Now there really is no need to jump, Katya. You are the reason I am here. I have news for you. Your father has come to visit you. Put your work away and go to my receiving chamber, now.' Mother Sophia was smiling as if she were a cat who had invaded the monastery dairy and supped up all the cream. 'He is waiting for you.'

Thea glanced up and sighed. If only someone from her past life would visit her, Edmund or Godwin, Padar or Gudrun, or even Earl Connor. It had been months since Padar and Gudrun had departed for Flanders. Mother Sophia moved on to a window alcove where several nuns were weaving on a horizontal loom passing their shuttles back and forwards, working the foot peddle with rhythmic thumps.

Katya packed away her gift belt. 'My father, Dimitri, I have not seen him since we left Denmark! He will have so much news,' she said breathlessly to Thea.

Thea caught Katya's arm before she followed the nun. 'Ask your father if he has seen my brothers. And Padar, too; their paths may have crossed.'

Katya sped off, unlatching the door into the hall and causing a chill draught to blast into the room. Thea bent her head and tried to concentrate on the pollarded trees she was stitching into her rushnyk. When it is spring I shall see you again, my prince, she thought to herself as she stitched another stunted tree onto her cloth. Would April ever arrive?

Thea flew from the window seat at the sound of Katya's tread on the stair. The girl opened the door and backed into the room. Thea ran to help her. 'What have you there?'

'A box of letters; my father has been to Flanders trading. He saw Padar and Gudrun. He was in Denmark too and met with your brother Edmund. He spoke with them all!' She laid the box on the wolfskin bedcover. 'These letters are for you, from everyone who loves you and wishes you well. There is even one from your grandmother, all the way from St Omer.'

'Why did your father not give these to me? Why to you?' Thea asked.

Katya said simply, 'Because they are secret. Mother Sophia might read them first.'

Thea thought about that for a moment. 'Why would she?'

'Mother Sophia might not be loyal to your interests. My father says it is best to be cautious.' Katya pointed to the casket, a plain wooden box with a lock. 'Here is the key.'

Thea bent down and inserted the key into the small lock. It fitted perfectly.

'My lady, would you like to read them alone? I can attend Vespers and say that you are indisposed. Mother Sophia is so pleased today that she will not notice your absence.'

'Why is Mother Sophia pleased?'

'My father has donated two hundred grivas to the convent and he has given her five bolts of undyed but very fine linen from Flanders for night shifts for the poor.'

'That is generous of your father. Well then, you attend Vespers and say that I am resting.'

Katya was not listening. Thea looked away from the box. Katya was peering out through the shutters, pushing the slates apart with her fingers. 'My lady, look, my father is walking in the garden with Mother Sophia,' she said, turning to Thea.

Thea desperately wanted to open the letters but for a

moment she stood beside her maid, looking through the window shutters at a tall man who appeared through the slates as if in broken lines. He looked stark outlined against the snow in a dark bearskin mantle and his brown furred cap. He was leaning towards Mother Sophia. If he was suspicious of the nun's loyalty he did not show it. They walked close together as if they were old friends. The merchant took Sophia's elbow and guided her along the wooden walkways that led between the two bare cherry trees bordering the herb beds. 'They are clearly friends?' she said to Katya, observing how the pair stood for a moment conversing near the gate.

'In his world, friends can easily become enemies. My father trusts no one. That is the way he survives, without giving his trust away, because he is trusted with the secrets of others. No one knows the secrets he carries, certainly not Mother Sophia.' After the merchant had reached the latch gate, he vanished into the courtyard.

'You must miss your family?'

Katya lingered by the shutters watching the last small flounce of her father's bearskin cloak disappear. 'We all miss our families, though we can pray for their good health and their happiness. My father is great fun. He is a sort of magician himself.'

'What sort of magic?'

'Oh, this and that. He is always experimenting with a recipe for dragon fire.'

'Greek fire. That sounds dangerous. No one knows that secret,' Thea said, thinking of how Gudrun was punished for owning a brooch with strange markings.

'Well, he clearly has not destroyed himself yet.'

Mother Sophia returned along the walkway. For a moment she looked up and Thea drew back. Katya allowed the slates to fall back into place and dropped the leather curtain over the shuttered window. Thea watched Katya hurry about lighting rush candles in the chamber. After she placed a lamp for Thea to read by on the table, she bowed to her mistress and said,

220

'Well then, I had best get to Vespers. You may not even be missed.'

Thea pulled a dry cloak from a peg by the doorway, and placed it around the girl's shoulders. 'They might even think you are me.'

'It is no sin not to attend Vespers.'

'Then let us hope no one comes looking for me.'

The casket was made of bleached pinewood with no decoration apart from a fine interlocking border of shells around its edges. Yet, the pale wood seemed to gleam invitingly in the lamp's glow.

Thea unlocked the box, opened the lid and slipped her hand inside. She felt something hard and circular. Using her finger and thumb she carefully withdrew the object. It was a small ring. She peered closer at it lying in her palm. This ring was a link to the three years she had spent with Grandmother Gytha. The amber stone in its centre glowed warmly and the silver setting gleamed. She turned it over and over, remembering it fondly, intrigued by it. She slipped it on the middle finger of her left hand. It fitted perfectly. It was not a large ring because her grandfather Earl Godwin had worn it on his little finger, but it was large enough for Grandmother Gytha to wear it on the middle finger of her left hand. She would wear it on that finger too.

Why has Grandmother Gytha sent me her favourite amber ring? Thea removed it from her finger and laid it on the nearest birch tablet. She drew three letters from the casket.

Trembling with excitement, she arranged the letters in the order in which she would read them. First, there was a letter from Grandmother Gytha, folded and sealed with her dragon seal. Next there was a letter with a seal she did not recognise. She scrutinised it. The seal appeared to show a small trading vessel. *It is more modest than King Sweyn's seal*. Finally, there was a third letter sealed with a blob of yellow wax bearing the imprint of a coin, possibly a dirham, pressed into it. *Padar, it is his.*

She opened Gytha's letter first, unfolding it carefully. Laying it out on the table, she bent over it, anxious to hear her grandmother's voice speak to her. She read it slowly.

Thea, my granddaughter, by the Grace of God in this summer of 1071, I send you greetings. There is not much time left. What is time but a chimera marked with great happiness and much sorrow. My life has been long and I shall depart it content in the knowledge that you are soon to make a great marriage. You will conduct yourself honourably and enter your new life with pride and honour.

It was a surprise when one who links our past to our present arrived this summer at St Omer, after a long journey from the north. With great joy, I say that I am pleased that the skald has married at last, and with our own little golden Gudrun. May the Virgin look over them and bring them safely back to your lands.

Your mother, Elditha, resides comfortably in Canterbury. My daughter Edith and your sister Gunnhild are at Wilton. Godwin has decided to remain in Ireland until he regains his kingdom. He was betrayed by Sweyn who has now granted ships and support to the Aetheling Edgar. Sweyn is not to be trusted and, by the Norns, he will never get a portion of England. He has backed the wrong prince. May the sisters who weave our lives confound his fate. Edmund is a merchant princeling, I hear. That is well since he must earn a living.

As my life reaches the end of its spinning, my great sadness is that my youngest son Wulfoth and your little brother Ulf remain hostages in the Norman court at Falaise. May the saint of travellers, Christopher, protect them and bring them home safely to their own land.

I send you my blessing and my ring. Remember me in your prayers and in your thoughts. And, my child, I have a final request. Name your first male child Harold, for no other name will do for the grandson of my greatest son.

Gytha, Countess of Wessex

When she came to the end of Grandmother Gytha's letter, Thea's heart was heavy for she loved her grandmother. Swallowing her sobs, she laid out her second letter. Glancing through it she saw it was from her brother, Edmund.

My sister, may God protect you in the foreign land where you now dwell. I hope to travel to Rus lands in the springtime with Earl Connor who has lived some months since in Roskilde. We have wool for Constantinople and many objects of great value to sell in the Byzantine markets. I have another mission in Kiev of which, at this time, I may not speak but which we may discuss when we meet again.

Edmund, son of Harold, once King of the English

Outside darkness had gathered. Thea could hear voices carrying through the corridors and up the stairways of Holy Trinity. Soon the refectory bell would ring for the final meal of the day, a supper of bread, kvass and honey. She must hurry. She broke the small seal on Padar's letter. It had been scribed several days after Gytha had written to her.

The Norns have woven the end threads of Countess Gytha's life. She has gone to the angels some days since. She requested that I write to you after her death and that I send her letter to you. Both letters will travel with us to Denmark where we shall find one whom we can trust to carry them safely to the Convent of the Holy Trinity.

Your Aunt Hilda attended her mother's passing. The great Countess Gytha was buried here on Saturday with great ceremony. May her soul rest in peace.

At her request, I enclose her favourite silver ring. She asked me to say that other jewels will, in the fullness of time, travel to England as a dowry for your sister, Gunnhild.

The Countess Gytha of Wessex will dwell in our prayers and thoughts always. Perhaps it is reassuring that your Aunt Hilda has taken vows, as has the countess's dedicated companion,

Lady Margaret. They remain for what time on this earth is theirs, in the Abbey of St Omer.

Lady Thea, may I intrude on your sadness at these grave tidings with our news? It is a joy to us that Gudrun is with child. We shall return to the Rus lands in the spring. I shall establish new business interests in Kiev where I hope for Prince Vsevolod's goodwill and kindness.

May Christ and his Holy Angels protect you, my lady.

I remain your servant, Padar

Thea's heart felt as if a stone had lodged in it. She did not know how she could attend supper but she must. It was good news that Padar and Gudrun were safe and that her companion was with child and that soon they would travel to Kiev. They linked her past to her present and she had wondered if she would ever see either of them again.

She folded the letters back into the box, locked it and slipped the key onto the silver chain from which the cunning woman's tiny swan dropped between her breasts. She did not return the amber ring to the pine box. Instead, she slipped Gytha's ring into her jewel box. She placed the pine box amongst others that included the bone-plated casket which her mother had given her long ago and which contained the Godwin christening gown.

The air stilled. She felt a strange peace descend. She wiped away the tears that had gathered in her eyes. It felt as if Grandmother Gytha was in the chamber, flesh and bone, breathing life into everything around her. And it was as if Grandmother Gytha's spirit was hovering with her own, guiding her and protecting her. Plucking her sable-trimmed mantle from the clothing pole, she slipped it about her shoulders. Softly closing her chamber door, she descended the stairway to the refectory.

As Thea ate her supper that evening in the monastery's customary silence, half an ear tuned to the sister who was reading, she felt as if shaken by an imagined jolt; what was Edmund planning? Her grandmother was dead and her heart was breaking because of it, yet she could not speak of this here. She desperately wanted to connect with her past tonight. She could write a letter to Elditha. There was just a whisper of a chance that one day it would reach her. She would also send Gudrun her greetings and suggest that her dearest friend return to Russia in time for her wedding to Prince Vladimir in the Great Cathedral of St Sophia in Kiev.

By candlelight she scratched out her letters on birch wood. She wrote deep into the night until her fingers were too cold to write another word.

Her letter to Elditha was short. She scribed,

My Lady Mother, by the grace of the Lady Mary, Queen of Heaven, I pray that you are in good health and in a place of safety as surely the nunnery at Canterbury remains. I am to be married to Prince Vladimir of Kiev. If we have a son we shall call him Harold for my father. May God and his Holy Angels protect you and may the Holy Spirit be with you. Although our lives have separated as lightning splits a tree in a storm, you dwell forever in my heart.

Your loving daughter, Thea.

To Gudrun and Padar she wrote that she hoped they would reach Kiev by Eastertide. She laid down her stylus and felt her eyes gather tears. I wanted a prince and a home, Grandmother, but in truth my home was with you, she said softly, thinking that perhaps her grandmother's soul would catch hold of her words.

She knew that she would forever hold her grandmother's memory in her heart.

The candle had burned down to a stump. Daylight was a long way off yet and she could hear the bells ring for Matins. In the morning she would insist that before the winter ice gathered the abbey priest would send her letters by Dimitri's ship to their destination.

23

April 1072

Gudrun stood by Padar's shoulder, peering over the long narrow stretch of parchment he had pinned with stones onto the table. Below them, she could hear the clanking of pots, trestles dragged into place in the inn's common room and the distant babble of men and women speaking in various tongues: Russian, Slavic, Polish, German, Norse, English and French. A cradle nestled in the corner of their bedchamber where Edith, their baby, slept peacefully.

Edith was a happy baby, born in St Omer, and loved by all the women of the monastery, who had been delighted to see Padar again when he had trailed in through the abbey gates, exhausted from a long overland journey from Novgorod. The women of St Omer were even happier that he had married Gudrun and their happiness at Edith's birth was only marred by the Countess Gytha's death.

Gudrun and Padar set out one early spring day filled with scudding clouds and a good southerly wind. Their ship slowly lagged northwards hugging land as near as they dared until they reached a small port near Hamburg. There, their vessel turned south-east, sailing along the wide snaking Vistula River through Poland. A short overland journey brought them to Lublin where there was a great market where Padar hoped to purchase salt and alum. From Lublin they planned to travel overland to Kiev with four packhorses, a comfortable wagon, the faithful boys from Novgorod and a substantial guard of thirty Danes.

They would reach Kiev in time for the wedding, which they had heard from Katya's father would take place after Easter. Padar had unfolded this map, provided by Earl Connor, to help them find their way from Lublin east to the Russian capital. He tapped the section that showed Lublin to be a town with a fortress and a market, then sliding his finger down the parchment close to a small river and what seemed to Gudrun to be mountain slopes painted with scree. After that, the trail seemed to pass through miniature fields of rye and barley, into woodland and on towards Kiev, which was marked by the Church of St Sophia.

Gudrun scrutinised the map. Here and there churches were named in mysterious letters. Villages were marked but unnamed. Only groups of small houses and churches were witness to the existence of humankind. There were no great towns between Lublin and Kiev, not on this route. On the edges of the map the mapmaker had inked-in not only crows, ravens and hawks but also tall, thin-legged storks, deer, beavers, boar, a grey wolf and a lynx. Gudrun hoped they did not encounter danger. She prayed that wolves, lynxes and great boars stayed in the depths of the forests.

'How can this guide us?' she asked touching the parchment, a frown creasing her forehead above her nose, just below her veil. 'There is no sense of distance.'

'You are right. It is only a list to help us. Tomorrow I shall hire a guide in the Thursday market, one who speaks Norse and Rus.'

'One we can trust?' Gudrun asked with doubt creeping into her voice. She had heard from her maid that the region was full of bandits.

'That is a risk we take.' Padar rolled the scroll back into its long wooden case.

Footsteps clattered up the stairs. Their maid, Lette, moved the curtain aside. The scent of frying bacon competed with that of baking bread. She peeped in. 'My lady, Mistress Katerina has sent me for you and the master to come and eat dinner. I think it is pork meat again.'

'Go, Lette,' Gudrun said. 'We shall follow in a moment.'

Padar had found Lette in Lund, chained to others. She was a slave and he had purchased her, freeing the girl before they had set sail on the Vistula. Gudrun had insisted and knew that she was right to insist. Lette had been a devoted companion to her mistress, happy because she was travelling through lands she knew, since Lette had been born in a village not far from Lublin.

When they arrived in Lublin Gudrun asked her servant, 'Do you wish to return to your village? Have you people there?'

'No, mistress, no. Bandits killed my father. They took all the women and children from my village as slaves. May I stay?'

'I am glad to have you, Lette.' Gudrun hugged her maid and was relieved that she did not have to look for a new servant.

Padar tossed his satchel across his shoulder. 'Come, Gudrun.' He smiled at his wife. 'We have been fortunate here. Dinner smells good. And at least Mistress Katerina keeps a clean house. I have not been bitten by too many fleas.' He lifted the door latch. 'We have sacks of salt stored away for the journey, but after dinner, I have one last task or two before setting out for Kiev.'

'What task?'

'Just a trip to the market place, to purchase alum, and find us a trustworthy guide.'

'We shall all be pleased to reach Kiev, Padar.'

'And we are not far away now.' Padar let the latch fall again. He hugged her. She hugged him back. The baby gurgled. She unpeeled his arms. Swooping up the drowsy Edith, Gudrun tucked her into a linen sling which she arranged so the baby was nestling against her breast. When he lifted the latch again, she stepped after him down the stairs to the inn's common chamber, happy in the knowledge that they would soon be in Kiev.

Two days later their cavalcade had reached the borderlands between Poland and Russia. Lette called out, 'I see shadows up in the rocks above us, mistress. I don't like it.' She lowered her voice and said nervously, 'This pass is perfect for a bandit attack.'

Gudrun followed her maid's upward look. 'There is nothing there,' she said as she scanned the horizon. She had been enjoying her reverie. The baby was asleep and Gudrun was drowsily dreaming of a steamy bath, attended by a Turk – she could not bring herself to ever use the word slave – to scrape the dirt off her flea-ridden, dust-covered limbs. Lette was just overly nervous.

'There is, I tell you. And we are lost.'

One of Padar's boys, Bryn, was driving their wagon. He flicked his stick anxiously at the two mules yoked to it as their wagons rattled along a stony track that twisted along a river path. Gudrun shook her head. Lette was nervous and now Bryn, who liked the maid, was making her worse by whipping the mules forward. So far the map was helpful. And, just as the map had been, their guide had so far been reliable. They were not lost, just travelling through a desolate territory. She patted Lette's knee and said as much.

As she looked up again, Gudrun noticed how the rocky heights merged with the sky, becoming a mountain range that stretched far beyond the visible horizon.

'Really, there is nothing there, Lette. Only rocks and sky.'

The boy scanned the rocks. 'I see nothing.' He added, 'But that guide, mistress, up front with Padar …'

'What about him?'

'I don't trust him.'

Lette nodded. 'See, Bryn believes me.'

'It is not the guide's fault if there is someone up there,' Gudrun said, hoping she was right and the guide trustworthy.

Padar had ridden ahead with the guide. Around half of his fighting men rode with them. These swordsmen and archers had accompanied them from Denmark hoping to sell their skill at the court of Prince Vsevolod. They had weapons, seaxes, swords and shields. Padar knew most of them to be strong fighters who could dismount and throw up a formidable shield wall anywhere in most circumstances, but this was formidable territory, and he hoped as he rode with a fast-flowing river to his left that they were not in any danger here.

Padar glanced back past his mercenaries to see Gudrun seated beside Bryn chattering and holding Edith in her sling. His eyes scanned the wagon. It looked safe. It bumped along but the wheels were strong, important in terrain where the ground was rough and rutted. He glanced at Gudrun again. She was now staring at an outcrop of boulders. Lette too, appeared to be watching the mountains and pointing. Bryn flicked the mules with his whip. Their upward gaze made him feel uneasy. He, too, looked up as they continued forward. There was nothing untoward up above the ravine. Yet, the rocks above were without doubt concealing. They needed to get over the river soon, before darkness fell like a trap. They needed a ford.

'The ford?' he said to his guide.

'Not far, by sunset,' the man said.

'I hope that is so. It is the third hour already.'

'Soon, master.'

None the less, as he trotted along, keeping close to his guide, Padar was thinking, *I hope we get through this stretch safely and do ford that river soon*. His hand instinctively slid down to his scabbard and to his sword, Gabriel.

A rear guard led by Gunor, the same warrior who had come with them to Denmark from Flatholm, followed the wagon. Also following the wagon were their five pack animals laden with sacks of precious salt and alum destined for Kiev's marketplace. The final half-dozen Danes rode at the rear.

Padar trotted back a little to check that the baggage train was secure, hoping now that the sacks were not leaking as the mules bumped along the rocky path. He nodded to Gunor. Gunor raised his hand to acknowledge Padar as he rode by. Padar thought that nothing looked amiss.

'There is no one there,' Gudrun said to Lette a little later, as she shaded her eyes again and scanned the rocks above. 'Do you see any creature or person, Gunor?' she remarked to the Dane who

231

had ridden up on her left.

Gunor edged his mount forward in front of the wagon and scrutinised the heights above. Stepping his stallion back, he said quietly, 'No, but it feels too silent. I don't like it. There isn't even birdsong.'

'There's a bird.' The boy jerked his reins. As he looked up, one of the mules neighed. Two long, lean Danish hounds, guard dogs, that always stayed close, raced in front of Gunor, and set up their barking. A hawk had taken wing and was careering across the sky just above them. It circled, dipped into the scree-covered foothills, then rose again and disappeared behind a rocky outcrop.

'I shall send one of the men forward to warn Padar,' Gunor said, his hand already on his sword hilt. 'The dogs sensed something other than a hawk. Could be shepherds.'

Lette said, anxiety creeping into her voice. 'If they were only shepherds they would show themselves.'

'Maybe, they are frightened of *us*. We are well-armed. Mutton for dinner would be very tasty,' Gunor said with a grin on his face. 'Don't you think so, little Lette?' he teased.

'No.' Lette looked away. Gunor rode forward for a while.

As they travelled on, trying to gather speed, the third hour after midday became the fourth, then the fifth and the sun grew lower in the sky; the rushing river raced close by on the one side and the mountains climbed towards the sky on the other. There was no sign of a ford.

Padar sent a message back that they must strike camp by twilight, but no one wanted to be trapped here between the river and the mountains. As the sky darkened, an inexplicable sense of unease began to travel down their line as fast as fire streaking through forest clearings. Padar sent scouts ahead to find a ford. They returned saying that there was no safe place to cross the gushing river. When he asked the guide, the man shrugged and pointed on along the track. 'Soon, soon,' was all he said, as he, too, appeared to watch the rocky scree as it stretched above.

The cavalcade moved forward methodically and silent. A

rider appeared up above on the scree and vanished. More appeared and they disappeared too. These others were armed with bows. Gudrun passed Edith over to Lette. 'Those are no shepherds. Take Baby Edith behind and stay out of sight. I can fire arrows if need be. Padar's second bow and sheaf is behind the kettles. Get it and place it right behind me within my reach.' Lette hesitated. 'Go, do it, do it. Edith is asleep. Put her in the cradle and stay with her,' she found herself hissing at Lette.

Bryn twisted around, jerking the reins again. 'I can fire an arrow too, mistress.'

Gudrun considered that it was very likely and maybe this boy had a better aim than she. He had come to Novgorod with his father after the Great Battle. Rhys, his father, rode up front with Padar. 'I am sure you can, Bryn,' she said, thinking that there were more bows and arrows on their pack horses. If they were attacked they could hold firm. She was sure they could. 'You can have your own bow. If we need them, Bryn, we can get more weapons from the pack ponies.'

Just after Lette had scrambled back into the wagon bed with the sleeping baby, Gudrun heard the soft thump of Padar's bow being placed behind her. Reaching behind, she felt it reassuringly leaning against the wagon's frame just behind her back. She glanced forward and saw Padar turning his horse back towards them. 'Hold steady, Bryn. Padar is coming back. He has seen something.'

Gunor rode forward to meet Padar. 'I have a bad feeling here. There is someone stalking us, more than one I am sure. I have seen weapons glinting up there, just a ghost of a glint in the lowering sun but lots of glints, flashing about the scree. And I sense something.' He pointed towards the furry-hatted guide. 'I have a bad feeling about that guide too.'

'Best we are prepared.' Padar swept his hand across his forehead. 'Warn the men we may have to fight. Distribute arms. You, Gunor, stay close to the wagon. Give Gudrun bows from the packs and give her as many arrows as you can. She can pass them forward should we have to stop and make a shield wall between the wagon and them.'

Padar looked behind from the riverbank to the lower boulders that marked the end of the track. There was maybe enough room for the pack animals there if they stopped now. They could have some advantage of a widened battle ground if their assailants' mounts swept down from above. *It depended on how many there were.* 'We may have to make a stand and shoot up at them. They have horses. Maybe we can fire arrows at their mounts' forelegs as they descend, if they *do* come down. They may hope we will ride further into a narrower place before they attack. They might not expect us to just stop and fight if we are outnumbered.' He looked along to where the guide was riding ahead as if there were no danger. 'There is no ford anywhere near either. And that guide is useless.'

He leaned across Gunor to Gudrun, whose face had drained of colour. She had paled with fear. 'Do not fear, lady wife, guard the bows Gunor gives you. Swords too, though I had hoped to sell those Frankish bastard swords, not put them to use first.' He circled his horse closer to the wagon, leaned down and kissed Gudrun's head. 'I shall not allow harm to come to us. You and I shall share a soft loving bed this night.' He shaded his forehead as he surveyed the river. 'On the Rus side.'

'I hope you are right,' Gudrun replied, concern creeping into her voice.

Padar rode further down the line to warn his mercenaries and organise the distribution of weaponry. They stopped briefly, organised a chain and unpacked spare bows and arrows. Finally he untied two bundles of precious Frankish swords. Soon, most of their spare weapons had been stowed in the back of the long wagon.

When Padar returned to her, Gudrun noted that this time he had his bow slung across his breast. His sword, Gabriel, hung from his sword belt in its leather scabbard. It was small comfort. They both glanced up. At the same moment they saw a banner with a crow depicted on it, black on crimson, rise above boulders on the hillside. Of one accord their mercenaries looked

234

towards it too and turning in their saddles set their bows. An arrow streaked from the outcrop of rocks and thunked into the wagon's cover.

The guide rode back to the wagon. He pulled his horse up short. 'Master, they will want your salt. That is all.'

'Go to hell with that,' Padar said to the guide and shouted up to the rocks, 'Show yourselves. We wish you no harm. You go on your way. We go ours. We have nothing of worth. We are pilgrims travelling to the Church of St Sophia in Kiev.' He turned to the guide again. 'Translate that if you can.' The guide cupped his hands around his mouth and called up in a Slavic tongue.

An answer echoed down the mountainside. The guide repeated, 'They do not believe you. They want your salt.'

'How do they know we have salt?' Padar scrutinised the guide's face. 'How could they know that?'

Lette stuck her head through the wagon's opening, looked up at Padar and said, 'They are slavers and thieves, that is why. The brigands that live in clans in these mountains trade with the Steppe Khans. They will take our goods and kill us all. They raid villages. Don't believe them or him. He is one of them.' She pointed at the guide. The guide kicked his horse towards the wagon and raised his hand. Padar drew Gabrielle from his scabbard, swiped the guide's hand away and hit the rump of his horse with the flat of his sword. 'Be off. Get up front.'

When the guide cantered off, his face thunderous, Padar said to Lette, 'They will not take our goods, nor will they take us. Not today,' Padar said firmly, his voice as grim as the banner that was winding its way down towards them.

Lette's words petrified Gudrun. When the mountain men appeared on the scree brandishing their crow banner, Gudrun stared at them with grim fascination as well as terror. Their ponies were scrawny, the sort that could scramble up rock walls like goats. They were dressed in animal skins and just a little chain mail. Their metal helmets had elk horns protruding from them and they carried bows and arrow quivers. A cold hand clutched at her heart and she immediately reached back for Padar's second bow.

Padar shouted to his guards and the boys seated on the mules, 'Off the horses and keep them hobbled together close to the wagon. We stop here.' He looked ahead for the guide but the traitor had melted away. He called along the line, 'Get the boys to deal with the horses. Close up ranks to give them protection.' The boys hobbled packhorses and stallions and roped them together and sent them between the wagon and the water. They unhitched the wagon mules in case they bolted. It was all done within moments.

This action came not a moment too soon. Facing the hillside, a dozen Danes ran in front of the wagon and immediately drew into formation, shields locking to make a protective shield wall. They had spears and axes.

Gudrun felt sweat trickle between her shoulderblades. Padar rode over to them again and said to Bryn, 'Boy, you will become a man this day. Protect the women. Stay in front of them. If need be, get them under the wagon.' Padar pulled a short sword from his belt and gave it to the boy. 'Take this but use a bow first if you can.'

Not waiting for a reply from the boy he ordered the rest of his mercenaries to form a second shield wall under Gunor's command. Now there was a tortoise of warriors, shields locked, three men deep, protecting the wagon and a huddle of pack animals roped together on the river bank.

Padar's strategy had not come too soon. The clatter of around two dozen armed men descending down the scree grew louder and closer, the noise growing thunderous as they reached the lower slope. Gudrun looked towards the river. Their pack animals were twitching beyond the wagon. As the descending noise of the horsemen grew greater, the horses began neighing. From the corner of her eye, she saw that it was all the lads could do to contain them. If an arrow flew over the wagon and caught one, the rest might try to bolt into the thunderous river. The two barking dogs bolted to hide underneath the wagon. Gudrun sent a prayer to the Virgin.

She glanced back trying to see Lette and her baby. 'Hide the cradle behind those bolts of cloth,' she called to her servant, trying to keep her voice firm, trying hard not to betray her terror, and she knew well from her experience after the Great Battle of 1066 that terror was a dangerous thing that would grip you like the plague if it was not reined in. She must retain her wits if they were to have a chance of survival.

A host of arrows now flew towards them. Every other man in the shield wall lifted his shield higher to deflect the onslaught. Those at the back hurled spears. Gudrun set an arrow into her bow ready to fire over the shield wall. She rose up above the boy at her side. She pulled back the string and allowed her arrow to fly. It soared over the top of the shield wall, over Padar whom she knew was, by now, in the thick of it. Her arrow soared straight and flew true into the face of one of the bandit leaders, a man with a helmet that had elk horns. She had aimed between his nose piece and the helmet's side guards, and it was an aim that was so true that her arrow gripped his face just below his eyes. He sat still. Slowly, very slowly he swayed to one side. Next he was dropping off his horse and she saw another chance. Setting her arrow into her bow again, she fired towards the horse. The horse went down, falling on top of its rider. A cheer went up from the tightly massed guard in their shield wall.

The brigands leapt off their horses and with a slap on their rumps sent their animals up the track with three of their servants to guard them. These guards drew the animals away from a volley of arrow fire that came from two Danes positioned at the flanks of the shield wall.

Both sides were now on foot and the battle began in earnest. The bandits attempted to push into the shield wall but every time they drew back, one of the Danes threw a spear at one of the assailants. Normally a shield wall would never open but Padar considered it necessary as long as his warriors were quick. He passed the word to Gunor who commanded the front line. Only every other man could leave the shield wall and only one at a time and only when Gunor ordered. The men were quick, the shield wall snapping open, closing over again just another crack to allow a Danish warrior to race back within its links. Two of their Danes fell in that first sortie. They missed the return opening in the shield wall.

Gudrun did not rise to shoot again. Bryn seized their bow, set an arrow and fired. She could not see where his arrow had landed. A heart-beat later, an arrow was returned. It soared above the shield wall, arched high and as if descending from the sky far above, fell and hit its mark. It caught Bryn on the shoulder. Bryn screamed and fell, almost capsizing the wagon. The wagon shook precariously. Gudrun could not hold on. She found herself falling out into the midst of the restless mounts that were neighing and jumping about on the river bank beyond the wagon. Stunned by her fall, avoiding their mules' kicks, she managed to crawl away from their hoofs and beneath the creaking wagon to where the dogs were cowering. She saw the running legs of the boys who were moving sacks of salt and alum under the wagon.

Gudrun needed to get into the wagon again but she had no strength. All around her there was deafening sound: the horses neighing and stamping, the boys shouting as they tried to calm them, the hammering of swords on shields followed by orders barked by Padar as his men moved forward as a mass. The brief sorties out from the shield wall were accompanied by the jeers and shouts of the enemy. And as all was amplified by the mountain range, the great clamour reverberated back as if it were a huge battle and not a skirmish. Would it soon be over? Were they going to die here? They would never see Kiev.

From the shelter of the wagon wheel, Gudrun tried to concentrate on the prancing horse legs and the moving legs of the Danes in front of her as they raced forwards and backwards like a wave breaking and then retreating on the shore. *She must try to climb back onto the wagon seat.* She then heard Lette. She was saying something like, 'Bite down, I must get the arrow out. Be still. Help me.' And above the shouts and roars of battle, Gudrun heard Edith's piercing cries. She had to get to Edith.

Another sack thumped down close to her. The two dogs sheltering below the wagon began to growl. She saw a boy fall as he tried to get back down the bank to the horses. She saw a second boy go down as he came to help his companion. Then, she saw the boots and a bearskin mantle belonging to a brigand flit past her hiding place. He must have sneaked around the shield wall.

She tried to grasp the wagon wheel, intending to pull herself up into the wagon, to get to the bow and shoot down at the bear-man who had attacked the boys, but she had banged her right side when she had fallen and any movement was painful. *I won't be shooting that bow again.* She gritted her teeth and hauled herself up until she was leaning against the wheel. This left her exposed. She felt for the seax in her belt. Withdrawing it she peered around the wagon and seeing the way clear she tried to climb onto the seat again.

She paused to catch her breath. At a glance she could see that the bastards meant to break the Danes' shield wall and force Padar's warriors into hand-to-hand combat. Her momentary delayed climb to safety was deadly. She felt a grip on her shoulder. Twisting to one side, she found herself looking at one of their attackers who looked back at her from under his horned helmet with cold black eyes. It was the bear-man. He growled incomprehensibly and seized her. With a knife in her side and a huge hand covering her mouth, he gripped her tightly and forced her back behind the horses. She bit down hard on his hand. She could taste blood. He swiped at her face with his free hand, growled a curse again and held her so tightly that she could not move at all.

Padar ducked in and out from the interlocked shields. He was small and he was fast. There had been no time to pull out his chain mail. He ran to the shield wall's front line, positioning himself on its left. He whispered a prayer to the Lady Mary, not that he was religious, and said a few words to the fates, the Norse Norns, not that he really believed in them either. But, when a man is fighting for his pack's survival, and, even more importantly, that of his own family, any help is worth a call upon.

He commanded the left flank. Gunor commanded the centre and another daring Dane, aptly called Beowulf, led the right. The wall had been, as the skirmish opened, three men deep and nine men long curving round on the flanks to protect their horses, the salt packs and importantly the long wagon with his wife, child and their maid. They were not three men deep now. Padar ordered his men to lock the shields and hold fast, to push forward as one. The ground was slippery with blood and guts and littered with dying and wounded. The horse Gudrun had shot with her arrow had stopped writhing and snorting. A brigand had put it out of its agony by slitting its throat but the battle raged around it. The man pinned beneath the animal and its blood added to the growing viscous mass of guts and fluid they felt underfoot.

The stench of the dying, the acrid smell of blood, and the unrelenting noise, the screams, the javelins thrusting into their shield wall and the clanging of seaxes against shields was overpowering. Twilight was falling. Padar knew that the fight must be over before the night slipped in, making their shield wall even more difficult to hold, and the possibility of enemy reinforcements tearing down the hillside, swooping in, destroying them all. They had been fighting for more than a notch of the hour candle already and these barbarians were more than a match for his men. Their curving swords and speed could win the next hour for the enemy – unless they could outwit the bastards.

Gunor recreated the shield wall two feet deep. Padar thought quickly. There was no room in the pass to fight on horseback. The shield wall, inadequate as it was, gave them one advantage. They held a greater stretch of ground. Padar allowed himself to glance over his shoulder beyond the wagon towards their horses. He could just see his stallion, Greyflank, back from the wagon, his tail flicking, his hoofs pawing the soil. He edged his way along their line behind his fighters, tapping four men with his short seax as, fast and light of foot he wove his way behind the first of two lines. 'You, you, you and you, move back there with me. I shall explain in a moment. Just follow.' Then he said, 'And the rest of you hold the wall!'

They doubled back through the second shield line. These men were accurate bowmen and able riders. If they could get up into the scree and behind the rock outcrop behind the enemy they could have the advantage of height. Padar gave this thought for a moment. The brigands could see them move as they exited their shield wall's protection. It must be done with speed. The crow-men's ponies were tethered up river where they were guarded. These animals were necessary for their enemy's exit from the ravine but if they could capture four of those ponies Padar's chosen warriors would climb faster up the steep mountain side. He thought quickly. If they were spotted the mountain ponies would give them the advantage of height. 'Can you ride and shoot at the same time?' he whispered to his companions. They nodded. He explained his strategy.

24

The bandit who held Gudrun's arms in a tight grip began to kick her forward. She had no option but to move or die. He was half-dragging, half-shoving her past the horses when, as if struck by a thunderbolt, he dropped to the ground. She was pinned beneath him, his mail digging painfully into her stomach. Ignoring pain, she elbowed, pushed and shoved and dragged herself from under his dead weight. She twisted around. Padar was pulling a bloodied Gabriel from the brigand's back.

He had freed his weapon, placed a finger to his lips and dragged her to her feet. She wanted to scream in agony but she dared not. 'Gudrun, thank Thor and Jesus both that I was coming towards the wagon. What by Freya are you doing here?' He saw her white, shocked countenance and held her to his breast for a breath or two, comforting her. 'Never mind, explanation later,' he whispered. 'Are you hurt?'

Gudrun shook her head and winced. She lied, 'Not that much.'

'Brave lass. Run for the wagon and stay there. When you get there, you must distribute arrows and fresh bows to the men at the back of the shield wall. Tell them to fire when they see us firing down from up there.' Padar pointed above.

'But how –'

'No matter how or why. Run.'

Ignoring her aching shoulder for a second time, Gudrun doubled over low and, half-running, half-hobbling, covered the few lengths it took to reach the wagon. Gulping for air, she worked her way behind the shrinking shield wall. She gabbled out Padar's strategy as she scuttled along ignoring her pained shoulder. The men nodded, passed the message down their line and locked shields again. An intake of breath and Beowulf had hoisted her back up onto the wagon. She crawled under the cover. The baby wailed.

Edith must wait. Edith is alive, she told herself. 'Lette, I must give them the spare bows,' she said as she crawled back along the wagon bed.

Lette was holding Bryn's head. He was moaning. Lette said, 'Can't you stop Edith's crying, mistress?'

'No, she can wait.'

Without going to her crying child, Gudrun began searching for the bows and arrows, frantically moving forward and reaching them down. She could hear the banging of shields, the cries, the clash of swords and curses, the shield wall opening and closing. As she worked, she prayed. *Please, Lady Mary. Keep him safe.*

Her baby was still screaming in the back of the wagon. Lette was using Edith's swaddling bands to staunch the boy's blood. The air tasted of death. Gudrun gulped for air as she came out from under the wagon cover. When she crawled back inside again, Lette had finished binding up the youth's wound and was rocking back on her heels. Just for a moment she rubbed her forehead and eased her back. As the frightened, hobbled mules tried to jerk forward, the wagon rocked and swayed.

'Let me do that. You must see to Edith,' Lette said, reaching for a bow. She began moving bows and arrows forwards. Two Danes climbed into the wagon, stood on its platform and used the advantage of their raised position to fire high, tilting their bows upwards so their arrows flew over the shield wall. Lette glanced down at the Welsh boy. 'If we don't die here, he could live.'

'You think so, Lette?' Gudrun said. She watched the youth's blood pool as it flowed from the bandage, whispered a prayer over him, pulled a small cross from about her neck and laid it on his breast. She placed an ear to his heart. 'He is fading, Lette. May the saints protect him.'

She looked into the little barricade of wool packs to where baby Edith was attempting to pull herself from her crib. 'Thank the angels she has not yet mastered that,' Lette said, looking down on the baby for a short moment, having seized the last sheaf of arrows.

Gudrun snatched Edith from her crib and rocked her. She gave Edith suck. The baby quietened.

Padar stumbled over someone, and glancing down saw the bodies of two of his boys behind the wagon. Their throats had been cut. He gently closed their eyes. Anger mingled with fear and boiled up inside him. Those boys had come all the way with him from Novgorod. But there was no time now. They had to move quickly. He must use cunning now to save the others. 'Let's go,' he said to his companions, his voice hoarse with emotion. 'We can do nothing for them.'

Padar and his men took a circuitous route down by the river beyond their horses. Like worms they crawled on their bellies along the river bank until they knew they could race over to the scree and grab five of the ponies guarded by the brigands' sentries. The guards were armed with vicious, long, curving blades.

'When I make a crow's caw, take them down,' Padar whispered, rising onto his knees. 'Irony it is indeed, by Odin's breath.' He glanced momentarily at the dark crow banner that still flew amongst their assailants. He jabbed each of his men in turn on their shoulders. 'You, you and you take each of the guards. Stop them shouting out. Move quick as wolves swooping on the sheep pen. All our lives depend on you three. Brian and I will let the ponies loose.' He pointed up to the rocks above. 'Ride up behind those rocks and pick off any of those bastards that try to climb after us.'

The men nodded.

At Padar's caw they ran one by one, keeping low, knowing they had the advantage of surprise as they each marked a guard. Padar and Brian crossed last. A breath later, Padar was sliding amongst the ponies whispering to them, a trick he had known from long ago. 'Just as religion can stun humans, I can soothe these creatures with poetry,' he laughed softly to himself. He whispered again into the ponies' ears, 'Now really, enough is enough. We don't want you lovelies too drowsy to climb those hills.' He loosened four of the animals and glanced through their legs. To his satisfaction, the guards were on the ground with their throats silently slit. *Revenge for my boys.* His men dragged them into a heap. Padar nodded his approval praying to both Freya and the Virgin that no one would glance down river from the battle and notice those guards gone. 'I could send the rest of these ponies on their way, liberate the creatures,' he said to Brian, as he mounted his pony. 'But that would cause too much unwanted attention. The animals might just thwart me and bolt. Here, take these two.'

The Danes stayed low against the ponies' backs. Stealthily, they climbed up into the rocks. 'Here,' Padar said, once they were above the battle. 'Come off the beasts. When I say "bows", set your arrows. And do not shoot our own men. Gudrun will have warned them to get behind the shields.'

From above the battle looked different. No one was running out from behind the shield wall now. He could see the barbarians pushing into it, trying to break it open, to burst it into two halves. It held firm. 'Bows,' he whispered and raised his bow, letting loose an arrow.

All at once the others fired down. Each Dane marked a different horn-helmeted man. Five of the attackers fell forward onto the shield wall. The Danes left in the shield wall sliced out at them with their swords and pushed them off with their shields. The surviving barbarians turned towards the hill. They set arrows and fired up but fell short of their mark. They were not the only warriors now shooting up. From behind the first line of their shield wall his men were shooting at the enemy. They were not as accurate as Padar and his four companions. Yet, they confused the barbarians since arrows were flying at them from all directions. For a moment the hissing of arrow fire paused and everything went silent. Padar whistled his crow's caw. His men set arrows once again and fired. An answering volley flew over the shield wall below. The same happened again and again. They were winning now. Just as it seemed to Padar that it would be easy for the men remaining below in the shield wall to finish off the job below, one of the barbarian leaders pointed up towards him.

'Get the ponies.' Padar spat his words. 'We can draw those bastards off. Once they go for their mounts to follow us they will get a surprise.'

'Should we have let the rest of their ponies go loose, Padar?' Brian whispered.

'Their ponies are as dopey as men in a brothel after a skinful of wine.' Padar watched the group of bandits run for their mounts. 'If they try to come up, we'll pick them off as we lead them along the scree.' Some of the Danes positioned below set arrows and fired but this time they only took down two of the men racing towards the horses, stragglers, since the others had darted out of reach.

The brigands clambered on their mounts and Padar thought they would head up to where he was positioned, but he had miscalculated. The bandits, some clearly wounded, galloped off down the river path, vanished around a bend and out of sight. Padar said, 'Wait here. Keep alert. They may have another way up behind us. Those animals are not as sleepy as I thought. I shall scout.'

He threw himself over a pony. Leaving his men with the others, he rode along the cliff top, scanning the river path for the crow men who had simply vanished. He looked back at the killing ground around the wagon. Survivors had begun to walk amongst the dead. There was no time to bury their own dead. They must get to a fording place before the crow men returned with reinforcements to finish off what they had begun. He tugged his horse's mane, turned its head and waved his men down the scree slope.

Rocking unsteadily on the stolen ponies, the Danes jogged down from the heights. Padar dismounted. Gudrun tumbled down from the wagon, hobbled to him and threw her arms around him. 'Oh, my love,' was all he could say. 'Leave their dead crows to the crows.' He glanced up at the sky. A horned moon was rising and darkness was falling. 'Is Edith safe?' he asked, anxiety seeping into those three bald words.

Gudrun nodded.

'We put our wounded on horses. We move on. There is no time to bury our dead, so we take them with us.' He turned to Gunor. 'How many are lost?'

'We have lost a half-dozen. We have a half-dozen wounded who will live.'

'Where is the guide?' Padar said looking around.

'Where, indeed? He ran for cover the moment the fighting started. They took him with them when they fled.' Gunor spat onto the earth.

'Good riddance. Someone knew we were coming when those crows attacked. We will find our way out of here without him. Send Beowulf and four others ahead. If we have to, we ride through the night. No matter how tired we are, we move on as quickly as we dare.' He added bitterly, 'We still have salt for the Kiev market.' He laughed a cynical laugh. 'And poor compensation it is for the loss of our companions!' He pointed at a tattered bloody pennant that lay on the ground. 'Take what is left of that. It is proof of their attack. Crows indeed! We out-crowed them. Pass water and bread around. Then move.' Padar looked up at the wagon, remembering that he had not seen Bryn. 'Where is the Welsh boy?'

'We could not save him. He died in Lette's arms. His father died in the shield wall.' Gudrun crossed herself. Padar saw tears in her eyes. He took her in his arms, tears smarting his own. He swallowed. 'Can you ride? And Lette, can she ride too?'

She nodded. 'Yes, I think so, and I can strap Edith across my breast.'

'Then we shall take their corpses with us in the wagon for burial.'

The scouts returned. The bandit group could have gone through a cave they had discovered some two leagues ahead. They had searched the cave but all they could see was a tunnel into the mountain. The bandits had vanished just as surely as the sun had descended below the earth.

'We shall follow that path with great caution,' Padar said to Beowulf and turned to Gunor. 'The women will ride the ponies. Wounded and dead in the wagon, hurry. You and Beowulf must guard the women.'

'With my life,' Gunor said, wiping the sweat from his forehead. 'Bran, Elf,' he called. The two hounds slipped out from under the wagon where they had been cowering during the battle. They licked Gunor's outstretched palm. 'They survived, Padar.'

'I would those three boys had survived too, never mind all the others who have died today,' Padar answered him.

Glad to leave the killing place behind, the remnants of Padar's cavalcade mounted their ponies and formed into a sad, nervous cortege. With cracking whips and rumbling wheels they moved off under the light of the horned moon and rode east. Before daybreak, the diminished band of travellers splashed across the river where it became wider and shallower. As they rode across the plains on the other side they avoided smoking villages that lay close to the river. As the sun swelled high in a pale sky they entered woods and rode on until, at last, Padar thought it was safe to stop, eat, rest and tend to their wounded. 'We were not the crow men's only targets but if we are not far from Kiev,' he said wryly, thinking of the ruined villages back by the riverbank, 'we should be safe.'

25

Kiev, May 1072

In April Thea removed from the Convent of St Trinity to
Novgorod where she was welcomed by Prince Vsevolod in the
terem's great hall. He told her that she was to travel to Kiev for
the translation of the two Russian saints, Boris and Gleb.
Shortly after that she would marry Prince Vladimir in the
Cathedral of St Sophia. During this meeting with Prince
Vsevolod, Thea kept her eyes lowered. She was determined to
impress him with her demeanour and her improved Russian.
She clearly succeeded, for he smiled upon her and spoke to her
in a voice softened with kindness.

A week later Princess Anya, her ladies and guards travelled
with Thea and Katya south towards Kiev. A fortnight later they
entered the great city fortress through the Lion's Gate.

Prince Vsevolod's palace in Kiev surpassed Thea's
expectations. She had never seen such extravagant, brightly
coloured hangings and so many glass windows inside a building
not a church. The rooms were filled with carved tables, chairs,
cushions. On chill April evenings warmth circulated the
chambers from corner stoves. Pipes climbed the walls and fed
into chimneys.

She stepped through an ornate doorway into Prince
Vsevolod's public room. It was grander, though not larger, than
the halls she was used to, and it was, without doubt, more
beautiful to behold than the halls belonging to King Sweyn. It
was, by far, more impressive than the hall in the Novgorod
kremlin. Mosaics covered the floors instead of rushes, and
Turkish carpets lay casually around on which to place her
slippered feet, so thick that she thought she could sit on them.

The prince swept forward to greet her, in his long fur-trimmed robe. He informed her during their short audience that Mother Sophia had confided in him that she was delighted with Thea's progress. He told her, still grasping her hands, that he was pleased that she could speak in complicated sentences and could also write Rus words on birch tablets. Mother Sophia reported that her knowledge of the Faith was excellent. She said that Thea carried herself proudly but discreetly. The English princess would indeed make a suitable wife for Prince Vladimir. Vsevolod allowed Thea's hands to drop, clapped his big hands together and announced that he was happy to bring her into the heart of the family.

What went unsaid was that he expected her to produce his son's heir. She knew that this was even more important here in Russia than anywhere else she had dwelled. According to Katya, women could be divorced if they were barren. She felt the prince studying her, his eyes appraising her, ravishing her flat belly, dwelling momentarily on her shapely hips, and so, remembering Katya's words, Thea suspected that was what he thought. She felt angry. It felt as if she were a brood mare and not a woman and certainly not as if she was an important English princess. She thought of her grandmother and how independent she had been. Her grandmother would never have been divorced by her grandfather, though he might have had sons by others had Grandmother not given him sons. Grandmother would still have been her grandfather's beloved wife and head of her household. Thea held her head high and matched Prince Vsevolod's appraising look with an icy stare. He had the grace to look away, though for a moment she wondered if she had made an enemy of her husband's father. Then he surprised her. 'You are a proud princess. That is good.' She waited and then without smiling slightly inclined her head. They had taught her well and she would match their chilly demeanour with equal frost. Frost for frost. Ice for ice. Pride for pride.

After the interview with Prince Vsevolod, Princess Anya sat companionably beside Thea on a long divan covered with rich cloth and littered with many silk cushions. Princess Anya told her that the family had chosen an auspicious day for her wedding. Mother Sophia had calculated the perfect date in accordance with the phases of the moon and Thea's menstrual period. The day chosen was to be a Friday which would be the first of the three days for the wedding ceremony. The Friday chosen was three weeks after the Easter canonisation of St Dimitri in the Kiev cathedral. Three was a fortunate number, one of religious significance. Princess Anya put on her most serious face and said firmly that although the prince and princess would be bedded on the first night, they must not consummate their union until the third.

'It is so much to remember,' Thea said feeling overwhelmed. 'Is all this necessary? I prefer a simpler wedding.'

'That is not our way, my dear. I must describe the ceremonies to you so that you make no mistakes,' she said.

Thea sighed. This was not going to be enjoyable. She had waited so long for her betrothal to end. She thought of the joyful weddings she had participated in when she had been younger. There had been flowers and a simple exchange of vows, sometimes with a priest present and sometimes not, and then a great feast with dancing and lots of mead and honeyed wine. She could not bear this. *I wish I was back in England with Elditha and grandmother and my sister and brothers. I wish I was marrying a thane and not a prince of a land stuffed full of stupid ceremony.* She found her mind drifting back to what seemed to her now sun-filled days with the scent of hay. She hardly heard what Anya was saying.

'First, is your rushnyk ready as you will kneel upon it there before the Iconostasis in St Sophia?' Anya, pregnant for the third time, folded her hands below her swelling stomach.

'Yes, it is.'

'That is good, Thea. And we have chosen your maidens.' *They have even chosen my bridesmaids. Let them. It can't get much worse. If only Gudrun were here.* Then she remembered …

253

'The stories!' Thea exclaimed excitedly. Her face fell. 'There is no Padar to judge them.' She had heard nothing further of Padar and Gudrun, not since her letters.

'I have chosen for him.' Princess Anya poured them a cup of kvass each.

She found herself smiling. Her lip curled. She had her own story ready for her prince, safely hidden away in her coffer. She took the cup from Princess Anya and sipped. She liked this Russian drink. In fact, she liked much about Russia, except for the fact that women were overly protected and she could not make her own decisions.

'Padar may be back in time for my wedding.' Thea spoke her wishful thought aloud.

'I hope so, Thea, but that would be too late. We had to decide on which girls must be your maidens without him.'

'So who are to be my maids?'

Anya folded her arms, her elegant silk sleeves trailing onto the carpet.

'Go on,' Thea said calmly though she did not feel peace in her heart.

Anya touched her lower lip with an elegantly ringed finger. 'Well now, let us see. Vera, Kalina, Vira, and Julia. I think we must include Katya. She has been your companion and her father stands high in my husband's estimation.'

Thea nodded. 'I like these girls well enough. May I hear the stories?' At least she was to have Katya.

'You will have a maidens' party. They will bathe you and prepare you for your wedding on the following day. On the night of your maidens' celebration we shall hear the stories. What do you think?' Anya said, smiling. She turned to face Thea and embraced her, folding her affectionately into the wide, trailing silken sleeves. She held Thea back. Thea could not return her warmth. She felt all this was happening to a puppet princess. She was not really present and Anya did not even notice it. 'The wedding is on the seventeenth day of May, the day selected by Mother Sophia,' Anya was saying. 'This is only fourteen nights away.' She released Thea and clapped her hands. 'And, the family has a gift for you and Vladimir, one you shall know first.'

'A gift?' *What could it be, another birthing stool?*

As Anya nodded, her eyes widened. 'Thea, you are to have your own house here in Kiev, not as grand a palace as this, but it is an elegant two-storeyed house with two wings, a tiled roof, rooms with glass windows or, at least windows of isinglass.' Thea came alive again, the puppet princess banished. She would have somewhere of her own, a home of her own. 'You can see the river with all its boats from all four tall windows. There are two courtyards, herb and fruit gardens and a small apple orchard. It has an encircling wall and do not worry ever. Even though Kiev can be dangerous, guards will be alert for trouble. You do not ever need to venture into the city streets.' *Ah, Thea thought. We shall see.* 'You will have a large part of the house for your terem and a new chapel for your own use.' Anya reached out and excitedly clasped Thea's hands. 'It is called the Chapel of St Theodora and it has been consecrated already. You will move into it soon so that you and Vladimir do not share the same palace before the ceremony. I shall stay with you to help you prepare.'

Thea said politely, 'It is more than I had wished for. I thought I would still share your terem here in the palace.'

'I think you will prefer to have your own household. Russian noblewomen organise the whole house. They travel around their castles and estates making sure everything is just so. By now, you must recognise that it is pleasanter for us to entertain guests in the terem and not to mingle with men at their feasting. Some foreign noblewomen find this strange, but it is a gentler way, I think.'

'I shall manage my household efficiently,' Thea said firmly, knowing that she was not convinced that she could ever enjoy confinement in a terem. She remembered the saints' days' feasts the women and children attended at her uncles' court at Westminster when she had been a child. She reflected wistfully on the jugglers, the harpists, the storytellers, the great central hearth and the sound of male voices singing. Pushing the memory away, she bit her lip and asked, 'Is Lady Olga to attend my wedding?'

'Yes, my dear, she must. Her husband is my husband's steward. Lady Olga is very important here and, although you may wish it otherwise, she will help you prepare for the wedding.'

Thea felt herself tense. Raising her head proudly, she rose from her cushions and stretched to her full height. 'Lady Olga treated Gudrun cruelly. I cannot forgive her.'

'Sit, Thea, such an outburst does not become you. Life can be unfair. I understand your frustration but you must swallow your pride. Let the past be the past. After your wedding you need not see Lady Olga unless she decides to visit you. You can choose your own servants. When the skald returns, you will see Gudrun once again. Do not allow Olga to spoil your wedding.' Anya poured another cup of cherry wine and offered it to Thea. Sensing defeat, Thea sank back onto the cushions. 'A wedding is a joyous occasion,' Anya added. Thea accepted the cup and slowly sipped the wine. The wine, at least, was sweet and soothing, if Olga was not.

Anya lifted her cup to her lips, sipped a little and set it down again. 'There, that is better. Now, there is something else I have intended to tell you.'

Thea gripped her cup tightly.

'My husband hopes that Padar and Earl Connor will establish new business interests in Kiev. Gudrun is forgiven for whatever magic she may have inclined towards. It was a bad year. Everyone suspected we had witches at court. I promise you, we believe she is innocent of spellmaking.'

'Of course Gudrun is innocent.' Thea almost dropped her cup. 'The women say that I am to save some of my bathwater from the maidens' party for my husband to drink on our wedding night so that he falls in love with me. Is that not spellmaking?'

'No, it is not,' Anya said. 'It is a harmless tradition. When Gudrun returns to our lands she comes back to us as Padar's wife. She is not part of the court. Olga claims that she, herself, acted in good faith.' Anya set her cup back on the table. She said in a quiet tone, 'I believe that she was wrong, but Lady Olga was only thinking of your interests. You broke the rules and when you did that you put yourself in great danger. It is fortunate for you that Vladimir took responsibility for that escapade.' Anya took Thea's now empty cup and placed it beside her own. 'Enough of past misdemeanours. Let us forget and forgive. Come and see my children. Eupraxia has grown fat as a piglet and is as stubborn as a mule. Rostislav is talking more and more every day. Soon you will have children of your own. Think happy thoughts and forget about Lady Olga.'

'I shall try.' As Thea made this difficult promise, doubts about Lady Olga remained securely lodged in the recesses of her mind. She determined that when Padar returned, Gudrun would stay close to her, under her own and Vladimir's protection.

Two days before her wedding Thea was carried in her litter to her new house. Princess Anya, Lady Olga and Mother Sophia accompanied the party. There had been no point in Princess Anya telling her that she would have her own choice of servants. Three score of these were in residence already. Thea determined that when her wedding was over she would make changes. Anya had chosen her cooks and seamstresses, laundrymaids, beekeepers, servers, personal attendants, sweepers, scrubbers, gardeners and cleaners.

'And, look at this. We unpacked your gifts from Denmark,' Princess Anya said.

Thea exclaimed over everything – the precious glassware that was laid out on top of an ash wood coffer in her chamber; the linen that had been stored into a great chest in her antechamber; her spoons; her tapestries and bolts of material which had also been unpacked and displayed. Then, as her eye

257

flew around her bedchamber, she saw the present she had actually found difficult to accept; the birthing chair, the gift from the Danish princesses, had been ominously stowed in an alcove where every morning she would see it on awakening.

She pointed at it. 'That will be kept from my sight until it is needed. Store it somewhere else. For me to even look on it before I conceive is bad luck.' It was probably a lie, but Thea thought St Theodosia would absolve her. She would never use that birthing chair. It was a gift given with ill-intent.

At Princess Anya's bidding, two maids ran to remove the offending chair. 'It is not appropriate for a birthing chair to be placed in a bedchamber. It will be brought to the bath-house when your time comes. Olga supervised the unpacking. She should know better.' Anya looked around at everything else approvingly. 'Yes, it is a beautiful room, perfect for your bridal nights.'

When the time comes I shall make other arrangements for that birthing chair. 'Is Vladimir to visit?' she said aloud. Vladimir had not sent her a letter while she was living in the Convent of the Holy Trinity and she had not been able to send him anything either. Often she had thought of tokens, a poem written on birch wood or a drawing but there had been no one to take it to him, not even Katya's father, who had melted away after that one visit. Occasionally, she had heard snippets of news from ladies who visited the convent. Prince Vladimir had been fighting the Steppe tribes south of Kiev or the brave warrior prince was out on the eastern borders near Chernigov.

Anya replied evenly, 'No. You must be patient.'

'I shall try but it is difficult. I have waited so long and now nothing feels as if it is really happening to me. If only I could see my betrothed, speak with him ...'

'No,' Anya said firmly. 'For the nobility, that is not our custom.'

Thea had prayed to St Theodosia nightly, before she drifted into sleep, that he still loved her.

As her wedding approached, Thea had fittings for her

258

wedding gown. She was to wear a deep crimson overdress with a long, trailing, gold mantle. This dress was of damask, covered with gold embroidery, its borders scattered with garnets from Bohemia. Her golden veil was so fine it was luminous, its hem embroidered with little seed pearls. Her belt was of plaited gold and studded with garnets and pearls and her undergown had opus anglicanum, tiny raised flowers with hearts of silver thread, scattered around the hem. Her night shift was silk and it, too, was heavily embroidered at the neck with opus anglicanum. When she enquired about the needlewomen who worked on these garments, she discovered that two English women who lived with their exiled merchant husbands in the city had embroidered them.

She learned that during the ceremony she would be crowned, not with flowers like an ordinary maiden, but rather, she must bear the weight of a princess's heavy, jewel-encrusted crown and walk with it on her head without allowing it to slip. She must glide through her wedding ceremony like a swan. Too many musts, she thought, feeling rebellious.

Her lessons in deportment continued under Lady Olga's supervision. Remembering Anya's advice, Thea listened, learned and never complained. An uneasy peace existed between them until one afternoon Olga entered her chamber uninvited. Tension hung in the air like a fragile glass bead ready to shatter if knocked to the floor.

'Lady Olga, I do not need any more lessons.' Thea looked over at Katya. 'We have planned a walk in the orchard today. I am sorry that you have made a wasted journey.'

Lady Olga shook her head. 'My lady, I come for the rushnyk today, not to coach you further in deportment, though as to whether you are ready or not remains to be seen on your wedding day,' she said. 'I shall take the rushnyk now since I am to carry it into St Sophia for you.'

'I see. Did Princess Anya say so? Yes, I expect she did,' Thea said and waved her hand towards her sewing chair. 'Of course, it is ready.' She turned to Katya. 'Katya, could you fetch it from my sewing chair.'

Once Lady Olga received the parcel, she bowed again to Thea and wished her a happy maidens' party.

The moment she was gone, Thea said, 'Fetch my mantle, Katya. We shall walk in the orchard. I feel uncomfortable. She is like an unpleasant odour.'

Katya said quietly, 'I feel her malevolence too.'

Weeks of waiting were over. Thea would have her bath in an enormous bath tub that was filled to the brim with warm scented water. Her skin would be scrubbed until it gleamed and her hair, that when unbound rippled past her hips, would be washed with her favourite rose soap. Her maidens would braid her hair into a single braid to represent her last night as a maid. Together, Thea and her maidens would eat pastries and sweetmeats and drink honey wine. As they ate, her bride's maidens would tell her their magical tales to enchant her sleep with pleasant dreams. Princess Anya warned, 'These stories must not go on like an endless ball of twine.'

'Yes, Princess Anya,' the maidens said in a chorus.

'Indeed, I must have my beauty sleep,' Thea laughed, feeling happier than she had felt for days. The palace had not felt as if it was her home. The servants were distant. The slaves were silent. They were not her servants and she did not like the idea of owning slaves. But soon all this would change.

The slaves lit the candles and vanished. The bath-house smelled of honey and wax. After Thea stepped from her bath and her hair had been braided, she lay back in the cushions that littered the colourful mosaic floor, ate sweetmeats from a silver dish, drank a cup of honey wine and looked forward to listening to her maidens' stories. The first tale went like this.

A crane and a heron lived in a marsh. Their huts stood on stilts at opposite ends of the bog. But the crane was very lonely. The heron was like him. She had a long nose and elegant legs. He flew over the marsh to the heron's house and asked for her hand in marriage. He waded up to her doorway and made his request. 'No crane,' she replied. 'I won't marry you. You have long legs. Your coat is too short. You fly badly. You can't provide for me. Go away, spindle-shanks!'

The crane went away dejected. The proud heron thought, but maybe I was wrong. I am so lonely. She fluttered and fluttered, hesitated, hesitated then, at last, decided. Off to the crane's house she flew and made her proposal to him. He refused her. Sometime later, feeling even lonelier than ever, he thought of his missed opportunity, and so he waded across the marsh to the crane's hut. This time, she put her nose into the air and declined but, of course, she regretted it later. And so, Lady Thea, it continues out there on the marsh. They keep proposing marriage to each other! And neither can say yes. Both are such lonely creatures. What is the sense in that!

'He should never have refused her. Trust a man to be so proud and regret his pride,' Thea said with firmness in her tone.

The next was a tale of Baba Yaga, the witch who lived in a house with clawed legs; she who haunted the sky with her pestle and mortar. Then a bridesmaid told Thea a story about the frog princess and, finally, another told her the story of Little Pigskin who had a wicked stepmother and who married her prince because she was really a princess. Thea kept her own story close to her heart because that one was only for her prince.

'So many tales,' Thea said as she began to feel sleep calling her.

'Enough now, to bed,' Princess Anya ordered. She shooed the maidens to the antechamber and put Thea to bed in the sleigh-shaped bed in the second room. 'Sleep well, little dove,' she said and kissed her brow. Thea was already drifting into her dreams. She drowsily thought of her prince, convinced that he would cherish her, as the princes in the tales her maidens had told her, guarded their princesses.

26

Thea awakened to the ringing of bells from St Sophia. Katya was already at her side with bread and honeyed milk. 'You must eat a little, Princess,' she said. 'It would not do to have a grumbling stomach today.'

As morning suffused the chamber with May sunshine, Thea was dressed by Katya and her maids, supervised by Lady Olga and Princess Anya. Each of the layers she wore below her wedding gown felt feather-light as they were sewn from delicate Byzantine silk.

Led by Anya and escorted by her maidens, Thea descended to the hall for the small and intimate meal that would precede her wedding. A priest from St Sophia entered the chamber from a side entrance. With a swaying incense burner that emitted the scent of frankincense, he approached the table where she sat at its head. He blessed her first and after he blessed the light meal of meat and cheese that was laid out for her bridal party. She could not touch a morsel. Her stomach was churning and her heart was beating too quickly. In case her nerves got the better of her, she drank a little wine to sustain her through the lengthy ceremony. Anya sent guards with Katya and Vera to fetch the prince from the palace. 'We are ready,' she said.

After the two maidens departed, Thea turned to her right side curious as to why an empty chair had been placed there. Perhaps it was for Vladimir but it was not. Moments after the deputation left to summon the groom, the great hall door burst open to reveal a solitary tall, fair-headed young man clad in a blue mantle, accompanied by one servant. For a moment he stood framed by the giant doorway. A heartbeat later he walked down to the table, his cloak falling in elegant folds behind him, a glittering sword hilt visible in the scabbard attached to a jewelled belt. Thea sucked in a breath as this beautiful man, her brother, Edmund, knelt in front of her, his fair head bowed. 'Sister, I am here at last,' he said, raising his head to look into her eyes.

Thea steadied herself, stood and said, 'By the Virgin, my beloved brother, you are welcome. I never thought to see you again on this earth and here you are.' Tears welled up in her eyes and she reached out her hand to him. 'Come, Edmund. This seat beside me can only be for you. If only Padar and Gudrun were here too and Earl Connor, my happiness would be complete. But they are not and I am more than overjoyed that you are here.'

'It is my honour to present you, beloved sister, to your husband today.'

'Is this your doing, Princess Anya?' Thea said turning to Anya.

'Our surprise,' Anya whispered. She then said loudly and with great formality, 'Edmund, son of Harold, brother to Thea, please join us.' She indicated the empty chair. 'Your page may sit on the lower benches.'

'Edmund, how come you here?' she said when Edmund was seated beside her.

Edmund said, 'We can talk later, Sister. Thanks to fair winds and a safe river journey I am here. Our parents would be proud of you today. Our murdered father had hoped to be the parent of a new dynasty. Mother is stuck in that Norman convent in Canterbury. It will be through yours and Prince Vladimir's children that we shall survive as princes. This will be our new dynasty, our destiny that through you, we live again to rule.'

Thea felt a great sense of responsibility. This was how she was to avenge her father's murder. Edmund lifted his cup and Thea saw a tear roll down his cheek. She leaned over and wiped it away with her thumb. 'Edmund, you are here and my happiness is complete.' She bit her lip and tasted a bitter droplet of blood on her tongue. All this ceremony. Would happiness really follow? Vladimir was not real any more. Had he ever been real?

A little bell chimed, reminding her of Grandmother Gytha's bell. For a moment she thought that the countess might have enjoyed her wedding and had she been there they could have joked about the ridiculous ceremony later, but her thought had no time to linger. She missed her mother. A mother should see her daughter married. Had Elditha even received her letter? There had been no reply though perhaps it was too soon for one. A tear edged its way onto her cheek. She swallowed hard. There must not be another, not today.

The great door swung open again. Everything now began to proceed too quickly. There was no time to feel sad. This was, after all, her wedding day. She had longed for this prince. Surely she was not feeling a sense of regret, not that she ever had the power to turn her back on this marriage.

A dozen candle bearers entered followed by a bearded priest in his sweeping embroidered robes. The candle bearers stood at the sides of the hall, six to one side and six to the other. The cleric held aloft an enormous cross of gold studded with enormous gems, yellow amber in the centre and blue sapphires and deep red garnets on the cross's arms. Moments later, Prince Vladimir's cousin, Sviatopolk, who was to be Vladimir's chief attendant, entered and stood behind the priest.

Her heart hammered against her rib cage because at last Vladimir had entered. It was the first time she had seen him since that stolen moment in the church in Novgorod. He stopped and knelt four times, each time facing in one of four directions. Her heart soared. The enchantment took hold of her again. *How beautiful he looks.* His long black hair fell softly onto his shoulders. His full-length gold damask gown and mantle fanned out into a triangular shape at his feet. She was sure his mouth twitched a smile as he looked her way and knelt at last to her, his chosen princess.

In order of age a procession of relatives followed. Uncle Iziaslav, who had been usurped what seemed a long time ago by the magician prince, looked kindly and very handsome. He was still greatly criticised, she had heard, by the boyars of Kiev. The difficulty, Katya claimed, was that he simply was not as clever as his father. The great Prince Yaroslav had developed trade in amber, furs, beeswax and slaves. He had controlled three great trade routes. Iziaslav's father had developed money-lending systems that made Rus merchants very wealthy. Iziaslav had done nothing to protect the merchants of Kiev from the Steppe tribes. In fact, the tribes demanded a toll on the merchandise that travelled on the rivers through the lands belonging to the Slav villages they had pillaged.

Trying to remain dignified, with the help her maidens and Katya gave her, Thea rose, waiting momentarily as the maidens adjusted her veil and arranged her trailing mantle. Once the maidens stood back, she walked from the table to a wide archway which divided two halls. She entered the adjacent hall where two chairs had been placed on a dais for herself and Edmund, dear Edmund. If only Padar and Gudrun were here. What could have happened to them? Under Anya's sharp eye, her maidens gently removed her veil, deftly undid her long single plait, separated it and neatly rebound it into two long tresses to symbolise her approaching union with Prince Vladimir.

Vladimir's close relatives entered the smaller chamber. Vladimir followed. He bowed to her and she inclined her head. She must not speak to him, not yet. It was forbidden. Servants moved around the nobles and offered bread and cheese to the family visitors. Katya had told her that the bread was important because it contained water from seven wells, flour from seven sacks, eggs from seven hens, butter from seven pots and so these wedding loaves would symbolise their approaching oneness.

'Everyone in the prince's family supports this marriage, so they will all eat the bread,' Katya had said some nights before.

'They condemn magic but practise it themselves,' had been Thea's terse response. Lady Olga, who had overheard this comment, glared at her. That day, Thea had felt the woman's antipathy cut into her and she remembered that Lady Olga had wanted her prince for her own daughter.

By the sixth hour all was ready. The bells of St Sophia were ringing again. Edmund led her out to where two caparisoned horses were waiting for her. She would ride beside Edmund through Kiev to the cathedral. Her closely guarded procession would follow in litters and on foot. Vladimir's procession was to take a shorter route. They would meet before the iconostasis inside St Sophia, since princely marriages were always conducted inside the cathedral.

The courtyard was covered with fresh hay, cornflowers and marigolds. Once Thea was helped up onto her white mare, she set off at a slow walk, led by a handsome young man who carried a pennant with the Wessex dragon embroidered upon it in gold and red. Edmund rode a pace behind his sister. What a day of triumph it was. Only a year before, Prince Vsevolod had threatened to return her to Denmark in disgrace. Six years before this day, her family had lost a throne. She thanked St Theodosia that fate had intervened. No one would come between her and her ambition to be become a great Rus princess. At the city's Golden Gate she paused as the citizens of Kiev cheered and tossed marigolds at her. Her heart filled with pride. They admired the young prince who was to be her bridegroom. She, therefore, because of the prince was their favourite princess. One day they will love me for myself, she determined, as she approached the Cathedral of St Sophia.

Together Thea and Edmund waited with the bridal party, which included Princess Anya, as Lady Olga hurried ahead with the rushnyk. After she spoke her vows, Thea would kneel on it for her crowning. As they waited she scanned the faces in the crowds by the cathedral. It was difficult to see them properly as she was veiled. She whispered to Edmund, 'Do you see them?' A moment later he replied, 'They are not here.'

One of the bishops appeared in the cathedral's entrance to lead her forward. Thea hesitated for a moment unsure. In England everything was so different. Handfasting was still the accepted form, except for weddings of the high nobility. And then, it was only after the wedding vows were said that a couple entered a church for a service and blessing. Princess Anya touched her lightly on the arm, and encouraging her, whispered that she must follow the bishop who had turned back into the cathedral.

The cathedral's five naves and five apses were highly decorated with icons and frescos, its floor covered with mosaics. As Thea glided through the pillars over a tapestry of gold to the main chancel she was momentarily blinded by colour and beauty. It was as well Princess Anya had brought her there before, so she understood exactly where she was to walk. She must remember not to step onto the mosaic floor. When she reached the iconostasis, Vladimir was waiting for her.

After she bowed her head for the ceremony, she thought of how three weeks earlier at Easter she had watched as Prince Vsevolod and his two brothers had taken the relics of St Boris and had carried the wooden casket that contained them on their shoulders into the cathedral. Monks had preceded the three princes holding candles aloft. Deacons waving censers, priests and bishops followed. They had watched as the casket was opened by the Metropolitan and the cathedral filled with fragrance. It was a miracle. But so was her wedding. Today incense was drifting lightly about the cathedral. Today it smelled of roses, her favourite flower.

Thea tried to concentrate on the Metropolitan's reading from Genesis, on his reading from St Paul to the Corinthians and the Miracle at Cana. The difficulty was Vladimir's proximity to her right, because she longed to reach out and touch him. At last, they were exchanging rings. Each received a burning candle. Now she must be very still. She knelt on her rushnyk. He knelt beside her. The Metropolitan placed the heavy jewelled crowns on their heads. Thea found that she had to shift her position because at the moment of their wedding crowning a sharp jabbing pain seared through her knee. If she moved too quickly, her crown could crash to the ground. She bit her lip so hard she tasted blood. She ignored the tears that gathered caused by a searing pain. If only she could stand.

At last she could breathe. She could rise to her feet. The ceremony was over.

She stood unsteadily, leaning slightly on Vladimir. He looked at her with a question in his eyes. She felt ungainly, awkward but, importantly, the heavy crown remained balanced on her head. That was all that mattered. She glanced down. The rushnyk had attached itself to her gown. Not only had something stabbed her knee but she could trip on the embroidered cloth if she tried to walk. Slowly, holding her tall candle carefully in her right hand, she moved her left hand along her gown towards her knee and tried to detach the cloth. The rushnyk was attached to her overgown by a sharp, long bronze pin. Its point had penetrated through her outer gown and her two fragile silk undergowns as she had knelt. She lowered herself slightly, stretched down and managed to pull the pin away, letting a small gasp escape her lips as the cloth dropped onto the floor.

Vladimir looked sideways. He could not but notice the bronze pin glinting on the floor amongst the crumpled embroidery. The Metropolitan nodded at her. No one else appeared to notice, and if they did they discreetly ignored it. She glanced sideways at Vladimir. He took her hand and pressed his reassurance into it.

Ignoring the pain that still assaulted her left knee, still holding her candle and proudly wearing her crown, Thea held her head steady. She tried to forget the throbbing pain in her knee. With grace, she walked beside her husband, her hand clasped in his, through the long nave and from the cathedral to their waiting horses.

Only Olga, who had been responsible for laying the rushnyk before the beautiful door into the sanctuary, could have done this to her on her wedding day.

On the third night of their marriage Thea and Vladimir made

love properly for the first time. For two days they had made love with hand pressings, with whispers of love, and with stolen fluttering kisses. Her maidens had fed them each night as they lay side by side, before discreetly removing themselves from the bedchamber. By then she had forgotten everyone else. They were together. The enchantment had returned.

On the first night, Vladimir gently kissed her and dared to whisper, 'I love you, Princess.'

She whispered back, 'And I thee.'

Vladimir fell into a deep sleep but she watched the moon sail across their window and the stars blink at her as they sat high in a dark cloudless sky. She fancied one star was her father and that others were Magnus and her three uncles who had died fighting in the battles of 1066. Her grandmother was there too. Thea felt her presence. She climbed out of the tall bed and opened the box in which she had placed her grandmother's ring. She slipped it onto the middle finger of her left hand. I shall wear it now always, Grandmother, she vowed to herself, and it will lend me your strength.

On the second day, Thea and Vladimir were surrounded by wedding guests who had celebrated far into the night, the men in the hall and the women in the terem. They received gifts sitting up in the great bed. On the second night, they whispered many words of love, vying with each other for the best ways to express their love. Vladimir won the game. His skills with languages were superior to hers. Vladimir asked her in a low whisper, 'Why was the pin in the wedding cloth? Did you leave it there by mistake?'

Thea confided, 'Of course I did not leave that pin in the cloth. How would I? It must have been Lady Olga. She wishes me ill. If I had allowed my crown to drop then I would be disgraced.' Feeling angry that he could think she would make such a mistake, she told Vladimir about how Lady Olga had treated Gudrun.

'If this is truth, then Olga must be held to account. I shall speak with my father and explain to him why Lady Olga will not be welcome in my household. Her plan failed because of your courage.' He squeezed Thea's hand. He kissed her on her lips. She longed for her husband.

He removed her veil and covered her face with kisses. She kissed him back passionately. He slid his hand beneath her embroidered night shift and touched her naked breast. 'I want to kiss you here and here,' he said, moving his fingers slowly over her breast. She flowed like honey at his touch. He took his hand away and she wished that they could discard the night shifts and sink into the bliss of lovemaking. Yet they must not. It was against the rules. She sighed; the rules again. There must be some way to distract themselves from this unbearable agony. To lie in a bed, side by side, hungry and unfulfilled was unbearable. Vladimir sighed. She felt him move away from her.

'This is torture,' he said. 'It is unnatural. I may have to sleep on the floor rug tonight.'

'No, no, stay. Do not do that. Listen, since we must remain chaste until tomorrow night, and since this day has been a day of gift giving, it is time for my gift to you.' Thea climbed down onto the step that was pushed against the great bed, lifted the dreadful though very lovely veil that lay crumpled there. She gathered it into a ball and mischievously threw it at him. He caught it and threw it back. She picked up a pillow stuffed with feathers and threw that. He tossed it back. Their game continued until the cover split and the feathers scattered over the wolfskin cover and the tiled floor. She laughed and ran to her coffer.

'What are you doing?'

'Wait and see.'

For a moment she felt around deep inside the chest, beneath her linen, further down below her jewel box, and deep into a corner, she found what she sought. Her six tablets were tied together with a crimson ribbon embroidered with golden thread.

She knelt beside him and placed the gift in his lap. Prince Vladimir pushed himself further up the bed and leaning back against the remaining pillows slowly untied them.

271

'It is my story for you,' Thea said softly, climbing back into bed. 'It is called The Little White Duck. In this story, a prince marries a beautiful princess. He tells her not to converse with any stranger while he is off fighting battles. A witch tempts the princess down from her tower to bathe in a crystal stream. She taps the princess on her shoulder with her stick and turns her into a duck. The witch disguises herself as the princess and the poor duck swims away. What else can she do? Soon she has children, but the witch finds her and destroys the ducklings. Yet, all is not lost. Fate is kind. When the mother duck laments the loss of her children, the prince recognises her crying, seeks her out and finds her lamenting her loss by the stream. When the duck flies into his hands, he says "Be a silver birch behind me, a fair maiden before me." A magpie flies down from the silver birch tree and shakes magic water from his wings onto the dead ducklings. Their children come alive again. The duck is a princess once more. They have found each other again. The prince and princess banish the witch from their lands and so that is the end of the terrible witch because her spellmaking is destroyed.'

Prince Vladimir kissed her, scattering the tablets about the bedcover. 'My princess, I shall banish all witches from our lives and I shall love you forever.'

'Just Olga,' Thea said, looking up at him with a wicked grin.

Collecting the tablets together, Thea crawled over the rumpled cover and placed them on the coffer at the foot of the bed. Later, she slid into his embrace. That night, Thea fell asleep in Vladimir's arms, her body longing for his. She wanted to remove her embroidered night shift but she must not, not yet. 'Goodnight, my prince,' she said instead, very softly.

'Princess, I dream of holding you and making love to you tomorrow night,' he whispered back.

'Sweet dreams then,' Thea said. Slowly she moved out of his arms and turned towards the window to watch the moon and stars again until she drifted into sleep.

The next day they arose just after dawn and attended masses

272

in St Sophia separately. Thea observed how Olga remained in Lady Anya's circle. They had all returned to Prince Vsevolod's palace where Anya kept her terem. Thea's ladies gathered around their mistress as if she were the queen in the centre of the hive. She certainly felt she was. The actuality of it all was not as terrible as she had feared. The atmosphere had lightened. There was a sense of gaiety. Yet, she did wish her mother could have been part of it. She wished her sister Gunnhild was with her and even more she longed for her grandmother. Where were Padar and Gudrun? By now they would have a baby too. She hoped they were all safe. If only all of them were with her, her wedding would be complete. As for Lady Olga, she would not be excused the evil she had tried to do to her.

That third day Thea and Vladimir held court in the hall of their new palace where, because it was the main wedding celebration, men and women feasted together instead of separately. Thea noticed Lady Olga watching her and wondered what she was thinking. The woman was fortunate today because Thea was not supposed to speak. No matter how important Olga was at court she would never allow that woman near her or those whom she loved. She studied the tall, thin steward, who was Lady Olga's husband, march about the hall pointing his jewelled staff at servants if he noticed an empty cup or a dish that should be removed. It was an odd marriage.

That evening, Vladimir swept into the bedchamber and everyone departed. She shared a cup of honey kvass with him and then they sank deep into the bed and removed each other's night attire. When they made love, Thea felt that she already knew her prince. She was not frightened of the marriage duty, as the terem women called lovemaking. How could making love be a debt or a duty when she wanted her prince so desperately to touch her? She was not disappointed. She had never known such joy. His caresses felt as if they were a gift from the angels. Vladimir gently eased a pillow beneath her hips. When he took her she felt as if she lived in a kingdom so sensual that she never wanted to leave it. There was a little hurt

273

at first, as she knew there would be, and there was blood as the women had warned, but Vladimir used a cloth left beside them as well as a basin of lavender-scented water. He carefully mopped away the blood and placed a dry cloth under her.

The second time they made love was absolutely perfect. The third time she felt bliss.

'One day, my father will make me Prince of Pereiaslavl, his fortress city to the south,' he whispered into her ear as they lay entwined in each other's arms. 'It guards the Steppe lands at the southern edge of our territory. In summer we can spend months in the country where poppies wave amongst tall green grasses, wheat grows in the dark rich soil, where woodland lends shade from the hot summer sun and where a river that runs through the estate has water so pure it looks like crystal. Your ladies will want to picnic by its banks and bathe in its waters.'

'Can we go there soon?' She longed for the country away from the court already.

'Yes, in a few months, I think.'

'No Lady Olga.'

'Absolutely no Olga.' He stroked her hair, drew her closer and kissed the top of her head. He said thoughtfully, 'I shall speak with my father. What she did was unacceptable. She must be punished.'

'At least she must be confronted,' Thea said. 'But Steward Michael is important at court. How can she be punished?'

'She is part of Anya's terem. It will be for my father to banish her.'

'What if Anya does not want her to go?'

'Nonetheless, Lady Olga has insulted my wife.'

'Will they believe me?'

'Perhaps not, but I saw her evil with my own eyes and in God's house too. She must go.'

'Yes,' Thea said. Even if Olga remained in Anya's terem, she would never be welcome in Thea's palace again.

Thea had made the right decision. Anya was furious when she discovered the evil Olga had done. She had no great love for Olga but Olga organised everything and Anya had never expected her to stoop to such depths of cunning. Arrangements would be made to send her back to Germany for a time. She had lands there. Any return to the Russian court would be dependent on her future humility and her sincere apologies. According to Vladimir, Michael was furious with his wife, and while Princess Anya was disillusioned he was broken-hearted, disappointed and sad.

Several days after Olga was dismissed, the steward came to Thea and begged for an audience with her. Thea granted it.

'I beg your pardon, Princess,' he said, falling to his knees on her tiled floor. 'I beg you to allow my wife to return. She is deeply sorry. Lady Olga says she had no idea how the needle got there but she takes responsibility for not removing it. My wife begs your forgiveness. Princess Anya says she will take her back but only if you grant her mercy.'

'Get up off your knees, Steward Michael. Let us be clear, my quarrel is not with you but with Lady Olga who ill-wished my wedding by neglect.'

The steward scrambled to his feet. She said, 'Your wife must beg my forgiveness before Prince Vsevolod, Princess Anya and my husband and all of my ladies.'

'Yes, Princess, she must.'

'And you must be henceforth responsible for her.'

'Yes, Princess, you are bountiful.'

'No, I am not. I cannot forget how she treated my maid, Gudrun. I hope that she sees the error of her ways. What I shall never understand is why she behaves as she does.' Thea waved her hand. 'Go, now. I have my own household to see to. My cook awaits my instructions. Go. After she apologises I do not want your wife near my palace.'

Steward Michael backed off bowing. Thea shuddered as he exited. It had not been a pleasant interview.

The apology was arranged for a week later. Vladimir was pleased that Thea could find it in her heart to show mercy to a lady of the court who had wronged her so cruelly. Olga would indeed make a journey to her German estates but in a year she would return to Anya's terem.

Vladimir sat up in bed that evening and looked at his wife with puzzlement. 'What was the answer to the riddle you told me last year in the Church of St Nicholias?'

'Well, after the grief that day caused me, I think you must work the answer out for yourself,' she said pulling him back into the bedcovers. 'A bird with a sleek coat and a strong song. There is a clue.'

'Nightingale?'

'No'

'Kingfisher?'

'No.'

'Raven, I think he is the raven.'

She kissed his mouth. 'Yes, it is. His coat as dark and sleek as your hair and his eyes shine like your own.'

'But I cannot sing.'

'No, matter, you are the jay.'

As she drifted into sleep, Thea thought, this is the miracle that God has intended for me, that I should love my husband; that he should love me too. Thank you, St Theodosia. Of a sudden, she sat up in bed as if she was pinched by a cross elf, *But I want more than children from this marriage. I want to rule our estates and cities alongside Vladimir, as his equal. I am beginning to accept what I shall not accept. I shall not lose myself in this court's spells with its terems and its traps and its nonsense about how its noblewomen must so constantly be protected that they cannot ride out into the orchards and fields without an army of men. My mother would never have endured it, nor my grandmother, nor shall I. Gudrun and Padar, please return to me soon.*

She looked down on his sleeping face and traced the line of his noble nose. 'And I shall,' she whispered. 'One day, I shall prove my worth to you, my lord, as my father's daughter and as a great princess,' she whispered.

27

When Olga entered Thea's great hall, her head was bowed and she was dressed in black from head to toe. She looked thinner and stooped. She had clearly suffered. Prince Vsevolod and Princess Anya sat on throne-like chairs. Thea and Prince Vladimir were seated on chairs with lower backs and carvings not quite so elaborate. Thea felt relieved because she knew that she had been believed.

Anya and Vsevolod remained stony faced as Olga fell on her knees. Vsevolod raised his hand in an impatient gesture and said, 'Lady Olga, you are fortunate that Princess Gita has a forgiving nature. You will direct your apology to her. You are fortunate too that my wife will take you back into her household as mistress of her bath-house after your visit to your estates. You will beg forgiveness for your betrayal of her trust.'

Olga turned to Thea and prostrated herself. Rising to her knees, she made her apology. She said that she simply could not understand what had possessed her to allow a needle to protrude from the rushnyk. Thea replied that she would forgive the crime but added, 'It is fortunate for you that Princess Anya is willing to have you return to her household, even as mistress of her bath-house rather than mistress of the terem.'

Anya stood, her face immobile. 'You, Lady Olga, will be accepted back for your family's sake. You will only return to me after you have been cleansed of your sin. To that end, before you set out for your estates, you will spend a month in prayer at the Monastery of the Caves where you will make whatever penance the monks prescribe for you.'

Later, Thea said to Vladimir, 'She begged our forgiveness with tears. But, I wonder why she is so bitter. Such bitterness must be a hard burden to bear.'

Vladimir buried his head in Thea's loosened hair, inhaling

her scent. Exhaling, he said, 'Lady Olga's elder daughters are dwelling in my uncle's wife's terem in Chernigov. Perhaps on her return to us, Olga might be happier there.'

Thea twisted round to look into the dark eyes she loved so passionately and saw his wisdom shining out of them. 'I care not where that woman goes as long as I have no further dealings with her.'

'Since my uncle will be the next Grand Prince, it would please Olga to be part of his wife's household.'

'Sounds like a reward, not a punishment,' Thea said with petulance in her tone. 'I hope that she will not try to scheme again.'

'If she does it will not be a comfortable visit to Germany for her next time. She will forfeit her life,' Vladimir said firmly, his arms folded behind his head.

Thea whispered into Vladimir's ear, 'I can think of better things for us to do than worry about Lady Olga's future.'

'You are bold, my beautiful wife, and I like it. Come closer.'

Some days later Edmund came to Thea's receiving chamber. He was living in a grand house with a tiled roof close to her palace and announced that it was so comfortable a living after years of exile, that he planned to remain in Kiev for the winter season if not for ever. He would travel south to Constantinople to trade for oil and spice.

'And,' he announced after Thea called for wine and pastries to be served. 'I have a surprise for you.'

'Oh.' Thea raised her eyebrows. 'I hope it is a good surprise.'

'The best of surprises, Sister. Padar and Gudrun have returned.'

She could not believe it. They had not returned in time for her wedding and she had missed them, but they were here now, several weeks too late. 'When will Padar and Gudrun come to me?' Thea asked, hardly able to contain her excitement.

'They are exhausted and are resting. Connor, as you know, owns my dwelling and so they came to it. They have a child, a little girl they call Edith for our mother. They will call on you on the morrow after Terce.'

'I hope they bring little Edith.'

'They will.'

'Edmund,' Thea said in a thoughtful way as she handed him a cup of sweet honey wine and offered him a pastry. 'What did you want to ask me, you remember in the letter that Katya's father brought me, you said that I could lend you help in an enterprise?' Thea bit into her pastry and, setting it back half-eaten on the silver platter, folded her hands in her lap and waited for Edmund to speak.

'Yes, I have been waiting for the opportunity.' He took a breath and plunged in. 'You are a great princess and Kiev is one of the richest cities in Europe. There is no doubt that Prince Vsevolod wants to make trading easy for us. He will grant us privileges. This request actually comes from Godwin.'

'Oh?' She was beginning to wish she had not asked. Godwin was intent on recovering England. She was not sure it could be possible without Sweyn's whole-hearted support. England was not united. William was building castles in every county and setting armies to guard them.

'Yes, our brother is in fine health in body, but broken in spirit. The north of England is suffering great hardship because Cousin Sweyn has made peace with the English bastard king. He levied a Dane gild on William the Bastard and in return for it our cousin of Denmark will stay away from England's shores.'

'But what has Duke William done in the north?'

'He has burned villages and fields, destroyed crops, killed the menfolk and left women and children to starve. The north is barren now. There will be no harvest. Those remaining will starve.'

Thea's stomach churned as she remembered how she had once sworn revenge on William of Normandy and how the wise woman had promised her that he would suffer in God's chosen time. All very well, but now the English people were suffering.

279

Her desire for revenge was rekindled. 'What can I do?' she found herself saying, leaning closer to Edmund so no one else could hear.

'Ask your prince to send soldiers and ships to England, to the north.' She heard the pleading in his voice and her heart softened.

'I can ask but I cannot promise that they will listen. They are fighting many battles of their own to keep enemies out of Russian lands. I think they could soon be fighting amongst themselves.' She lowered her voice further. 'The noblemen and the council that they call the Veche do not like Prince Iziaslav. They want a strong ruler who can keep the Steppe tribes out of Russia.'

'Who would that be, sister?' Edmund sounded extremely interested in the internal conflicts of the Russian court.

She stood and poured two cups of kvass and handed one to Edmund. She sipped her own and after she had placed the gold drinking cup on her side bench she said, 'They want Prince Sviatoslav and Prince Vsevolod to rule together. Vladimir tells me that we are moving to an estate south of Kiev. He does not want me to remain in Kiev if there is to be a civil war.'

'Nice cup, gold, wealth, riches,' Edmund remarked as he turned his cup in his hand and for a moment studied the patterns of vines engraved on it. 'Stinking rich as once England was too, a country of beautiful things and now one of lost hopes. Ask him for help, Thea, for Godwin's sake. I promised him.'

'You have no right to promise Godwin my husband's help. Where is Godwin now?' Thea said sharply.

'He lives in the house our mother was granted in Dublinia by King Dairmaid. He is finished with Cousin Sweyn.'

'I see. I shall make your request on your behalf.' Thea sank back into her cushions. 'So Padar and Gudrun are well?' she asked, turning the subject back to her friends.

'They suffered an attack between Poland and your lands. Gudrun will tell you all about it. Padar has salt to trade, and alum which is used to dye cloth. He must get it sold. And more news, Earl Connor is setting up his own trading house here in Kiev. We are a triumvirate.'

'You, Padar and the earl?'

'I can think of none better. We are the Meath Trading Company, a first!' He laughed. 'Now I must get back. We shall speak further about Godwin.'

After Edmund had gone, Thea frowned and bit her lip. It was unlikely that the Rus princes would want involvement in England's woes but she must try.

The next day Gudrun and Padar visited bearing gifts and profuse apologies for missing the wedding. She embraced Gudrun and made a fuss of tiny Edith.

'You will soon have one of your own, my lady.'

'Sit, both of you. Later you must seek out Katya. Padar, Edmund told me how you were attacked.'

'We are safe now. It was dangerous and not an experience I ever wish to repeat,' Gudrun said and shuddered.

Padar sat close to Gudrun on a divan with the baby between them. They were clearly so in love. She could see Gudrun's happiness on her countenance and was glad.

Padar said, 'My lady, I have brought you Flanders wool.'

'No, no, you brought me a greater gift.' Thea reached out to Gudrun and took her hand. They both wept tears of relief and joy. They chattered on about the ladies of St Omer, about the countess, about Thea's time at Holy Trinity and about little Edith. Thea begged Gudrun to join her terem when Padar was away on his travels.

'I shall. And baby Edith will come too.' Gudrun frowned. 'But will I be welcome?'

'If you are thinking of Lady Olga, she is spending the autumn in Germany and then she will be moving into Prince Sviatoslav's household in Chernigov.'

'How have you managed that, my lady?' Gudrun said.

A silk curtain blew against the isinglass window as a door opened and Katya came in. She bowed to Thea but as soon as she saw Gudrun and Padar, she was all eyes for the baby who slept on the divan by their sides. She lifted Edith. 'May I?'

Gudrun nodded. For a moment Katya buried her face in little Edith's shawls.

'Katya will tell you all about Lady Olga,' Thea said to Gudrun and turned to Katya. 'Katya, show Gudrun and Edith the garden. I wish to talk with Padar for a moment. I need his advice concerning my brothers Godwin and Edmund.'

After Gudrun and Katya hurried out into the garden, Padar listened intently to what Thea had to confide.

'I knew it was so but I fear that it is too late. Rebellion in England will never be consolidated. There are Norman castles and stronger defences everywhere and there are parts of the land where people are adjusting to Norman rule. I think Edmund agrees, but Godwin is broken. He feels that he has betrayed his father if he does not recover his kingdom.'

'And you feel it is an impossible venture.'

'There is little desire for war. There has been so much suffering.'

'But that is a defeatist attitude,' she said fiercely.

'It is a realistic one. The English thanes left to England must now work from within to improve the peoples' lives.'

'Oh, Padar. How sad all this is.'

'My lady, it is change, some good and some bad. That is how one day the future will judge it all. For now we must live as well as we can. Peace is precious.'

Some days passed and Thea thought she would never find the best opportunity to discuss Edmund's request with her husband. At last an opportunity did arrive. It was a fasting day, which meant eating lightly and not meat. They had shared a goblet of watered wine. He reclined against feathered cushions that had come from Denmark with Thea.

'Play for me this afternoon, my sweet.'

'With pleasure, my lord.' Thea lifted her harp onto her knee. Plucking the strings she began to sing a song she had been taught by her Danish music master. Vladimir told her that her voice was as beautiful as that of the nightingale.

'Thank you, my lord. One day I shall sing songs for our children.'

'They will be enchanted children if you sing to them as you sing for me. They must learn to play instruments. You must teach them.' His eyes were filled with genuine admiration.

On an impulse she laid aside her harp and crossed the chamber to a great oak coffer. She lifted the lid, and dug deep below the tapestries she stored there. She withdrew her mother's bone-plated casket. From the casket, she lifted out one of her most precious possessions and held aloft the Godwin christening garment, so fragile that sunlight shone right through it. 'My grandmother asked if our first son could be called Harold for my father.'

Vladimir watched the sunlight shine on the precious garment. 'All this way, and all that time ago and it survives.' He smiled at her adoringly. 'Yes, we shall call him Harold amongst the family but I think his name for formal occasions must be Mstislav. This way we keep the boyars happy and my father content.'

'If that is your wish. In the terem he will always be Harold.'

'Of course, that is as will be.' He kissed her on her lips and pulled her onto his lap. 'One day we shall have many children.'

'My mother had four, though one, our beautiful Magnus, is dead and another is a prisoner in Normandy. I wish you could help him. I wish you could spare an army to invade England and take my country back for my brothers.' There it was said and she could not take back her words, though she knew they were futile.

This was no simple request such as a baby's name or that her child would be christened in an English christening robe. He gently pushed her off his lap and rose from the bench. Slowly he paced the length of the room, his boots tapping as he walked. His raven's head was bent in thought and his hands were folded in front of his long gown. Occasionally he raised a hand to touch the cross he wore about his neck. Something about the frown on his countenance and the sound of his boots clacking over the tiled floor made her feel extremely uneasy. Thea let go a sigh, sensing that she was about to be rebuffed.

Vladimir sank down beside her again, lifted her hand and kissed it. 'It is not a decision for me alone. The boyars have a council and even our freed men have a say. It would have to be their decision.' Vladimir pulled her close. 'I shall send a letter to the King of England asking him to free your younger brother into our care, though I suspect he will refuse.' He took both her hands into his own. She felt gripped by sorrow for Godwin, for her sister in Wilton Abbey, for her mother in a nunnery in Canterbury and she felt sad for Ulf because she suspected that he would not be set free.

Vladimir continued, 'We cannot spare any soldiers for a foreign war.' He looked at her with sadness in his eyes. 'Perhaps we can organise a ship to bring back survivors from the English rebellions, those who need a new land for their home, though unless they have their own way of living in Rus lands as mercenaries or as craftsmen, they could find life very difficult here.'

'But ...'

'No *but*. Edmund is welcome here as a merchant, but only that. He cannot interfere in our political decisions. You, my wife, must not involve yourself in the ruling of our lands. You are mistress of your terem. As such you will rule fairly and by example, just as I, my father and uncles and cousins rule our land. Your task is to guide our children and our noblewomen. That is all I ask. Our women do not meddle in politics. Do you understand?' He lifted her hands to his lips and kissed them. 'It is not right for women to try to behave like men and you are now a Russian princess. You will rule the politics of your terem and oversee my household and I know you will do this well. The women already respect you and, well, Lady Olga. I think you handled that incident very well too.'

Thea bit back her protest. She did not want a quarrel. 'I had to ask.' A feeling of irritation welled up deep inside her. A snake had entered her garden. She was a woman and a Rus princess who must not think about politics. It was unfair. For now she would hold her tongue but things must change if they were to continue to live in harmony. 'I shall tell Edmund,' she said aloud.

'No, I shall,' he said. 'In a month you will travel to Pereiaslavl. The skald, Padar, requests that Gudrun and their child accompany you. Will that make you happy?'

'I am glad to have Gudrun back. Even though she has her own household now, she will always be part of mine. She dwells in my heart.'

'Not as much as I, my sweet.' He pushed his hands into her hair and drawing her close kissed her forehead and then her lips as if to silence her. She returned the kiss but as they kissed she remembered how she had once lived through a terrible siege. She had learned too much about politics to not be curious about how a country worked. Her grandmother had been a politician. Her mother had been courageous. That night she wished as she looked through her chamber window at a rising full moon that one day she, too, would prove her worth in the world of men.

Part Three
Marriage

Oleg and Boris advanced on Chernigov. Vsevolod joined Iziaslav in Kiev and these brothers reunited …

Oleg and Boris led pagans to attack the Rus. Many Rus died …

Boris, Oleg and their uncles met in Battle at Nezhata meadow where the carnage was terrible and Boris fell … Iziaslav died, struck on the shoulder by a spear …

The Russian Primary Chronicle, entry *1078,* translated and edited by Samuel Hazzard Cross and Olberg P. Sherbowitz-Wetzor, Medieval Academy of America, Cambridge, Mass. 1930

28

Kiev, December 1076

Sviatoslav died from the cutting of a sore and was buried in Chernigov.

Russian Primary Chronicle, entry, 1076, trans. and edited by Samuel Hazzard Cross and Olberg P. Sherbowitz-Wetzor, 1930.

For almost five years, despite many separations, Thea and Vladimir's apparent happiness was smiled upon by all who knew them. They were sensual by nature but it was more than that – Thea delighted in his vigour, determination and in his sense of justice. He spoke many languages and knew poetry. They discussed Greek poets long into the night. She learned to speak Russian with increased fluency. He was ambitious but not overly so. He was fair-minded. Often he discussed matters of law with her but when she tried to change his opinion the discussions ceased. To Thea's mind, his one fault was that for him her main role in their partnership was that of wife and mother but as the years passed she began to possess an increasingly strong sense of her identity as an admired and clever princess of a great land. She was her father's daughter and she wanted to rule.

She knew that Vladimir admired her intelligence as well as her beauty. One day, she decided, he would need her clever mind to help him rule Russia.

The merchants of Kiev and many of the noblemen expected that in time Vladimir would be their grand prince. Thea heard whispers to this effect amongst her ladies, many of whom visited their families who lived in the city's great houses. Katya, too, carried stories to Thea from her merchant father,

Dimitri, who returned often from his travels to dwell with her Rus mother in a grand house situated below the hill of palaces, in the merchant's quarter in Kiev.

This Christmastide everybody was anxious – merchants, noblemen and Prince Vsevolod's immediate family, in fact, all of Kiev. Prince Sviatoslav lay ill. It had been only three years since he had seized his brother Iziaslav's throne and Iziaslav was thrown out of Kiev for a second time. For three years Sviatoslav ruled. It was not to last. Over this past Christmas, the sense of apprehension amongst the nobility reminded Thea of the atmosphere in King Edward's palace of Westminster ten years before when *he* lay dying. Who would succeed to England's throne? This question had caused the terrible succession crisis that had eventually caused her father's death, their family to be scattered, her exile, and her younger brother Ulf, now sixteen years old, then six years of age, to be taken into Normandy, never to be set free.

Padar, a regular visitor to Thea's terem, said that Iziaslav had it coming. He had raised taxes to build monasteries. He had helped the poor but he refused to provide the merchants with an army to protect them as they traded south along the Dnieper. That decision was unpopular. Tribes from the Steppe lands were attacking ships and demanding tribute. Padar insisted that Iziaslav was weak and Prince Vladimir agreed, but he considered also that his father was foolish for supporting Uncle Sviatoslav and his greedy sons Boris and Oleg. Gleb had already quietly moved south, away from trouble.

When the Kiev Council, led by Sviatoslav and Vsevolod, demanded that Grand Prince Iziaslav leave the city or face imprisonment, Prince Iziaslav had taken as much gold and jewels from the palace as he could pack into fifty closely guarded carts and had set off for Poland, his wife's country. The Poles who had helped Iziaslav the first time he was exiled from his kingdom chose not help him this time. They refused him sanctuary and made an alliance with Prince Sviatoslav. Iziaslav found his sanctuary in Italy.

Who knew what could happen now, Thea mused, if Sviatoslav died. Padar said that Sviatoslav's sons, who ruled in Chernigov, would fight to inherit the throne of Kiev. The Kiev Council had found Sviatoslav as much of a disappointment as his elder brother. Padar reported how this grand prince did not protect the merchants from attacks on the River Dnieper from the Cuman tribes. Earl Connor complained that Sviatoslav refused them guards. Edmund growled that if Prince Vladimir had real courage he would raise an army and throw the Sviatoslav family out of Kiev.

'Hush, Edmund you speak treason. Anyway they spend most of their time in Chernigov.' Then, Thea would warn, 'Have a care where you say such things. There are spies everywhere.'

Edmund would simply say, 'The Cumans attack our ships. Soon it will be our cities.' Thea noted how Russian her brother had become but even so he had no rights in this his adopted country. Despite the attacks the triumvirate of Padar, Connor and Edmund thrived and they grew wealthy.

Now they were reassured as Sviatoslav weakened. It was increasingly clear from court talk that the boyars would have none of Sviatoslav's family to rule if he died. They might instead select the fair-minded and astute Vsevolod as their new grand prince, rather than the Sviatoslavichi sons, whom they considered sly imitations of their father.

Thea sat in her sewing chamber stitching a shirt for her husband. Companionably, she shared the window seat with Katya as the room was warm. The isinglass kept the draughts out and allowed a little natural light to seep through. Harold, her first son, only eighteen months old, was contentedly playing with wooden animals that Earl Connor had given him as a gift. Wrapped in soft furs, her tiny baby, Iziaslav, was sleeping in his cradle as his nurse applied a gentle pressure with her felt-slippered foot to the cradle's rockers.

Snow twirled against the window. Thea loved watching the snow fall. It would soon be piled up about the courtyards, until a few months later it would melt into unpleasant rivers of slush.

But for a time it was beautiful, like a fairy tale.

She stretched her hands towards the coals that glowed in one of the many braziers the servants had brought into her large sewing chamber earlier that afternoon. She could feel her forehead crinkle into worry folds. If there was unrest after Sviatoslav died Vladimir might send her to safety in Novgorod? If he did, she decided that she would refuse to go.

'How can it be?' Katya broke into her thought. 'That in Russia a prince can only become a grand prince if his father has held the throne in Kiev.'

Thea smiled, looking over at little Harold. It was an interesting thought since one day, Harold, grandson of King Harold of England, could become the Grand Prince of all Russia.

She had no love for the grossly overweight, mean-spirited Sviatoslav, nor did she like his sons. She avoided his wife, the German Oda of Trier, whose ladies included Thea's old enemy, Lady Olga. Every time she thought of Lady Olga, she felt that deadly prick in her knee again and anger seeped into her heart.

Vladimir had said that Sviatoslav had once been a great warrior and that long ago when he was a little boy, the three brothers, Sviatoslav, Iziaslav and Vsevolod, a young warrior triumvirate, had together fought off Russia's enemies, wealthy tribes called Cumans who owned enormous sweeps of territory out on the Steppes. His father and uncles were all impressive influences on him, he told Thea, as he grew up. However, as Vladimir explained to Thea, his Uncle Sviatoslav had become greedy and harsh. In truth, he had not been a good influence on Vladimir's father.

If Uncle Sviatoslav died of the sore that had caused poison to seep through his blood, there would be a terrible dispute between her father-in-law, Vsevolod, and his nephews. They would never agree over succession to Kiev's throne. Life in Kiev could become dangerous. Yes, Vladimir would think of his baby sons and send her to safety.

'If Prince Sviatoslav dies, my father says that his sons will not inherit Kiev,' Katya was saying.

'Prince Vsevolod will be grand prince. Sviatoslav stole his brother's throne. Find out all you can, Katya. Your father is the keeper of many secrets.' She wished that Vladimir would confide political secrets to her. If he had, she would not have to listen to the constant speculation that flew about the terem like fire racing through a wheat field.

Thea bit off a length of blue silk from a spool and rethreaded her needle. 'He may not die,' she said as she hemmed the shirt. She smiled over at the four ladies who were embroidering close to the corner stove. 'My ladies will soon want supper. Katya, go downstairs to the kitchens and tell the cooks that since the sewing room is warm, we shall dine here this afternoon rather than in the refectory. Take Harold with you. He might like a ginger pastry.'

Harold tottered over and took hold of Katya's hand when Thea mentioned the words ginger pastry. Not even glancing at his mama, he toddled by Katya's side to the stairway. *A listener. Intelligent child. He knows what he wants*. Thea could hear him chattering nonsense as Katya picked him up to carry him down the wooden staircase. He looks like Edmund, she thought, and Edmund looks like our father. *My father lives on through my son*. She stretched her feet towards the brazier and, as she became mesmerised by the baby's cradle rocking close by, she puzzled the first five years of her marriage. Where had those years gone?

For a time, she had thought that she could not conceive. She was glad that Vladimir never blamed her. Nor should he, she thought one night when he whispered, 'We have time,' as they made love under her silver wolf cover. This bed was reached by steps which Vladimir claimed led him to heaven. Sighing, she remembered how at first she had lain in his arms and traced circles with her fingers amongst the curls that sprouted in a dark entanglement on his chest. All the same, she had longed for a child. Watching Gudrun fall pregnant again caused her to long for her own children with such intensity she thought she was

293

losing her sense of herself inside this one particular longing.

Gudrun told her that it was because her husband was never with her at the right time during her moon cycle. Thea tried various remedies. She wore prayers on her girdle. She carried a small crystal ball in her belt purse as a charm to aid conception. Katya came to her with a remedy her mother swore by. 'On the Holy Icon of St Margaret, she swears this recipe will work,' Katya declared.

'What recipe, Katya? I have no time for spells or concoctions anymore. None work.'

Katya said with conviction, 'This might. My lady, do try it. Take the testicles of an uncastrated pig and dry them and make a powder. If you drink this with wine after the purgation of your menses and cohabit with your lover, my mother says you will conceive.' Katya procured the powder and insisted that her mistress try it.

When Thea threw the powder away, she had not the heart to tell Katya that she had rejected her mother's help. She attended the Cathedral of St Sophia with regularity. There, in the golden light that hung as long shafts at midday Sext, Thea knelt before the jewelled icons depicting her favourite saints, St Margaret, St Cecilia, St Sophia and St Theodosia, their gilded faces illuminated by a hundred glowing candles. She prayed for a child, and as she prostrated herself in prayer she felt the saints' almond-shaped eyes looking down on her with sympathy. Surely they were listening to the longing she held within her heart?

They moved to Smolensk north of Kiev and east of Novgorod for a couple of years. She spent much time with her husband, who had been appointed governor of the region and who received tribute from tribesmen and taxes from merchants. He supervised Council decisions and administered justice. She became pregnant at last.

When she approached her mid-term Vladimir sent her to Novgorod. It would be better for her to give birth in that city where Princess Anya was in residence. There were more luxuries than in a provincial town like Smolensk which was really just a fortress. At first she had refused to transport the birthing chair that had been gifted to her in Denmark because she associated it with Ingegerd, but when she examined it more closely she saw inscribed on it a prayer to St Margaret of Antioch, saint to birthing mothers. The words, *Ease be with you in your labour and may St Margaret protect this mother* followed the curving dragon's tail that circumnavigated the chair's rim. Since her labour happened to fall in July close to St Margaret's feast day she knew that she must use it. She called for it and afterwards she considered that not only had it been right to do so, but it was just to add Ingegerd and the Danish princesses as recipients of her future prayers. Forgiveness was a noble emotion and after the safe delivery of her child, she felt blessed and her sense of forgiveness towards those who had once been unkind swelled in her proud breast.

In the bath-house of Princess Anya's terem, she gave birth to a boy. They called him Harold, but to please the boyars, his official name was Mstislav. He had slipped from her easily as the candle clock turned between daybreak and the dinner hour and she been thankful for the fortune-blessed, comfortable birthing chair for allowing her such ease.

She had not attended her son's christening. Vladimir had not visited her until ten days after the birth. This was another tradition that made her cross but then such traditions existed in England also. By this time the bath-house, where she had given birth and the terem chamber, where she slept and ate, were purified. The purification ritual took place on St Margaret's feast day. The priest stood on the threshold, muttered prayers and sprinkled holy water over everything in the chamber including herself. Afterwards she, to her great relief, was churched and permitted to move freely around the fortress.

Importantly her husband, who had travelled to Novgorod to be close to his wife and his son, returned to her bed. They did not have intercourse for another month but again Lady Fortune smiled on her. Fifteen months later, Thea gave birth to a second child, another son using the twice-blessed birthing chair. They named him Iziaslav for his banished uncle. He was two months old when she had come out of seclusion just in time for Kiev's Christmas feasts, just in time to know that her life at court was about to change. Importantly, now, she was able to talk with Padar and Earl Connor and consider their thoughts on the grand prince's illness.

Padar was often in the north buying furs or selling spices, nuts and oils from Byzantium. Edmund returned to Ireland promising to return soon. Earl Connor, who lived mostly in Novgorod, married at last. He had chosen one of the English exiles, a flaxen-headed young widow whose rich merchant husband had been executed by Bishop Odo of Bayeux in York. The merchant had been in the wrong place at the wrong time and was accused of hiding English rebels. The widow had escaped with her baby son and with as much jewellery and silver as she could secrete in her luggage. She came to Russia on a rescue ship that Vladimir had organised with Earl Connor.

Vladimir had never secured Thea's little brother Ulf's release from Normandy. Despite the secret request he had sent to King William, he was refused. Ulf was much too valuable a hostage and besides, William had his scribe write that the boy was receiving an education in Normandy. He would neither want to leave his religion nor his Norman friends. Ulf, the king's scribe wrote, was destined for the monastery.

'I am sure that is not true,' Thea said when the letter with this response arrived in Kiev. 'I shall write to him.'

'Maybe so, but at least he is safe and in good health. Leave well alone. You will not write.' That was clearly a battle Thea was not going to win. Instead she had angrily fingered the swan amulet she wore about her neck. She could not find it in her heart to forgive the Bastard William, even though it was the past and no amount of ill-wishing could bring her father back. Nothing would happen to reunite her with her mother this side of heaven.

Her mother had never responded to her letter of years before.

She was sure that Elditha had not received it. If she was not permitted to write to William the Bastard then she would write to her mother once more. She simply wrote that she hoped her mother was well and that she had given birth to a son whom they called Harold. She sent her letter secretly with Katya's father who had known priests whom he asked to find a way to get it to Canterbury. No reply came. She despaired and cursed William. When Iziaslav was born she wrote another letter similar to the first announcing the birth of her second son. This time she entrusted it to Earl Connor who would that spring return to his wife in Novgorod and because one of his ships was sailing to England.

Her little brother, Ulf, was lost in a dark Norman world. Against her better judgement and the teachings of her adopted Russian Church, Thea once again ill-wished William who had destroyed her family and whose family she hoped would one day destroy each other.

29

January 1078

'Will there be a coronation?' Thea asked Vladimir as they sat on a cushioned bench in the palace hall. Her feet were freezing after having stood in the church nave all morning through Uncle Sviatoslav's long funeral service. She raised her slippered feet towards the fire, and thankfully sipped from the warming cup of kvass her husband offered her, before passing him back the cup. He drank deeply. He had not answered her question. 'Will they crown your father?' she asked quietly.

Vladimir set the cup down on the bench between them and hunched over the blaze, his head close to hers. She felt his breath on her hair causing her veil to slightly move. 'Unlikely,' he muttered into her ear. 'There is much to be considered.'

She turned her head and held his dark eyes with a quizzical look. His forehead had creased. He was tense. She felt his concern. She saw it on his countenance. 'I hope they consider soon. I dislike indecision.'

'I do not think your likes or dislikes will be considered, my wife,' Vladimir said as he shifted along the bench slightly. His voice was kindly but firm. Women, of course, she remembered, had no place involving themselves in decisions made by men. Well one day that must change, she decided there and then. *My time will come. If Vladimir ever rules this land, I shall have my say.*

Soon enough, she knew that the women would retire to the terem. The men would remain in the hall where they would discuss the future. And that future, to Thea's mind, now looked extremely unsettled.

Sviatoslav's sons and Vsevolod, her father-in-law, would not agree about the succession. After all, Iziaslav was still an exile.

He had sons as well. Perhaps his sons would return to Kiev from Italy, where they had sought shelter, to claim their inheritance.

Sviatoslav's coffin was to be taken by sleigh to Chernigov where it would be laid to rest in the Holy Saviour Cathedral. Prince Vsevolod would ride north with the funeral procession in the company of the Chernigov boyars. Vladimir was to remain in Kiev just in case there were the usual disputes over land and property between the nobles and merchants who sat on the town council. Thea was glad he was to stay behind and she determined to make him discuss the more interesting disputes with her. Who knows what disputes could erupt in Chernigov? *Best to stay on the margins of those.*

It is still Christmas, she thought, and it is not going to end happily. There had been none of the usual festivities, great feasts or dancing and storytelling. All that had been banished because Prince Sviatoslav had lain dying in a darkened chamber. Instead, over Christmas, the court of Kiev attended endless candlelit church services praying for his recovery, but despite everyone's prayers, Sviatoslav had died anyway.

Across the room noblemen had gathered in huddles, whispering. Many nobles said that God had frowned upon this grand prince who had stolen his brother's throne. Serious-faced priests carrying tall crosses moved between groups. Vladimir glanced over at the young noblemen who were his cousins, Sviatoslav's sons, Boris, Gleb and Oleg. The princes were deep in conversation with their own boyars who had travelled in bitter weather to Kiev for the funeral. In a few days they would escort the coffin back for the interment in Holy Saviour at Chernigov. At least it was so cold the corpse would not go putrid. And when the Chernigov priests opened the coffin lid to place a relic inside to help Sviatoslav on his way to heaven his rigid body would not stink.

Thea's eyes followed her husband's watchful glances.

'No coronation,' Vladimir repeated. He lifted a poker and stirred a log into life, creating a myriad of sparks. 'Sviatoslav's family will remain in Chernigov. It controls the Dnieper trade north, a bigger land than that surrounding Kiev. Just think of the taxes! My cousins will want to hold onto it. However … Katya's father, Dimitri, has been sent to Germany to bring Uncle Iziaslav back.' His eyes looked stern as he placed two long, manicured fingers on his lips. 'Do not breathe a word of it, my love, not even to Katya who has no idea where her father has gone.'

'Katya's father … go on,' she whispered, leaning forward with her feet now planted firmly on the tiled floor.

'If my father brings Uncle Iziaslav back to Kiev and supports him, my father will get …'

Seeing what he was saying, she finished his sentence, 'Chernigov. He will be next in line for Chernigov.'

'Shush, Thea. Do not say it so loudly.'

She shook her head as she thought for a moment. 'But if our noble father becomes grand prince after Iziaslav, it could be *you* who gets Chernigov.'

He smiled at her. 'Exactly! You are quick, my sweet wife. Chernigov is a prize. But you see, it is not just about Chernigov. My father does not want to be grand prince. He believes that God would frown on him if he sat on Kiev's throne while the rightful grand prince lives in exile. He regretted supporting Sviatoslav in the end; backed the wrong brother.'

Sometimes Thea did not believe that God cared. He had not cared that Duke William had taken the throne of England. He had allowed the dispossessed English to suffer. Some said it had been her father's fault. In 1066, worried nobles had said that the long-tailed star that had shone in the Easter night sky had been proof of God's displeasure with the English for allowing Harold Godwinson to be crowned as their king. He had broken a promise to recognise Duke William as King of England, a promise made over relics. 'I doubt God *would* be displeased if your father kept peace in the land and exercised fair rule and even-handed judgement over his people.'

A tall, cross-carrying priest passed close to their bench and

301

bowed to them. 'Best stop this conversation, my lady,' Vladimir said. 'There may be ears in the walls.' He glanced across the room again. Again, she followed his watchful eyes. The women were assembling behind the widow.

'You must go and join them,' Vladimir remarked.

Thea noticed Olga hovering beside Princess Oda. 'Must I? Well, I suppose it is expected.' She was irritated that she must leave the comfort of the hearth. She felt resentful at being banished from male conversation.

'You must, my sweet.' He turned to her and patted her hand. 'And I must put on a semblance of sorrow for my deceased uncle, especially around my cousins.'

Boris, Gleb and Oleg were approaching their bench. They moved together as if one, same pace, same gait. Well, trouble brews there for us all, Thea mused. When they learn Vsevolod's plans for Kiev, they will be furious and, in a way, she could not help thinking, as one who had, herself, been dispossessed, one cannot blame them. Rus law decreed that Chernigov went to the second senior prince and if Iziaslav returned Vsevolod would without doubt take up that position and rule Russia's richest city after Kiev.

'I shall find Katya and bring her with me,' she said quickly, standing up. 'Though, my prince, I have no desire to be forced into conversation with those women.'

'It is only one afternoon.' Vladimir sighed, and turned to speak to his cousins.

The widow's ladies began to exit the hall as if they were a pack of pups clinging to a protective mother bear. Except Oda was not protective; she was vulnerable. Her stepsons' wives were the she-wolves of the palace. Thea knew them to be greedy, silly and scheming.

As she made ready to find Katya and her warm mantle, Thea wondered what protection Oda of Germany would get, now that she was a widow. She would depend upon the goodwill of her stepsons. Thea quickly wove her way through the press of people and called to Katya, who stood amongst the female servants, to fetch her boots and her mantle. She bowed to Prince Vsevolod but her father-in-law was deep in conversation with one of his boyars and never noticed her. She was, after all, only a woman.

Feeling annoyed by his dismissive attitude, she reached the entrance where Katya was waiting with her boots and mantle. Katya helped Thea remove her slippers and replace these with her boots. By the time Thea had her mantle gathered around her shoulders and her brooch pin securing it closed, Princess Anya had already disappeared through the outer doorway with her ladies. *I expect she does not want to speak with them either today.*

They climbed an outer staircase to the terem. Off came boots and on went the slippers again. The widow sat on the winged chair closest to the heat of a huge stove. The other women were seated on benches that were placed in a large circle close to the stove. Thea joined them after sending Katya to sit with the lesser ladies near the door.

They drank honeyed wine and ate cakes. At first the conversation was about the sadness of Sviatoslav's illness. Afterwards it turned to the funeral and how chill St Sophia had been. 'My poor bones,' one elderly noblewoman remarked. 'I cannot do it anymore,' she complained. 'The cathedral is draughty.'

You could be next, Thea considered, but did not say it of course.

A servant hurried over to the elderly lady with a hot brick wrapped in cloth to warm her feet. 'I shall have chilblains,' she said by way of explanation.

The women close to her sympathised but as the wine loosened their tongues they forgot the old lady and were soon commenting on who was present that day and who was missing. Many nobles lived on estates in outlying districts from where only narrow snowy tracks led to Kiev. They had sent outriders ahead to say that they could not break through and had returned from whence they came.

Soon they ran out of comfortable conversation. It was apparent that all wondered about the succession, though because none spoke of it in Princess Anya's presence, they sat in silence.

Anya, herself, was first to break it by saying to Oda, the German widow, 'What do you intend to do now?' As she spoke it felt as if a chill wind had entered the chamber. The widow looked through Anya as if she had not heard the question. Anya tried again. 'I just mean, Oda, will you chose to dwell in Kiev or Chernigov?'

'What a great question that is,' the widow said at last. She shifted her considerable bulk in her winged chair and grasped the arms.

'I am sorry. It was insensitive of me to ask,' Anya said.

After a moment's pause Oda said in her thickly accented Russian, 'No, it is best to speak about it.' Everyone's eyes were on her. Everyone was waiting for her to speak her mind. No one liked her stepdaughters. She took a breath and said, 'Yaroslav, my child, is only ten years old. His three stepbrothers insist on keeping him with them. But, there is clearly no place for me here. I must return to my homeland.' It was obvious that she did not want to go back to Trier because tears welled up in her eyes.

Oda was Sviatoslav's second wife. Though she was very plump, she was young and handsome, particularly when she smiled her sad smile. It was likely that her important relation, the third Henry, the Holy Roman Emperor, would find her another husband soon enough.

The two young foolish wives of Oleg and Gleb looked at Oda from where they sat on the opposite bench. 'Yaroslav will have two mothers now instead of one,' Oleg's wife ventured in a honeyed voice.

Thea doubted that the young woman cared for Oda's child one bit. It would be the boy's nurses and tutors who would care for him. She wondered how the poor, sad German widow really felt about the family's plans for her son. If those silly princesses tried to be mother to Harold, Thea knew that *she* would fight

304

against them with freshly grown talons for the occasion.

'Your son will no doubt visit you, Princess Oda,' she said in as gentle manner as she could manage.

'Indeed, my dear, indeed, and that is a great comfort.' Princess Oda reached out to Lady Olga who was seated beside her during the exchange and clasped Olga's hand. 'My loving Olga is to travel with me. She will remain by my side until I am settled.' The widow turned to Olga with pleading eyes. 'Won't you, Olga?'

The widow was too trusting. Thea was sure that Olga only cared about herself.

Yet, to her surprise, Olga tenderly stroked Princess Oda's head. 'Princess, it is agreed. I shall stay with you.'

Anya exchanged a glance with Thea as if to say 'good riddance to Lady Olga,' before addressing Princess Oda again, 'In a fair world your son should remain with you. If you like I shall speak with my husband on the matter. You will not be departing Rus lands before summer.'

Oda smiled. 'You are kind, Anya.'

'Princess Oda, tell us this, do your stepsons intend to remain in Chernigov until the succession is decided?' Anya ventured.

Thea saw frowns on the wives' faces as Anya spoke. Oda said, 'My stepsons say that Chernigov is their principality. Until Gleb inherits Kiev after Vsevolod's death, they say, they have insisted that they shall remain there. In that event, Gleb will be the senior prince of his generation, will he not? As for Boris, he is a monk.'

Gleb's wife was nodding vehemently. 'Absolutely, and when he has Kiev, our son will inherit Chernigov.'

Anya smiled serenely and said smoothly, 'Not quite, my dear. Do not forget how their cousin, Sviatopolk, who is exiled with his father to the German Empire, is first in line of their generation, more senior than they. The boyars of Kiev have not yet decided which prince will succeed. Prince Iziaslav may yet return to Kiev.'

'A returned much-hated prince. I think not.' Lady Olga

305

leaned forward and spoke clearly as if it was all decided already. 'No, Princess Anya, you will be the next grand princess here. The boyars will choose Prince Vsevolod. My husband has that on good authority.' She added rudely, 'Just think how the Kiev nobles will love to have a Steppe Kipchak princess as their queen.'

'I think they would like it very well, especially a princess as kind, beautiful and as educated as Princess Anya,' Thea ventured. She turned to Anya before Olga said another word. 'My lady Anya, perhaps we should leave and return to my palace now. The hour is late. Some of these ladies have much to do before they depart for Chernigov in the morning.'

In that moment Thea was glad that Princess Anya had chosen to stay with her while Sviatoslav's widow, her stepnephews and their retainers occupied the princely Kiev palace.

Anya nodded, 'Indeed, daughter, it is growing chillier here. My children have not seen their mother all day.'

She turned her head and clicking her fingers she called for her waiting women. Katya rushed forward to Thea surrounded by Princess Anya's ladies. They bundled Thea and Princess Anya into their mantles. The women of the Sviatoslavichi rose from their stools and politely bowed. Thea bowed back. She felt sorry for Princess Oda, unloved by that family and apparently dependent on Lady Olga. There were false smiles on the Sviatoslavichi women's faces as Anya and Thea departed for their waiting sleighs. Thea thought, *poor unwanted German Oda.*

The Sviatoslavichi women were not Thea's friends. When Oleg's and Gleb's two wives found out that they were to leave wealthy Chernigov for nondescript principalities in the Rus hinterlands, their verbal swords would be bloodied and, as Thea confided to Anya, she hoped that her family would be out of the line of attack when the battle began.

30

February 1078

In February, there were ceaseless quarrels amongst the boyars and increased pressure on Vsevolod to rule. Vladimir and Thea argued because he told her to mind her own business when she gave him her kopekworth of advice. He stayed away from her and she ignored him as she walked boldly into the hall followed by Katya, sometimes with Gudrun, and greeted whomever she chose to greet. On crisp mornings she accompanied Gudrun out into market places wrapped in a concealing mantle with only a page to carry her parcels. That way she was able to find out the peoples' thoughts. She listened and she watched. They were afraid that when spring came the Sviatoslavichi brothers would burn their homes and destroy their trade and if they did not the Steppe tribes would burst through the gates and fire the city. Thea wondered what her silent husband's equally silent father intended to do about the complaints. They must talk. However there seemed to be no resolution to their own quarrel. They passed each other in the palace halls and only greeted each other briefly. He did not, as she had expected him to do, banish her to the terem.

At last Vladimir broke their impasse. To her great surprise, he joined her in her comfortable private chambers one chilly wintry afternoon. She greeted him coolly and carried on with her sewing as he attempted to make conversation, asking about the children and remarking on how he knew that she had been out into the markets with Gudrun. He asked her what she had heard. He looked worried, his brow furrowing as she answered him with concise sentences, saying how the people feared the Sviatoslavichi. Evidently her freedom was watched. He had her followed secretly by his armed bodyguards who were instructed to watch over her.

'You had me what …' she protested.

'The streets are unsafe and anyway, now, I am pleased that you are observant and can report back so succinctly.'

'I am clearly not observant enough,' she said tersely thinking of the shadows whom she had *not* observed following her. He shrugged and seeing her angry look he smiled, lifted her hand and kissed it. She snatched it back.

'How would you like to travel to Pereiaslavl, and I don't just mean the fortress, how would you like to stay on our estate close by?' he said.

'Why?' Thea said. She carefully threaded her needle with a deep blue silken thread as she thought about the suggestion. She liked it, but was not quite ready to admit it. She slipped her needle into her linen tapestry and looked up at him quizzically.

'I want you and the boys to be safe if there is a rebellion in Kiev. Prince Iziaslav and his son, Sviatopolk, are returning to the city.'

'I heard something of the sort.' She made another dainty stitch. She was stitching a new length for her rushnyk, adding the birth of her second child in blue cross-stitching. Looking up again from her needlework, she enquired, 'Do the boyars agree he should come back here?'

Vladimir shook back his long black hair and frowned. 'It is a solution. If my father remains to advise him, yes; there will be conditions attached to his return.'

'Such as?'

'Really, Thea, must you concern yourself with politics?'

'Yes,' she said firmly. 'I must.'

'Well then, if you must. If there are threats from the Steppe tribes, Prince Iziaslav must grant the boyars arms and freedom to protect the city. He must safeguard the merchant ships travelling north through the trade route from Chernigov and south through Pereiaslavl to Byzantium.' He took a breath. 'Now you know.'

'I see,' she said thoughtfully. 'There need not be any

308

ceremony because thanks to your father's negotiations Prince Iziaslav will simply quietly return from exile. I don't have to stay in Kiev, nor do I have to go north to Smolensk or Novgorod again because our interests lie in keeping Pereiaslavl safe.' She felt herself smiling at her deliberate use of the second person.

He was quick to respond. '*Our interests*? Let us be clear, *only* through *me* do your interests matter, but to me those interests are always important, and to be truthful I do value your intelligence and advice, well, sometimes.' He opened his hands in a supplicant's gesture. His eyes, those brown velvet eyes, his soft smiling mouth would win her when he let go of his masculine haughtiness. She raised her eyebrow into a curve and gave him her firmest glare. She was not quite ready to acquiesce. 'Look,' he went on, 'Thea, I know you prefer the estate in Pereiaslavl to the fortress in Novgorod.' He touched her stomach which was still flat. 'Are you with child again, my love?'

'I am not.'

'It is just that you seem so irritable. Well, hopefully you might be soon. I know you want more children and we cannot get them if we continue this quarrel. Our third child might be born in Pereiaslavl. We can have time together and share things we used to share, stories, music, hunting, picnics in the woods.'

'Another child will not be so easy if I am in Pereiaslavl and you are here. How can we share our lives if you must be here?' She considered for a heartbeat. 'Yet, I would be very happy to be in the country for the summer.' She laid her sewing aside. 'I shall bring Gudrun with me. Padar will be in Constantinople buying silks and spices. Katya's father will be trading. He could return by Pereiaslavl. The arrangement is perfect.' She did not mention Earl Connor who was trading north and whom she hoped would see that her mother received a letter from her. She thought again. 'And if Anya wanted to come too ...'

'She might prefer to remain in Kiev for now, but later my stepmother would perhaps appreciate the country air. I shall speak with my father.'

'We would be such a company of women.'

'You would, except that I intend coming too, at least until the summer. I have a desire for a season of hunting, and this way I can oversee the Steppe borderlands.' He kissed her ear. 'We shall be together and you can bring your falcons. As for a complicated terem with its rumours and politics, since that hardly exists in such a small country palace, we can sleep together every night without comment.' She felt desire creep up through her body. She could never resist him.

'But what about Smolensk?' she asked, turning to face him.

'There is a governor in place until we send one of the junior princes there.' He leaned over, caught her arms and kissed her mouth. For a moment their tongues flicked together. She felt the old desire rise again.

'You mean Boris, Gleb or Oleg,' she said after he drew back.

He frowned, his forehead crumpling into a rippling sea of worry lines. 'Indeed, we should separate my cousins. They have been together in Chernigov for too long.' He thoughtfully stroked his recently grown moustache. He asked brightly, 'Sleigh or ship? You have a travel choice.'

She found herself longing to glide over the snow-filled tracks that stretched south of Kiev. 'Sleigh because the children will love to fly over the snow. And it is only a short distance. But we must leave soon before there is a thaw.'

'Sleigh it is. We shall leave within a week. Can you get us packed within a space of three days?'

'I shall start to pack now, this very moment,' she said joyfully, anticipating the adventure they would share.

'No, not just yet,' he said, covering her face with fluttering little kisses. They tickled. She laughed and touched his moustaches. He kissed her again. 'Why don't we spend the rest of this afternoon under that wolfskin of yours?'

'It is a holy day. And it *is* the afternoon.'

'I think God will look the other way.' He grinned wickedly

at her and his dark eyes filled with mischief. He learned down and whispered, 'Send your women away.'

'They will criticise us. It is scandalous,' she said with a tease in her voice.

'Nonsense. I shall send them to the sewing room if you will not.' He cast a mischievous glance over at Thea's ladies who were gathered around a brazier stitching shirts for the poor. 'Ladies, perhaps you could retire,' he called down the antechamber to them. They glanced up from the embroidery they were working with a glint of amusement in their eyes. 'Your lady and I want a little privacy this afternoon,' he added. 'Take the children with you.'

Lady Sabrina, who had joined Thea's household, nodded, and as her senior lady replied, 'My lord, we shall retire to the workroom at once.'

Katya tugged Harold by the hand. A nursemaid lifted a protesting little Iziaslav into her arms. A second lifted up his cradle and the women trooped out with Lady Sabrina leading them, the nursemaids glancing back with amused glances.

Vladimir called after his elder son, 'I shall see you later, young Harold, after your nap. Behave for Katya or the whip will come out. If I get a report that you are a good little boy, you can have ginger cakes instead.'

'Ginger cakes now,' Harold insisted as Katya hurried him from the room.

'You should not scare him,' Thea said to her husband after they had gone and she could hear them climbing the staircase to the work rooms above.

'Nonsense, I promised him ginger cakes. You saw how his eyes opened at the suggestion of them.' He took her hands in his own and tugged her up from the bench. She tried to pull away but he said, 'Now you … shall I take my riding whip to you, my lady, for your daring to question me or shall we …?'

He slipped her veil away and pushed his hands into her hair, loosening its rich abundance. Pins fell to the floor. Her hair floated in a golden-red cloud around her face. He drew her into his arms and began to untie the laces at the sides of her outer gown. It dropped in a pile of soft sage-coloured wool to her feet. 'I think I would prefer the wolfskin to the whip,' she murmured as she stepped out of her second gown.

After her second gown was discarded, she found herself pulling him through the curtain that separated her two chambers, untying the silk laces of his shirt, kissing the curling hair on his chest, falling against him, tempted into a frenzy of desire.

He pulled off her plain linen undergown and swept her from the floor as if she were a feather. He swirled her around, her red hair fanning out as he carried her to their bed. Not bothering to mount the steps up to her bed, he tossed her onto the covers. She was wearing her shift, the final garment of four. While she had been kissing him, she had managed to remove his two garments. They made a trail across the tiles of her antechamber and through the rich curtain that separated bedchamber from antechamber. As he tossed her onto the bed, her embroidered silken slippers dropped from her feet to be lost in the bedcovers.

'I adore you,' he told her as he climbed up after her and stretched her out on the silvery wolfskin. Gently he removed her very last shift and delicately laid kisses on her breasts.

'And I thee, my beautiful prince,' she whispered back, her previous irritation forgotten in the midst of their lovemaking. Though when she did remember she felt she had won the siege if not the battle. He had come to her contrite, well almost so.

Snow blew up in clouds as they travelled in sleighs pulled by strong little horses over tracks that snaked back and forth, narrowed, came near to a river and curved back again. Through skeletal trees of pine, birch, beech and oak, Thea caught glimpses of the frozen river. The ice floating on the water reflected the woods and the sky in a revolving blur of blues, browns and green. She thought it perfect.

She snuggled in deep below thick furs beside Gudrun. Harold nestled between them. Iziaslav was wrapped in a sack of marten fur and for most of the journey remained fast asleep in his wet nurse's arms except when he was hungry.

The grown children were all wrapped so warmly against the winter cold that only their noses showed. Gudrun's trio of little girls travelled with Katya and their maids in the second sleigh. Vladimir rode his horse at the head of their guards, often doubling back over the hardened snow track checking along the column of six long horse-driven sleighs to ensure their safety.

The sun shone in the middle of the day causing the snow to glisten. Vladimir's sword hilt reflected the sunlight, and his black hair, which fell long onto his shoulders, appeared like a raven's glossy coat. Thea found herself filled with admiration and her heart filled with joy at the thought of the romantic days that stretched before them in their small, remote country retreat. Her heart sang because they were journeying through a wooded landscape that belonged to fairy tales and today she felt that she belonged within it.

They stopped at a boyar's modest estate on the first night. The nobleman and his wife had given up the best bed, a curtained box bed in the hall close to the hearth, for the prince and his lady. Their two small boys slept with them, Iziaslav in his cradle and Harold snuggled in the bed between his parents. Vladimir looked down on her, smiling through the glow of a stumpy candle, as she cuddled tiny Iziaslav.

'Sleep?' he whispered as the child seemed to sleep.

'Yes, pinch the candle, my lord.'

Leaning across Vladimir, she slipped the sleeping baby into his cradle close to his nurse's pallet.

The room grew peaceful. All about them, throughout the old-fashioned hall she could hear others snoring. It was a comforting sound that reminded her of the halls she had known in her childhood. As she began to fall into a half-sleep, she dwelled on the past and sleepily wondered how her mother, Elditha, fared and how her sister Gunnhild lived now. She must find a secret channel by which they could communicate and recently she had wondered if Katya's father could help her again.

Some time ago Thea heard a rumour from Edmund who had got it from Denmark. After Dowager Queen Edith, her aunt, had died a year before at Wilton, Thea's sister, Gunnhild, had run away with the same wicked Breton count who had courted their mother. Thea started out of her half-sleep. *What, by the virgin, was Gunnhild doing with that man?*

Thea could remember with clarity how the flame-headed knight, Alain of Brittany, watched her when she was only fifteen in Countess Gytha's palace in Exeter, before the women of Exeter had gone into exile on Flatholm. *He wanted one of us.* That knight wanted us for my mother's lands, first, my mother, then me, and now Gunnhild.

For a short while her mind pushed sleep away. She listened to Harold breathing beside her and to Vladimir, who was beginning to snore in company with the other men in the hall. She wondered what Gunnhild looked like now she was grown up. Was she fair and slender like their mother, tall like Elditha, tall like me? *I have not seen my little sister since she was eight years old and I had only thirteen summers, so long ago, long before all our lives were turned inside out by war, but Lady Fortune smiles on me. I have a prince, kinder than many others.*

She whispered a prayer into the darkness, *St Theodosia, protect my sister and watch over my mother.* Then she touched the Godwin ring on the middle finger of her left hand and added a special plea, *Grandmother, wherever you may be, and may it be beyond St Peter's gate, ask my saint to intercede with the King of Heaven for us all.*

That night, Thea dreamed her father was seated on a noble brown stallion. He was wearing a chain mail overshirt that was so heavy only he could lift it. His great blond moustaches were drooping below his nose plate. She saw his eyes, so blue and clear that when he fixed them on anyone, servant or thane, or his sons and daughters, none dared ever to lie to him. In her sleep she felt little Harold shift a little beside her. Her ghost father looked at her through his piercing eyes, and then they travelled down to rest upon her sleeping son. Staring at her with tears misting over his eyes, he said, 'Gytha, my daughter, remember that you are our future. Remember it well.'

She sighed in her sleep. It was a message filled with both defeat and promise. If she were to believe it, Godwin's was a lost cause. Edmund had followed the best course possible by becoming a merchant trader sailing with Earl Connor, trading north to Iceland and south to Constantinople. She opened her eyes wide for a moment and this time saw the night cloaking her family safely together. At last she fell into a second deeper, dreamless sleep.

31

Summer 1078

Thea was overjoyed when, just before midsummer, Edmund
rode to the estate with news from England. Earl Waltheof, the
last English earl in England, and two Breton earls had rebelled
and had attempted to destroy William's hold on England.

'What?' Thea said astounded, gripping the arms of her
garden chair. So they could talk privately she had swept him out
into the pear orchard, her sanctuary.

'But it was not to be. The plot was foiled. Earl Waltheof has
been executed for his pains, one of the rebellious Breton earls is
held prisoner in a dark dungeon. The other has fled to Brittany.'
For a moment she listened to bees buzzing and a finch singing
above in a pear tree.

'The thanes will never rebel again,' she said at last.

'Best look to the future. Our sister has. She is with that
Breton, Alain of Brittany. And I heard she has done rather well
for herself; a castle in Brittany and another in Yorkshire.'

Thea shrugged. 'Good for her. I wish her well of him. He is
after our mother's properties again.'

Edmund nodded. 'Afraid so, but poor Godwin. Let us hope
he finds some happiness too now he has given up rebellions. I
heard that he will marry an Irish noblewoman. It will bring our
brother a new life,' he said to Thea.

'I hope he marries soon. The Irish king still holds much of
my father's wealth. Our brother should get himself a great
estate.'

'If our silver has not all disappeared into thwarted rebellions,
he might. We should have used our wealth in a different way
and offered a ransom for Ulf instead,' Edmund said bitterly.

'It is doubtful that a ransom would be acceptable to William.
Vladimir tried to get Ulf back and was refused. Maybe Ulf is

happy where he is. He must be nearly eighteen years old now. Normandy is his home. He has forgotten us.' She swiped at a bee. 'Go back to your queen, bee.'

'I shall never forget Ulf,' Edmund said with sadness in his voice.

'You hardly knew him and nor did I. Now, come inside and enjoy supper. We have strawberries tonight and cream and as much of last year's pear cider as you can drink. And I think our Katya will be pleased to see you.'

She noticed he had the grace to blush when she mentioned Katya.

On Midsummer's Day, the prince organised a hunting expedition. He was proud of his roosts. Vladimir, as Harold, Thea's father had done, kept hawks, goshawks and even a golden eagle that he had recently procured from a territory far to the east. This was the bird he wanted most of all to fly. When he mentioned a hunt on Midsummer's Day, Thea said she would come too. 'I want to fly Juno,' she said.

'My dear, really you should not. Not now that you are with child again. What if the excitement caused us to lose him?'

'Him? I hope *this* baby is a daughter,' she said, 'Nonsense, my mother often rode out with my father when he flew his hawks. Edmund will remember it if you do not believe *me*.'

'This is Rus, Thea, not England. Ladies here …'

'Do not fly hawks. Well I do, which is precisely why I have Juno. You have taken me out hawking before and you shall now,' she insisted, arguing back and even sulking. As she knew he eventually would, he gave in.

'If you promise to take great care, my love; Juno is a well-trained goshawk but I do not want you galloping after her when she brings down her prey. Those marshes can be deadly. A horse can stumble off the path.'

'I won't gallop, I promise. I shall wait patiently. I shall not race after her. And Gudrun, she is not with child, may she come too? If she and Katya promise to take care of the children, why not let them both join us, and the maids and children? It is St

John's Day, after all. It would be a treat for our household and especially for Edmund who has been sad about our brothers.'

'Well, yes, put so prettily, if you insist. Katya too, huh.' There was a twinkle in his eye. Katya was twenty-five summers old and although she was no longer young it was obvious that Edmund had taken a liking to her.

'Harold is three years old and well able to sit on his pony as long as he does as he is told. It is time he saw the hawking.' Vladimir glanced up at the cloudless sky. 'And a great day for it too. Get the servants to make us up a picnic. The other children can follow in a wagon.'

After Prime, Vladimir went off to the barns muttering. Thea watched him disappear through the door.

She smiled as she climbed up the ladder to her solar, named so after the new continental fashion. A heavy curtain separated the solar from a bedchamber which she shared with Vladimir. Since life on the estate was more carefree and informal than life in the family's city palaces, she hoped that they would stay here for a very, very long time.

In the solar, she found Katya and Gudrun giggling like young girls over a posy of summer flowers that they were arranging in a jar. Gudrun had lifted up a stem, inhaling its scent. Peeping over the bouquet she teased. 'Katya, he loves you.' She gave it to Katya to arrange. There was a pretty wild rose amongst a collection of maidenhair and daisies. 'Well, why else would he send you these flowers on St John's feast day, especially this rose?'

Katya daintily touched a roseleaf. 'Shall I send this leaf back to him?'

'*Who* is *he*?' Thea asked as she approached the chest.

Both women looked up, their hands fumbling with delicate daisy stems, the maidenhair scattering all over the coffer. Katya held the rose so tightly it looked as if the thorns might cause her pain.

'My brother?' Thea queried when there was no immediate reply. 'Is Edmund responsible for your midsummer posy?'

They nodded together. She began to laugh. So, Edmund *was* wooing Katya.

'He sent his page with them and gave them to Gudrun for me after Prime. Should I send them back, my lady?'

'No, you may keep the gift. It is St John's feast day, a day for flowers, but you need to hurry because we are all spending the day on our horses.' She touched Gudrun's arm. 'Gudrun, go down to the kitchens at once. Ask for pies and pastries and apples, if there are any to be had. Tell them to fill some flasks with water and others with watered kvass. Collect the children. Change into something comfortable. You can travel in the wagon with the little ones and two of their nurses. We are going out to the marshes to watch the hawking. Rub the children's skin well with lemon juice. Then rub your own. A waste of a precious lemon, but 'tis best we all protect ourselves today from biting creatures.'

After Gudrun hurried off, Thea turned to Katya. 'I think you might like to ride with me. Edmund can be our escort. You can have Koshka as your mount.' 'Koshka' meant cat, though this Koshka was no cat but a sturdy white pony. Katya narrowed her almond-shaped eyes at the news that she was riding with Edmund. 'Katya, best not to send him back the posy. He might die of longing for your attention and that would never do.'

Thea laughed again when a blush as red as the rose Katya was holding settled on her cheeks. She said quietly, 'Let me say now that we would have no objection to you and Edmund becoming betrothed. Love is precious. His life has yielded to him much heartache, difficulty and sorrow. He does not need you to bring him a dowry. We shall provide for you both. My brother, as you know, is part of a great merchant business running up and down our rivers and another across the seas sailing between Ireland and Iceland. Edmund would not always be by your side. But in those times, I hope you will return to me. After all, I shall become your sister.'

She heard Katya exhale a long breath. The girl's eyes shone like silk. She was crushing the rose. The thorns were biting into her skin. Thea noticed a crimson droplet fall to the coffer.

'That rose is causing you pain.'

'My lady,' Katya said simply, laying the rose down on the coffer, 'I am far below him. He is a Saxon prince.' Then her cat-like green eyes opened wide. 'Has he asked?'

'No, Katya, not yet, but I think he might.' Thea involuntarily lifted her hand to stroke the swan pendant that fell below her throat. Surely, it granted wishes. She looked up and smiled. 'Yes, I think he will. Now come and help me change my clothing into something comfortable for the ride.'

They found a woody glade shaded from the sun by beech trees, back from the river, so that the biting insects which hovered around watery places were fewer. Pages hobbled the horses and their maids unpacked the long covered wagon. Gudrun laid out a linen cloth and opened their baskets. Gudrun's little girls fashioned posies of daisies and placed them on the cloth.

Vladimir lifted Harold onto his own horse and together they watched as Thea allowed her goshawk to soar high into the blue sky. It flew along the river southwards through the marshes. Now a speck in the sky she thought she saw it pounce on a tiny bird, maybe a thrush. She was right. The goshawk returned with the poor trapped creature, obediently allowing it to drop by Thea's feet. Harold shouted and clapped his hands. 'Again, again! Send Juno up again,' he chorused in a frenzy of excitement.

Thea rewarded her bird with a mouse from a basket of dead creatures and her page popped the thrush into a reed basket kept aside for the day's catch. Already they had collected a dozen small birds.

'After this next flight, we stop to eat,' Vladimir said firmly. 'You mother must rest too. Later, I shall release my eagle. I have seen several pheasant flying up there today. I want some of those.' He turned to Thea. 'You may fly Juno again, my wife. Perhaps she will catch our supper.'

'Here we go,' Thea said as she released Juno into the skies.

Juno swooped from above taking her prey, another small bird. Just as she soared back with it, Thea said, 'Horse hoofs are approaching.' A moment later, horsemen broke through a stand of ash trees to their right. They must have ridden out to the marshes from the estate buildings. As he wheeled his stallion around to face them, Vladimir held protectively onto Harold. Edmund and the guards drew swords. They created a semi-circle around the prince and princess. A servant deftly hooded Juno and carefully secured the bird onto its travelling perch beside a rook and a sparrow-hawk.

'Hakim.' Vladimir relaxed and Thea recognised the guard as one who was with Prince Vsevolod. 'Why are you here?'

The leader of the riders dismounted and removed his helmet. He knelt in front of Vladimir. When he looked up again there was anxiety on his countenance.

The man called Hakim said, 'We are sorry to startle you, my lord, we come in peace. We should be wearing your father's colours. However, we thought to leave Kiev inconspicuously. They told us at the hall back there that you would be here ... There is a rebellion in Chernigov. Your cousins refuse to depart the city. The boyars of Kiev are rebelling against Prince Iziaslav again. They demand arms. There will be bloodshed. '

'Why should my uncle Iziaslav arm the boyars of Kiev this time if the rebellion is in Chernigov? What is so important that it cannot wait until after tonight's feast for St John?'

'Alas, my lord, it cannot wait.' Hakim quickly withdrew a parchment from his belt. He handed it up to Vladimir who snatched it from him. 'My prince, your father has departed with Prince Iziaslav for Chernigov. Prince Gleb has fortified Chernigov and refuses to submit to Grand Prince Iziaslav's ruling that your father is to control the principality. The Sviatoslavichi refuse Smolensk and there is worse ...'

'Spit it out, Hakim.' Vladimir was still holding onto Harold tightly. Harold began to wriggle and complain.

Hakim glanced over at Thea. 'Women should not ...'

'She is my wife. She has seen war before. Continue.' His horse paced restlessly. Harold buried his head in his father's woollen tunic but refused to cry, though he was clearly frightened. Thea reached out for him and Vladimir lifted him from his horse and gave him over to Thea, who took Harold onto her own mare and soothed him. She did not ride back to the servants who stood amongst the trees as Hakim obviously expected she would. Edmund sheathed his sword again. The pages and guards drew back.

'Prince Boris has ridden out east of Chernigov onto the Steppes to incite the tribesmen to fight against your father, promising slaves and riches as reward. The boyars of Kiev want protection. Your father wants *you* to take over from him where he is besieging Chernigov. He will return to Kiev and protect the city from invading Steppe tribes. You are to ride back with us immediately. All is in that document. It is war.'

Vladimir broke the seal with his knife and unrolled the small scroll. He read it and nodded.

'Are *we* safe here?' Thea asked Hakim as Vladimir read his father's letter.

'Safer than in Kiev. You should remain here, my lady, or in the fortress of Pereiaslavl. Prince Vsevolod has sent Princess Anya and his three children south to Pereiaslavl already.'

Vladimir rolled the scroll up and tucked it into his belt. Worry lines criss-crossing his face he said, 'We set out tonight. Hakim, let us discuss this over refreshments.' He called over to the horsemen following Lord Hakim. 'Dismount. Another hour will make no difference.' He turned to the pages and hawk-keepers. 'Return to the palace now with Lord Edmund. Edmund, warn the grooms that we will all need fresh horses.'

'Do I ride to Kiev with you, my lord?'

'No, Edmund, stay here with the women. The estate could be endangered. If so, get the women and children into the fortress at Pereiaslavl and send messengers to Kiev. Set guards on the palisades; send patrols out to the Steppe edges, the river and the woods. You will take charge here in my absence. I place my family in your care.'

'As you wish, brother.' Edmund inclined his head to Vladimir.

'Thank you, Edmund. I thank you from the depths of my heart. Guard them well.'

Thea ventured a smile at her husband. 'It will all be over by Michaelmas and you will be back. Besides, I would like to visit Anya and the children in Pereiaslavl,' she added in an attempt to lighten the seriousness of everything. 'We should go to Anya anyway.'

'If it is safe to travel; I trust Edmund to make that decision with you. The Cumans never come to our estate and farms. Besides, the route north to Pereiaslavl may not be safe for travel. Only leave if there is a serious threat of attack.'

When he docked his ships at Pereiaslavl on a blistering August morning, Padar heard about the battles gathering force in the north around Chernigov. Princess Anya and her children were in the fortress. He wondered why she was there and not in Kiev. Gudrun and his daughters! They were on the estate with the princess. They must not remain there. None of them should, though Chernigov was up the river north of Kiev. He would seek an audience with the princess.

Princess Anya greeted him in the hall she called her blue chamber, named so because the great reception room possessed walls of blue tiles and colourful floor mosaics and opened into a courtyard edged with palm trees and fountains. She invited Padar to walk with her in the courtyard and sent for Steward Michael whom, she explained, had recently come from Chernigov to her court in Pereiaslavl and knew more than she. He came bustling along the pathways moments later. Tugging at his moustaches, he said thoughtfully, 'The tribes are fighting again. You cannot sail up river north of Kiev. The Chernigov region is unsafe. The tribes have been called out by the Sviatoslavichi. They are intent on destroying us all and seizing power for themselves. There is an army of Cuman tribesmen out to the north-east of us here too.'

'My wife and children, are they safe? Where is Princess Thea?'

Princess Anya laid a hand reassuringly on his arm, 'They are all at the estate south-west of here but now they are coming north to the fortress. They are in no immediate danger but if the Cumans move south-west as surely they will they must be safely inside the fortress. You have arrived in time to see your wife because only yesterday we sent a guard south to bring them to us. We expect them to arrive soon. Edmund is with them.'

'I must ride out to meet them.'

Suddenly a parrot, perched on a palm branch above, shrieked. Taken unawares, Padar almost leapt out of his loose gown.

Princess Anya laughed and shook her head. 'That was Signor Tomas protesting. He can talk too, you know.' She looked at Padar thoughtfully. 'There is no real danger south of Pereiaslavl yet. It is best to be safe so we summoned the princess and her ladies here. Allow them a few days to close up the estate palace and to leave it under guard and they will ride in soon.' She reached out and touched Padar's arm. 'Store your goods in our warehouses. And, Padar,' she added brightly, clearly not wanting to distress him, though he did feel distress, 'there are quarters here which you may have for your family and servants. There is no need for Gudrun to stay with us in my terem now that you are here. You can have a courtyard dwelling. There is one for guests, like a pavilion. It has a garden. Michael will take you to it. The Cuman army is just sitting out there on the plain. They have not moved and we think they will not reach us for some days yet. We're making preparations here. We can sustain a siege until my husband brings his army south to destroy them. Messengers are already riding north to him.'

'And Princess Thea, is she well?' Padar asked, trying to contain his concern, trying to sound relaxed about threats he could not help fearing, as he sensed Princess Anya was more concerned than she revealed.

'Is she well? Is she well?' The parrot mimicked Padar's northern accent.

'Be quiet, Signor Tomas,' Princess Anya ordered the bird, who responded by fluffing up his feathers in a small rebellion. She led them along the path away from the parrot. The bird remained chained to his perch. 'She is with child,' she said quietly.

Padar began thinking about when he and Gudrun were last together. It had been before she set out for Pereiaslavl. It was unlikely that Gudrun was with child too. At five months, or was it six? Anya would have known. 'I hope they are all safe,' was all he said.

Steward Michael, who followed behind them as they walked, said, 'We will secure our bridges north and south of the river. No tribesmen will be allowed to cross over. We have enough provisions to see us through many months should a siege threaten.'

'I really ought to ride out and meet the princess and my wife.'

'If they are not here within three days then ride forth by all means. They will come. Go now, Padar, secure your vessels, store your goods and look forward to a few days rest here with your wife. All will be well,' Anya said optimistically, clearly summoning up all her courage, clearly determined to remain calm and in control.

'I hope you are right,' Padar muttered, thinking how they would not be resting if a siege threatened. He bowed before taking leave of the princess. He remembered something, 'The merchant Dimitri is sailing north from the Southern Sea. He has a large cargo.'

'Let's hope he reaches us before the river is completely closed. He has only a few days to do so.'

She reached out and touched Padar's arm. 'God go with you and may He be with us all.'

32

Pereiaslavl Fortress

Thea rode on her ambling mare, Asha, at the head of a long cavalcade of wagons and carts. She thought to herself how dangerous it was that they must travel across open country, and into the beech woods, taking her whole household into the safety of the river fort, leaving only a skeleton guard to defend their estate should it be attacked.

She had heard rumours from country folk. The Cuman army were sweeping south and west. On hearing these, some of her people had hurried back to their farms and villages. Others joined her retinue, following her with oxen-drawn carts, on donkeys and on foot carrying their bundles and their children, swelling her number, needing to be fed. She prayed to her saint that the fortress could shelter them all. Katya said her father should be back from trading down the Dnieper soon. He might even have reached the fortress. Gudrun remarked that maybe Padar was returning from the spring trading and may have pulled in at Pereiaslavl. He had said that he would come to the estate for her before Michaelmas.

The fort at Pereiaslavl was heavily guarded by warriors. Pereiaslavl was a naval city. Pushing the thought of immediate danger into the recesses of her mind, she allowed herself to think instead of seeing Princess Anya and her children. She managed to convince herself that it was as if they were simply making a summer social visit. They would enjoy their children. There was seven-year-old Rostislav, already an arrogant though endearing boy, eight-year-old Eupraxia, a strong-willed little girl, and two engaging little girls, Catherine and Maria, who were five and three years old. Rostislav would be a companion for Harold, who this summer was fast growing out of his babyhood.

Harold had fallen asleep, leaning against his nurse, exhausted by the journey. He had persistently begged to ride his pony, Urchin, and his determination to ride had slowed them down. In the end, despite his protests Thea insisted that he rode in the wagon. They should arrive before darkness fell if they could keep a faster pace. Every now and then she would catch sight of the river snaking through the Steppe far to their right, glinting in the sunshine, like a beacon guiding them to safety. By sunset they should be riding through Pereiaslavl's great eastern gate.

Edmund led a group of scouts forward to make sure that the road was kept clear for their long train of riders, carts and wagons. Shortly after noon he galloped back from the direction of the Dnieper. Thea raised her hand to stop her cavalcade. A moment later, Edmund drew up sharply in front of her.

She listened as he breathlessly told her, 'There are no boats on the river, save Pereiaslavl vessels. Far to the east, across the river ... smoke from cooking fires curling into the skies ...' Edmund paused for breath. He had confirmed her worst fears. 'Sister, there is an army out there. I have the same uneasy feeling I had in Wessex when a Norman patrol was approaching. We must get inside the city gates as fast as we can.'

She remembered another time ten years before when she was almost caught by a Norman army. She had been approaching Exeter with Alfred, the sword forger, seated precariously on his fast-moving wagon. They managed to enter the city's western gate just in time but were besieged inside for several weeks. Now her first thought was for her children. 'Edmund, then we must get the children inside the fortress quickly.' She hesitated. 'But wait, could you actually see warriors? Do you think it is an army on the move? Could they just be a caravan camping on the Steppes, grazing their herds?' she asked, holding a desperate hope in her heart that this was the case.

He shook his head. 'It will be the army that Princess Anya's messenger spoke about when she ordered us into Pereiaslavl. You know as well as I how terrible that will be for the fortress and, indeed, all of us, unless we are sent an army from Kiev to break a siege. Why would so many soldiers guard the bridges over the river into the city if those smoking fires were innocent?' Edmund glanced up at the sun which was slowly crawling down the sky. He looked back at her. 'If we hurry we can be safely in the fortress by sunset.'

His speech was interrupted by a complaint from the first wagon. Harold had woken up and was demanding to ride his pony.

Edmund dismounted and walked his stallion to the wagon. 'No, not now, lad,' he said firmly. 'You will stay in there with your nurses and your brother. Urchin will slow us up. Your step-grandmother is expecting you before nightfall.'

The dark look on Edmund's face clearly frightened young Harold. He buried his face in his nurse's mantle. Katya peered out from the cover's shade where she was seated inside with little Iziaslav and Gudrun and her girls. Edmund began to explain that there was an army out on the Steppes. 'They are far to the east and the river between us and them is a half-mile wide. We are safe, Katya, for today.'

As he tried to reassure her, Katya gave the toddler over to his nurse and scrambled forwards. She squeezed in on the wagon's broad bench beside the driver, a frightened-looking, sharp-faced man who kept a tight hold on the horse's reins. Peering towards the river, screwing up her eyes, she looked quizzically at Edmund. 'I can see nothing.'

'They are too far away, for now. Do not fear, Katya.' He frowned at the driver. 'Don't look so terrified, man. The enemy are across the river. They are not coming for you.'

The driver muttered something incomprehensible but remained worried.

That driver is a sack of grain, Thea thought to herself. He can drive at the back of my line of wagons next time. If there is a next time.

Edmund remounted his horse, 'We need to get going again. If the children need to eat, they can eat and drink as we move. No more stops between here and Pereiaslavl.'

Thea shouted at the frightened driver to move on. She flicked her whip impatiently and led the long line of wagons, horses and guards forward. Edmund sent scouts out again but this time he stayed with his sister. For the rest of the afternoon the riders came galloping back to Edmund reporting that all was as it had been at noon. They reported that they had met a messenger from the city who said that Padar the skald was returned from trading and awaited his wife in Pereiaslavl.

'Where is this messenger?' Thea said, looking beyond them.

'We sent him back to the fortress to say that you were on your way, Princess. They will keep the gates open past dusk if necessary.'

'You did well. Go and tell Gudrun now. She will be overjoyed.'

I wish that Vladimir was there too, Thea thought, as the rider went back to tell Gudrun this unexpected news.

As they came closer to the city Thea felt an uneasy sense of impending doom. The river was unusually quiet, though they passed others approaching the city on horses, with carts filled with sacks of grain and families on foot carrying bundles, leading children even though the Cumans were too distant to be an immediate threat. If she looked hard she could see that all the bridges north and south of Pereiaslavl were guarded and secure. This included the small bridge they must cross at the river's southern bend which took them over a tributary of the Dnieper so that they entered the city through a water gate.

Thea breathed her relief. This tributary exited through a similar channel cut into the city's north-western walls. The small river divided the city into two sections connected by humped bridges. It also ensured Pereiaslavl's water supply. The city possessed many deep wells. Peasants with carts filled with turnips and barrels of apples pulled their wagons to the side and, bowing their heads, silently waited for Thea's armed and protected cavalcade to pass through the water gate. One cart carried cages with small birds. Their chirruping eerily reached out into the late afternoon shadows. It was clear to them all that Pereiaslavl was preparing for a siege.

Their horses clattered over the bridge on the river's bend just as church bells began ringing for evening Vespers. The city stockades rose high, one behind the other to protect those fortunate enough to escape inside the fortress before the Cumans attacked their villages. Thea glanced up. Warriors in chain mail had positioned themselves on the palisade walkways. The city's two great towers appeared impenetrable. They called the tall outer tower the Wolf Tower because a wolf pennant always flew from its battlements. The further one, even taller, the Oak Bear Tower, dipped its wooden feet into the great Dnieper where it swung close to the far outer northern stockade. The names appealed to Thea's imagination.

The fortress city slanted like one of Aristotle's parallelograms towards the west. Two small square towers stood on the south-western corner and at the north-western turn of the battlements. She saw lookouts and guards up on all of the fortress towers visible from the southern route into the city.

Once they had passed over the water gate, they entered the city through the first strong gate of three set into the outer stockade. Thea glanced back. Across the wide Dnieper, on the eastern horizon, smoke curled up into the sky from encampments. Shuddering, she knew in her bones that the enemy would not be retreating for some time. They could be besieged in Pereiaslavl for weeks.

Passing through the city's three southern gates did make her feel more secure. Their children would have protection. Her ladies would be safe. The last gate banged shut behind their wagons, their twelve riders and the limping kulak company that followed in their wake. Their carts rumbled over a wide paved road, past gawking citizens who were pushing barrels through their yard gates and building up sacks filled with sand by their fences. By the curiosity that showed on their faces, Thea could

331

see that they were not sure who she actually was. She had deliberately chosen not to fly her well-known banner with its stork on a blue background. With only a dozen riders to protect her journey she could be attacked out in the woods, taken as prisoner by roving tribesmen and sold for ransom or into slavery.

The great keep itself was situated on the northern side of the town. A high, covered walkway connected it to the city's Oak Bear Tower. It was with a sense of relief that she rode at the head of her cavalcade in through the gates of the wooden-built keep and they had no sooner entered a second courtyard than Princess Anya appeared, accompanied by her steward, Lord Michael, Ivan Ilyich who was the castle's governor, and Padar. Servants followed, bearing copper basins of water and linen cloths so that they could cool their faces and wash their hands before entering the castle.

Gudrun leapt from the wagon and ran to Padar. Ceremony was forgotten in that moment as he held Gudrun close. Though she was not tall, she was a little taller than he. He reached up and kissed her and she bowed her head to reach his mouth. Moments later their small daughters had clambered from their wagon and had surrounded him. Watching Padar forget the presence of the Rus nobility to kiss his wife publicly and Padar's children throw themselves into his arms, Thea's throat constricted. She longed for Vladimir. She bit her lip and, steeling herself to be brave, she acknowledged Padar with smiles. She bowed to Governor Ilyich who suggested that the princess's brother, Edmund, should accompany him to the comfortable chambers he was to occupy. Steward Michael helped settle Harold by taking a soft, damp, linen cloth to wipe the little boy's face and hands. Thea smiled her widest smile as she threw herself into Princess Anya's arms. All ceremony was indeed forgotten in those moments and Thea felt a great relief overwhelm her.

'Thank the saints, you have arrived safely. Come inside and eat. You must be famished,' Anya said after they had embraced.

Thea found sleeping places within the fortress for her household. She settled her exhausted children and their nurses in a chamber close to her own but Katya was to share her own comfortable chamber. Leaving Katya to unpack their baskets and travelling coffers, Thea hurried down the wooden staircase that kept turning at sharp angles as it descended and searched for Anya. She discovered her in the blue-tiled antechamber with Edmund, just as they were breaking off a meeting with Governor Ilyich, and a general whom she introduced to Thea as Lord Luke.

After he bowed to take his leave, the general said, 'Should Pereiaslavl come under attack, we can defend it. We have enough grain, meat, milk and water to withstand a siege here until help reaches us.'

'Should,' Princess Anya said in a clear voice. 'Even the townspeople are preparing for a siege. The country kulaks have descended on the city today in great numbers to swell its population. Surely you mean, when we are attacked? Loaves of bread will not stop them bringing their ballista and trebuchets to destroy our walls.'

'We hope to keep them away from our walls, my lady.'

'You have not enough men.' She turned to Edmund. 'Tell them what your scouts have observed. If the Cumans move closer to our city we must be better prepared.'

Thea and Edmund added their concerns to Anya's own. Edmund said that the army out on the Steppe was enormous.

General Luke said, 'I am waiting for my spies to return. They will estimate their numbers.'

Anya said curtly, 'I sent a messenger to Kiev days ago and he has not returned. I hope your scouts will keep their distance from the enemy. If they are captured they may be forced to reveal our weaknesses.' She stood and faced her general. 'So, my lord, we must wait on your decision on our strategy. Make it soon. We may be defending our city within days. I shall send my personal guards into the town to oversee preparations for a siege. They can take an account of what provisions the monasteries have.' She lightly touched Thea's shoulder. 'Come, Thea, we shall collect Katya and the children. I promised you supper a long time ago.' She glanced at the hour candle. 'At least two notches of that candle have burned down since. Supper will be served in my terem chambers tonight. Best to keep all as normal as we can. The general has much to discuss with Edmund and with his captains.'

Thea felt Anya's firmness and her strength. Despite the pervading tension in the fortress, Anya was organising everyone. She was arranging food and medicines to be carried to the fortress from the monasteries and defences inside the city. Thea could not but feel admiration for her.

After supper, the steward, the city's patriarch, Padar and Edmund met in the cool blue-tiled hall again. To her chagrin Princess Anya was not invited, nor was Thea.

They sent the nurses, children and Katya away so that they could converse in private.

'This is the way of men. They think we have nothing of value to contribute to a discussion,' Princess Anya said as they walked through the moonlit garden.

Thea sank onto a stone garden seat. She had no sooner sat by a sheltering palm tree than the resident parrot, Signor Tomas, echoed Anya's voice, causing her to jump up.

'The way of men,' it parroted. 'The way of men,' it squawked over and again, as if trying to ram the message home. Thea peered up into the palm tree above and covered her ears with her hands. 'How can you stand that parrot?' she asked, irritated beyond belief.

'He can be amusing sometimes,' Anya began to apologise. 'A diplomat brought him to us from Aragon. I shall have him removed.'

She hurried to the doorway that led back into the terem and called for a servant to catch Signor Tomas and shut him up in his cage. For a moment they watched the creature's removal, grateful and annoyed in turn, but relieved to discover laughter as the man enticed Signor Tomas down with a fruit. He placed the bird in a huge cage which two servants carried between them through an archway out of the garden.

'At least he was quietened by a fig,' Thea remarked. 'Thank Heaven that bird is gone. Remind me never to keep a parrot.' Anya laughed again and their mood lightened.

Although they had the garden to themselves, they spoke in hushed tones.

'Will we survive an attack, do you think?' Anya asked. 'I feel abandoned here and the children ...' There were tears in her eyes. She was obviously feeling very stressed. Thea took Anya's hands in her own.

'I hope so. I don't think Prince Vsevolod suspected that the Cumans were on their way south. Vladimir was anxious, but only a little. He said we would be safe in the fortress if the Cumans raided the countryside. I don't think he expected them to attack the fortress city itself. Surely we can protect ourselves until messengers break through and he sends us reinforcements?'

Anya took her hand away and made a steeple of her hands, leaning her chin on them thoughtfully. '*If* messengers reach Kiev.' She glanced up at Thea with a hopeful look in her eyes. 'We *do* have our own troops, just not enough.'

Thea thought for a while. She jumped up. In the distance she could hear shouts.

'It is the guard changing, up in the two towers. That is all,' Anya said.

Thea sat down beside Anya again. 'Thank heaven that is all.'

The night-time scent of lilies and jasmine permeated the garden. For a few heartbeats Thea breathed it in, half-listened to the night and drifted into thought. The evening had now closed protectively about them. Something was occurring to her, a far-fetched thought but she couldn't let go and it refused to leave. It was something Katya had once told her. At last it grew into spoken words. 'You know, I believe I have an idea.' Thea clasped and unclasped her hands. She leaned over, resting her chin on them. She looked up and turned to face Anya. 'It is possible we can destroy this enemy completely.'

'How can we without help from Kiev?'

'No, listen to me, Anya. We can if we must.'

'I'm listening.' Anya looked at her quizzically.

'You know that Katya says her father is on his way ...'

Anya broke in, 'If he is sailing from the Black Sea ports he will be turned back far down the river. The rest of the trading vessels have all been turned back for their safety. How can the merchant possibly help?'

'She says he knows many secrets.' Thea leaned closer to Anya. 'Listen, I have been thinking just how. Katya once told me that her father knows the secret of liquid fire. He used to experiment with it. I was thinking how we might avoid a siege if we made it and sent it into the heart of the enemy.'

Anya's eyes opened wide in amazement. 'How can he know such a secret?'

'If not the whole secret, he certainly knows something of it. He can make explosions.'

Anya's eyes became as wide as two great ponds. 'Does Katya know how to make explosions?'

'I asked her that question years ago when she was talking of it. She knows the ingredients her father has used for liquid fire. I think not his formula, however.'

'That is the point, you see.' Anya sighed. 'Many know the ingredients but not the formula. Then there is the method of dispensing such a weapon, even if her father does know the formula. And we would have to have those ingredients here in the fortress or nearby. Even so, it would be much too dangerous. If that explosive mixture hits water we could destroy *ourselves*.'

'It does not have to hit water!' Thea exclaimed, clutching onto Anya's arm with excitement at a new thought. 'It can work if we fire it from the water *at* the enemy. We can fire it before they get a chance to cross our bridges and lay siege to us.' She clutched Anya's arm even harder. 'If we entice the enemy south beyond the bridges, we can use fire against them. I am sure we can. We can send it out from the ships and make them flee. Our horsemen could come down from the north bridge and attack them from behind. They will *want* to cross the bridges. We must make them think the south bridge is not so well protected and tempt them towards it. There is a valley cutting into the hills from the east bank of the river just beyond the water gate. I saw it today as we rode from the south-west.'

Anya replied, 'Trap them in the eastern valley!' She laughed. 'What a strategist you are. It is a good plan and it sounds simple. Perhaps it is too simple.' An owl hooted. Anya looked beyond the trees towards the tower. 'That is a good omen. The wisdom of owls, that was thrice it hooted, I believe,' Anya said, glancing up towards the top of the terem tower. Looking back at Thea again, she said, 'You may have something here. A part of our cavalry and infantry would draw them down the river. The other part would need to encircle them once they began to flee. There would be much noise and terrible smoke.' She voiced another objection. 'Our horses would panic and toss their riders.'

'Our throwers can mask their horses. A flask of water and a damp cloth will do that. They must stay back once they hurl the fire at the enemy.'

'The riders hurl the fire?' Anya looked surprised.

'Yes, they *can*. It has been done that way in ancient battles. My father spoke of them. They hurl it in pots. They ignite a taper from the pot first and then they throw it into the enemy. Assuming we can make the liquid fire and get it into clay pots, we aim accurately and from as much distance as it will allow because if we do not, we destroy ourselves as well as the enemy.'

Anya said, 'It is best if *we* destroy *them* first and only a small number need to use the fire pots. We have some amongst our horsemen who can outride the Cumans' best riders, but not many.' She thought for a moment. 'But we must try. Let us find Katya and ask her to make a list of ingredients.' Anya rose from the bench. 'We have told the cargo ships to wait in Miskenk or

337

return to Byzantium. Dimitri may be amongst the ships in Miskenk, just down river, out of immediate danger. '

Thea felt more positive than she had since her arrival in Pereiaslavl. 'It is possible that he is still on the river,' she said.

'Then we must find him. I know of a smith called Peter who understands alchemy. Vsevolod always says that Peter forges the greatest swords. He has spoken of how he thought he could turn base metal into gold if he could work out a formula. Maybe he can make our fire.'

'There is no need for alchemy, just the right formula. There is no magic in this.'

'I shall send a scout down river to search for Katya's father. Padar did say he saw him in Byzantium as he was setting out. Padar said he was on his way, close behind his own vessel.'

'Katya will be pleased at that news.'

'The Cuman army is still miles away to the east. With good fortune he will be here by mid-morning.' Anya's eyes shone with hope. 'Come, let us see if we can collect up the right ingredients.' She hurried Thea along the garden pathway. 'We shall speak to Katya and then you must get some sleep. You have been travelling all day. Besides, you are too far with child not to need rest. Does he move?'

'*She*,' Thea said. 'I am going to have a girl. I think she is moving now.' Thea placed Anya's hand on her belly.

'She is full of hope and life.' She drew Thea close and linked arms. 'Just like her mother. For the sake of our children, we will destroy our enemies.' She glanced up at the sickle moon that hung high in the sky. 'The Moon Goddess is for us as well,' Anya said smiling. 'And maybe my husband will bring us a large army.'

Thea had a feeling that whatever was happening in the Chernigov region and in Kiev, Vsevolod would not ride south. The Cuman presence was a cunning strategy designed to divide Vsevolod's armies and take hostages from Pereiaslavl. The prince could not leave until he had taken Chernigov.

They climbed the terem stairs to Thea's chamber. Thea

gently shook Katya awake and confided their plan to her.

'So Father is on his way to us.'

'Padar thinks he was close behind his own vessel.' Thea paused. 'Does he know how to make the mixture? Does he truly know the secret?'

'He knows something of it. I can remember those items, my princess, I recollect them because my father was obsessed by it, the weapon, I mean. He used to make me gather the ingredients. Bring me writing tools,' she said, her excitement clearly beginning to mount. 'I can make a list.'

Thea searched through her travelling chest until she found a birch tablet and stylus. She passed it to Katya, who climbed down from the bed they were sharing, sat at the table in the window and scratched away by the moon's light. After chewing the top of her stylus for a moment she placed it in front of her on the table beside her list. 'I think that is it; all these items will be to hand, that is the joy of it. We need my father to bring them together.' She handed the birch bark and stylus to Thea. 'You must bring him back to us.'

'We shall find him. Go back to sleep. I'll come to bed soon.'

Katya nodded. 'Find my father,' she repeated, turning to Princess Anya.

'I intend to,' the princess replied. 'I shall send a messenger tonight.' She frowned. 'And I shall call a council to discuss this, in the morning,' she added before softly closing the door. 'You must both be present.'

Thea read the list over and over – pine resin, naphtha, a dozen copper cauldrons, pots, copper tubes, stoves, and so the list went on. These were common enough items in Pereiaslavl but they would need time to make the concoction, assuming they found Dimitri, who would have the formula. When she looked away from the list and glanced out of the window, she observed Padar and Edmund walking towards the outer courtyard, deep in conversation. She pulled the slatted shutters closed, wondering what the council had decided, and climbed into bed beside Katya. She must speak to Edmund at Prime

339

before Anya demanded the meeting of the inner council. They needed his support. Reticent men would always be an obstacle. They would assume they knew better. Subtlety was the best approach, with Edmund helping them to put over their idea.

The next day, after Prime, when Anya sent a servant to fetch Thea, Thea carried the list to the meeting. Followed by Katya, she entered the blue antechamber to see that the city's patriarch, the governor, the general, Padar and Edmund were already present. Katya slipped away to sit on the bench by the wall beside Anya's steward. The others, the important ones, were seated on cushioned low stools around a long, low, mosaic table. The men rose politely and bowed to Thea.

'Thea, sit here beside me,' Anya said, nodding to a stool by her side. Thea placed the missive with the list on the table in front of Princess Anya.

Governor Ilyich threw a puzzled look at the birch tablet lying on the table.

'Your report first, General Luke, then we shall explain that,' Anya said, looking at the birch tablet which contained what clearly seemed to be a shopping list.

The general stood and cleared his throat. Governor Ilyich was not looking at the general. Thea noted that rather he could not lift his eyes from the list. She was sure he was trying to read it upside down as the general cleared his throat again and began to speak.

'My spies returned after we spoke yesterday.' The general bowed again in an obsequious manner to Princess Anya. It was an unnecessarily low bow. 'Safely, Princess, since they kept out of sight. They have reported that a great Cuman army are organising their horsemen far out on the Steppes, to the east. Within a day, two at most, this army will move forward to surround Pereiaslavl.'

Edmund gestured his impatience. He muttered, 'As if we were unaware of that.'

Anya frowned at him, and then returned her attention to

340

General Luke. 'This much we know already,' she said quietly. 'Tell us what we don't yet know.'

'We have decided to send both cavalry and infantry out to give battle rather than allow a siege to commence. That has been the council's decision. There is no alternative unless Prince Vsevolod reaches us with reinforcements. Otherwise, our chances of keeping their troops off our bridges are slim,' he said grimly.

Princess Anya shook her head. 'My husband will surely advance once he knows we are under attack, but our messengers may not have broken through to Kiev never mind Chernigov.'

The governor tugged at his neat little beard with fingers that Thea observed were perfectly manicured. A bemused smile played about her mouth. He was vain. He tore his eyes from the missive. Thea reached over and pulled it towards her.

'We have no option, Princess,' he said. He studied Thea. 'May I ask what is the purpose of –' he pointed at the list '– that shopping list?'

The patriarch raised a hand. 'I think I know, Governor. Princess Gita's brother told me at Prime that she has a suggestion that might stop the Steppe tribes from besieging us.' He nodded to her. 'You could explain, Princess.'

Thea took a deep breath. She rose to her feet.

'Be seated, General Luke, you will listen to the princess,' Anya said firmly. The general pulled his stool back and sat. Thea could see a thunderous look gathering between his bushy brows, as if to say, how dare a woman, even a princess, tell me to sit.

'It is just an idea,' she said quickly. 'My lords, if the army that is camped out on the Steppes fights its way into this fortress we will be sold into slavery or worse.'

'If my strategy is followed we can fend them off,' General Luke said, looking even more furiously at Thea.

Thea said in a confident voice that was more assured than she truly felt, 'No, you cannot. We are outnumbered. Even I know that.'

The governor said, 'What do you suggest then, Princess? I expect the missive lying there is part of something.'

Thea opened her hands and directed her eyes at the men seated around the table, looking from one to the other. 'My lords, have you heard of Greek fire, siphons sending fire through ships' figureheads and warriors riding into battle carrying throwing pots?'

Eyebrows raised, mouths moved, but did not open. The general grunted. The governor muttered the word, 'Insane.'

Anya said quietly, 'Continue. Princess Gita, explain further.'

'If we make the liquid fire, we can destroy our enemy.' She glanced about her.

'No such weapon, not nowadays, anyway,' the governor remarked and shrugged his heavy-looking shoulders.

Thea braved a smile. 'That is not true. We all know about liquid fire and I think Katya might help with this.' She turned to where Katya sat on the bench beside the steward. 'Katya, come forward.'

Katya rose, nervousness showing in her face, her hands clasped to stop them shaking. Edmund smiled reassurance at her as she came to stand by Thea. 'Katya, what are the ingredients used in Greek fire?' Thea asked, as at last she lifted the missive with its list of ingredients. She passed it to Katya. 'These are the ingredients you wrote down last night. Read them aloud.'

Katya's voice was so quiet, it was hardly audible. The men around the table leaned closer to listen.

'Speak up, girl, these men don't eat women,' the patriarch demanded.

Katya said clearly, 'Naphtha and pine resin will work in combination. My father knows more about that. His may not be the Greeks' secret recipe but it will work.' She glanced at her list. 'We need metal containers, cauldrons, charcoal, siphons, containers and tap mechanisms, nails and copper for tubes.'

'Why does Prince Vsevolod not know this?' General Luke asked.

342

'Because, my lord, it is dangerous; it is difficult to control,' Katya replied. 'My father has not perfected its making. I have seen him construct siphons and I have seen him fill small jars to throw. They contained the dragon fire. He once took it out into a pool in a wood and said afterwards that he could not reveal the recipe he used until he discovered a way to stop the flames running wild. He said that sand would work, my lord. It would stop it running wild.'

'Well, well,' Governor Ilyich said scratching at the bald patch on his head. 'What an idea!'

Thea addressed them. 'We have no time to test it but, my lords, do we have these ingredients?'

For a moment no one spoke. Steward Michael coughed from the bench. He stepped forward. 'May I speak?' he said in a soft voice. They all turned to hear what he was about to say. 'We *do* have the resin and the oil, lots of it, for our lamps. As I see it, if we can find the girl's father we can provide the items on her list.'

'I have already sent a guarded vessel of my own down river to find Katya's father,' Anya said.

'Without our advice?'

'Yes, and he should be here soon if he is to be found.'

The general and the governor muttered amongst themselves for a moment. Thea heard mutterings of 'Too dangerous, what nonsense; it is a woman's idea and it won't work.'

'It can work,' Princess Anya said, her voice so scissor-sharp they looked up at her in shocked horror. 'Let us vote – including myself, Katya and Princess Gita. Who is in favour of trying it?' The patriarch, Padar and Edmund raised their hands. They would be six, seven with Steward Michael supporting the plan. He would not go against Anya.

The governor lifted the tablet from the table and studied the list scratched on it. He laid it down again, shaking his head. Gradually, his blue eyes filled with anticipation, followed by something close to hope. At last he broke into the silence. 'Perhaps it is possible. We have alchemists in this city.' He

343

unlocked his clenched fingers and clapped one huge fist to his forehead. 'Greek alchemists, by the saints; I know of several.'

'Then send for them, sir,' Steward Michael said. 'It is a chance. It is a difficult and dangerous chance, but it is all we have and we must take it. I vote for it.'

'It is our only chance of survival,' Padar ventured. 'I vote for it. If we make enough liquid fire we will need siphons to attach the containers to the dragons and griffons on our ships' prows. And ... be aware ... we can only pray that the fire shoots away from the water.'

'I have thought of that,' Thea said with increasing confidence.

Five pairs of ears were now clearly ready to listen. Anya was smiling. Having now captured their complete attention, Thea now explained her strategy.

'Princess Gita, you would make a fine general if you were not a princess,' General Luke said in a conciliatory manner. He was smiling at her when she finished speaking. 'We can use our ships as well as the throwing pots. It is the only way we can do this.'

'Our cavalry should disperse from the north bridge behind the Cuman army,' Edmund lifted his head and suggested.

'Let me lead them,' Padar interrupted. 'I am good with horses.'

'How is your throwing technique?'

'I can lead the throwers,' Padar said.

'And if you allow me, I can command the ships containing the fire siphons,' Edmund suggested. 'The wind has blown from the north-west for days so that will be in our favour.'

There was a knock. Governor Ilyich drew the precious list towards him and turned it over. Princess Anya called out, 'Enter.'

A moment later, Earl Connor, looking as if he had not slept for a week, unkempt and bearded and wearing a huge grey mantle trimmed with green velvet, stood in the doorway.

Thea gasped her shock. Earl Connor was not expected. The

Rus council stared, surprised at the Irishman as if he were an ancient giant come to haunt them and would gather them up into his elegant cloak as easily as they all took in a sharp breath. They drew back. Anya looked at Thea. Thea looked at Padar and then at Edmund. Edmund pushed his stool back and crossed to the door and embraced Connor.

'Lord Edmund, my lady.' Earl Connor's eyes returned to rest on Thea.

Thea rose. 'Earl Connor, I thought you were in Novgorod ...' His presence had filled the chamber and for a moment it felt as if it were only she and Earl Connor.

He shook his head. 'I was on the river. They let me through. And you here also with the *Arctic Fox*, well ahead of me. How could I allow that, Padar?' He glanced around the chamber. 'And Edmund too, well, well. The guards told me messengers were looking for Dimitri.'

'Do you have knowledge of Katya's father?'

'No, I do not, but I can see my sword may be put to good use here.'

'We need more than your sword. We need a miracle,' Padar said.

'We saved another city from destruction long ago, if I remember, Princess Gita and Padar. With God's grace we shall again.'

'We do have a plan, Earl Connor,' Thea announced 'My brother will explain our strategy to you both,' she said. She leaned down and lightly touched Anya's sleeve.

Seeing her intent, Princess Anya rose from her chair. 'Dine with us later, Earl Connor. Come, Princess Gita and Lady Katya. We women shall pass the afternoon with our children and wait for news of Dimitri.'

33

An anxious day passed. Preparations continued within the city. The nunneries and monasteries prepared dormitories to house those who had entered the city from the countryside and were seeking shelter. The price of grain inflated to double within a day. Chickens and small birds went in the markets at a premium expense to those prepared to pay highly to eat flesh. Blacksmiths sold weapons at enormous cost to those who looked to purchase swords and daggers. The sound of knife grinding joined the general hubbub in the market place.

There was no movement out on the Steppe to the east. The smoke from thousands of cooking pots rose calmly into the skies and the distant encampment appeared as if it had settled comfortably for a clan gathering. When Katya remarked on this, Anya said, 'It is doubtful they are gathering to sell goats. Your father will need to arrive soon if we are to stop General Luke changing his mind and riding forth to attack. That would be a disaster. Have we collected the ingredients, Katya?'

'At a huge cost to the treasury here,' Katya said. 'No one is selling anything cheap. Padar, Gudrun and Padar's crew set about that task. If my father does not come I doubt I can do anything with them. They will sit below the fortress waiting for the Cumans' attention. I doubt those alchemists Governor Ilyich summoned into the keep know how.'

'And no news from Kiev either,' Thea said morosely.

At last Dimitri appeared accompanied by castle guards and the messengers. His dragon ship had been turned back and he was about to return to the great Dark Sea trading ports when, after much searching and enquiry along the river, he was discovered. There was no time for reunions. Dimitri had an audience with General Luke, Governor Ilyich, Thea and Princess Anya. He confirmed that he had a recipe, not the recipe, but a possible formula, if the ingredients were to hand.

'Your daughter has given us a list,' Thea said. 'We had thought we might have to make the fire ourselves.'

'And you think you could achieve that?' Dimitri grunted doubtfully. 'Even my clever daughter cannot make Greek fire. Where are these ingredients stored?'

Two days later, exhausted, Thea leaned against the battlements at the top of the Wolf Tower and surveyed the broad river. Ten boats could span this river, she thought, prow drawn up to stern. Her eye was pulled northwards to the upper bridge over the Dnieper. It was guarded by bowmen. She could see how heavily armoured they were, how the sun was reflecting off their pointed metal helmets as it eased its way out of the eastern horizon. The enemy would see them too.

Beyond the keep tower, a great town gate usually opened towards the North Bridge was closed. It was a hot August morning with cerulean skies. Beyond the city gates, the kulaks should be overseeing a wheat harvest on such a morning, not preparing for battle. Instead they had gathered what grain they could save and transported it on carts and mules into the fort. Amongst the pastures surrounding Pereiaslavl, the rest of the harvest wheat shone like pale amber. Not a single peasant was working the fields. Many of them had begged shelter within the fortress palisades. Others had closed up their homes and businesses in the small outer town that had crept up against the city's western edge.

Stealthily, others, mostly traders, had taken boats down river towards the safety of Byzantine territories. *They have little faith*, Thea thought to herself. *They will be returning soon enough*. Another inner voice whispered in her ear. *As long as the dragon fire does not turn on us and destroy us all.*

To the east, the Oak Bear Tower protruded beyond the stockades. One corner reached down into the river. A postern gate led from the south face of the other tower to a wharf area that stretched between the Dnieper and the city stockades.

Beside the postern gate, small boats were able to navigate through water gates set deep into the palisades and pass into the city itself. All the gates had been closed to traffic.

Before dawn, Thea had fallen to her knees in the small church dedicated to St Sylvester, whom she was told took care of the human race. She had begged the saint to protect them. She prayed that their use of the dragon fire would be a success and that it would save the city from a siege.

In the fortress cellars, Dimitri had worked hard for two days and two nights as the enemy slowly moved closer over the north-eastern Steppes down through the grassland, poppy-scattered plain towards the city. While the citizens of Pereiaslavl had prepared for a siege, collecting water in buckets, baking bread, putting food into padlocked stores within the fortress and building sand barricades around their courtyards, Dimitri, his potters, blacksmiths and his alchemists had worked ceaselessly, crafting suitable pots, creating metal siphons and manufacturing liquid fire.

Only trusted flame throwers and experienced marksmen would operate the siphons when the time came to use them. Led by Padar, the city's most agile and fast cavalrymen would ignite and throw the pots. When Dimitri's fire was ready, the city's leaders met under the fortress.

Thea, Edmund, Earl Connor and General Luke visited the cellars under the fortress to see Dimitri's progress.

Dimitri lifted a clay pot from a makeshift shelf. He looked at them, his hand cradling the small vessel. 'Once filled with the mixture and ignited you will be able to throw these and force the enemy down towards our ships. Then, as soon as the Cumans reach the wharf area where we shall be waiting for them, your men, General, must retreat back to the North Bridge. We shall then let loose chaos through those siphons over there.' He pointed to the metal tubes. 'That fire is for them, not you, not unless you fancy being roasted alive.'

The general thoughtfully stroked his moustaches. 'I shall retreat,' he said. 'Though it pains me to do so.'

'Good. It will pain you more if you do not. This mixture will be lethal.'

Padar nodded. 'General, we can succeed and we can be controlled.'

General Luke said, 'Then, God willing, these unbelievers will be washed in front of us as wheat bending in the wind.'

Dimitri walked them through the cellars where his equipment was neatly stored. He touched the tubes that would connect the contraption containing the liquid to the figureheads belonging to the ships. General Luke touched these and praised the two blacksmiths who had worked relentlessly through the night to make them. Thea felt hope grow and grow. Dimitri sounded so confident. She was sure the plan could work. The enemy would not be permitted the opportunity to break their defences.

Looking at Edmund, who was examining the barrels of the liquid that when ignited would become deadly fire, Dimitri said, 'And since you, Lord Edmund, will command the fire ships, I shall be on hand to see that the liquid is fed into the siphons from our fire contraptions.' He pointed to a line of stove-like contraptions that had taps and attachments for the metal tube-like pipes. 'You will deliver the fire onto the river bank from the ships' figureheads and into the heart of the enemy.' He folded his arms.

General Luke thanked the alchemists who had helped Dimitri make up the liquid. He turned to Earl Connor. 'Your archers and swordsmen will wait for tribesmen who survive the onslaught of dragon fire. You will cut them down in the valley.'

Earl Connor said, 'We can get our troops up into the hills before the Cumans draw closer.'

General Luke nodded. 'All must be done with stealth and under cover of darkness, loading the ships and riding out of the city into the valley. Now we shall dine and then set to work.'

Edmund bowed to the general. 'Come, Sister,' he said to Thea, offering her his hand to aid her mount the cellar steps. She gathered her skirts into her free hand, turned back to

Dimitri and said, 'Thank you, you may be our saviour.'

Turning to Edmund she said, 'God give us all strength, brother mine.' With those words she dropped his hand and headed away from the cellar steps, along a corridor towards a staircase that led up to the terem.

The following day, Thea thought she saw the Cumans move closer. She was sure that their pennants were unfurling and she could see the glimmer of their helmets as they rode across the plains. There was a rattle reverberating from the stairway. She spun around to see who it was. It was only Edmund. His sword was hitting the wall.

He sniffed the wind. 'A breeze from the north-west. Let us hope that it does not change direction. If it does, our plan falls short. We cannot risk burning our own ships.'

'Perhaps Prince Vsevolod will come to relieve us,' Thea said, less confident now she had seen the large army out on the Steppe drawing closer.

'We cannot depend on it. We must save ourselves. All is ready. You look exhausted. Go and rest. Stay with your ladies and the children. Find shelter in the garden. There is nothing to be gained by watching that army come forward.'

She placed her hand on Edmund's sleeve. 'We have sent for linen and herbs from the monastery infirmaries and set up our own hospital.'

'It may not be necessary. If fortune favours the bold, it will favour us. The siphons and the barrels are already on board *The Mary*, *Hope*, *Faith*, *The Great Bear*, *Wolfsan*, *Swordfish, River Rat* and *Scimitar*, oh, and the *Sea-Dragon* as well.' He rattled off the names of the ships that would carry dragon fire.

'Our best ships. And you can name all of them. And the ship we sailed to Denmark all those years ago. The *Sea-Dragon* has come all the way here?'

'Old, yes, but still a fine ship and now adapted for the Rus rivers. The ships need to ride high enough to fire safely. We had to use the steadiest and most competently manned of the fleet.

And I offered my own ship.' Edmund gazed around the tower and then at an army that was steadily riding over the sunlit plain in disciplined lines.

Thea said, 'There are so many of them, so many banners.'

'Look, there is a Cuman general.' Edmund pointed at a group of riders that had detached themselves from the front line of horsemen. 'He is riding towards the bridge. They carry a white pennant. By Christ's holy blood, Thea, they want a parley. I had best hurry.' Edmund turned and raced down the endless, steep, narrow, wooden stairways that turned at right angles as they descended. She could hear his sword knocking again against the stairwell walls as he ran.

Thea glanced across the plain and again towards the south-east at the long, straggling, ribbon-like flags fluttering behind ranks of well-ordered archers and cavalrymen. They wore chain mail and leather. They were carrying javelins. Pommels protruded from scabbards. She saw bows on warriors' shoulders and then caught her breath for a moment. They bore round shields similar to the Saxon shields she had once known so well, though these seemed to be smaller. If so, and from this distance she could not be sure, they would be lighter. Those shields would never hamper their agility. They were not intended for an interlocking shield wall but to simply protect riders.

She tore her gaze from the waiting enemy and followed Edmund. She called for a messenger. 'Find Princess Anya. Bring her here at once. Tell her to wear a crown.'

She did not have to wait long because Princess Anya hurried to join her. The princess wore a small coronet over her veil. She handed Thea a jewelled band to wear over her own veil. Already there was an enormous stir by the fortress's inner gate. The general bustled past them on his horse. He was wearing full chain mail. He pulled his stallion up and said gruffly, with anger blazing in his eyes, 'You intend showing yourselves at the parley? Much good will that do; they will know you are here and try to take you hostage.'

'They will already know that since doubtless they have spies,' Thea said with firmness.

The patriarch approached bearing his huge staff, his elaborate jewelled cross bouncing on his rich robe. He would be sweating under those stiffened damask gowns, Thea thought, thankful for her light linen gown.

He stopped and said to the general, 'Let the princesses come with us. It will remind the heathens that God and our princes own Pereiaslavl. She speaks true. They will know who is in the city.'

'Hopefully not who has left,' the general said, referring to the battalion out in the hills.

'I say we are coming,' Princess Anya said, crossing her arms and holding her crowned head high.

The general snapped to a groom, 'Bring them mounts and be quick about it. There is no time to dither.'

Thea raised her very mobile eyebrow as the general moved off.

The Cuman envoys stood on the bridge. They were watching the Rus bows trained on them from the gatehouses and towers. Their khan wore partial armour, mail and a strong, decorated, leather breast vest, his yellow silk tunic and ballooning hose flowing out from under it. Other envoys wore no armour but instead were dressed in stiffly embroidered gowns and decorated coats. They wore leather caps with furred flaps. Sweat glistened on their foreheads. A young shaman stood by their side. His head was shaved except for a long flaxen plait that hung from the centre of his crown. Although he was richly clad, strings of shells, bones and beads rattled when he moved. Behind the group a standard-carrier held a huge red banner with an enormous goshawk embroidered on it. Its stitched eyes were as furious and as piercing as the shaman's real eyes. For a moment, Thea – absurdly – wondered at the skill of the embroiderers, that they could make such an eye appear so life-like. The wind dropped and the goshawk eye vanished into the banner's folds.

The Rus archers lowered their bows.

'We stand for our lands,' the khan, said in perfect Russian. So that was the lie that the Sviatoslavichi had spun to make these tribes attack Pereiaslavl.

Princess Anya raised her right hand and stepped her horse forward. She spoke in a Cuman language and in a reasoned tone, as the patriarch translated for the rest of them. Most likely, he had learned the Cuman speech to set an example to missionaries he sent out to convert the Eastern Steppe-lands. He whispered to Thea. 'She tells them that they are deceived. Her husband, the great Vsevolod of Kiev, who is the rightful ruler of Chernigov and Pereiaslavl, has no plan to take their Steppe grazing lands for Russia. She says it is all a Sviatoslavichi plot.'

'So it is,' Thea replied, thinking how the tribes were deceived.

There was a gasp from the patriarch after the Steppe khan's response. 'He tells her she is deluded. In marrying a Russian princeling she has betrayed the Steppe people. Her father, a Christian khan, is no friend of his. They are not brothers. His tribe will destroy her father's tribe after they have taken the fortress and the fertile lands on the west bank of the Dnieper. If she surrenders the fortress she and her court may depart for Kiev. He does not wage war on women. Her army will become his army or they will be slaughtered.'

'This is *our* city and we do not intend leaving it to *your* plunder,' Anya said clearly in Russian.

'You will die before my warriors' swords.'

She shook her head and said in Russian for all to hear. 'We shall not surrender our city. We stand for all whom we protect. You would do well to broker peace with us because, otherwise, you will never use our great river for trade again.' For a moment she looked more regal than Thea had ever seen her appear. The Cuman khan spat on the ground and said, 'So be it.' He said something else in his own language.

Any colour Anya had owned drained from her face. Her stance went rigid. Her horse pawed the ground. Her eyes blazed fury. She looked as if she were about to explode into flames as fierce as those the dragon fire they promised to deliver. The Cuman khan swept his party around and had trotted off the bridge by the time Anya appeared to recover her usual countenance. The parley was over. The battle for Pereiaslavl was about to begin.

When they had returned to Anya's apartments in the terem, Thea asked Princess Anya what the khan had said that was so upsetting.

'He said he would take us into slavery.'

Thea felt physically sick when she learned that the khan would take the English princess as a junior wife because her hair, he could see, was the colour of flame. Thea swallowed her bile and glanced down at her swelling belly. She whispered another prayer to St Sylvester for deliverance.

34

Before midday, Padar and Argon, his stallion, clattered over the Dnieper Bridge, riding close to General Luke. He prayed to all the gods whose names he could remember for protection, crossed his breast, saying in English, 'By Christ, we shall succeed.'

Chosen riders with calm horses carried the deadly substance, the mix of resin and naphtha, in small pots. These were secreted in the chosen riders' saddlebags along with flints. Since they planned to ignite them and cause chaos by throwing the small pots into the enemy they rode towards the front line. The idea was to drive the khan's horsemen first towards the river bank, then down river to the southern bridge close to where the ships lay waiting ready to let loose their streams of liquid fire. Padar glanced down the river. For now, the ships waited, hidden from the north by the bend in the river, by the southern bridge and the wharfs.

The khan's army had gathered on the Steppe to the east. They spread over flat, grassy territory north of the eastern valley cut. This was to General Luke's advantage. As long as his army could be disciplined enough to obey his orders when he gave the sound to retreat, there was a chance of success. The Cumans would hope to capture the southern bridge. Padar knew that his warriors must ride back to the North Bridge which was behind them and defended, once their commanders gave a signal by using two blasts of the horn. This would allow Padar's throwers to get their missiles into the ranks of the Cuman cavalry with minimal damage to their own ranks.

Padar glanced back. His fire-hurlers were riding close behind him, primed to act once he gave his command. His command was different to other commands. He had decided on a long wailing blow from his pipe, the sound so high-pitched it would be easily heard above the clamour of battle. He was convinced that it would work. In theory it should, but out in the midst of hurling spears, arrow fire and cutting swords this strategy had yet to be proved. It was their only hope of success. The enemy army was large. They also possessed siege weapons – mangonels and trebuchets ready to come forward to breach the city walls. It must not come to that. The time to destroy the enemy was now. Padar made another quick prayer to Woden and another to the Virgin, before he looked again and realised that he was looking into the enemy.

Within moments they were forming up in lines facing the khan's troops, at a right angle to the bridge. General Luke had wheeled them into a semi-circle that reached behind the Cuman army. No doubt, the khan gleefully thought this was madness. How could they defend the city's two bridges, if they permitted his Cuman warriors an advantageous position this close to the city between the two great bridges?

Lightly touching the padded scabbard that held his Frankish sword, Gabriel, Padar moved his horsemen into a front position on the army's right flank, close to their formation of foot archers. Drums banged, curses flew across from army to army. Pennants flew like colourful birds' wings, black, red, purple and a vivid yellow. These were ghastly warnings of impending destruction. As they flapped open and shut, Padar glimpsed parts of animal heads, wolves' ears, bears' snouts, lean cats that prowled the grasslands, crows and buzzards, hawks and falcons. The Rus banners were simpler. Their pennants depicted colourful castles, occasionally a hawk. Mostly they were similar to Norman pennants, since they were split into geometric sections.

There was a moment of eerie silence followed by the snap of hundreds of bowstrings. At once, a sound that began as a soft whistle of air passing through feathers became the rushing of a great Steppe wind storm. Arrows whipped in arcs through the sky. When they struck wood, they made a clatter against enemy shields. This was so loud it was as if Thor was throwing hailstones. Their fire was quickly returned. Two great storms of arrows reached the height of their trajectory before falling and striking targets. This happened several times over. The sun beat down relentlessly from the heavens. The two armies moved forwards and engaged.

'Stay close,' Padar yelled to his men. 'Keep me in sight until I gave the signal.' He felt for his flint. No one could create a spark as easily as Padar. Years of experience travelling the isolated and lesser known route-ways of England on secret missions for Harold Godwinson had given him much practice. Not only was Padar a skald, a storyteller, a harpist, and a merchant, he never forgot that he had been a spy and always a warrior. Momentarily, he thought of Gudrun and his daughters who had joined Thea in the fortress terem. He breathed in, exhaled and charged.

He passed through his own lines, avoiding arrow fire, lunging javelins and wide, deadly sword swipes. He glanced back. His men were leaning low over their horses, intent on following him. The wind of their movement caressed his face. He smelled the battle. They were in the thick of it. Around him he heard the noise of pain. Javelins came plunging towards him but he was small and fast and avoided their thrusts. Others were not so fortunate. Too soon the battlefield had become a weaving advance of swords, lances, battle-axes and deadly maces with spiked heads. Many fell about him. His horse reared and whinnied. He held fast. As the assault raged around him Padar, having regained control over Argon, criss-crossed his way towards the centre.

An enemy's horse screamed. An arrow had lodged in its neck. It bolted, reared up and tossed its leather-clad rider about in his saddle. The rider lost his conical helmet and his javelin as he attempted to rein in his mount. It was futile because it was catching. Other horses pursued the bolting creature, despite their riders' efforts to control their mounts. It was only a small incident in one small section of the battle but Padar took heart. The time had come to deliver more chaos. He whipped his delicate bone pipe from its wool-lined case, hung it around his neck, placed it to his lips and gave his signal. It was followed by General Luke's blast calling his men to fall back. Padar lifted his head and with great skill wheeled Argon around as if he were about to retreat. For a heartbeat he caught sight of a flock of geese fly southwards, crossing the blue sky in a neat formation, moving with speed, as if intent on escaping the killing field. He saw his men reaching for their missiles.

He turned forward, ducking enemy spears. Seeing his throwers spread themselves along the chaotic disentangling ranks of Cumans and Rus, before hurling their first missiles, Padar dropped his pipe, struck his flint, lit the cord that connected with the lethal, sticky mixture inside the pot and threw his fire into the heart of the enemy. As the missile exploded, the section of horsemen nearest Padar fell into panic. Horses reared as flames caught their horsemen. They bolted back through their ranks, creating more chaos as they threw their riders.

Ahead, Padar saw one rider frantically trying to beat off the flames. It was as much as he could do to keep control of his own horse. As he glanced from side to side he saw his companions courageously and systematically igniting and launching second and third missiles brought out from their saddlebags. Once these pots gained their marks it was as if lightning had descended from God's heavens to ignite a whole section of the khan's army. Padar's riders created turmoil. All at once the khan's army turned down river towards the southern bend. Commanded by experienced men, the Rus army moved forward again to pursue the Cumans forwards towards the southern bridge.

As he galloped, his sword now drawn and held forward in one hand, Padar allowed himself a glance upwards. The Wolf Tower loomed up from the river to his right. He was sure that by the battlements he could make out three mantles flapping in the wind. For the intake of a breath he could make out Gudrun with her gold hair, loosened from its plait, streaming behind her.

He felt a fierce renewal of his flagging energy. He was not only fighting for the survival of a Godwin princess, he was fighting for his own family's survival. He was fighting for the freedom to trade along the Russian rivers and he was fighting for a future in a new land. Most of all he was fighting for Gudrun and for their girls' birthright to live in peace. He plunged forward, but as the galloping horses in front of him approached the bend in the river where the ships were waiting, he signalled for his men to slow, fall back and let the Cumans, unhindered, approach the bridge.

Thea watched from the tower, standing alongside the governor, Michael, Anya, the patriarch, Katya and Gudrun. She saw the khan's army wheel around and race along the far river bank, galloping towards the bend. Through the flames from the thrown missiles that stretched plumes of smoke over the river she discerned movement on the dark waters below. She leaned over the parapet, peering through the smoke barrier, trying to see more clearly. The ships were ready. She glanced up at the sky. The sun was falling and sunset was almost upon them. Vespers had passed. Soon it would be the hour of Compline.

She watched the Rus ships sneakily glide across the water. Within moments, a cloud of arrows were flying from the ships into the midst of the fleeing army. It was the usual strategy of a Steppe army to operate a feigned retreat and wheel around again into a crescent to engulf the horsemen pursuing it. She watched for this. Before the Steppe horde performed such an operation their dragon fire must stop it. She grasped hold of Anya's hand and prayed that they could send out their Greek fire as soon as the enemy reached the river bend. Somewhere down there, on the ships, Edmund was in command. For a moment she thought she had glimpsed him. She prayed to St Theodosia. There was a gasp from Gudrun.

'Look,' Gudrun cried out. 'The dragon fire.'

The patriarch lifted his great jewelled cross high and shouted

361

up towards the reddening sky, 'May God destroy the infidels.'

Anya's steward, Michael, looking in the opposite direction, cried out. Thea turned about. He was pointing towards the north. Far in the distance she saw what appeared to be dust kicked up by horsemen riding along the wide river. They were so far away. She could not make out whose horsemen they were. If this was a second Steppe army, their own army would be caught in a trap. Her heart sank. Her optimism was shattered.

She turned southwards again. The Rus were falling back. Great billows of smoke rose from the fire that issued forth from the ships lined along the river. Ghastly flames of yellow belching fire had been launched from the prow heads of their ships. Within the time it took for a ragged-looking crow to flee overhead, fire appeared to be snaking along the ranks of the fleeing Cuman army. A moment later, smoke obscured the armies. Thea could hear a thunder of hoofs passing below the tower, the horses' neighing, agonised shouts, cries of the armies as the enemy tried to turn their horses away from the flames; the clang of their weapons as they sought blindly for their Rus opponents was terrifying. Thea could smell the khan's army burning. She watched, fascinated and terrified by the sickening noxious yellow flames that licked upwards, as if they seeped through fishing nets. She was glimpsing them through gaps in the dark smoke. The flames seemed to stretch along the length of the river. She drew her veil across her face in an attempt to escape the stink that rose up towards the very heights where she was standing. She watched the scene below obliterated by flame and smoke.

'What must it like be down there?' Gudrun cried, coughing and clutching hold of Thea.

'Victory for us. Defeat for them.'

Tears were streaming down Katya's face. Katya's lips began moving in silent prayer. Thea knew she was praying for both Edmund and Dimitri. There were no comforting words that she could lend. She glanced towards the wooded flatlands to the north where the air was clearer. The distant horsemen appeared to have paused, but ghostly ships seemed to be moving very slowly along the wide Dnieper from the northern horizon, still too far away to completely discern. Something uncanny stirred in her breast and her heart beat faster. What if Vladimir was coming to save them? Were the Sviatoslavichi moving south towards Pereiaslavl to help the Cuman army to destroy them? She shuddered.

Below her, momentarily smoke cleared again. Despite the launch of dragon fire through the prow heads of dragons, griffons and great bear heads, the khan's army were fighting back, launching an arrow attack on the ships. The sky that had been dark with smoke was now dark again, this time with arrows. She prayed that these arrows would not carry flames back onto their ships. If this happened the remaining siphons of dragon fire would ignite. All of hell would be loosened into a river of fire.

It appeared now that the ships were holding back the dragon fire. Instead, they were returning arrow fire. At last, the remnant of the burning army was racing towards the cut beyond the heavily defended southern bridge. Cuman ranks swerved. For a moment she held her breath. They might attempt a crescent. Suspense hung amongst the smoke. Then, the great burning army moved as one away from the river and the Cumans were galloping into the low hills to their left. Once their broken army turned into the valley, the Rus ships let loose another deadly round of Greek fire into the back of the retreating cavalry.

Smoke began pluming upwards once again. Falling to her knees on the tower's platform, Thea prayed for the souls of their slain. Many of their own cavalry would have also been destroyed by the dragon fire's merciless havoc. 'Please ask our Lord to spare us, St Theodosia. If Pereiaslavl is saved, I promise that I will found my own nunnery.' She twisted her grandmother's ring. 'I swear by my grandmother and on my mother's life that I shall devote my life to God's work.'

Padar made an impulsive, strange and deadly decision. When

the Rus army held back, close to the southern bridge, he turned Argon's head away from the Dnieper. Concealed by smoke, he guided his horse forward. He allowed himself a glance over his shoulder and saw General Luke still erect on his brown stallion with his sword raised high. He was urging his army back from the flames pouring out of the ships. Padar edged his horse to the right, and with as much speed as he could get Argon to make, he rode through the fleeing Cuman horsemen, leaning low over his stallion's neck, holding on for his life. He knew it was taking a great risk but the enemy were too intent on fleeing from danger to pay attention to what appeared to be a lone horse running loose. There were so many of their own horses without riders by now. The Cuman retreat had become chaotic. In chaos danger beckoned. Padar needed to get up into the hills if he was to follow his impulsive plan to join Earl Connor. There were enemy horsemen all about him – shouts, screams, coughing and dying as many simply gave up, fell over their mounts or were enflamed. Others were intent on returning to their camp to the east. Padar cantered through many small groups of warriors who were riding forward into the valley, attempting to beat off flames, their horses maddened and uncontrollable.

Padar tore away a sleeve from below his chain mail shirt and held the cloth over his horse's muzzle. He rode away from the fleeing horsemen and along the river valley trying to find a crossing. The tributary ran fast as he steadily worked his way down its sloping banks into its stony, fast-flowing shallows, seeking a bridge he knew lay by a corn mill. He was ahead of the fleeing horsemen by the time he found it. He urged Argon over the wooden bridge and whispering into the stallion's ears, persuaded him up into the hills beyond the mill to where the air was clearer.

Once Padar gained the top of the hillside, he was exposed. Moments later, a small band of Cuman horsemen, who clearly had found relief by riding through water along the river, crossed by the same bridge and began to climb the hill after him. Padar thought, as glanced over his shoulder, I must be bold if I am to reach Connor alive. As the three horsemen picked their way up the slope, he spurred Argon onwards. For an intake of breath he looked back again. He had miscalculated these horsemen's ability. They were fast gaining on him. A moment later the horsemen were reaching for their bows and within the time it took to mutter a curse, arrows were clattering and banging about him. He raised his shield to protect his head.

He desperately dropped his shield as the riders set arrows again. He spurred Argon onwards faster but his horse was exhausted. Steam poured from Argon's nostrils. Then his stallion roared. Before Padar could create enough distance to reach for his own bow, Argon was falling, an arrow piercing his rump. Several more arrows lodged in Argon's flesh as the horse fell with a great, heart-aching whinny. Padar threw himself off and rolled behind the stallion's heaving body. Peering around his dying beast, he knew that he could not fend off the advancing horsemen. Nor could he outrun them on foot. He glanced up at the heavens. His hope of reaching Earl Connor with news of the fleeing Cumans now faded as fast as the last rays of today's dying sun. Darkness was only moments away.

There were three assailants. He was but one. He would go down facing his enemy. Could he delay them until night enclosed them? Maybe he could escape. He felt for his bow. He cursed his bad luck. It had fallen and was trapped under his horse. There was no way he could dislodge it.

Drawing Gabriel from his padded leather sheath, he stumbled to his feet. With both hands clutching the sword's leather hilt he raised Gabriel high. The Frankish sword caught the last dying light rays and flashed. His pursuers stopped and stared. The fire flames were now far behind them. He could still hear Cuman horsemen shrieking like devils as they raced along the cut. His assailants let loose another round of arrow fire. As their arrows fell all around him, he dropped low behind his fallen horse, praying for deliverance. God answered his prayer. The arrow fire paused. Taking advantage of the sudden lull

Padar peered out from behind Argon.

One of his pursuers had leapt off his horse, the two others following his lead. Leaving their bows aside, they advanced on Padar, swords reaching out for him, points flicking up and down. They clearly intended to tease him just as a cat would amuse itself catching a mouse. He shuddered. His death would be slow, menacing and hideous as they tore his flesh to shreds. Yet, in that moment, Padar knew that just as he could shoot an arrow with accuracy, despite his small stature, he could also thrust his sword with precision, jump aside and outwit his enemy, except for one problem – it was one against three.

Padar raised himself up to stand facing his enemy, his sword lifted high. The riders were taken aback at this feat of courage. Padar saw this and before the three riders caught breath again, he bent his back and charged, running into the one to his right, taking him off guard. Striking with Gabriel where the man had no chain mail covering, through the legs just above the knees, Padar put all his strength into an upward thrust. With a scream the assailant dropped his weapon and fell to the turf, screaming in agony. Padar held on to his sword hilt as his enemy collapsed. He pulled Gabriel back. His sword came out covered with gore. He lifted it high again.

Immediately, the other two assailants shouted in fury and began to circle him so that he felt like an insect caught in a spider's web. These men had deadlier swords than he. Their blades were double-edged and longer than his. The one to his right, a giant of a man with a leather helmet and blackened face, a look of fury crossing his countenance, advanced and withdrew. The other laughed, dropped and kicked away his long sword, reached for and lifted high a scimitar, nonchalantly waiting aside, ready to swipe off Padar's head. This rider, Padar saw at a glance, wore no helmet. He was tall and blond, his hair plaited like a Viking of old, his eyes filled with deadly concentration as he approached and paused. He was casually waiting until his companion was done playing with Padar.

Padar jumped back, drawing the sword-wielding giant

towards him. Their weapons met and whipped each other above his chest. Steel clashed on steel. He fought on, returning his assailant's sword strokes with well-measured and accurate sword play of his own. He moved with speed but his arms were aching. Gudrun's serene face momentarily flashed through his mind. In that moment he was off guard and his enemy sliced out at his sword arm. Instinctively, Padar leapt to one side but not quickly enough. Gabriel dropped onto the ground. Padar was weaponless.

The blond Cuman flew into action, bringing his scimitar closer, daring him forward. In that moment, Padar remembered something. He had been so stupid. He drew back, dropped to the ground and rolled towards the bag that hung from his horse's saddle. He reached inside the great leather pouch and felt around. He still had one pot and he had his flint. He could have saved himself and Argon. Miraculously the last pot had not broken.

He reached over his damaged arm, held the flint in his aching wrist and sparked off flint against flint and hay. Miraculously, within a breath he had ignited the cord on the pot. He hurled it just as his assailant was almost on top of him. Pulling himself from the ground he raced along the slope, away from the huge burst of flame that enveloped both the vicious blond swordsman and his own dying horse. He heard screams of agony as the Cuman burned. He felt the heat of the fire he had thrown scorching the bastard's leather jerkin. His nostrils filled with the suffocating odour of singing hair and cooking horse. He collapsed.

Blood obscured his vison. He smelled sulphur. This time it was suffocating like a stinking devil's cauldron. He coughed and spat mucus as he heard the canter of horses. They were coming for him now. It is the end, he thought. By Christos, make it quick. Sweet Lord, protect my wife and children.

A familiar voice reached through the roar of smoke and fire. 'For the love of God's saints, Christ and all his holy angels, Padar, what are you thinking of?' Padar could not reply. He felt

367

water slide down his throat. Someone was wiping his face with great gentleness. Imagining Gudrun, he muttered her name. 'Are we in heaven?' he heard himself say. Someone was feeling his left arm.

'You'll live. An arm injury but that is all, I think,' the voice said gruffly. Earl Connor gently lifted Padar onto his own horse. 'Hold tight until we catch you another.' He turned to one of his men. Padar heard him order, 'Bring me that sword over there if it is not too hot to lift.'

'My weapon and my horse,' he mumbled in confusion, forgetting the smell of the burning animal, hardly able to grab hold of the horse's mane because his arm and sword hand were in agony.

He heard Connor say gruffly, 'We have your sword. Argon is dead, burning nobly as a Viking steed should, and if we don't hurry we will be too.'

Every bump caused Padar further agonies as Earl Connor rode furiously down the slope towards his own troops. The earl's men had already cut off the fleeing Cuman army. As Padar regained partial sight, he saw two Cuman messengers ride forward bearing a white flag. The khan was surrendering.

Padar glanced back. Flames from his horse's last pyre lit up the dark sky with a yellow light that obliterated the stars. A ghastly hush ensued as, surrounded by torch light, the khan rode forward from his bedraggled and defeated army to meet Earl Connor. Though he hurt terribly, Padar sat erect on the horse Connor had given him and sighed his relief.

Later, as they were returning to the city, Padar said, 'Earl Connor, what was that secret mission?'

'If I told you it would not be a secret. I think you had better not say another word until we get you safely into the city. You are in need of a woman's touch, Padar. Never mind what missions I was on in Constantinople.'

For a while they rode in silence. Connor leaned over and whispered. 'I was seeking an alliance for my wife's brother is all. There is a Saxon silversmith down in Constantinople. His

368

name is Alfred. He was once a coiner. He has a wife called Gertrude.' He smiled at Padar's gasp. 'Ah, I see you remember them from Exeter. They had a daughter though they never thought to. God has blessed them. She is now eleven years old ...' Connor laid a finger on his lips. 'Not a word, Padar, until this alliance is forged. They named the girl Margaret. So there you have it. They are considering. If they can bear to let her go, one day Alfred's daughter will come to dwell in Novgorod.'

Some secret, thought Padar, not knowing whether to believe a word of it.

35

The Hall

Thea stood in the midst of the outer hall, shocked into utter silence, stunned by the great numbers of their injured. By nightfall they had won the battle, but at a price. Some of their own dead had been consumed by flames but most had been injured by arrow fire. Others were sliced through by swords or speared with javelins. How could she console these men's wives and mothers? For a moment she watched Gudrun, who was helping Anya organise their makeshift infirmary. Lifting an urn, she went to help.

Gudrun was ashen faced as she trailed from pallet to pallet with water and a sponge. As Thea held the urn and Gudrun helped each wounded man she asked about Padar, who had not returned. No one had seen him since he had led the fire attack during the afternoon. The outbursts of fire and the smoke that followed, the nitrous smell, the cries of the burning and dying had confused them all. 'You could not see for smoke, you could not breathe. I did not see him,' one said.

Another man gasped that it was impossible to even see the river once the fires started. It was with great difficulty that he found the bridge and struggled back into the fortress. He had not seen Padar either.

After many more men had returned, badly burned and with similar reports, Thea climbed to the top of the tower, leaving Anya and an anxious Gudrun in the hall. To her horror, the dragon fire was snaking over the water south of the bridge, its green tongue catching cogs, carracks and galleys that were anchored by the southern wharfs. She watched horrified until smoke gathered again, obliterating the scene. There was nothing to be done except hope and pray that the ships that carried the fire machines were spared. Concerned for her brother's safety as well as Padar's survival, her heart heavy, she dragged herself down from the tower and sent two guards out onto the wharfs to see what was happening. They returned, reporting that all was chaos out there. She feared that it was not yet over.

A messenger returned to say that the enemy was in flight. She grasped her hands so tightly with relief that her knuckles turned white. The messenger said that they could bring the dragon fire under control by using sand. The fire that was licking the water, swallowing up their barges, appeared more fearful than it actually was. Lord Edmund would remain on the *Lady Maria*, until the cogs and galleys that had ignited, burned themselves out. They must save what lives they could. The messenger breathlessly added, 'My lady, if you could send salves and strips of linen to bind the wounds our sailors have taken it would help.' He bowed low, and rose again with difficulty, his face creased with the agony of his effort.

'Go to the kitchen and ask for food and drink.' Thea reached forward to help him to his feet. She clasped the man's rough hands for a moment in her own and added in a quieter voice, 'You have fought with great courage.' The bruises on the boy's face, his singed hair, the terror in his eyes and his exhaustion spoke of a terrible fight. 'Stay in the fortress now. I shall send help to the ships, water and food. In fact, I shall take them myself.'

She ordered the steward to organise goatskins with fresh water and bread. 'Take the provisions out immediately. The medicines will follow.' Steward Michael hurried off, promising that he would send them forthwith.

Thea wasted not a moment. She ran from the great antechamber into the outer hall. At the entrance, she stopped short as her eyes took in a frantic sight. Many kneeling women who had come in looking for husbands, brothers, sons and fathers, tended to those who lay on the mattresses. Moans and cries filled the hall. Priests waving censers and muttering prayers wandered about and bent over mattresses to offer solace here, a prayer there. Gudrun was twitching the corners of the blankets covering those who had not survived. She glanced up as Thea approached her. 'Padar is not here.' She reached for Thea. 'Please God, may my Padar live.'

'Gudrun, we can only hope, but for now we must help where we can. If we keep busy…it is better…Gather up salves and fetch the powdered opiate of poppy from my chamber. You know where I keep it. Look in my bone chest. At the bottom there is powered root of mandrake. It may still retain potency. Fetch these now. I am going out onto the wharves.'

Gudrun sped off towards the stairway that led to a walkway which connected the central keep to the terem tower.

Anya glanced up from the dying warrior she was tending on a mattress close by. 'Thea, you must be insane. You cannot leave the citadel. They will quench the flames, and if they do not, the fires will burn themselves out. To go down there now is madness.'

'I want to see Edmund. I must see him. There may be news of Padar,' she said desperately. 'He might have boarded one of our ships. I shall take Katya.'

'We can send servants.'

Thea folded her arms across her chest. She was resolute.

Anya shook her head. 'Promise me you will return as soon as you deliver the medicines. Promise me.' She grabbed Thea's arm. 'Vladimir would never forgive me if you were placed in danger.'

'And where *is* my husband?' Thea retorted angrily. 'I have *already* been placed in great danger. We all have. And we *have* survived.'

Anya said, 'There will be a reason why he has not come. Our messengers may not have even reached Kiev.' She looked over at the stairway. 'Here is Gudrun returned. I shall fetch Katya for you.'

Thea called after her. 'No promises, none at all, not after all we have been through today. Believe me when I say that I intend returning safely.'

Anya stopped, turned round. Her countenance was furious. 'Then, I relinquish responsibility for your safety. You are very stubborn.'

'I am, and I *do* take responsibility for my actions, Anya.'

The women hurried out of the postern gate leading onto the wharf. As they sped down the sloping pathway to the wharf, they passed struggling blackened men returning to the fortress. 'We sent them, packing, my lady,' one said, recognising her. Another fell to his knees, crying, 'The dragon fire has saved the city, Princess.'

They also met a great number of shrouded women who had gathered about the wharf seeking their kin amongst the returning wounded. The patriarch had sent two elderly bearded priests with her. As the priests limped along, their chasubles flying behind them, they tried to give words of comfort to the women. Carrying tall crosses they reached out and blessed them. Thea's servants carried torches but there was no need for these since the river was bright with flames.

Thea's party boarded two small rowing boats that were being used to ferry the worst of the injured to shore. Slowly, they made their way over the half-mile wide river through debris and bloated floating bodies, smoke and wreckage, towards the *Lady Maria*. Edmund ran to help the priests climb on board first. They began moving amongst the injured with their incense and prayers.

Then he reached over the ship's side and hauled his sister up the boat's ladder saying, 'You did not need to do this.'

'I had to come; Katya too. Have you seen Padar?'

Shaking his head he replied, 'I have been too busy to see anybody but those on the water.'

Once Katya had tumbled on board she fell into Edmund's arms. He embraced her tightly and turning her around said, 'Your father is hurt but refuses to leave. Go to him.'

Katya and Thea cast their gaze across the deck to a squat iron furnace from which a tube ran to the ship's prow to enter the rear-side of the ship's figurehead, a bear. Its mouth was open, its gilding blackened. She made out Katya's father. He was bent over the portable stove with its spouts and taps. He must have been wounded as he had stood by the siphon directing the launch of the last round of fire into and out of the bear's mouth.

'Here!' Thea withdrew the bag of powdered mugwort from her leather satchel and thrust it to her. 'Use this on your father's wounds.' She pressed a tiny pot containing a honey and lavender salve into Katya's free hand. 'And this; mix the powder into it and take the water pitcher too. It's there.' She pointed to where pitchers sat collected under linen cloth.

On the deck the wounded lay groaning. Thea paused to help where she could. She heard Katya's father say, 'This is no place for you, little one, or the princess either. Your father ... must see this machine made safe.' He was out of breath with pain and anxiety. 'It is still too hot,' he moaned.

She saw Katya's father wince. She went over to them with a clean piece of sponge which she silently gave to Katya before returning to the dying man whom she was helping.

'Rest for a bit, my father,' Katya replied. 'Others will finish this when the furnace cools.' She drew her father away to a bench, sat him down and began to wash away the dirt on his arm. Once the dirt was cleaned away, Dimitri's arm showed an angry burn. He leaned against the ship's side clearly exhausted. He gasped as Katya touched his blackened suppurating skin and gently rubbed the salve into it. His burns reached up from wrist to shoulder. 'Oh, Papa, you should have returned to the hall,' Katya said.

'Not yet. I started this ... I must see the fire off the water. If the wind turns ...' He managed a smile between hoarse breaths. He called to Thea. 'Princess, we did it. We ... have ... defeated them,' he attempted to say. 'They have ridden into the cut. Connor – the earl – he will destroy what is left of the bastards.' Tears streamed from his pale eyes. 'It worked. The fire worked.' His voice creaked. 'We have saved Pereiaslavl.'

Thea glanced up at him. 'Yes, we have.'

She returned her attention to one who was clearly not going to survive. He was burned from head to toe. His clothes had melted from his agonised body. He died in her arms clutching a small wooden cross. 'At a great cost,' she said sadly, looking up again.

She heard Edmund shout an order to the ship's rowers. 'Turn us back now. The horsemen are not returning. I shall take one of the rowing boats down the river.'

Across the plain, through the fading fires, Thea glimpsed dead horses and bodies. Already buzzards were circling. 'Ours?' she asked Edmund.

'Some, but mostly theirs,' Edmund said hoarsely as the sailors manoeuvred the *Lady Maria* around and back towards the wharf. 'Tell Gudrun, Padar will return. He is a survivor.'

Thea nodded, but she had worry in her heart for Padar's safety.

Later that night, once the ships had been docked and the last of the survivors had been taken to the keep, Thea removed herself to the receiving hall to rest before returning to help in the makeshift infirmary. She was mopping at her face and shoulders with a dampened cloth when she heard horses' hoofs entering the courtyard below the shuttered window.

She hurried to the chamber entrance into the hall to see what was happening. Vladimir, sweat pouring down his face, his eyes wild with concern, came striding through the pallets of wounded, past the women who knelt by them, circling the wounded and the dying. She stood as if frozen. He was clearly desperately intent on reaching her. Anya followed, trying to keep up with his strides. Behind her Steward Michael, Governor Olaf and Vladimir's guards stumbled through the hall. Thea thought with sudden realisation, of course, the distant horsemen they had seen far, far up the river that afternoon – it was *him*. She sank to the tiled floor clasping her hands together in a prayer of thanks.

Prince Vladimir lifted Thea to her feet and embraced her. He waved the governor and steward away. 'I want to speak with my wife alone.' He looked at Anya. 'Stay, Princess. Come with us into the private chamber.'

Once away from public gaze, Vladimir embraced his wife again. 'I hear from the governor that you saved the city.' He held her elbows, tears gathering in his yes. 'Look at you. How could I have deserted you?' He looked from Thea to Anya. 'Did you send to Kiev for help?'

'Yes,' she said.

'Then your messengers were captured.'

'We suspected as much. Where is my husband?'

'He is in Kiev. I am to bring you both there. This is why I am here. I had no idea until we rode towards Pereiaslavl that the city was under threat of siege. In fact I was not even sure that you were here, Thea.' He searched his wife's face. 'You look exhausted. You should lie down. Thea, you are with child.' He looked towards the terem stairway. 'Our sons – are they safe?'

She nodded, overcome with exhaustion and unable to speak, but she felt a great weight lift from her shoulders. Her tears of relief flowed freely. He gathered her into his arms again and a moment later reached towards Anya too. 'You are both brave, courageous women.'

'By the grace of God, we are all safe,' Anya said reaching out her hand to him.

Anya's hand was caked with drying blood. 'It was because of your wife's strategy that we were able to prevent a siege,' she said.

Vladimir looked down at Anya's blood-stained, filthy garments. 'I am sorry. I was not here to protect you.'

'It is war, so many wasted lives, such loss,' Anya said, gesturing towards the door into the outer hall. 'We have paid a great price for this victory.'

Vladimir bowed his head in sorrow. 'God save their souls for they have saved us.' He gently touched Thea's ash-grimed face. 'It seemed to us when we were back along the river as if the whole of Pereiaslavl was on fire.' He swallowed. 'Let others tend to the fallen. You must rest, both of you, after I explain why I came to find you.'

After they were seated, he said, 'I am here, not because messengers came, because clearly they did not make it through to Kiev. There is both good and bad to explain.' He looked at them gravely and took Thea's hand. 'I was riding south to conduct you to Kiev. We paused to break bread. The men were tired and hungry so I sent ships ahead. They returned to say that the river was on fire, that the Cumans were attacking. As far as they could see the bastards were getting the worst of the fight. We saddled up again and arrived close to the North Bridge only to find that the Cuman army had vanished. There is a killing field on the far banks of the river. I feared the worst. Never did I guess Greek fire caused the flames on the water, not until we reached the city. The flames were licking along the water just as the ancients described it, green, blue and yellow tongues of fire.'

Thea interrupted, 'Katya's father knew a formula. We pushed the liquid fire through siphons from a container and through the ships' figureheads into the heart of the Cuman cavalry. We sent it into the horsemen riding to capture the southern bridge. Edmund is still quenching the flames. They are using sand. It is effective, but we have lost lives because of it.'

'Fewer than if the city was sacked.' Vladimir sank onto the bench beside them.

'We have won the day, but the price has been so great.' She mopped tears away with her sleeve. 'Earl Connor is out there and we have not seen Padar. Gudrun is beside herself.'

Everything conspired to cause her tears to flow – his presence, her exhaustion, memories of the aftermath of the Great Battle for England when she had seen her father's body in King William's encampment at Senlac. The winter siege of Exeter, their exile and her difficult betrothal. They flowed because of her marriage into a family where women lived secluded lives. Finally, she wept with relief for the safety of her children. She swallowed back those tears. There was still much to do. Earl Connor and Padar had not returned. Part of their army was still fighting out on the plains. She wiped her tears away, breathed deeply and waited for him to speak again.

'It could be worse,' he said, holding her hand.

She nodded, snatched her hand away and managed a weak smile. 'I shall recover, my lord.'

'We have another journey ahead. We have been betrayed by your nephews. While they engaged us up in Chernigov, Gleb sent the khan that attacked you with orders to destroy Pereiaslavl, control the river, meet with him back up the river and take Kiev.'

Anya said, 'So, exactly where is Prince Vsevolod?'

Vladimir stood again. 'My father is safe in Kiev but ...' He paused and breathed deeply. 'But I have grave news.'

Anya's eyes betrayed her terror as to what was to come next.

Thea quaked at what he might say. Her hand momentarily went to the swan pendant that hung under her mantle. He said softly, 'Prince Iziaslav died in the battle at the Nezhata Meadows. He was not quick enough to avoid an enemy spear. He had ridden forward from his guard, into the thick of the battle.' Vladimir crossed himself. 'My uncle was braver at the end than any of us were that day.'

Thea said with firmness, 'If there is more, Vladimir, do not spare us.'

'We took Chernigov and my cousins have fled. My father has taken his brother's body to Kiev for burial. The merchants and the armies want my father to be crowned grand prince.' Vladimir knelt before Anya. 'He has sent me, my lady, to fetch you and my stepbrother and sisters home to Kiev.'

'My husband has never wanted to be the grand prince and you do not need to kneel before me.'

Vladimir took Anya's hand and kissed it. 'Accept, he must. He is the senior member of the family now. We have won this round of battles. Unless we broker a fair peace there may be more.' He turned from Anya to Thea. 'I think you, my wife, have proved the greatest general of us all today, though I fear this may not be the end of the Steppe tribes. They will return unless we can bring the khans around to a sensible way of thinking. They must know that they are better off making peace with my father in Kiev than lingering in an ill-fated alliance with the Sviatoslavichi.'

He stretched his hands towards Anya, palms up in a supplicant's gesture. 'Your own father, a Steppe khan who joined with us, understands this well. The battle for Pereiaslavl may not be ended for all time but, because of you both, it is over for now.' He took Thea's hands again, kissed her forehead. 'In the morning there will be a defeated khan waiting to offer his surrender to *you*,' he said. 'You will both meet him with me. We shall accept his truce. Have either of you any terms in mind?'

For years Thea had wanted to help him rule his kingdom, or rather his father's kingdom. Now, it seemed not so important. 'I embrace the opportunity to show you that I am the daughter of the great King Harold of England, able to sit by your side and discuss matters of diplomacy with an enemy, though the cause saddens me.'

'Then we shall do so.' Vladimir's eyes were twinkling as he stood. 'I shall visit our children. I shall ride out to find Earl Connor. When I return with the Cuman khan, we shall tell him that he must pay us tribute.' He slapped his fist into his hands. 'Otherwise, his people will face destruction.' Vladimir bowed to his wife and stepmother and walked to the doorway of the great receiving hall, his retainers opening up a space for him to pass through them into the hall.

Thea called after her husband, 'The khan must free any of our women he has taken into slavery, those stolen from our villages.'

Vladimir looked back and nodded. 'We shall also charge the Cumans much silver for the loss of Rus lives.'

'Money will never replace husbands, brothers and fathers, but it will ease their lives.'

The sun rose in a burst of rose-coloured light when Vladimir rode back to the fortress in the company of Earl Connor and the khan. Padar was immediately hurried away by Gudrun who insisted that she tend to his wounded arm. The khan was placed under guard, comfortably, with food and drink, in an antechamber until Vladimir, Earl Connor and Edmund washed, rested and dined. The peace conference convened late in the afternoon.

It was held in the blue hall. Thea and Vladimir both wore crowns. The khan fell onto his knees before them. Vladimir nodded to her. For a moment her voice felt as if it was about to vanish but then, just as she felt a heartbeat of despair, her speech returned to her. She admonished the khan for waging war on Pereiaslavl. She then said that his women would not be molested when they removed their dead from the killing grounds. 'We did not seek this conflict, Khan. You imposed it upon us. The fault is yours.' She demanded that he compensate the widows of Pereiaslavl for their loss. At this, the khan pointed at Edmund. 'He released the fire on my fighting men. That prince from the western lands is the messenger of the evil ones. One day, he shall reap what he has sown.'

'Not so.' Thea stood and moved to Edmund's side. She could feel the khan's eyes following her. 'My brother did not plan the use of dragon fire. *I* gave the order for the fire to be released. Had I not, you would have destroyed our city, taken us as prisoners and hostages or massacred all of us. Accept our terms.'

The khan grunted and shuffled around on his knees so that he was facing Vladimir. 'We shall pay tribute and sign your treaty.'

Later, during the negotiations, she saw the khan's eyes descend to her belly. He said, 'If your wife has a daughter I would have the princess wed to one of my sons. That would establish a lasting peace between our peoples.'

'That, we may consider, but it is far in the future,' Vladimir diplomatically replied. 'You will free any Russians you have taken and grant us hostages.' He smiled. 'One of these must be the son of whom you speak. You will grant us the silver we ask. You will sign a treaty with us that for six months you will not seek access to the river trade. That is all.' He touched Thea's hand and stood after she stood, leaving the great khan humbled and on his knees before her chair.

The next day Vladimir and the khan signed a treaty document agreeing the hostages Vladimir demanded, freeing any Russian slaves the Cumans had taken from villages near Pereiaslavl and granting Vladimir two large sacks of Cuman silver, which he promised Thea would be used to help compensate the wives and families of Pereiaslavl's fallen warriors.

36

Kiev, January 1079

Forty days had passed since she had given birth in the warmth of the bathhouse. It was long enough. The purification ritual had been held a few days previously. Her Danish birthing chair was removed and stored away. At last, she could enter the world again.

Tiny Elizaveta had slipped from her mother like a ball of silk. She had not suffered because of the terrible events in September. The baby came to the world crying lustily as early winter snow batted against chamber shutters and piled up in mounds outside in the courtyards. She possessed a great fortune because her hair was a fluffy halo of pale golden red and her eyes were the blue of summer cornflowers.

Thea held her baby daughter in her arms when Vladimir came into her chamber. He reached out and she carefully gave tiny swaddled Elizaveta to her adoring father.

The damp wool smell of Thea's warrior husband mingled with that of cleansing herbs – thyme and rosemary. Amulets still hung about her bed. A mother could take childbed fever at any time during the first month following a birth. Thea reached up and touched an ivory-and-amber figurine of the Virgin. Smiling, she said, 'The Lady Mary has kept me safe.'

'She has protected us all.'

'I promised her a monastery if we survived the battle for Pereiaslavl.'

'You shall have it,' Vladimir said, kissing Elizaveta's soft head and placing his daughter back into her mother's arms. 'We shall speak with the patriarch and to my father and I think we can begin work once the springtime returns to Kiev. You saved Pereiaslavl, Thea. It is to be a mark of the respect in which I hold you, my thanks to you. '

'And when it is built I should like to pass some months of every year there.'

'That, I grant you.'

She tucked Elizaveta into her cradle. 'There is another request.'

He smiled at her, his eyes filled with respect for her. 'Today is the day for granting wishes.'

'As you know, Edmund wishes to marry Katya. He says he will take her to Novgorod after their wedding. My brother intends to continue trading with Earl Connor.'

'It shall be one of the most elegant weddings the royal house of Kiev has ever witnessed.' Vladimir began to anxiously feel about his person, slapping his great hands here and there. 'I have something that came for you during your lying in.' He slid his hand into a slit in his triangular-shaped outer robe. 'There has been a messenger from the English.' He withdrew his hand and began fumbling about the voluminous cloak he had left on a bench. 'Here it is.' He withdrew a small, sealed package from the lining of the furred mantle. 'I think you have waited a long time to hear news from England.'

'Years.' She tapped the cradle with her foot, setting it to rock. 'Is it to do with Godwin?'

'No, not Godwin. It is from your mother and it is a secret letter. She is still not permitted letters. What rebellions a nun could incite I do wonder. It was written back in the summer. Can you read it?'

'My mother!' she whispered. 'Elditha?' Thea's hands were shaking as she reached for the package.

'Take it,' he said. 'I shall leave you and return later. You will want to be on your own. And you should rest. You must be well enough to help Edmund and Katya plan their wedding.' He winked. She smiled. As he took her hands, the letter with its plain seal fell to the floor between them. 'You are my heaven, my moon and my stars and our children are my jewels, more precious than rubies and jade. A soothsayer predicted only last week that we would have many more boys – only boys, he said – so this little one will be our golden princess. She is indeed most precious of them all.'

'You flatter me.' She smiled. 'I think it should ever be so. But a soothsayer …?' she said, recollecting the Rus fear of wizards and sorcerers. 'What would the patriarch say?'

'I think the patriarch has consulted this one more than once himself. I hear that the same fortune teller promised him he would have a new nunnery for the city. Apparently, this will come to pass.'

'I see.' She released her hands and rescued her letter from the floor rug. She could not wait to break the seal. 'Go,' she said. 'Return later. And when you return, bring the boys. They have not seen their sister yet.'

'They will adore her. She is beautiful and most important of all she will be wise like her mother.' He paused at the door. 'We could dine together tonight, all of us, here in your chamber, without anyone to serve us. Would you like that? A family supper.'

'It would bring me great pleasure, Vladimir. Afterwards I shall tell stories. I have a new book, one about a great khan whose wife was under sentence of death but delayed it for ever by telling him stories, one for each night. There are one thousand and one stories in all. This khan was so infatuated by her stories that his wife lived to be very old. I shall tell you one of her tales later. She was clever, patient and very wise.'

After Vladimir departed, Thea sank into her chair, her heart fluttering like the leaf that shivers from a branch in an October breeze. She cut the letter's seal with her jewelled knife and unfolded this treasure that had travelled so far to reach her. She smoothed open the single page. As she read, she listened to the one voice from her past that she had for many years longed to hear. Savouring every word, she slowly devoured her beloved mother's words.

My dearest daughter, Princess Gita of the Rus,

Greetings. May this letter find you in good health.

I am filled with happiness to hear from you. My life contains many moments of great joy. One such moment was when I learned that you are safe, that you, daughter, are married to a great Rus prince. By now you may even have a new child, your third, I am told by the messenger who brought me your letter in the spring. The Godwin christening robe, I understand, has travelled far and has been put to good use. Your father, King Harold, would be proud to have Russian princes and princesses to continue our noble line. You carry our future with you.

Godwin, so I am informed, will soon be married to an Irish nobleman's daughter. Edmund, I hear, has travelled to the Rus lands. I hope that he remains with you. My sweet child Gunnhild has married the Count of Brittany, Count Alain, the King of England's cousin. Unfortunately, as you know, he is one who has long wished to join with our family. It is not a union of which I approve. Least said in this letter the better. As for Ulf, my stolen child, I listen every day of my life for news of him. I pray that Ulf is well-cared for. His loss is a great ache in my heart. And I pray that one day he must return to me. Not so Magnus, for I shall not see him again in this world.

I wish I were able to travel to see my grandchildren. It is not to be. I have chosen my life in Canterbury. The plainsong chanted for the offices in the chapel cheers me when I am saddened by all my memories. Nunnery life is simple but it is comforting. My apartment is hung with tapestries. I have a warming fire in winter. I eat well. The nuns are kind. They hail from many countries – Denmark, Ireland, France, Normandy and England.

In the summer season I look after my bees and tend the herb gardens. I embroider and I stitch winter gowns for poor women – simple woollen gowns. On each one, I embroider a swan in pale linen thread. It is a good ending for a life which has observed much happiness as well as much loss.

The light is fading now so I shall finish. Autumn leaves rattle against my shutters. The trees are golden with fruit. The world passes through its seasons and it will still be here when we are long gone from it. To each of us there is granted a season. Mine was with your father. My dearest, your mother is at peace.

May God and all his saints protect you. Bells ring for Vespers. The sun's last rays slant through my opened window. I think it will be a starry night. Up there, far above the heavens, your father, my great love, watches down on us all.

Edith of Canterbury, known as Elditha.

Epilogue

January 1079

That afternoon, Thea tries to remember her mother's face. The candle burns down and winter darkness gathers. The wet nurse enters her chamber and tiptoes around her chair. She lifts the baby from her cradle, whisks her away and quietly feeds tiny Elizaveta by the fire. Thea sits on, not stirring, until she hears her boys' chatter on the stairs and the tread of their father's footsteps. Then Vladimir is calling to the maids to bring them supper.

Her mother's treasure box lies on a mosaic table where on a blue background tiny tiles are fashioned into an angel. She opens the lid of the bone-plated silver casket and places her letter inside; she carefully places it on top of the Godwin christening gown which has so recently been used for Elizaveta's christening in the Cathedral of St Sophia. She says a prayer to St Theodosia. She prays that in time Ulf will return home and that Elditha will see her stolen child once again.

'Ah, my mother,' she whispers as she gently drops the silver lid on the letter, 'how wise you are and how fortunate I am to have a husband whom I love and who loves me back, the father of my father's grandchildren.' She sighs wistfully, and smiles to herself. 'If there is one constant in our brief lives, it is change.'

Feeling joy in her heart, she steps to the window and opens it wide. It is a clear night though a few flakes of snow flutter into her chamber. She peers out. The stars are glowing in a great firmament above the courtyard. Out there, far above the pole star, her father is watching over them and smiling. She closes over the shutters. There is no desire for revenge in her heart any more. Her longing for it died as her happiness and her understanding of her place in her world increased.

389

She knows that their lives will go on. Her rushnyk lies unfinished by her chair but one day, she thinks, as she picks it up and studies it, one day this will tell my story from its beginning to its end.

The End

Glossary

Handfasting	a form of secular marriage which while legal was not a church wedding
Skald	a poet who has Scandinavian origins
Terem	the Russian equivalent of the bower or solar where the women lived
Rushnyk	an embroidery that follows a woman throughout her life and which contains events from her life in cross stitching and couch stitching for the most part.
Boyar	a Russian nobleman
Veche	a council
Grand Prince	the most important prince from the Riurikid dynasty. He was the most senior family member whose father had also been a Grand Prince. His seat was Kiev.
Steppe	the great plain of Russia through which runs the Dnieper river.
Cumans	a loose confederation of Steppe

tribes. Some groups were friendly to the Rus princes. Others were their enemies. By the late eleventh century the Rus princes sometimes married Steppe princesses. Vsevolod's second wife was Anya, a Cuman princess.

Kremlin	a Russian castle
Iconostasis	the screen before the altar in Orthodox churches
The Patriarch	a senior member of the Rus clergy, a little akin to an archbishop

Author's Note

Thea's story haunted me from the moment I read that she married a Russian prince of Kiev after she had travelled into exile with her grandmother and her brothers, ending up at Sweyn's court in Denmark. Her Russian wedding took place in the early 1070s.

As women are the footnotes of history, Thea's real story was not easy to excavate. I relied on what I could discover about a noblewoman's life in medieval Russia and on the political events which are the background to this novel. I did not take the novel's narrative through to the last days of Thea's life although the prologue implies that by this much later date she had not long to live and that Thea tells her own story through her rushnyk. Finally, that she tells this narrative to include the voices of others, a creative license on my part.

It is a fact that although Thea is said to have had a good marriage she did, indeed, enter a convent during the final years of her life. I chose to end my story's narrative twenty years before her death and focus on the early years of her betrothal and her brilliant marriage. I wanted to end this narrative at a point when she surely must have been very happy because her world within the context of the story's narrative scope had been put to rights. Russia was an alien world and one she would have both enjoyed and disliked. It was, for women, an even more restrictive world than that of Western Europe. Yet, there were laws laid down to establish respect for women in Russia at this time. These were established by Vladimir's grandfather.

I read Russian Studies at university and I have visited Russia on many occasions. The Slavonic Studies Department in Oxford had texts I could consult and for this I am grateful. It was there that I was able to consult the *Russian Primary Chronicle* which is a little akin to the *Anglo-Saxon Chronicle* but with a greater amount of Church stories, all beautifully told in the vernacular. I read it in translation.

The *Russian Primary Chronicle* was my main source for the political events of the 1070s in Russia and for the atmosphere of the period, for the laws to protect women, the fear of wizards and the belief in miracles, the monasteries and the great churches, especially St Sophia in Novgorod and Kiev, built along the lines of that in Constantinople, today known as Istanbul.

Thea, who is referred to as Gita, only gets a brief mention in this Chronicle. Her marriage to Prince Vladimir, who was her exact age, is recorded in the Chronicle and her children get a mention too. Her death dates are confused and two dates are offered.

Thea (Gytha or Gita) went into exile after the Siege of Exeter in 1068, when her grandmother, the formidable mother of King Harold, held out in that city for three weeks, refusing to pay King William's tax. It is probable that her daughter, Dowager Queen Edith, who held a pragmatic attitude towards the Normans, arranged her exile. She may have spent time at the Danish Court where, amazingly, King Sweyn, her nephew, had married a third wife. There exist two theories about Sweyn's third marriage. Some historians suggest his third marriage was to Tora, the concubine or handfasted wife of Harold Harthrada of Norway, who was killed by Harold of England at Stamford Bridge. Others say it was Elizaveta, the Russian legal wife of Harold Harthrada. I suspect it was the latter. Her daughter positively married one of Sweyn's sons.

The fact that Sweyn probably organised Thea's marriage to Elizaveta's nephew in Kiev suggests to me that this third wife was indeed Elizaveta. She was recorded as having had a stormy relationship with Harthrada who had elevated his concubine's status. Tora was the mother of Harthrada's sons. The policies of Novgorodian/Kiev princes was to develop and protect trade routes north from the Black Sea to the Baltic. They had strong links with Scandinavian neighbours and this was confirmed through inter-dynastic marriages.

Janet Martin, expert on Medieval Russia, writes in *Medieval Russia 980-1584* 'Prince Iaroslav Vladimirovich married the daughter of the Swedish king, Olaf. He strengthened his bonds with the Scandinavian world by arranging the marriage of his daughter Elizaveta to the King of Norway, then to a king of Denmark.' Vladimir Monomakh's marriage to Gyda (Thea), the daughter of Harold II of England, reflected the prince's ties with the King of Denmark more than England. Also it was the Danish king who gave refuge to Harold's family after he was defeated and killed at the Battle of Hastings in 1066. It is likely that Sweyn arranged the betrothal and marriage.'

The political events in Russia during the seventh decade of the eleventh century were dominated by internecine conflict. Those elements of these conflicts between uncles and nephews and between cousins that enter the pages of this novel absolutely belong to the realms of fact. I have simply integrated the history into the story's narrative. Wars continued between the Sviatoslavichi and the Monomakhichi long after the pages of this novel close. The Steppe tribes collectively known as Cumans were courted by both sides. Chernigov was a great prize, as was Kiev. Kiev in the eleventh century surpassed London and Paris. It was extremely sophisticated and wealthy. Pereiaslavl was located on the Trubezh river close to the Dnieper. Its territories bordered the Steppe and the fortress city bore the brunt of raids from Steppe nomads. The region was one of the main principalities within Kievan Rus and was assigned to Vladimir's father, Vsevolod, and later to Vladimir.

It is true that in 1078, after the death of their father, the Sviatoslavichi made deals with the Cumans of the Steppe to weaken Vsevolod and Iziaslav. What is invented here is the particular attack on Pereiaslavl that claims the final chapters of *The Betrothed Sister*. The battle for Pereiaslavl is representative of such attacks, though, of course, I invented the use of Greek fire. Even so, Greek fire was a researched invention and not implausible. The attacks around Chernigov in 1078 did happen and Grand Prince Iziaslav did lose his life at Nezhata Meadows.

So you might ask, what happened to Vladimir? My story ends in 1078. Vladimir had caused Oleg Sviatoslavich to flee to Timutarakan, now in Crimea. By the end of the seventh decade political order was restored. However, peace did not last. By the 1090s Prince Oleg and the Cuman tribes had resumed their attacks on the southern Rus frontier. They carried terror to the heart of Kievan territories. They reached Kiev in 1096 where they pillaged the Cave Monastery. Vladimir made a treaty with Prince Oleg and the attacks were called off for a time. The Grand Prince Vsevolod died in 1093 and Prince Iziaslav's elder son then ruled Kiev until he died.

The feud between the Sviatoslavichi and Vladimir and Vladimir and Thea's sons who were, by the ninth decade, grown up, continued until Vladimir made his own tribal alliances and engineered peace in 1097 with a conference at Liubech. Vladimir ruled Pereiaslavl throughout these two decades. It was complex because the Rus princes often intermarried with Cuman princesses to preserve peace and protect trade routes. Vladimir's son Iuri (the third son) married the daughter of a Polovsky (Cuman) khan. It may be of interest here too that after Thea's death, circa 1107, Vladimir remarried, unsurprisingly to a Cuman princess. He was elected Grand Prince of Kiev in 1113. He died in 1125 and was succeeded by Mstislav, whom the family had named Harold. Prince Vladimir left a beautiful and wise testimony, a letter to his sons, which can be read in the *Russian Primary Chronicle*. He was a warrior prince but he was also sincerely religious, philosophical and thoughtful.

The domestic details of the novel, both in Denmark and in Russia, are researched in depth to lend authenticity to what is imagined within its pages. The Russian princesses did dwell in the terem that really equates to a bower or a solar. Most of the time women did not attend social gatherings in their own houses. Women were expected to be chaste, obedient, pious and to take care of servants and children. They were extremely protected and mixed less with men than their Western European counterparts. Women could own property. They ran their estates but they never interfered in politics. By the Rus law codes if a woman accused a man of rape her testimony was believed. There was severe punishment for rape. Rape was unreligious and it violated the honour of the woman's clan.

The rushnyk is an embroidery tradition that goes back long before the times I write about. It reaches back to Herodotus. Originally rushnyks were folk embroidery symbolic of beliefs and superstitions. Yet they evolved. The rushnyk held ancestral memories and followed a woman throughout her life. The act of spinning the thread for the rushnyk embodied spiritual power for, after all, three fingers, a trinity, were used to twist the thread. The path of life starts at the bottom and continues to the top. They represented a cycle of life. They were used at weddings as I describe in the novel. They were used to lower the coffin after death. Every colour had its own needle and the colours represent different qualities. A needle was never loaned but left hidden. The idea was that thousands of tiny stitches can create great energy. I wanted Thea to have a rushnyk to contain her memories and to follow the life that she had once she became a Russian princess. I felt that along with Thea's love of storytelling it is an important trope for this fictitious historical story which is, as far as I can make it, a symbol rooted in many of the actual facts and in the atmosphere I felt belonged to this story.

Thea's story illustrates too how the Godwine line survived through her. She was the great-grandmother many times removed of the last Russian royal family, the Romanovs, and also connected to our own royal family through Philippa of Hainault who married Edward III.

We do not know what happened to her brothers. We know that Magnus died as I have told it. Godwin sought help from Sweyn over and over. He did have connections to Ireland and may have lived his life out in Ireland or possibly in Denmark or possibly Russia. Many Anglo-Saxon dispossessed were scattered throughout Europe after 1066. The same applies to Edmund. Since there was a strong English presence in Novgorod and in Kiev after the Battle of Hastings, I allowed Edmund the luxury of being a merchant trader. Ulf was not released until after the death of King William in 1086. He was knighted by William's eldest estranged son, Robert. He possibly accompanied Robert of Normandy on the First Crusade. Ulf is the stolen Godwin princeling, forever in the background of these novels. Gytha died at St Omer or in Denmark. Her daughter Hilda died in St Omer where she had taken the veil.

This is where the series ends. I have loved writing all three stories. It is difficult to say goodbye to them but I am delighted that apparently they have found their readers. Thank you, my readers. They are, I emphasise, a retelling of events that happened so long ago that often these women's stories as I tell them belong to the realms of fiction as well as fact. However, I wanted to bring them to life so they are not shadows forgotten in the footnotes of history. Please do be aware that in each book I blend fact with invention. There is just not enough fact available about them and remember that I am, after all, writing Historical Fiction, albeit thoroughly researched and thus informed fiction.

Short Bibliography

Medieval Russia 980-1584, Janet Martin, Cambridge University Press, 1995, 2011

Borderland: A Journey through the History of Ukraine, Anna Reid, Basic Books, new edition, 2000

Russia's Women, edited by Barbara Evans Clements, Barbara Alpern Engel and Christina D. Worobec, Indiana University Press, 2012

Reinterpreting Russian History Readings 860-1880s, compiled and edited by Daniel H. Kaiser and Gary Marker, Oxford University Press, 1994

Russian Magic Tales from Pushkin to Platonov, edited by Robert Chandler, Penguin Classics, 2012

The Vikings, Else Roesdahl, Penguin, 1998

The Elder Edda: Myths, Gods and Heroes from the Viking World, translated by Andy Orchard, Penguin Classics, 2013

The Russian Primary Chronicle, Nestor the Chronicler, translated and edited by Samuel Hazzard Cross and Olgerd P. Sherbowitz-Wetzor, 1930

The Anglo-Saxon Chronicle, translated and edited by Michael Swanton, Phoenix Press, 2000

Russian Proverbs, Chris Skillen, Appletree Press, 1994

These are only a few of the scores of texts I consulted when writing this novel. I must thank the Department of Slavonic Studies, Oxford where I read *The Russian Primary Chronicle* which I found utterly absorbing not only because of what it said but because of the poetry of those voices reaching down through the centuries to us from that very distant world. How can we ever forget them!

Carol McGrath

Carol's passion has always been reading and writing historical fiction. She lives in Oxfordshire with her husband and family. She taught History in an Oxfordshire comprehensive until she took an MA in Creative Writing at The Seamus Heaney Centre, Queens University Belfast. This was quickly followed by an MPhil in Creative Writing at Royal Holloway, University of London. Her debut novel, *The Handfasted Wife*, first in a trilogy about the royal women of 1066, was shortlisted for the RoNAS, 2014 in the historical category. *The Swan-Daughter* is the second in the trilogy. It is also a stand-alone novel. Carol can often be discovered in Oxford's famous Bodleian Library where she undertakes meticulous research for her novels.

Find Carol on her website: www.carolcmcgrath.co.uk.

The Handfasted Wife

The Handfasted Wife is the story of the Norman Conquest from the perspective of Edith (Elditha) Swanneck, Harold's common-law wife. She is set aside for a political marriage when Harold becomes king in 1066. Determined to protect her children's destinies and control her economic future, she is taken to William's camp when her estate is sacked on the eve of the Battle of Hastings. She later identifies Harold's body on the battlefield and her youngest son becomes a Norman hostage.

Elditha avoids an arranged marriage with a Breton knight by which her son might or might not be given into his care. She makes her own choice and sets out through strife-torn England to seek help from her sons in Dublin. However, events again overtake her.

Harold's mother, Gytha, holds up in her city of Exeter with other aristocratic women, including Elditha's eldest daughter. The girl is at risk, drawing Elditha back to Exeter and resistance. Initially supported by Exeter's burghers the women withstand William's siege. However, after three horrific weeks they negotiate exile and the removal of their treasure. Elditha takes sanctuary in a convent where eventually she is reunited with her hostage son.

The Swan-Daughter

A marriage made in Heaven or Hell.

1075 and Dowager Queen Edith has died. Gunnhild longs to leave Wilton Abbey but is her suitor Breton knight Count Alain of Richmond interested in her inheritance as the daughter of King Harold and Edith Swan-Neck or does he love her for herself? And is her own love for Count Alain an enduring love or has she made a mistake? The Swan Daughter is a true 11th C tale of elopement and a love triangle.

The Swan-Daughter

Root of the Tudor Rose

1421: Henry V and his young bride, Catherine de Valois, are blessed with the birth of a son – but their happiness is short-lived. Catherine is widowed and when her father, the French king, also dies, her son inherits the crowns of France and England. Just ten months old, Henry VI needs all his mother's watchful care to protect him from political intrigue.

But Catherine is a foreigner at the English Court. Lonely and vulnerable, she is held in suspicion by those with their own claims to the throne. Only with another outsider, a young Welshman named Owen Tudor, does Catherine find true friendship but their liaison must be kept secret at all costs. Catherine, Queen of England is forbidden to remarry and she is in love with a servant...

The Witch of Eye

A love that leads to treason …

1435, England. Eleanor Cobham has married into the highest ranks of the aristocracy – she is now the Duchess of Gloucester. She and her husband, the Duke Humphrey, set up a court of their own to rival the royal court in London, surrounding themselves with fascinating and influential people.

But Eleanor craves the one thing she lacks: a son and heir, and with him a possible route to the throne of England. Desperate, Eleanor turns to the one person she believes can help her: Margery Jourdemayne, a woman now remembered as the infamous Witch of Eye.

Such help comes at a high price …

Scorpion Sunset

1916, Mesopotamia. The Turks order prisoners from the siege of Kut to march the hundreds of miles to Baghdad. The men are weak from starvation after the five-month siege, with many suffering from dysentery, scabies, and malaria. Hundreds of men die on the march, the stragglers killed by Arab tribesmen; those too ill to move are left behind to die.

Soon, though, the tide of war turns, and eventually the British march victorious into Baghdad. Having taken control of Mesopotamia, the British find they do not have the resources to govern it. What will be the country's fate? Meanwhile, the POWs who survived imprisonment re-enter an uncertain world – among them John Mason, his health ruined and future unsure.

His old friend Charles Reid is more optimistic as love blossoms. But nothing is clear-cut anymore ...Harry Downe remains with his Bedouin wife's tribe: how much of his past does he truly remember? His journalist brother Michael seeks answers amidst the ruins of war as, for their friends and comrades, the struggle to survive goes on despite the conflict's end.

The Daughters of Hastings Trilogy

Carol McGrath

For more information about **Carol McGrath**
and other **Accent Press** titles
please visit

www.accentpress.co.uk

Find more from **Carol McGrath** at

http://scribbling-inthemargins.blogspot.co.uk/

www.carolcmcgrath.co.uk